GraveYard Wars

VOLUME 1

CREATED & WRITTEN BY
AJ LIEBERMAN

ART/COLORS BY
ANDREW SEBASTIAN KWAN

LETTERS/COLORS BY
DARREN RAWLINGS

FOR ABLAZE
MANAGING EDITOR
RICH YOUNG
DESIGNER
RODOLFO MURAGUCHI

Publisher's Cataloging-in-Publication Data

Names: Lieberman, A. J., author. | Kwan, Andrew Sebastian, illustrator. | Rawlings, Darren, illustrator.
Title: Graveyard Wars , Volume 1. / A.J. Lieberman; illustrated by Andrew Sebastian Kwan and Darren Rawlings.
Series: Graveyard Wars
Description: Portland, OR: Ablaze Publishing, 2020.
Identifiers: ISBN: 978-1-950912-13-1 (Hardcover) | 978-1-950912-14-8 (pbk.)
Subjects: LCSH Death—Fiction. | Twins—Fiction. | Family—Fiction. | Graphic novels. | Horror comic books, strips, etc. | Horror.
BISAC COMICS & GRAPHIC NOVELS / Horror
Classification: LCC PN6728.G72265 L54 | DDC 741.5—dc23

Graveyard Wars Volume 1. First printing. Published by Ablaze Publishing, 11222 SE Main St. #22906 Portland, OR 97269. Graveyard Wars © 2020 Doppleganger Publishing LLC. Ablaze TM & © 2019 ABLAZE, LLC. All rights reserved. Ablaze and its logo TM & (C) 2019 Ablaze, LLC. All Rights Reserved. All names, characters, events, and locales in this publication are entirely fictional. Any resemblance to actual persons (living or dead), events or places, without satiric intent is coincidental. No portion of this book may be reproduced by any means (digital or print) without the written permission of Ablaze Publishing except for review purposes. Printed in China.

For advertising and licensing email: info@ablazepublishing.com

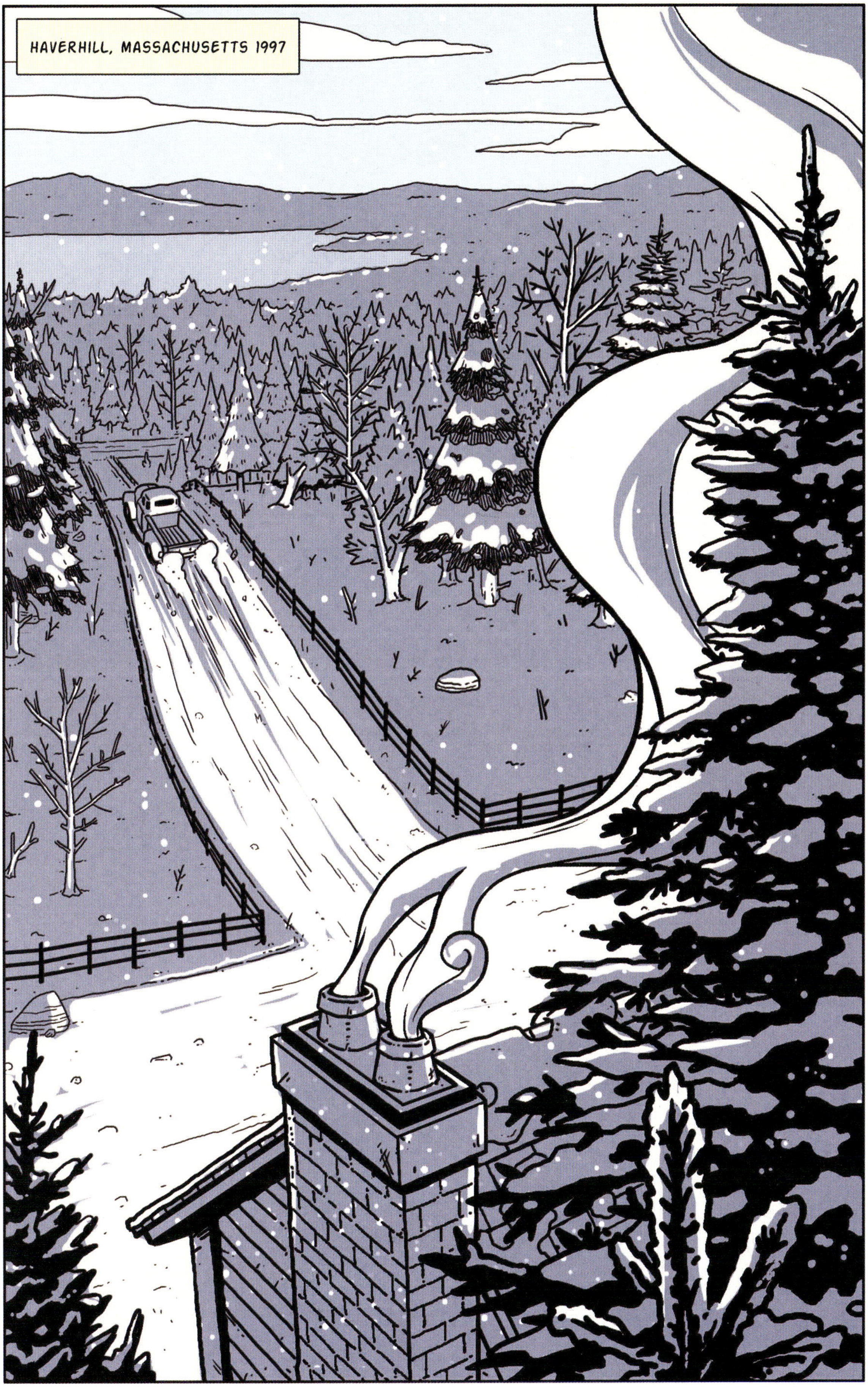
HAVERHILL, MASSACHUSETTS 1997

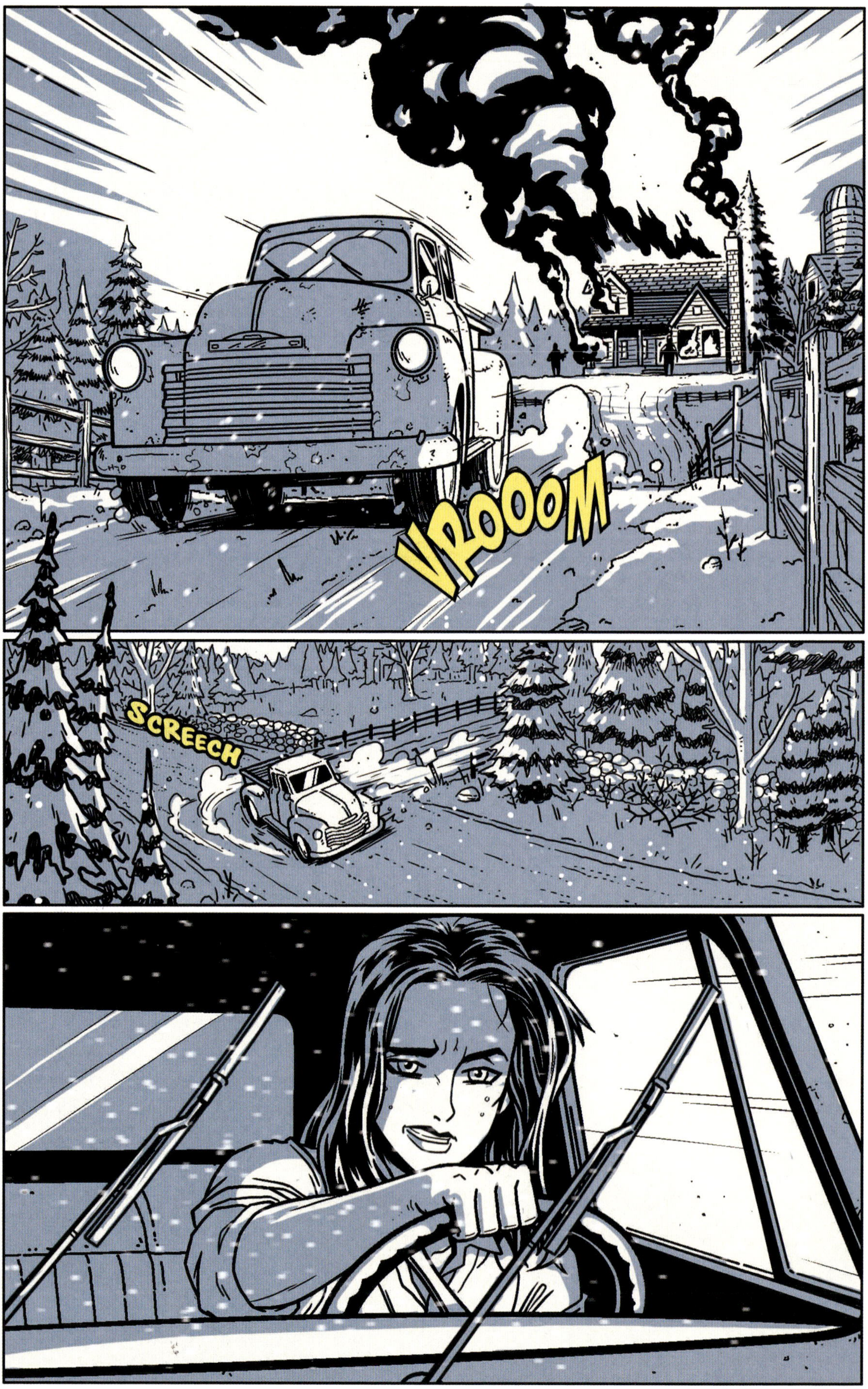
VROOOM
SCREECH

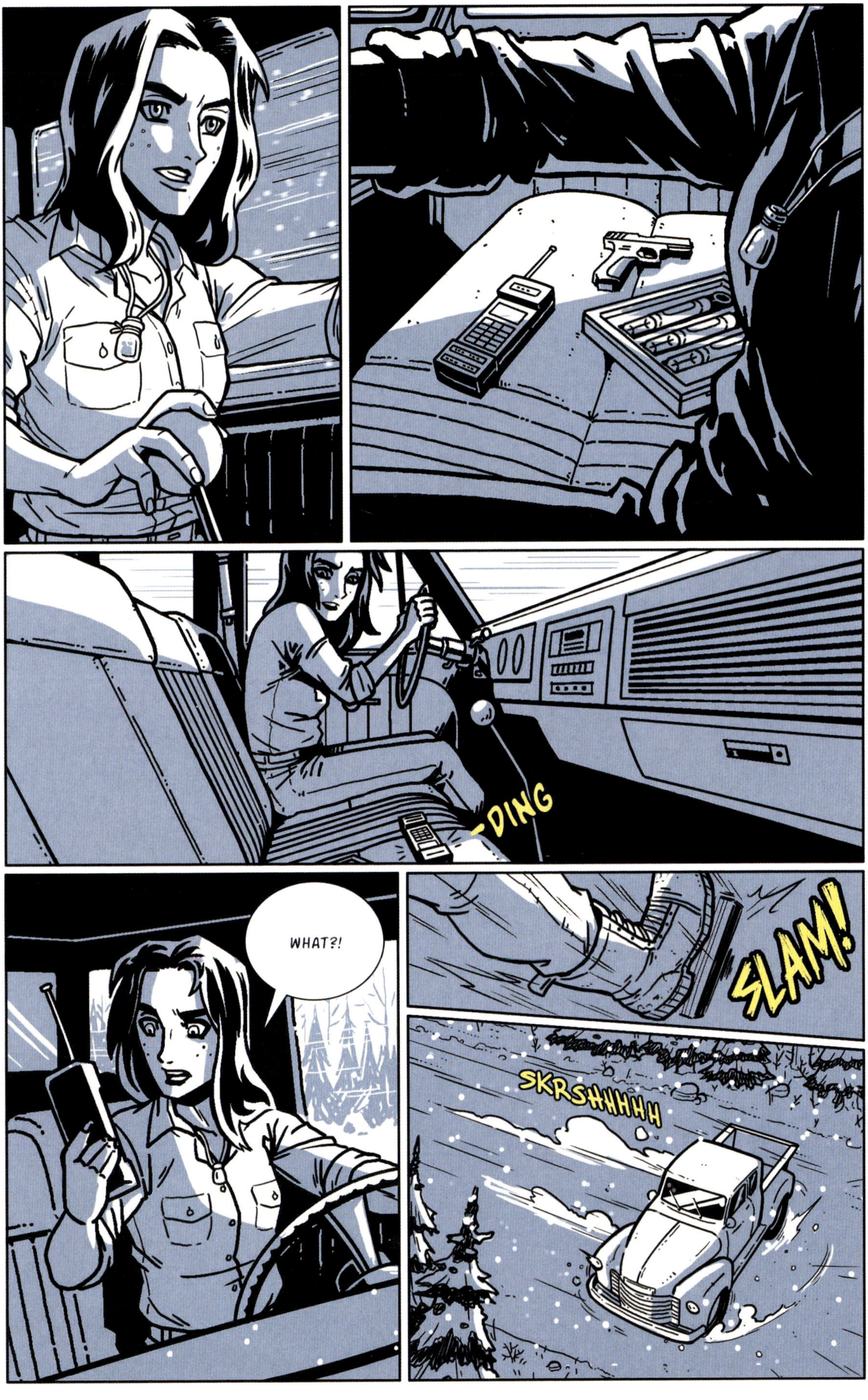

-DING
WHAT?!
SLAM!
SKRSHHHHHH

UNKNOWN:
Test came back negative.
NO...
NO THERE HAS
TO BE--
DING
UNKNOWN:
Test came back negative.
YOU:
R U sure
YOU:
R U sure
UNKNOWN:
Yes.
UNKNOWN:
Yes.
YOU:
How many..?
YOU:
How many..?
UNKNOWN:
All of them.

RING RING

WHERE ARE YOU?

OLD BROOK ROAD. BY THE MILL.

I'M ALMOST THERE. DON'T MOVE.

SEBASTIAN, SOMETHING'S WRONG.

JUST DON'T MOVE UNTIL--

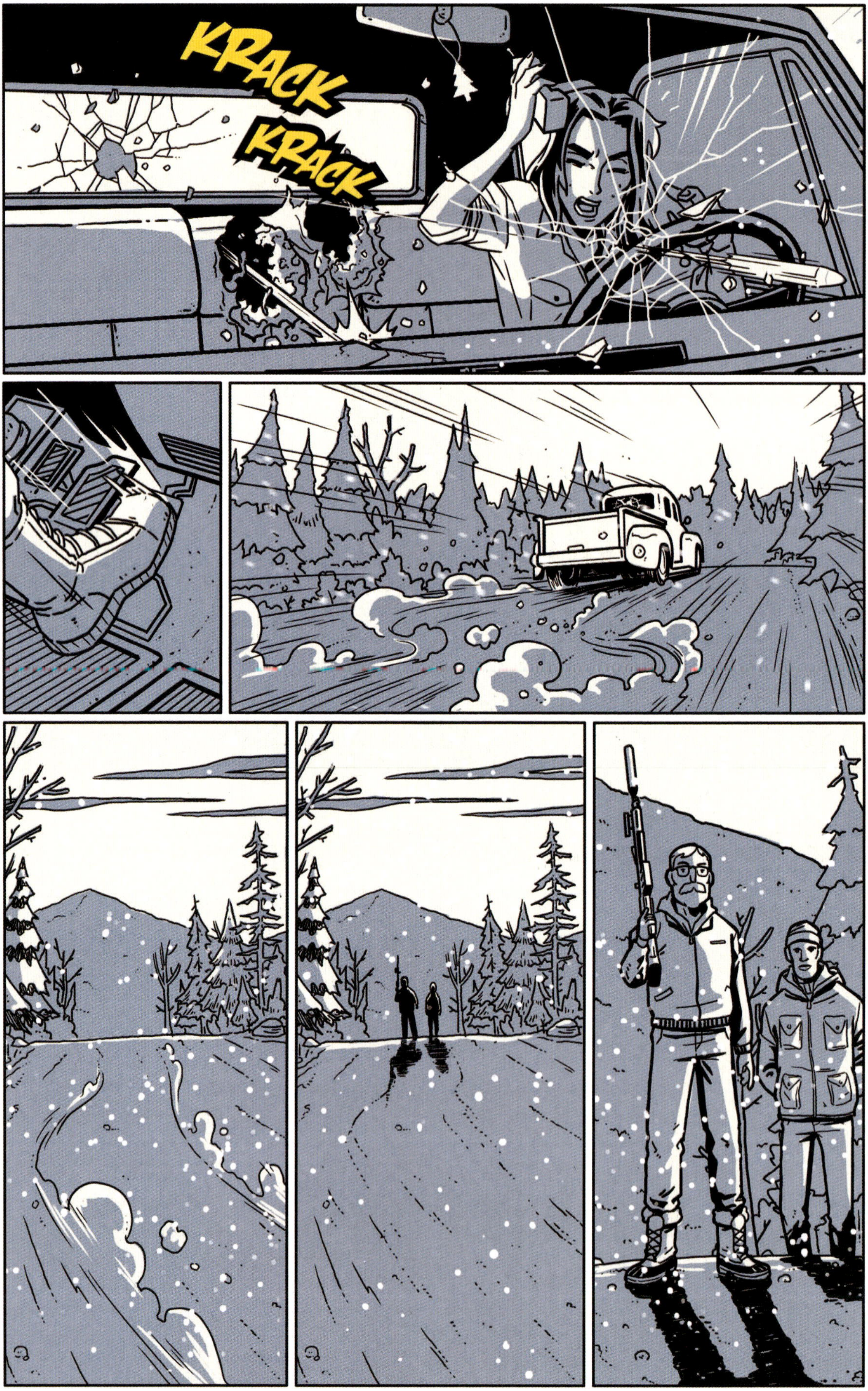
KRACK
KRACK

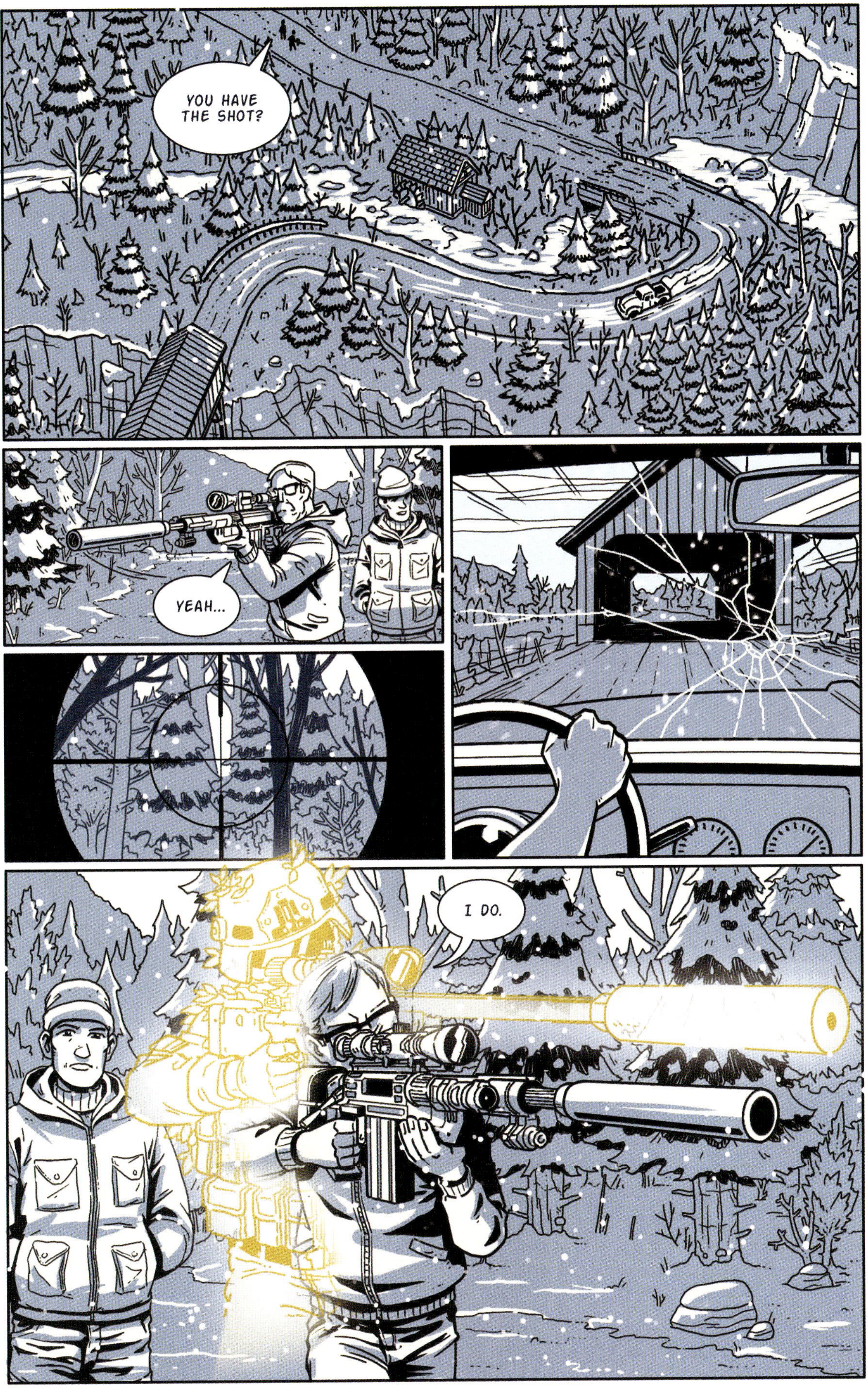
YOU HAVE THE SHOT?
YEAH...
I DO.

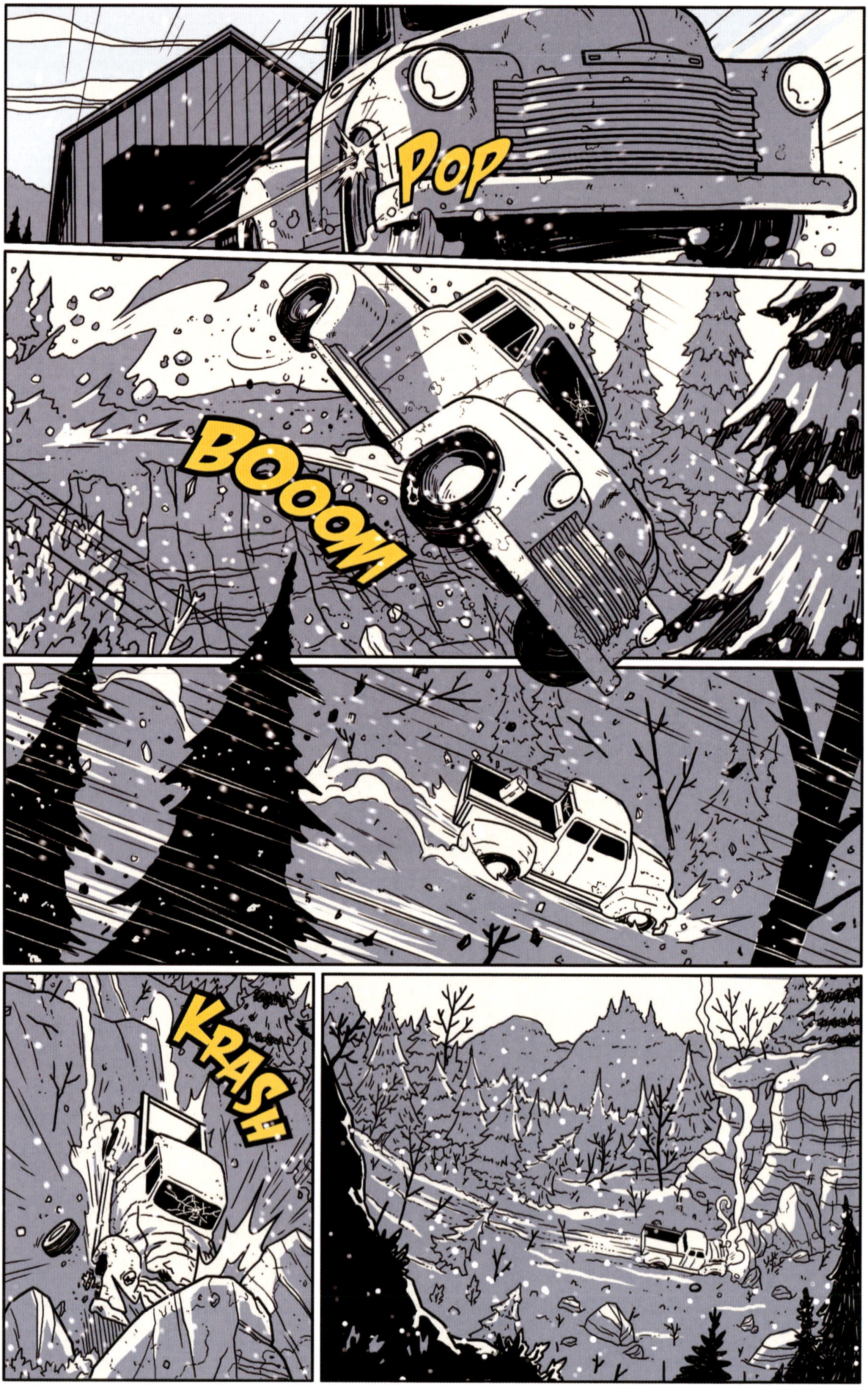
POP
BOOOOM
KRASH

CARTER...

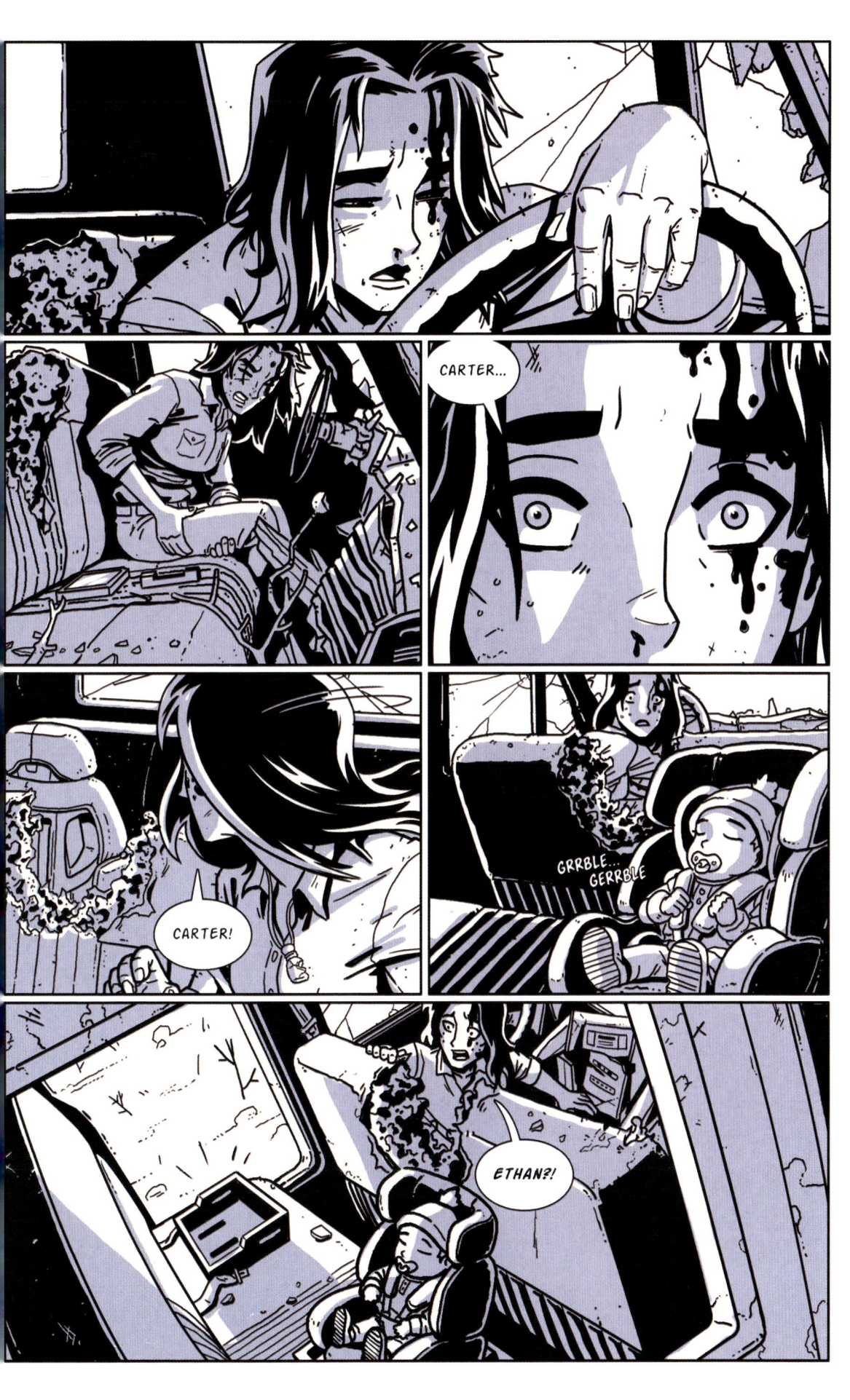

CARTER!

GRRBLE... GERRBLE

ETHAN?!

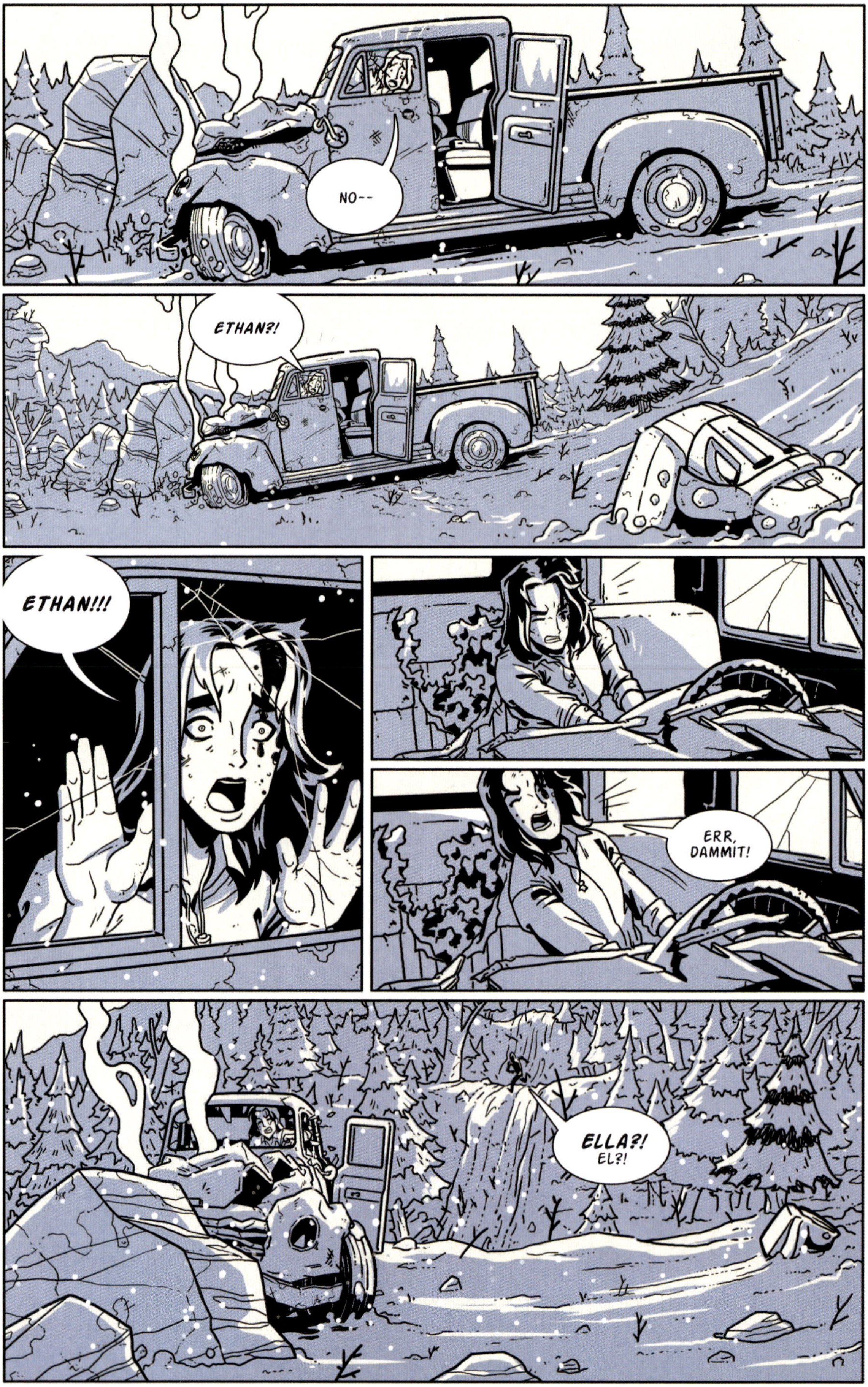
NO--
ETHAN?!
ETHAN!!!
ERR, DAMMIT!
ELLA?! EL?!

EL!
SEBASTIAN!
THE TWINS?
CARTER'S... SHE'S GOOD, BUT ETHAN, HE...
...HE'S OVER THERE!
SEBASTIAN...?
H-HOLD ON.

SEBASTIAN...
...I NEED TO KNOW!
HE'S GOOD! HE'S BREATHING.
'BASTIAN, THEY WERE NEGATIVE.
WHICH?
ALL OF THEM. IT DIDN'T WORK.
SO... WE MIGHT HAVE A PROBLEM.
OKAY, DON'T... LET'S JUST GET YOU OUTTA THERE AND DEAL WITH THAT LATER.
'BASTIAN...
MY SAFE SOIL IS GONE.
I HAVE MINE. WE CAN STILL MAKE IT--
'BASTIAN, TAKE THE TWINS AND GO, *BEFORE* THEY FIND US!
I'LL GET YOU OUT AND THEN WE'LL GO.
ALL OF US.

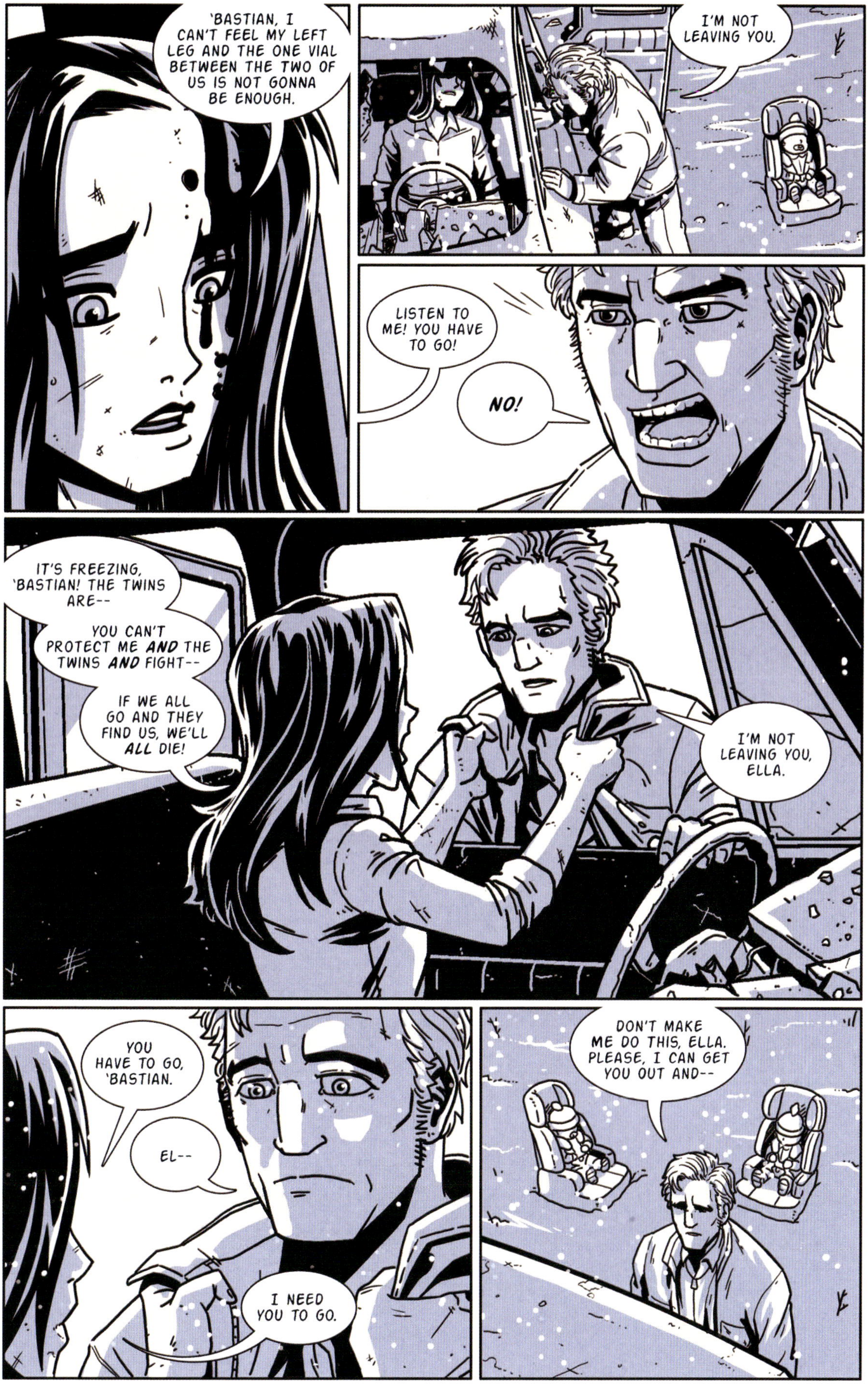
'BASTIAN, I CAN'T FEEL MY LEFT LEG AND THE ONE VIAL BETWEEN THE TWO OF US IS NOT GONNA BE ENOUGH.
I'M NOT LEAVING YOU.
LISTEN TO ME! YOU HAVE TO GO!
NO!
IT'S FREEZING, 'BASTIAN! THE TWINS ARE--
YOU CAN'T PROTECT ME AND THE TWINS AND FIGHT--
IF WE ALL GO AND THEY FIND US, WE'LL ALL DIE!
I'M NOT LEAVING YOU, ELLA.
YOU HAVE TO GO, 'BASTIAN.
EL--
I NEED YOU TO GO.
DON'T MAKE ME DO THIS, ELLA. PLEASE, I CAN GET YOU OUT AND--

PROMISE ME YOU'LL KEEP THEM SAFE.
EL--
PROMISE, SEBASTIAN!
DON'T MAKE ME DO THIS.
SEBASTIAN, EITHER I DIE OR WE ALL DIE.

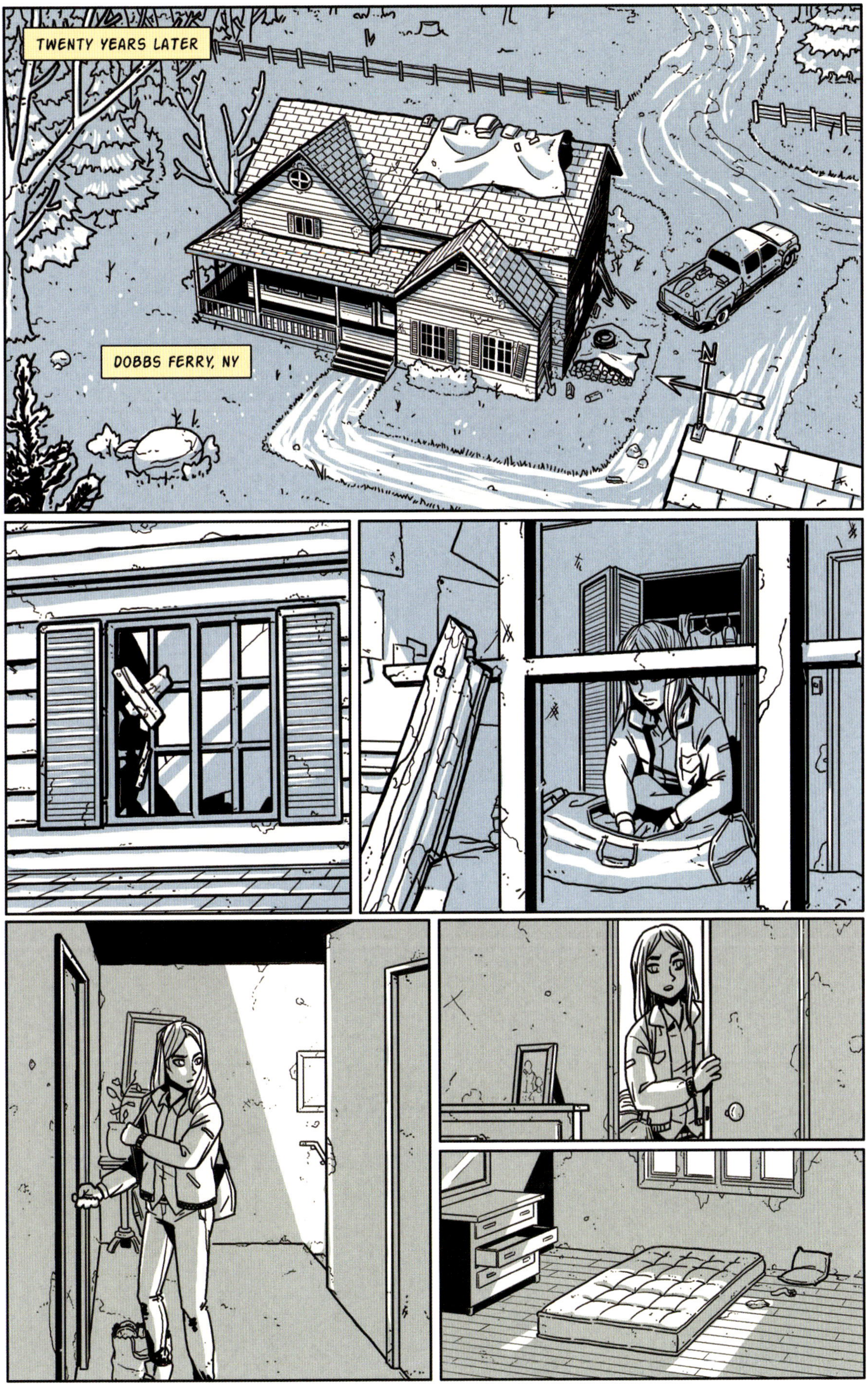
TWENTY YEARS LATER
DOBBS FERRY, NY

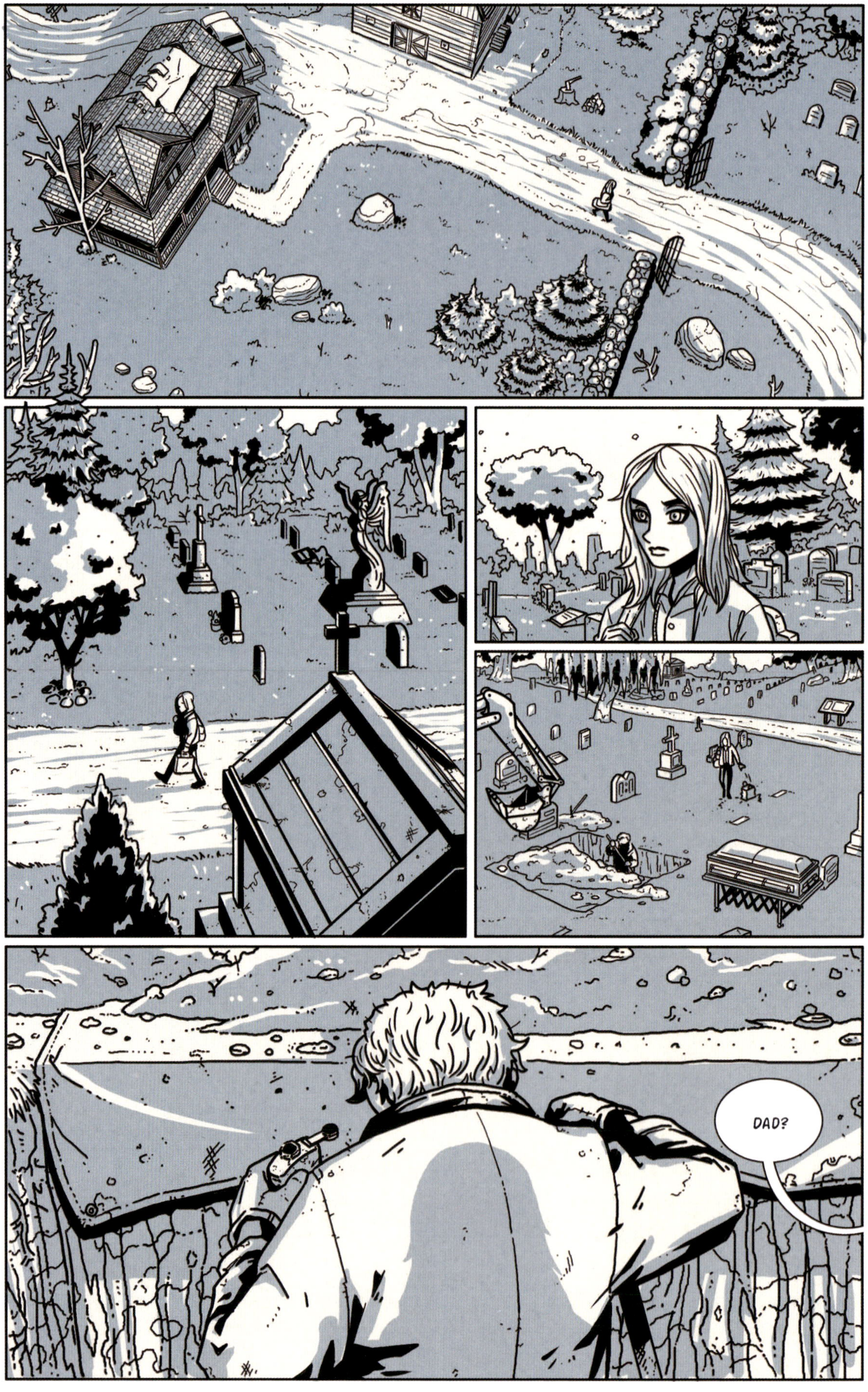
DAD?

CARTER.
YOU HAVE NO FOOD.
WHERE?
ANYWHERE. I MADE YOU A LIST.
OKAY.
TAKE THE LIST TO THE MARKET. THEN, Y'KNOW...
...*BUY* THE THINGS ON THE LIST.
YOU HEADING BACK ALREADY? THOUGHT THAT WAS NEXT WEEK.
IT *IS* NEXT WEEK.
YOU GONNA GO SEE HIM?
CARTER--
ARE YOU?

Panel 1: WHAT HAPPENED TO THE LITTLE GIRL WHO'D RUN INTO MY ARMS, KISS ME ON THE HEAD AND SKIP AWAY?

Panel 2: YEAH, NOT ME. BUT IF YOU HAVE ANOTHER FAMILY, I'D LOVE TO MEET'EM. GO SEE HIM.

CARTER.

DAD.

RING

Panel 3: YEAH? WHERE?

WE FOUND ANOTHER ONE.

Panel 4: UPSTATE.

I'LL CALL YOU RIGHT BACK.

Panel 5: YOU HAVEN'T BEEN THERE IN--

Panel 6: CARTER, I'M NOT SURE ME GOING TO SEE YOUR BROTHER IS SUCH A GOOD THING.

Panel 7: NOT GOOD FOR YOU OR FOR HIM?

Panel 8: IS THIS HEADING TOWARDS A LECTURE?

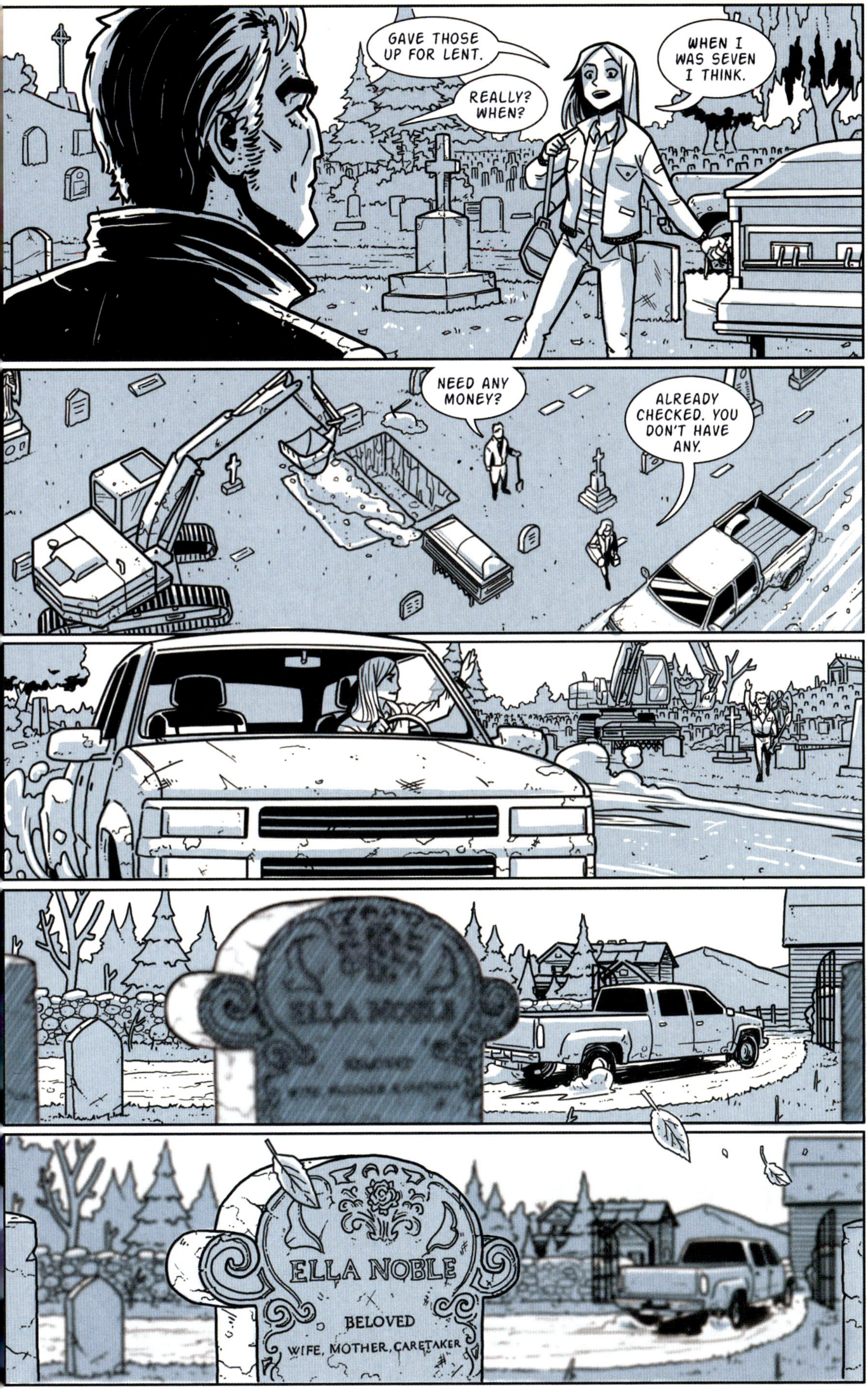
GAVE THOSE UP FOR LENT.
REALLY? WHEN?
WHEN I WAS SEVEN I THINK.
NEED ANY MONEY?
ALREADY CHECKED. YOU DON'T HAVE ANY.
ELLA NOBLE
BELOVED
WIFE, MOTHER, CARETAKER

BROADMOOR PSYCHIATRIC FACILITY
NOBLE. YA'GOT A VISITOR!
WHERE'S DAD?
HE WANTED TO COME.
NO HE DIDN'T.
HE'S WORKING.
BUSIEST GRAVEYARD DIGGER IN THE WORLD.
IT'S GOOD TO SEE YOU.

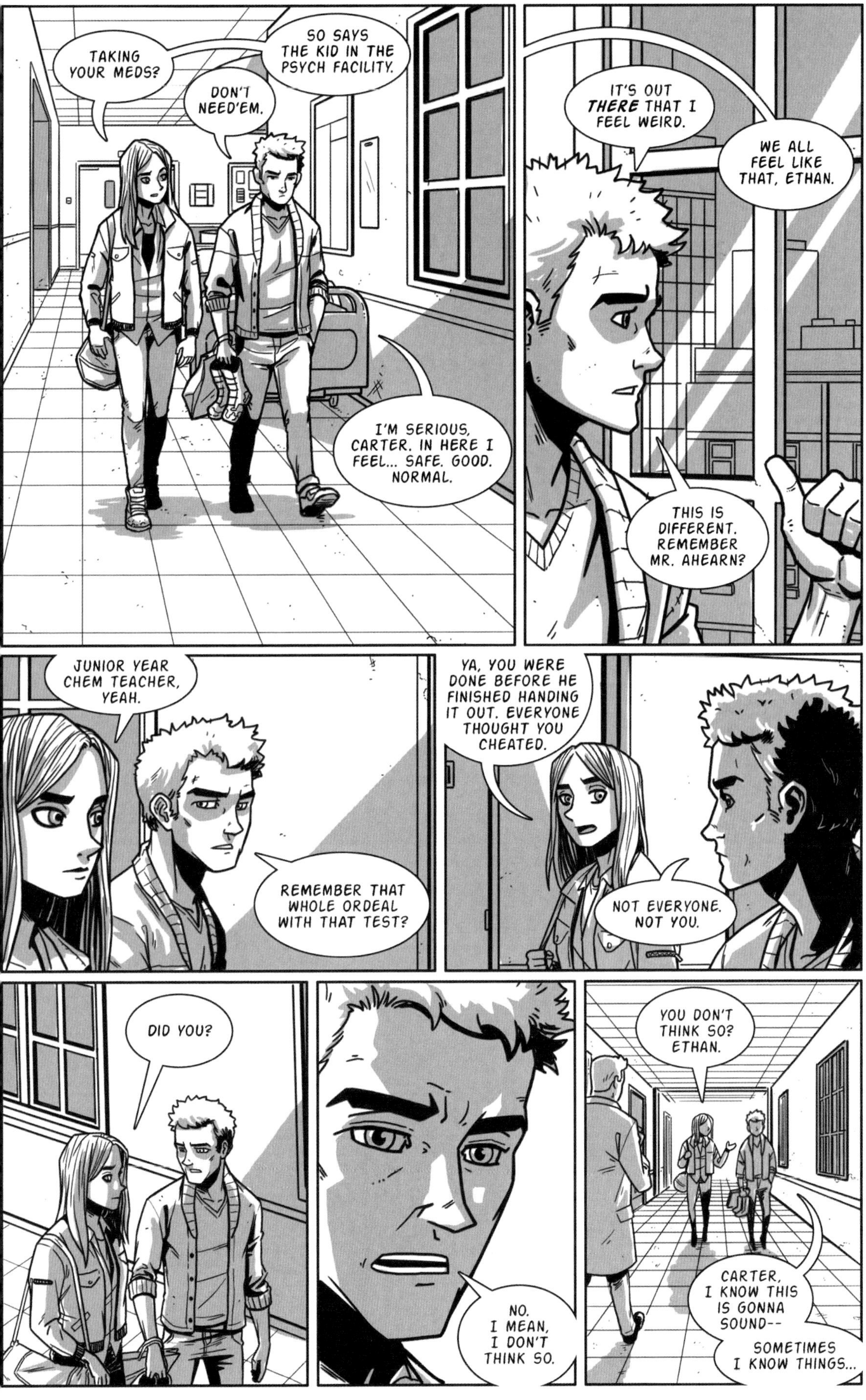
TAKING YOUR MEDS?
DON'T NEED'EM.
SO SAYS THE KID IN THE PSYCH FACILITY.
I'M SERIOUS, CARTER. IN HERE I FEEL... SAFE. GOOD. NORMAL.
IT'S OUT *THERE* THAT I FEEL WEIRD.
WE ALL FEEL LIKE THAT, ETHAN.
THIS IS DIFFERENT. REMEMBER MR. AHEARN?
JUNIOR YEAR CHEM TEACHER, YEAH.
REMEMBER THAT WHOLE ORDEAL WITH THAT TEST?
YA, YOU WERE DONE BEFORE HE FINISHED HANDING IT OUT. EVERYONE THOUGHT YOU CHEATED.
NOT EVERYONE. NOT YOU.
DID YOU?
NO. I MEAN, I DON'T THINK SO.
YOU DON'T THINK SO? ETHAN.
CARTER, I KNOW THIS IS GONNA SOUND--
SOMETIMES I KNOW THINGS...

...THINGS I SHOULDN'T KNOW. CAN DO THINGS I KNOW I SHOULDN'T BE ABLE TO DO.
THAT TEST. THE THING WITH THE MOTORCYCLE. SOMETHING JUST HAPPENS AND ALL THIS INFORMATION JUST... FILLS ME.
I DON'T UNDER--
AND NOT JUST RANDOM FACTS, C. I KNOW STUFF LIKE I'D BEEN STUDYING IT MY WHOLE LIFE. LIKE I LIVED IT.
AHEARN LET YOU TAKE THE TEST AGAIN, E. YOU GOT, LIKE, THREE RIGHT.
IT... IT WASN'T THERE ANY MORE.
WHAT WASN'T?
ANY OF IT. WHIPLASH OF NOT KNOWING WHY OR HOW-- IT'S AS IF SOMEONE WAS FLICKING A LIGHT SWITCH THAT TURNED MY LIFE ON AND OFF.
AND IN HERE?
NOTHING. I FEEL NOTHING.
IS THAT HOW YOU WANT TO SPEND THE REST OF YOUR LIFE?
DAD THINKS I'M WEAK, RIGHT?
FORGET DAD. I KNOW YOU, ETHAN. ALL MY LIFE I'VE KNOWN YOU.
YOU'RE NOT LIKE THE OTHER PEOPLE IN HERE. I KNOW IT.
HAPPY EARLY BIRTHDAY, BIG BROTHER.

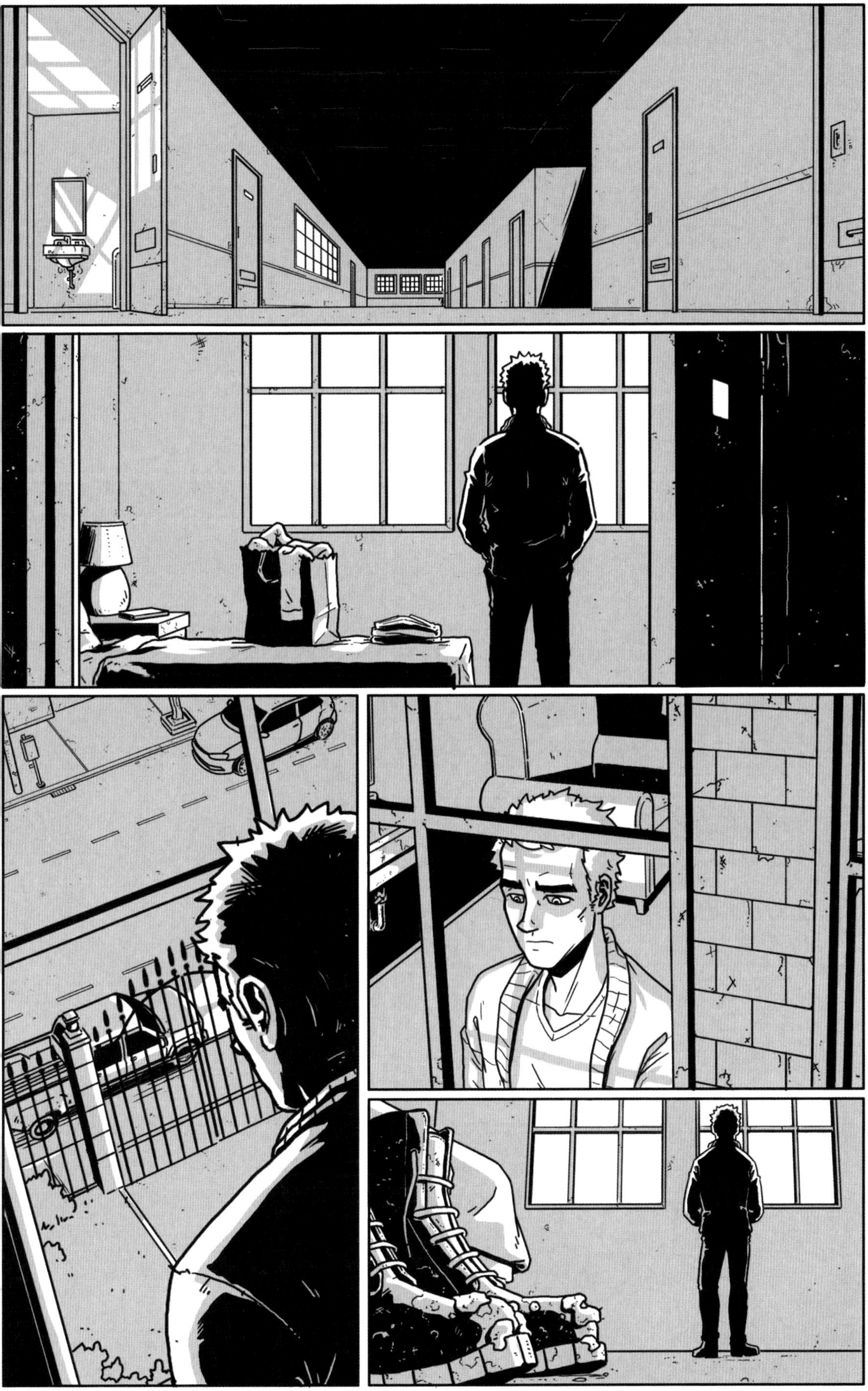

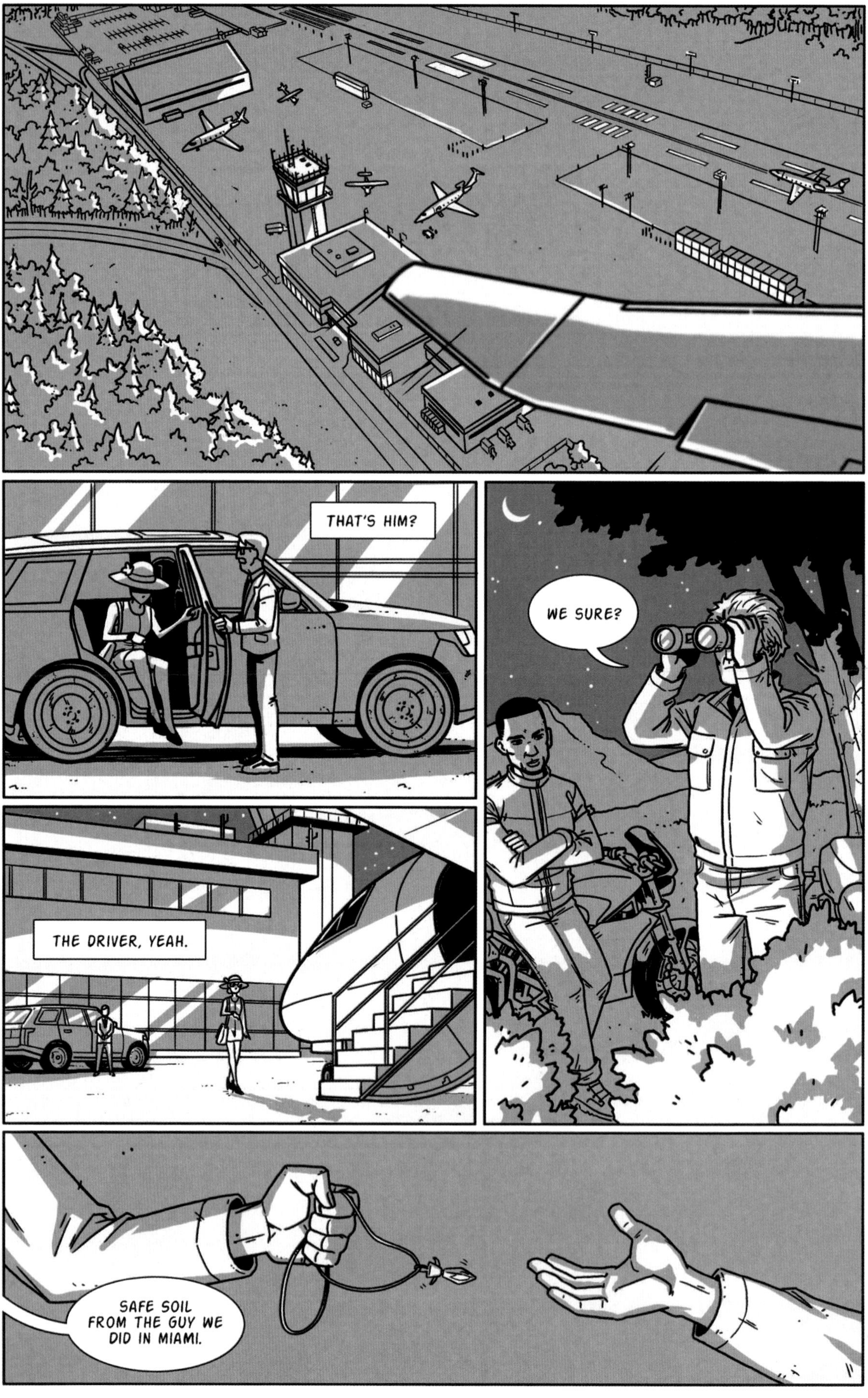
THAT'S HIM?
WE SURE?
THE DRIVER, YEAH.
SAFE SOIL FROM THE GUY WE DID IN MIAMI.

IT'S HIM. HE WAS IN THE WOODS LOOKING FOR ELLA THAT NIGHT.

CAN I JUST SAY ONE THING?

WHAT?

MAYBE WE TRY TO DO THIS ONE A LITTLE MORE... SUBTLE.

SUBTLE?

I'M JUST SAYING YOU DON'T NEED THE COUNCIL STARING AT YOU ANY HARDER THEN THEY ALREADY ARE.

LOW KEY.

I KNOW WHAT SUBTLE-- MIAMI WASN'T LOW KEY?

NO, MAIMI WAS *NOT* LOW KEY. NEITHER WAS PORTLAND.

LINCOLN, PORTLAND WASN'T MY FAULT.

FINE. BUT PORTLAND WAS NOT MY FAULT.

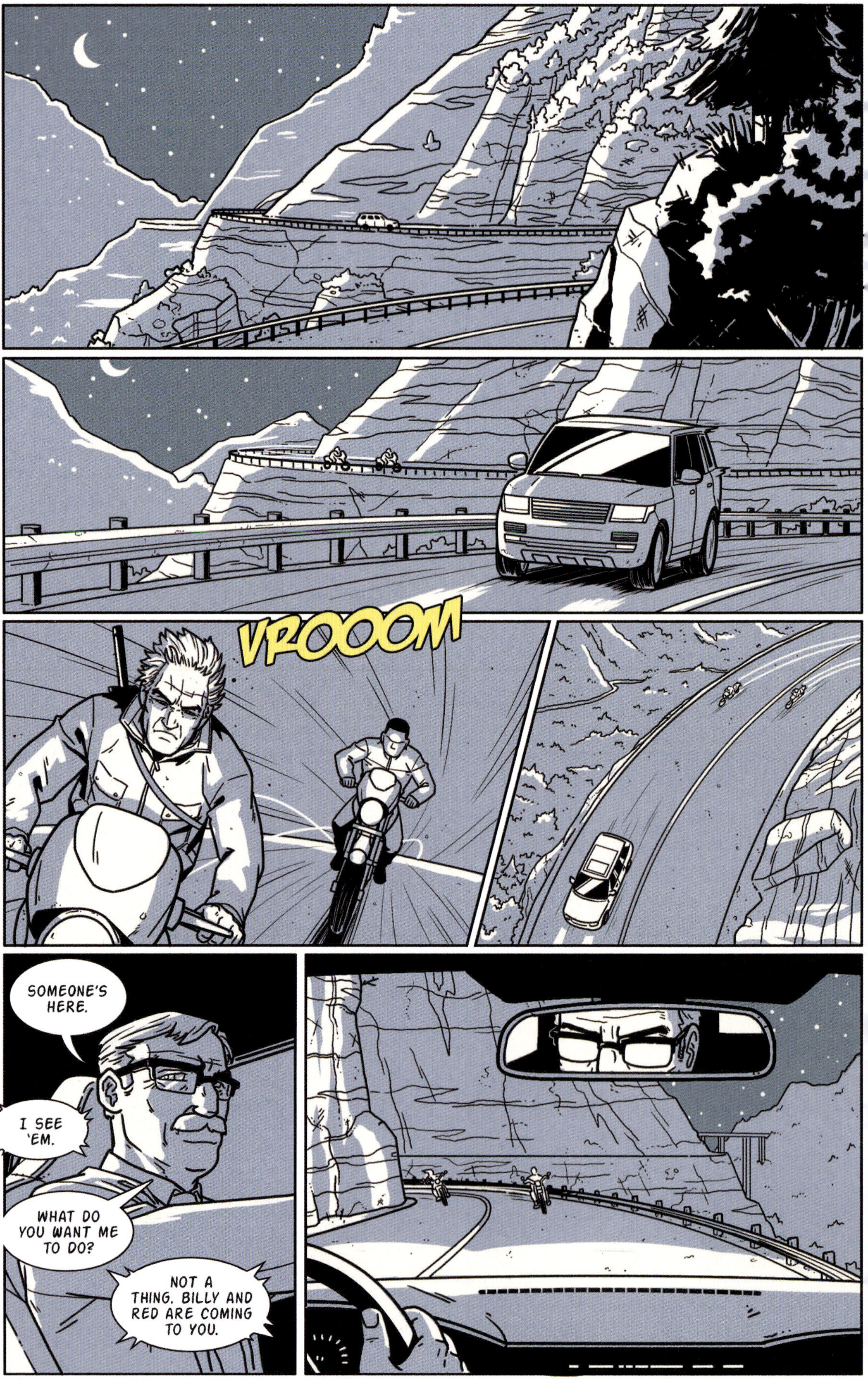
VROOOM
SOMEONE'S HERE.
I SEE 'EM.
WHAT DO YOU WANT ME TO DO?
NOT A THING. BILLY AND RED ARE COMING TO YOU.

VVVRRRMMM

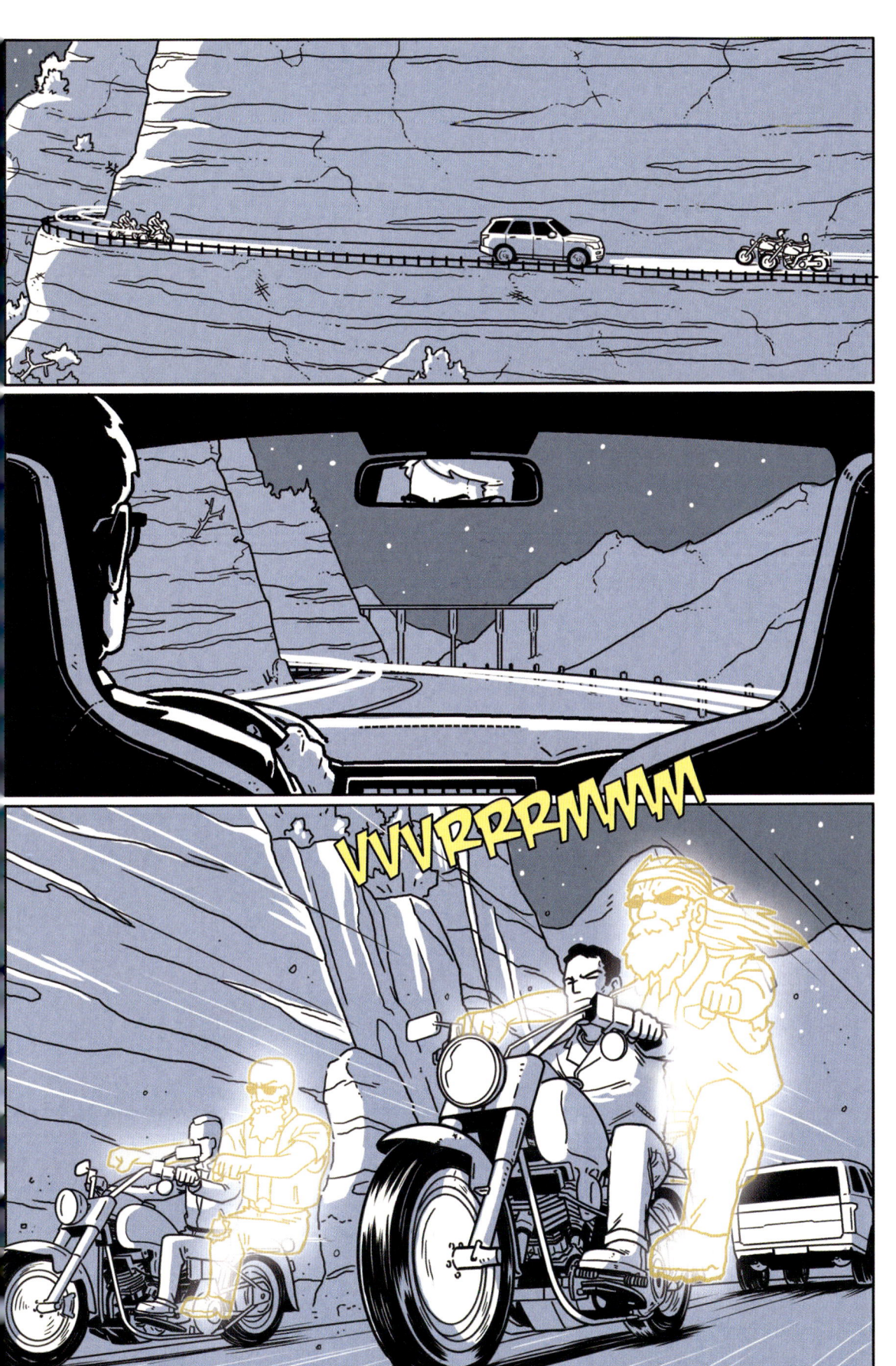

BLAM BLAM BLAM BLAM BLAM BLAM

SHHHHNG

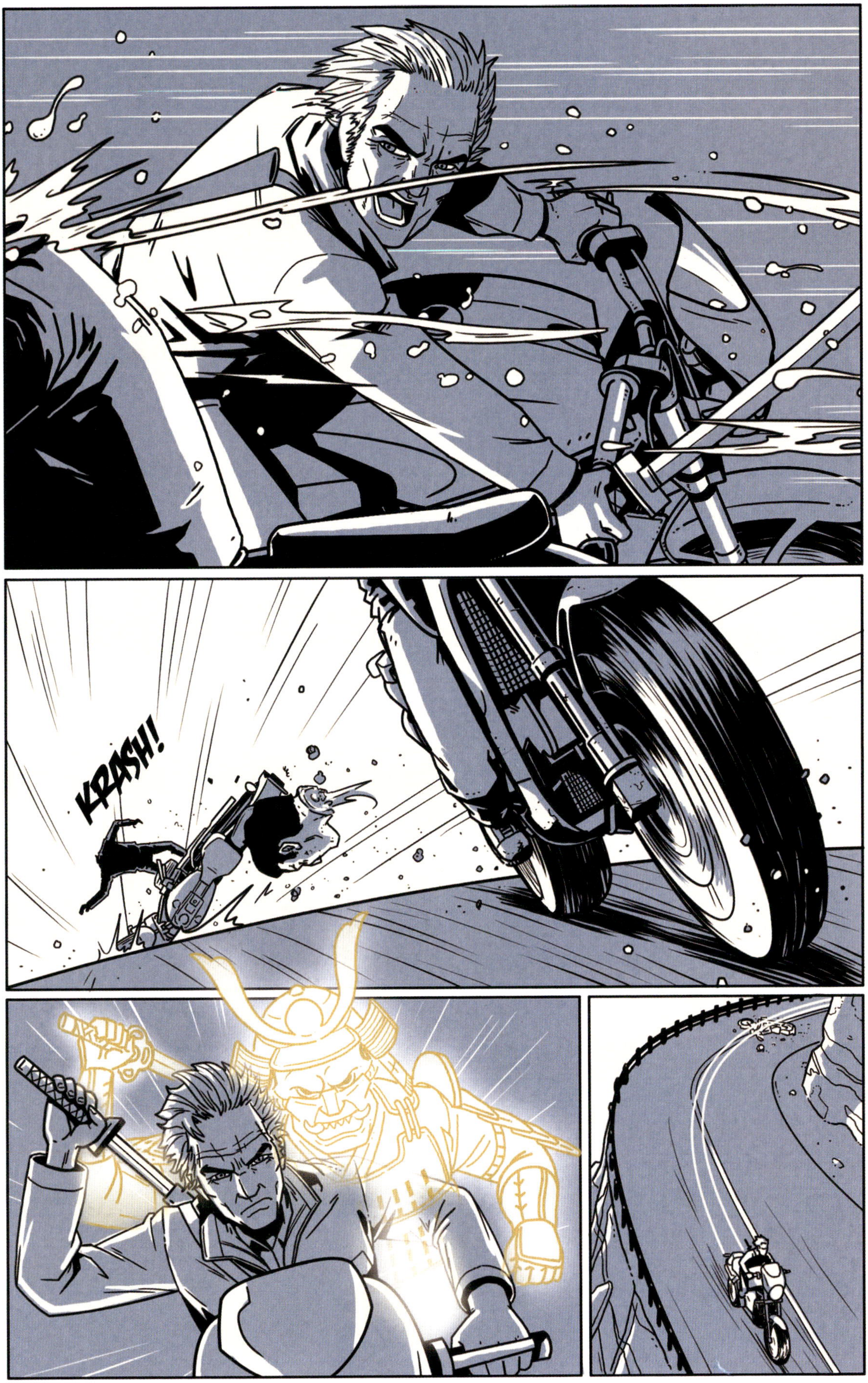
KRASH!

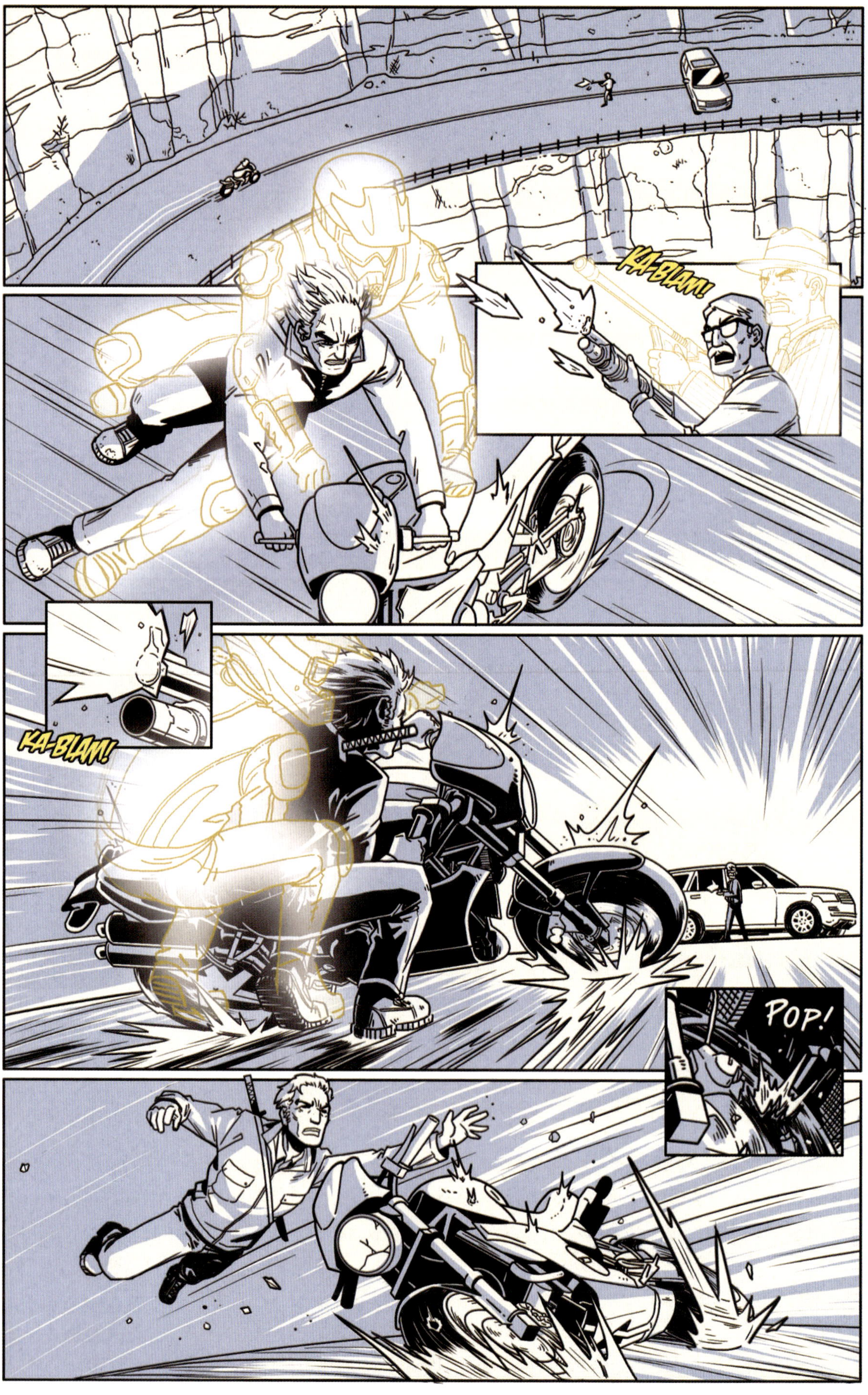
KA-BLAM!
KA-BLAM!
POP!

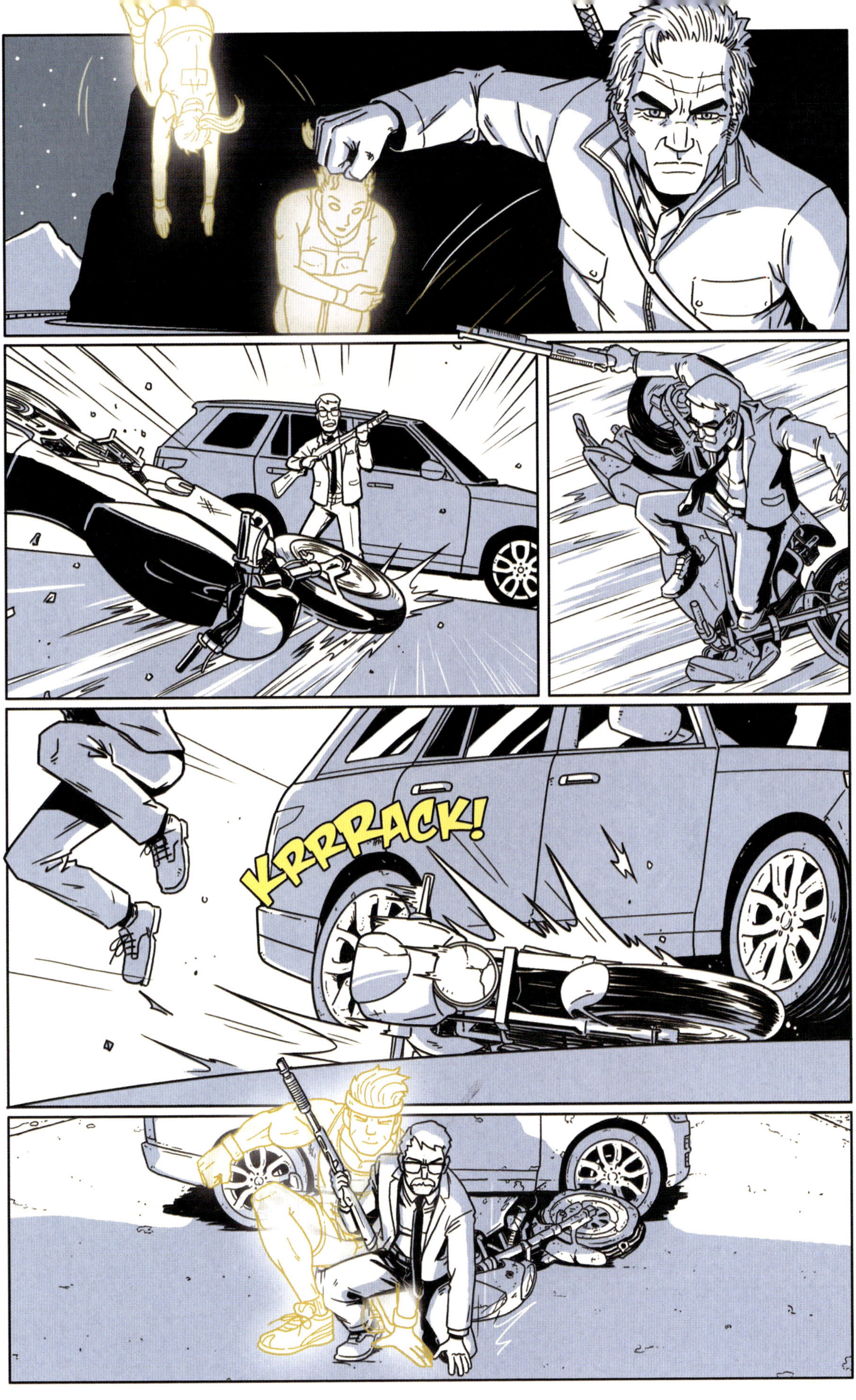
KRRRACK!

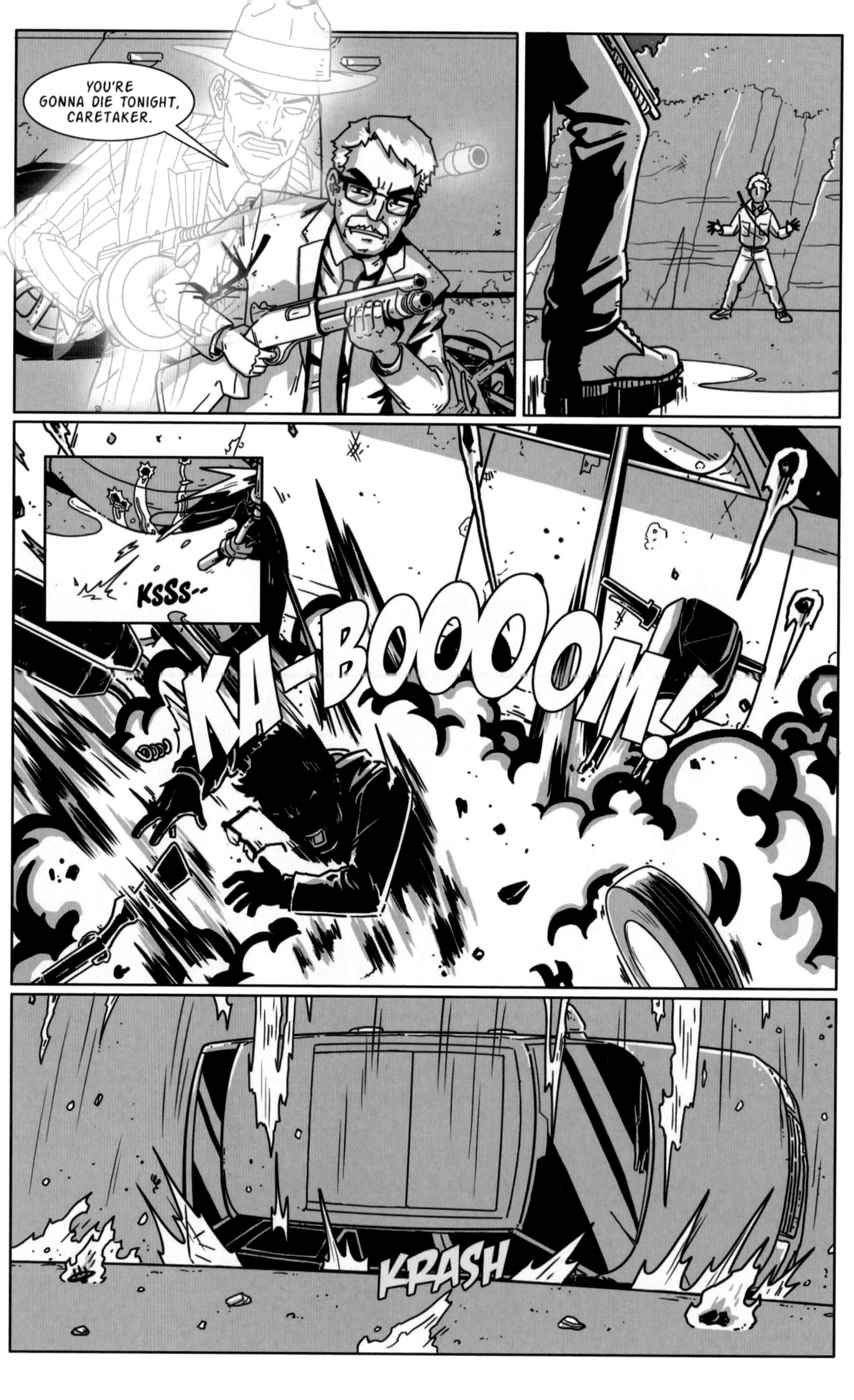
YOU'RE GONNA DIE TONIGHT, CARETAKER.
KSSS--
KA-BOOOOM!
KRASH

SERIOUSLY?!
SHUT UP.
THIS IS WORSE THAN PORTLAND!
PORTLAND WASN'T MY FAULT--
WAIT.
WHAT?
SOMEONE'S IN THERE!

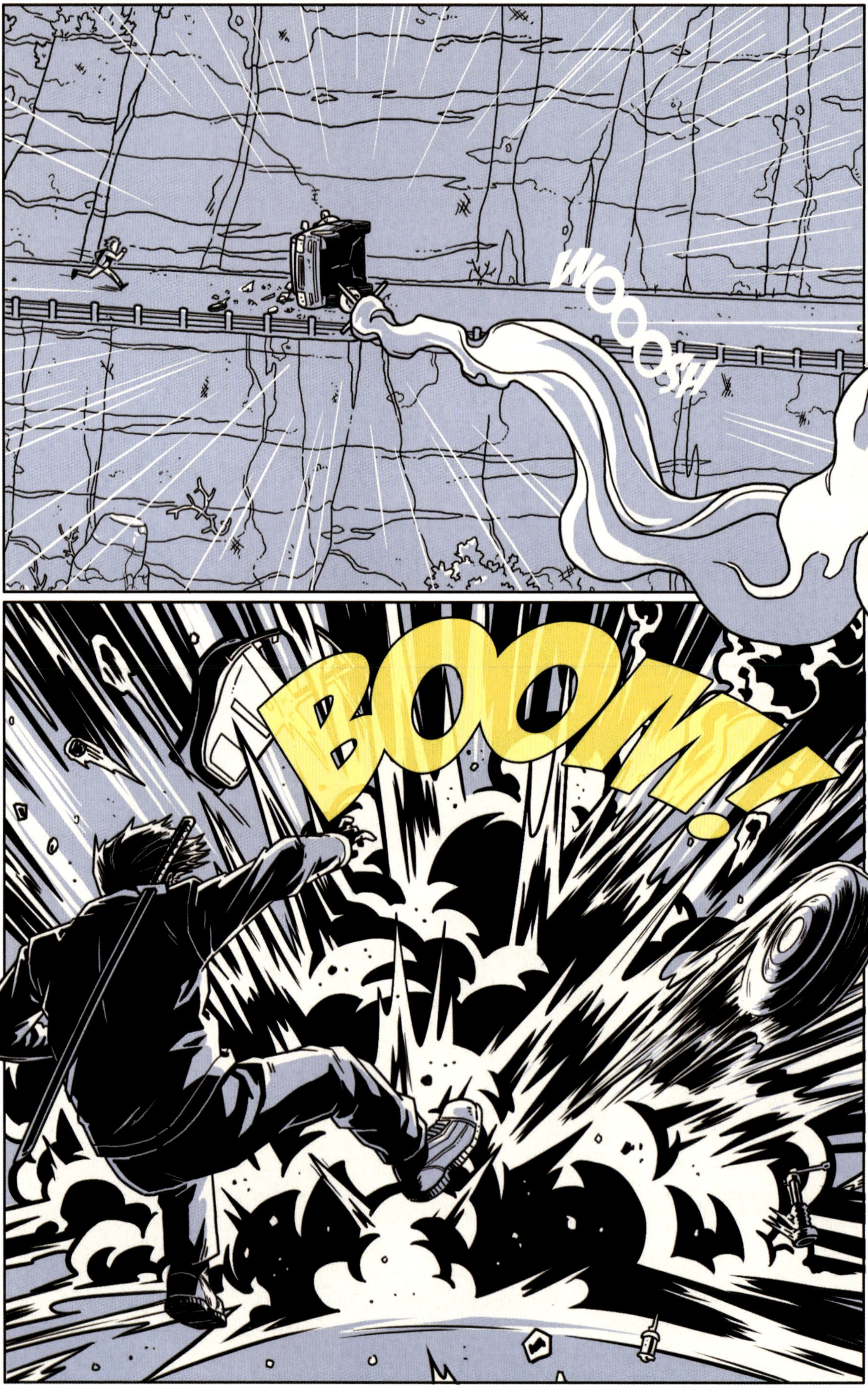
WOOOOSH
BOOM!!

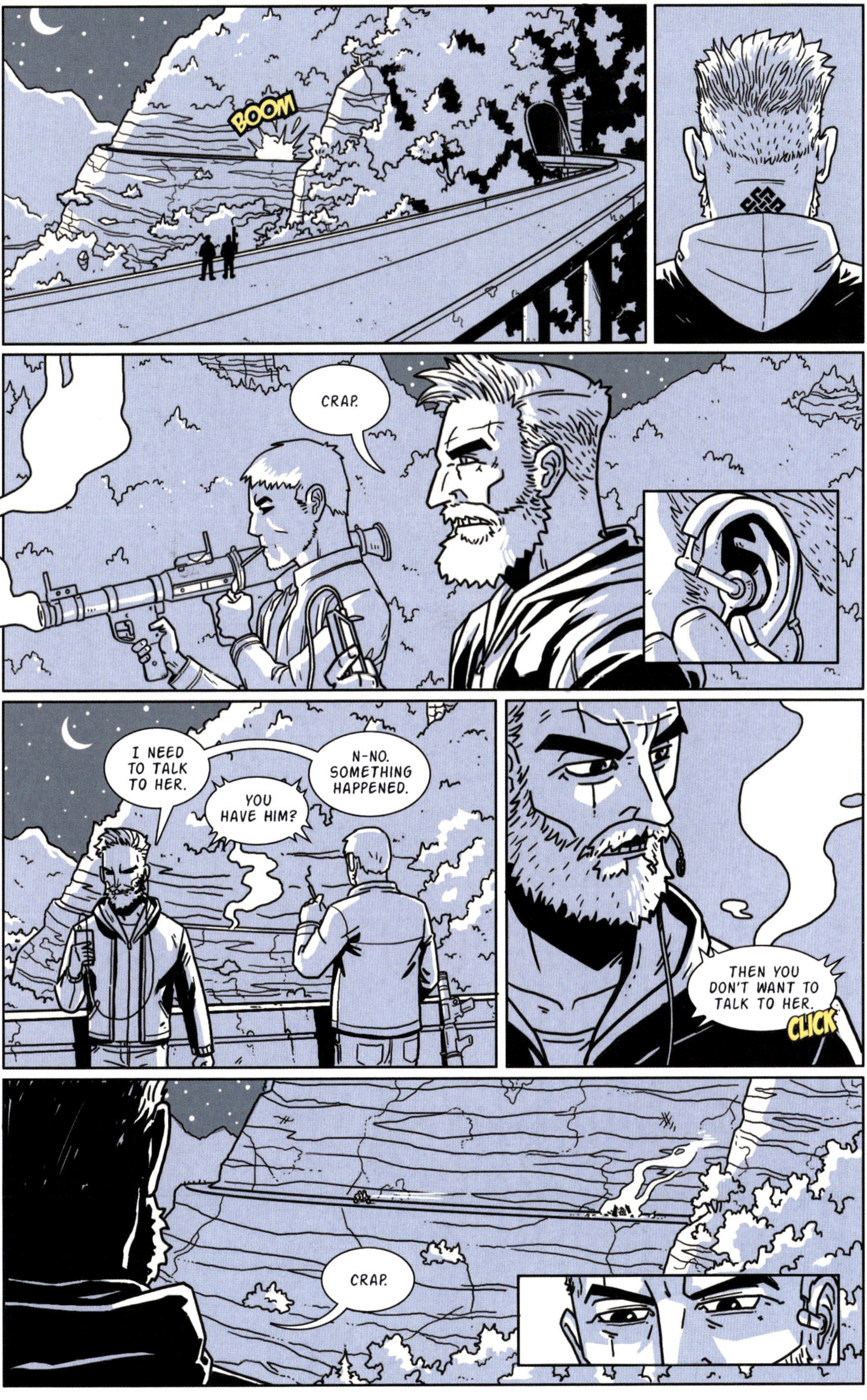
BOOM
CRAP.
I NEED TO TALK TO HER.
YOU HAVE HIM?
N-NO. SOMETHING HAPPENED.
THEN YOU DON'T WANT TO TALK TO HER.
CLICK
CRAP.

BRONX, NEW YORK
YOU KNOW WHO I AM?
I DO, YEAH.
THEN YOU KNOW WHAT THE STREETS SAY ABOUT ME, YEAH?
WOULDN'T BE HERE IF I DIDN'T.
AND YOU STILL WANNA GO THRU WIT' THIS?
NAZ, WHERE'S THE MONEY?
CAN I GIVE YOU SOME ADVICE?
SURE, WHY NOT.
DON'T KNOW HOW YOU GOT THIS FAR, BUT CREDIT GIVEN WHERE CREDIT BE DUE.
BUT I TELL YOU THIS, YOU SURE AS HELL MIGHT WANNA RETHINK YOUR GAME PLAN.

'CAUSE I'M TELLIN YOU, IF THIS DON'T GO DOWN EXACTLY INCH PERFECT...
I'M GONNA COME FIND YOU AND WE GONNA SET RECORDS ON THE AMOUNT OF PAIN A PERSON CAN INFLICT ON ANOTHER INDIVIDUAL. YOU DIG?
I DIG. NOW WHERE'S THE MONEY?

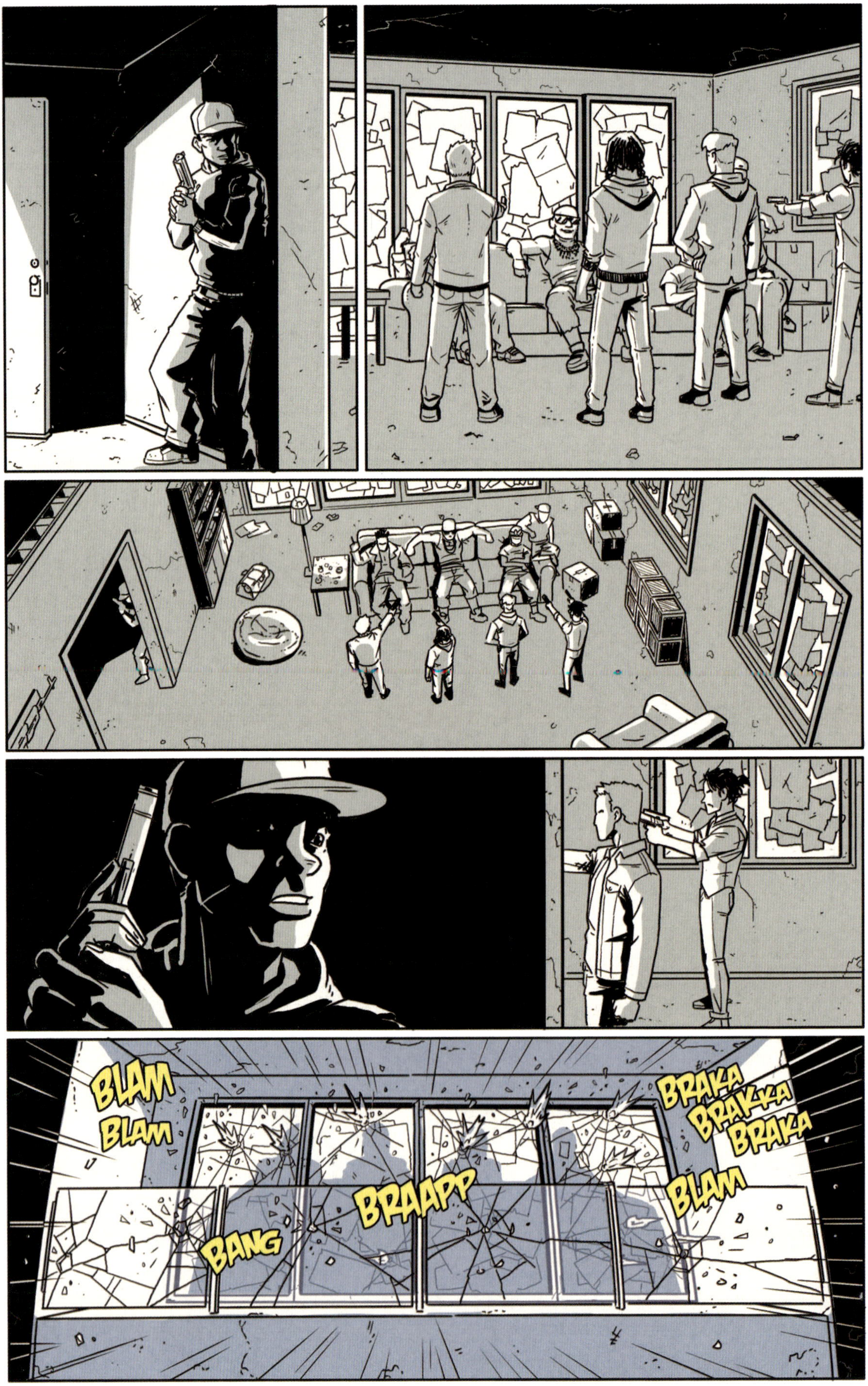
BLAM
BLAM
BRAKA
BRAKKA
BRAKA
BRAAPP
BLAM
BANG

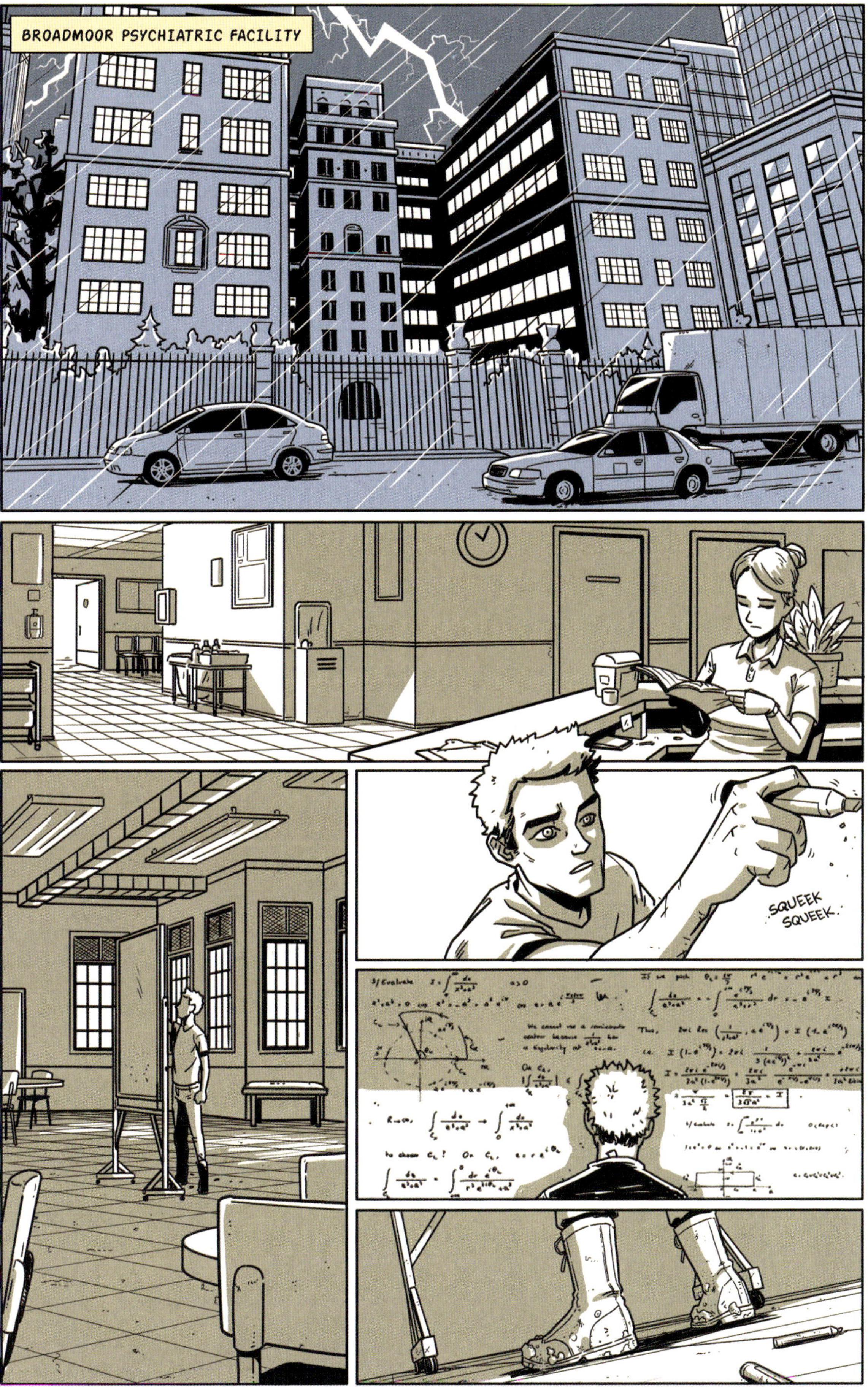
BROADMOOR PSYCHIATRIC FACILITY
SQUEEK
SQUEEK

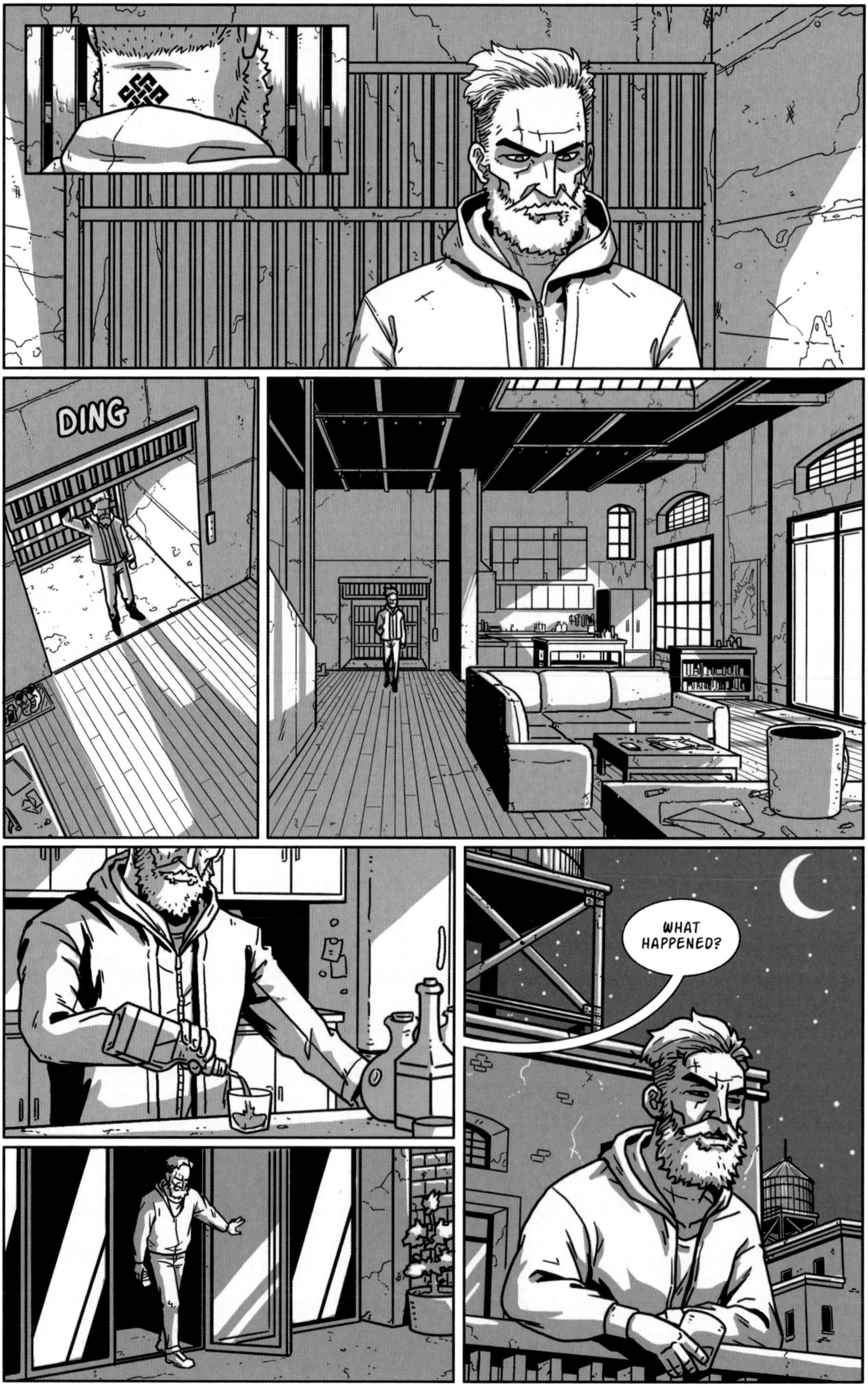
DING
WHAT HAPPENED?

I DON'T KNOW. WE'RE STILL LOOKING INTO IT. THE GUILD HAD PEOPLE WAITING.
FOR VOGEL? HOW COULD THEY KNOW WE WANTED HIM?
I DON'T THAT'S NOT PART OF MY JOB.
WHICH YOU HAD FOUR PEOPLE TO DO.
SHUT UP, KEATON, I NEEDED SIX!
AND VOGEL'S BODY?
VOGEL IS-- THE BODY WAS TORCHED.
WHAT?!
THE SUV HE WAS IN EXPLODED. IT'S GONE. I TRIED TO--
TELL ME YOU HAVE IT.

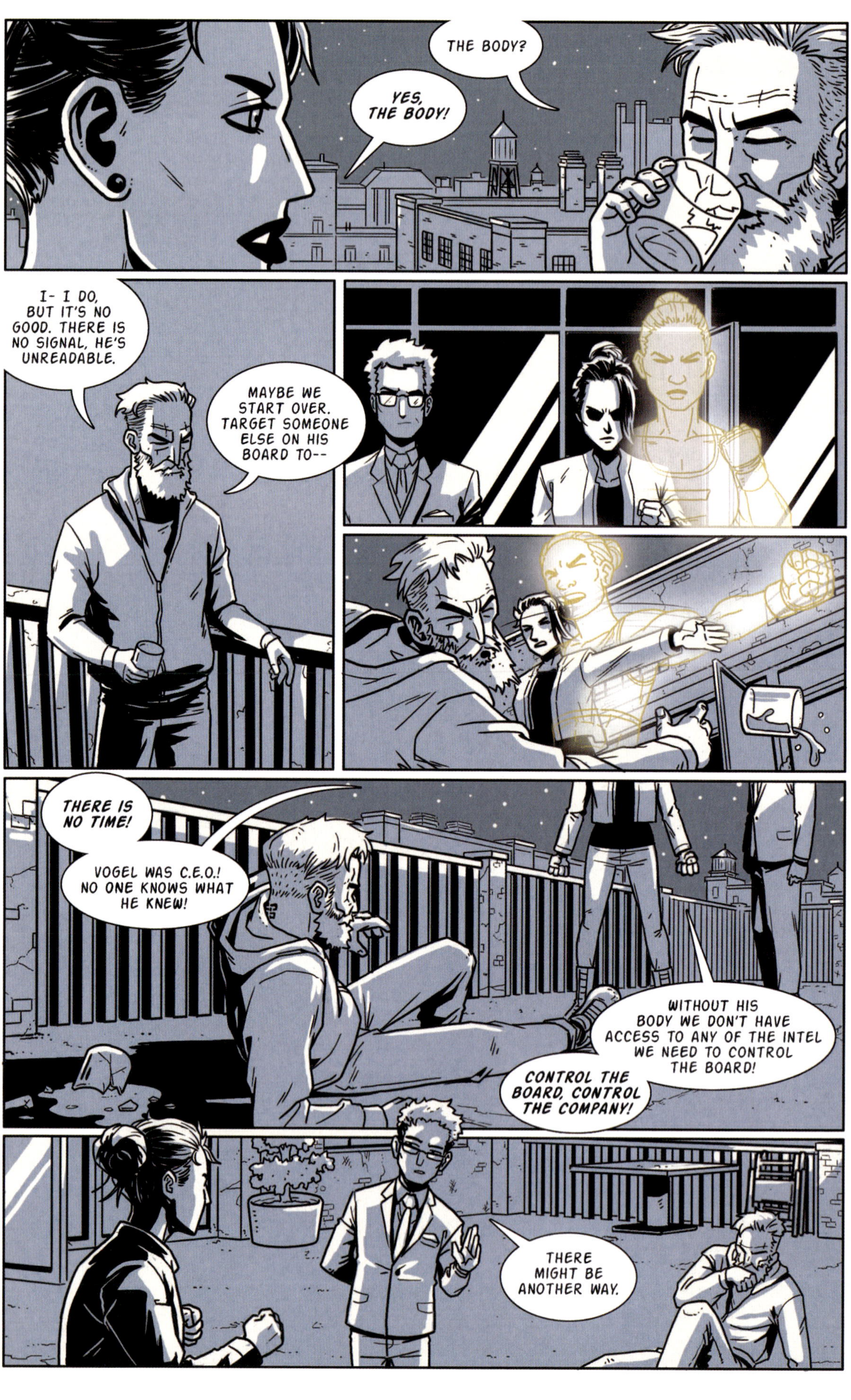
THE BODY?
YES, THE BODY!
I- I DO, BUT IT'S NO GOOD. THERE IS NO SIGNAL, HE'S UNREADABLE.
MAYBE WE START OVER. TARGET SOMEONE ELSE ON HIS BOARD TO--
THERE IS NO TIME!
VOGEL WAS C.E.O.! NO ONE KNOWS WHAT HE KNEW!
WITHOUT HIS BODY WE DON'T HAVE ACCESS TO ANY OF THE INTEL WE NEED TO CONTROL THE BOARD!
CONTROL THE BOARD, CONTROL THE COMPANY!
THERE MIGHT BE ANOTHER WAY.

Panel 1
WE WOULD NEED-- THERE'S A CHANCE WE CAN ACCESS THE ASHES EVEN THOUGH THE BODY WAS BURNED.

Panel 2
HOW?

WE'D NEED A FAMILY MEMBER.

HE'S GOT A WIFE. AN EX-WIFE.

Panel 3
NO, IT HAS TO BE A BLOOD RELATIVE. A SIBLING. A PARENT.

THROUGH THEM WE MIGHT BE ABLE TO TAP INTO SOMETHING.

Panel 4
WHAT ABOUT A KID? WOULD A KID WORK?

IT SHOULD, YEAH. WHY?

Panel 5
'CAUSE HE'S GOT A DAUGHTER.

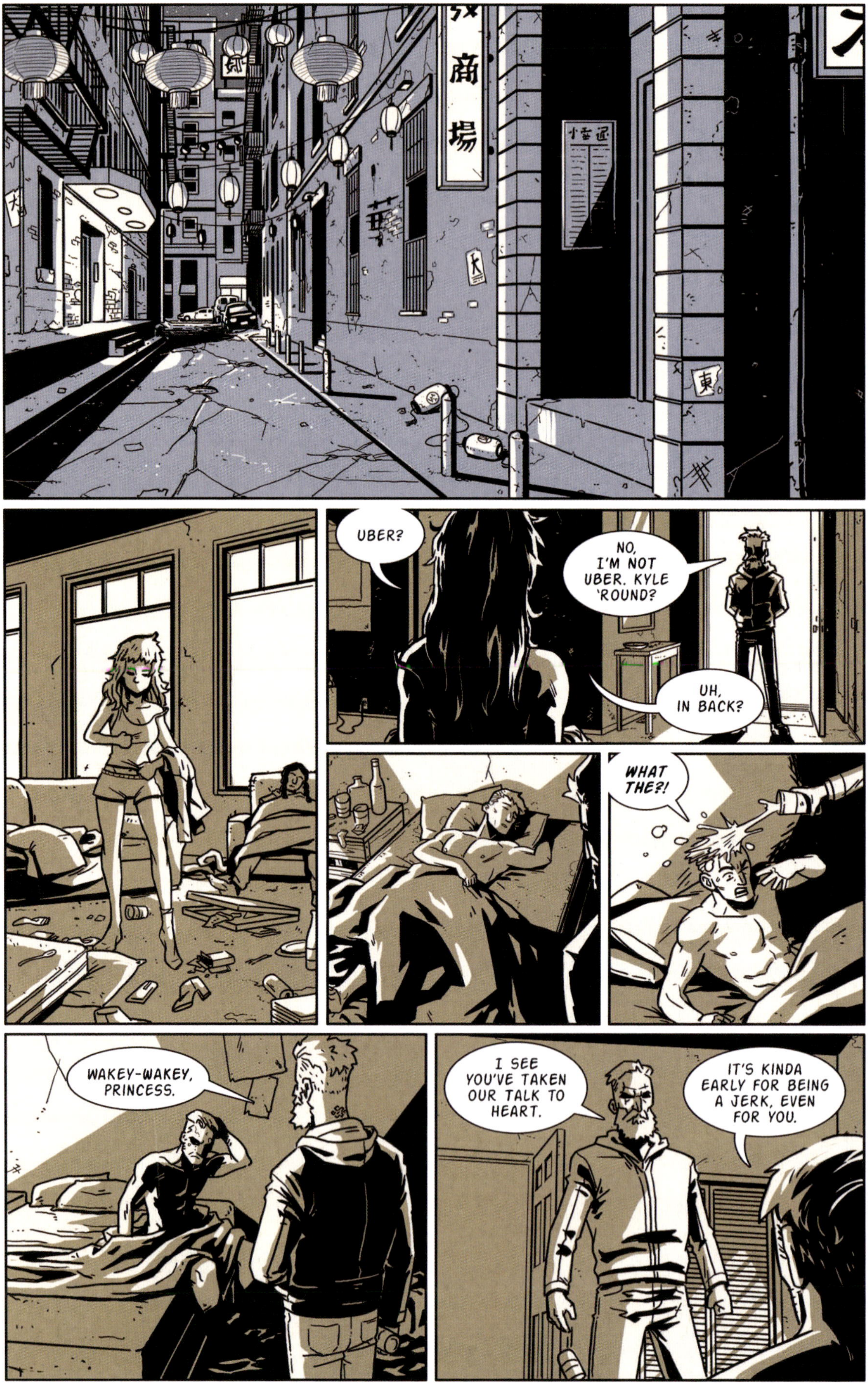
UBER?
NO, I'M NOT UBER. KYLE 'ROUND?
UH, IN BACK?
WHAT THE?!
WAKEY-WAKEY, PRINCESS.
I SEE YOU'VE TAKEN OUR TALK TO HEART.
IT'S KINDA EARLY FOR BEING A JERK, EVEN FOR YOU.

WHAM
IS IT TOO EARLY FOR ME TO PUT MY SON'S HEAD THROUGH THE WALL?
RUMOUR HAS IT, SOMEONE TOOK THIRTY GRAND OFF A DRUG DEALER. YOU BACK TO OLD HABITS?
UGH... L- LOOK AROUND AND YOU TELL ME.
LISTEN TO ME, KYLE, I KNOW THIS LIFE CAN BE COMPLICATED...
...BUT I CAN'T PROTECT YOU IF THE COMMITEE CATCHES YOU AGAIN.
CAN'T OR WON'T?
WHAT DO YOU WANT?
I HAVE A JOB FOR YOU.

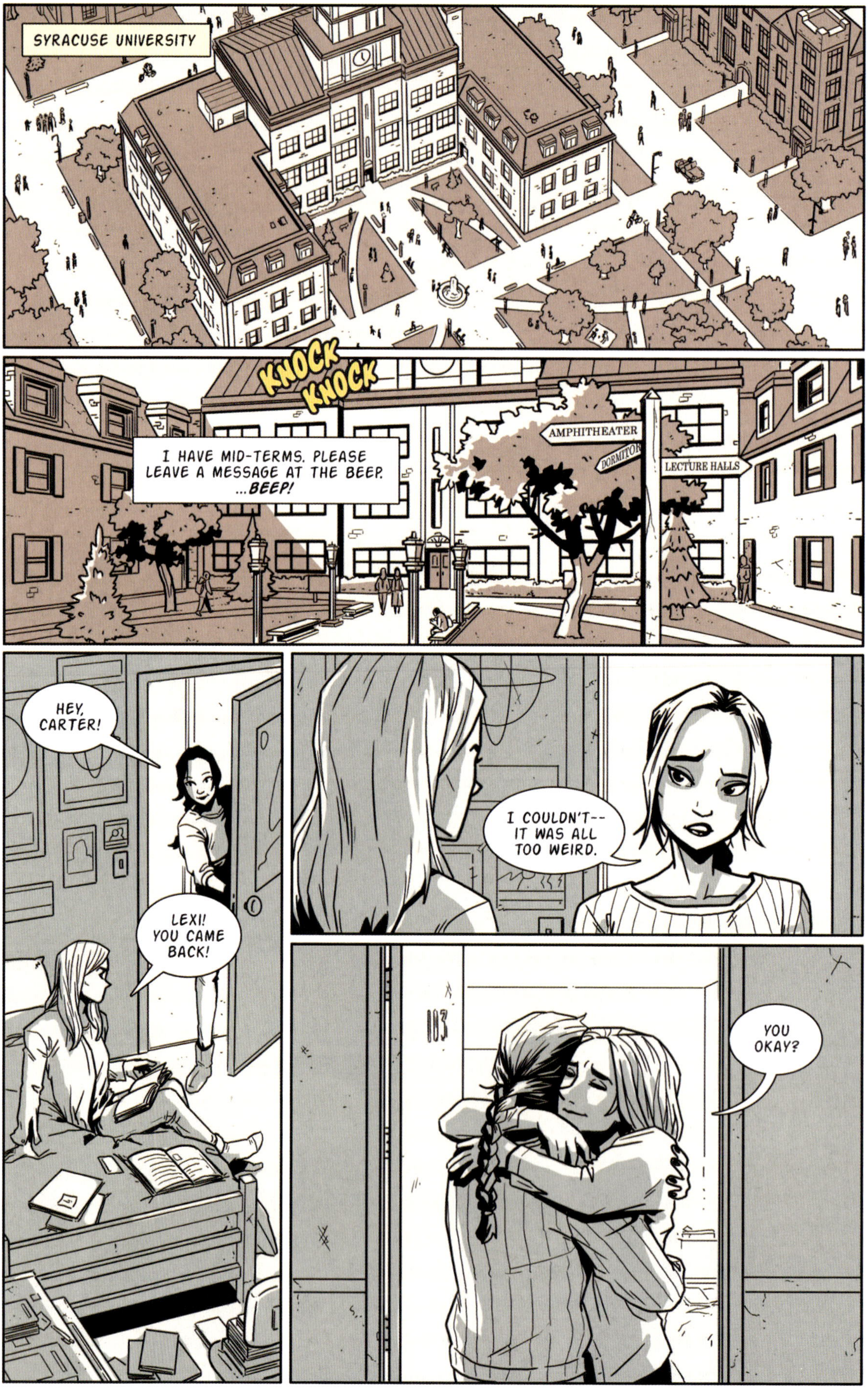
SYRACUSE UNIVERSITY
KNOCK KNOCK
I HAVE MID-TERMS. PLEASE LEAVE A MESSAGE AT THE BEEP. ...BEEP!
AMPHITHEATER
DORMITORY
LECTURE HALLS
HEY, CARTER!
LEXI! YOU CAME BACK!
I COULDN'T-- IT WAS ALL TOO WEIRD.
103
YOU OKAY?

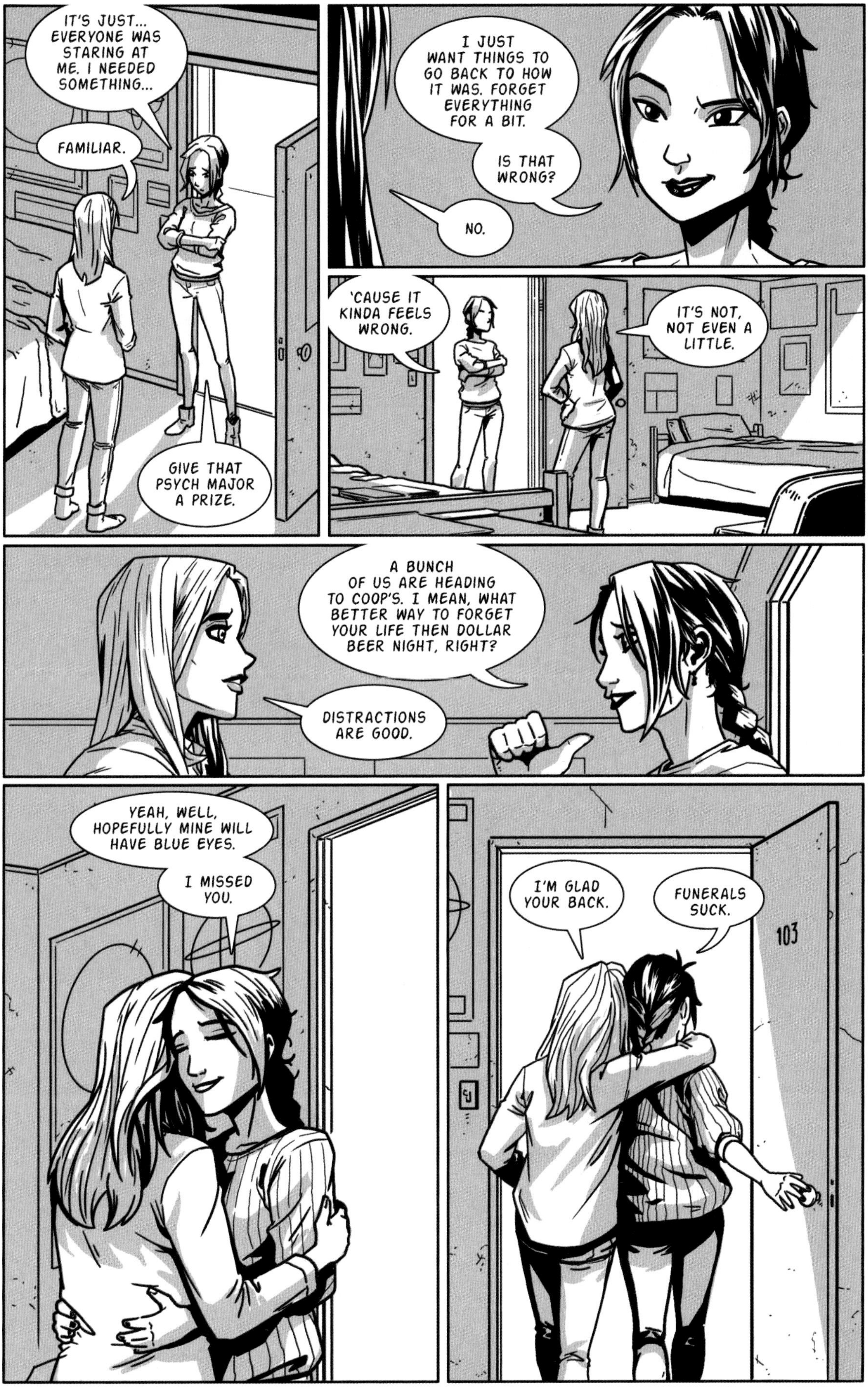
IT'S JUST... EVERYONE WAS STARING AT ME. I NEEDED SOMETHING...
FAMILIAR.
GIVE THAT PSYCH MAJOR A PRIZE.
I JUST WANT THINGS TO GO BACK TO HOW IT WAS. FORGET EVERYTHING FOR A BIT.
IS THAT WRONG?
NO.
'CAUSE IT KINDA FEELS WRONG.
IT'S NOT, NOT EVEN A LITTLE.
A BUNCH OF US ARE HEADING TO COOP'S. I MEAN, WHAT BETTER WAY TO FORGET YOUR LIFE THEN DOLLAR BEER NIGHT, RIGHT?
DISTRACTIONS ARE GOOD.
YEAH, WELL, HOPEFULLY MINE WILL HAVE BLUE EYES.
I MISSED YOU.
I'M GLAD YOUR BACK.
FUNERALS SUCK.
103

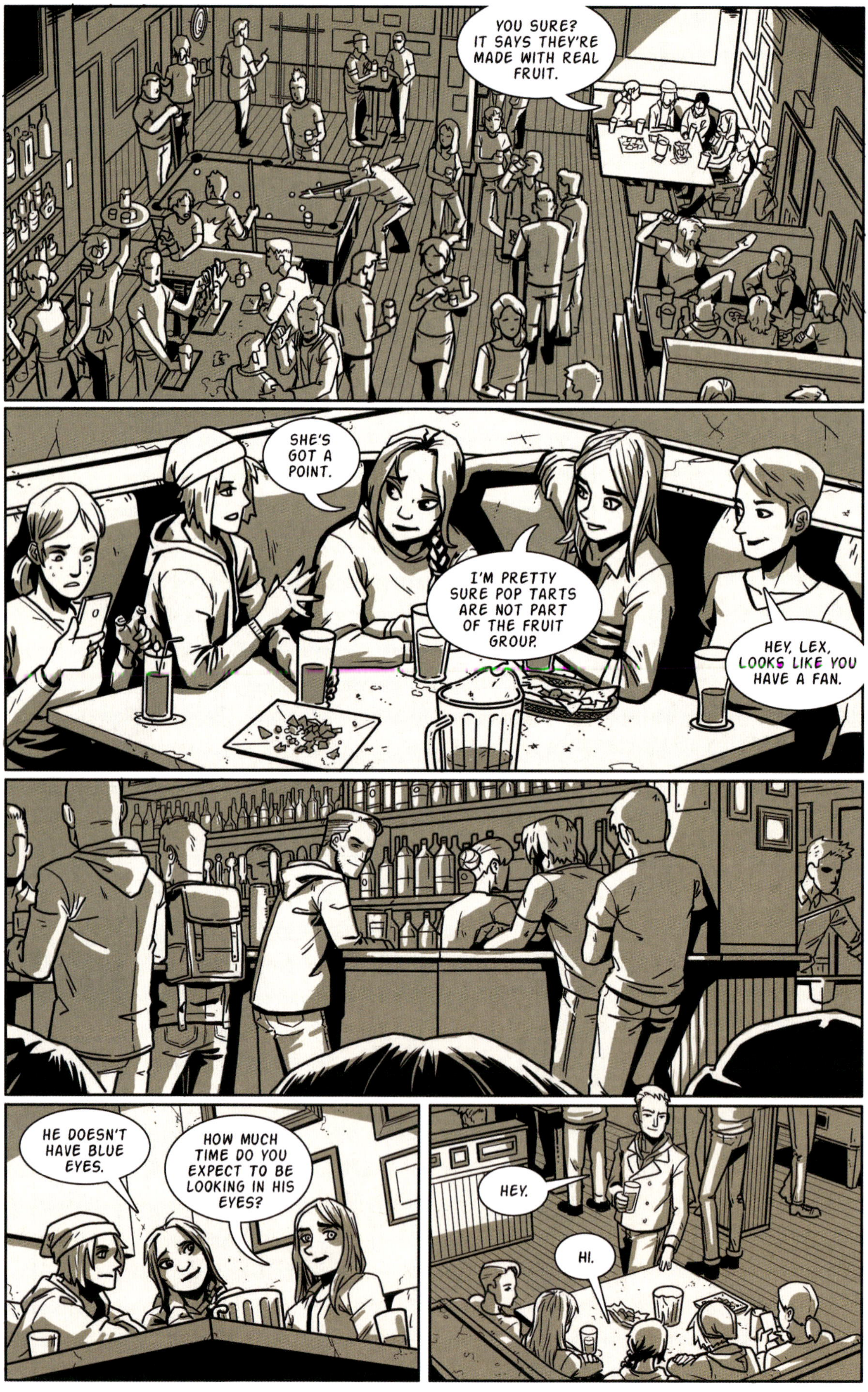
YOU SURE? IT SAYS THEY'RE MADE WITH REAL FRUIT.
SHE'S GOT A POINT.
I'M PRETTY SURE POP TARTS ARE NOT PART OF THE FRUIT GROUP.
HEY, LEX, LOOKS LIKE YOU HAVE A FAN.
HE DOESN'T HAVE BLUE EYES.
HOW MUCH TIME DO YOU EXPECT TO BE LOOKING IN HIS EYES?
HEY.
HI.

BULLS-EYE AND YOU LET ME BUY YOU A DRINK.
ALREADY HAVE ONE.
AND IF I UP THE DEGREE OF DIFFICULTY TO IMPRESS YOU?
WHAT DID YOU HAVE IN MIND?
WHO ARE YOU?
ME? I'M HER AGENT.
I NEGOTIATE ALL HER HOOK-UPS. SO, WHAT ARE WE THINKING?
I'LL DO IT FROM HERE.
RIGHT HERE?
RIGHT HERE.
OKAY. I'LL TAKE IT TO MY CLIENT.
WITH YOUR EYES CLOSED.

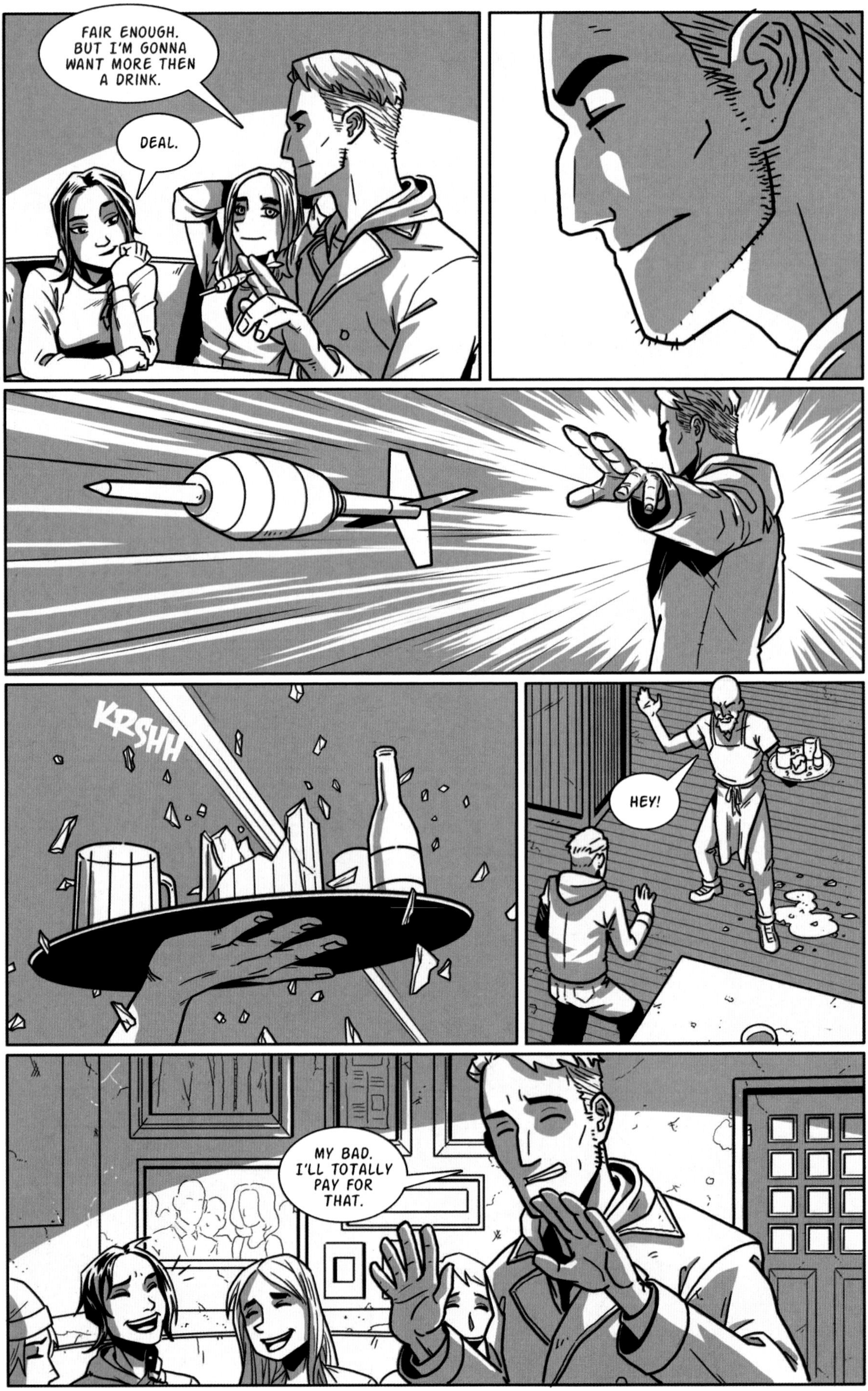
FAIR ENOUGH. BUT I'M GONNA WANT MORE THEN A DRINK.
DEAL.
KRSHH
HEY!
MY BAD. I'LL TOTALLY PAY FOR THAT.

LATER THAT NIGHT
WE'RE ONE OF FORTY COLLEGES WITH ONE OF THESE ON CAMPUS.
REALLY? DIDN'T SEE IT ON THE TOUR.
KINDA FEELS LIKE WE SHOULD GET A TUTION DISCOUNT, RIGHT?
HEY, WHAT'S THE MATTER?
N- NOTHING. IT'S --
MY DAD JUST DIED.
OH! I'M *SO* SORRY.
IT'S OKAY. IT'S JUST... IT JUST HAPPENED IS ALL.
I'LL TAKE YOU BACK.
IT'S FINE. WE CAN WALK.
HOW DID IT-- I MEAN, WAS IT...
CAR ACCIDENT.

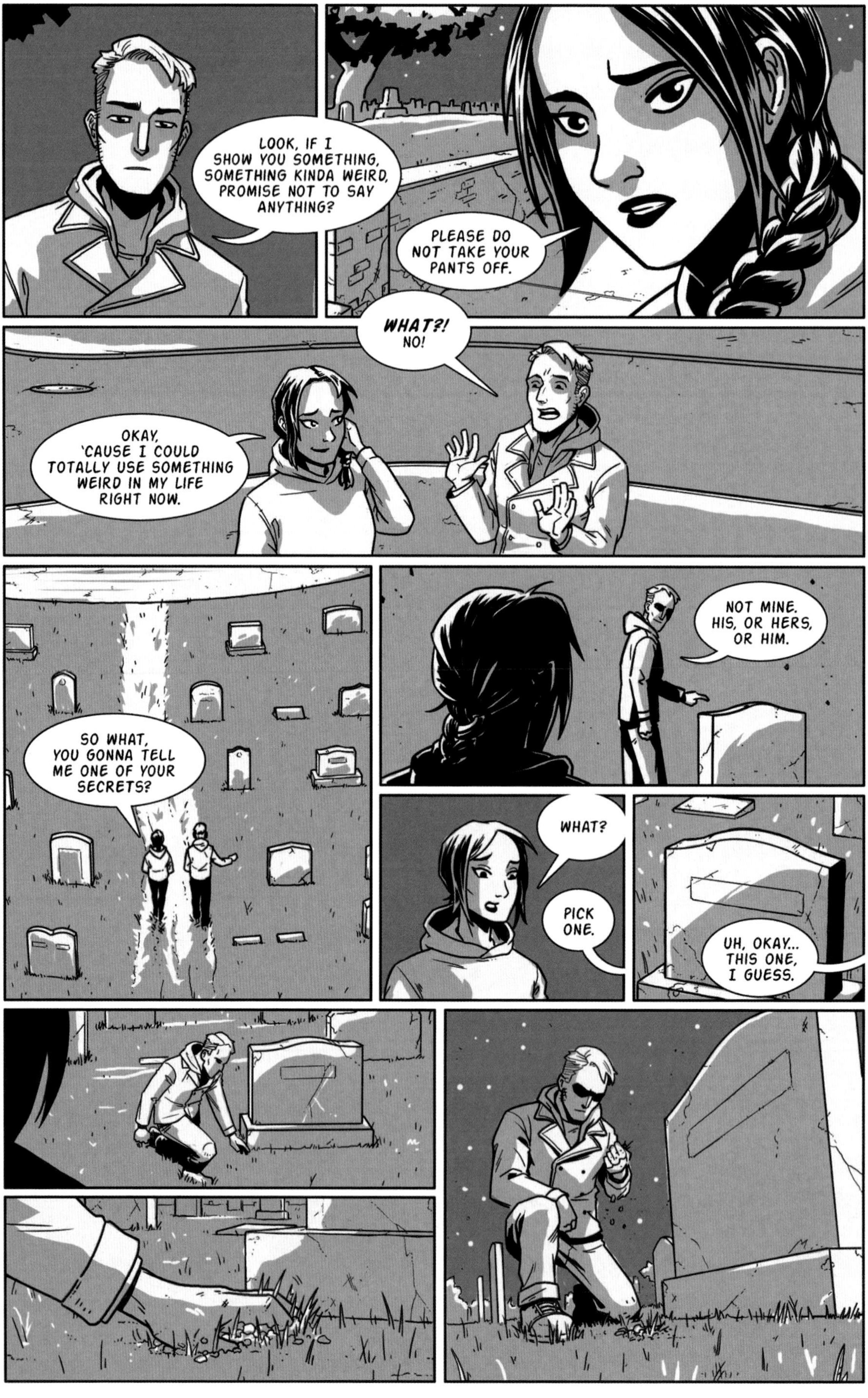
LOOK, IF I SHOW YOU SOMETHING, SOMETHING KINDA WEIRD, PROMISE NOT TO SAY ANYTHING?
PLEASE DO NOT TAKE YOUR PANTS OFF.
WHAT?! NO!
OKAY, 'CAUSE I COULD TOTALLY USE SOMETHING WEIRD IN MY LIFE RIGHT NOW.
SO WHAT, YOU GONNA TELL ME ONE OF YOUR SECRETS?
NOT MINE. HIS, OR HERS, OR HIM.
WHAT?
PICK ONE.
UH, OKAY... THIS ONE, I GUESS.

EDDIE MCDONALD, HE WAS A MECHANIC. DIED IN THE PACIFIC WHEN A JAPANESE SUBMARINE SANK THE TRANSPORT SHIP HE WAS ON.
I DON'T UNDER-- YOU KNEW HIM?
NOT EXACTLY.
THEN HOW DO YOU KNOW ANY OF THAT?
PICK ANOTHER ONE.
THAT ONE, THERE.
CATCHER BLOCK, GRADUATED THIS UNIVERSITY IN 1956, LETTERMAN, BASEBALL AND TRACK.
WENT TO NEW YORK AND BECAME AN AD-EXEC. WROTE A NOVEL HE THOUGHT WAS GOOD AND NO ONE ELSE DID AND MOVED BACK HERE.
HOW DO YOU KNOW THIS STUFF?
IT'S A GIFT, I GUESS. ONE THAT MIGHT HELP YOU WITH YOUR FATHER.
I TOLD YOU MY FATHER IS DEAD.
I KNOW. OFFER STILL STANDS.

IS THIS SOME KIND OF JOKE?
NO.
THEN HOW ARE YOU DOING IT?
I'M ACCESSING THE LIVES THEY LIVED.
THEY'RE DEAD.
LIKE I SAID, WEIRD.
ARE YOU TELLING ME YOU CAN MAKE IT SO I CAN... WHAT?
TALK TO MY FATHER?
NOT TALK... EXPERIENCE.
WHAT'S THE CATCH?
YOU HAVE TO TRUST ME.
WITH WHAT?
YOUR LIFE.

BRONX, NEW YORK
WHY AM I HERE, RUIZ?
WHY, WERE YOU BUSY, NOLITO?
I WAS, YEAH.
WITH WHAT? WAITING FOR YOUR LAW-$-ORDER CALL BACK?
WITH A NICE LADY WHO ASSURED ME SHE WOULDN'T PASS JUDGMENT...
...WHEN INFORMED THAT I WOULD, IN ALL LIKELIHOOD...
...FALL ASLEEP AFTER WE WERE DONE HAVING SEX.
SHE SOUNDS SPECIAL.
YOU KNOW WHO THIS IS?
YEAH, NAZ WASHINGTON. EVERYONE KNOWS HIM.
BUT SEEING AS I AIN'T IN NARCOTICS NO MORE, CAN'T SAY THAT I CARE ALL THAT MUCH.

YOUR NOT HERE 'CAUSE OF NAZ.
YOU'RE HERE 'CAUSE OF HIM.
AND WHO'S THIS?
THAT, IS DETECTIVE EDDIE MCFADDEN, UNDERCOVER UNIT AT THE TWO-FOUR.
DAMN.

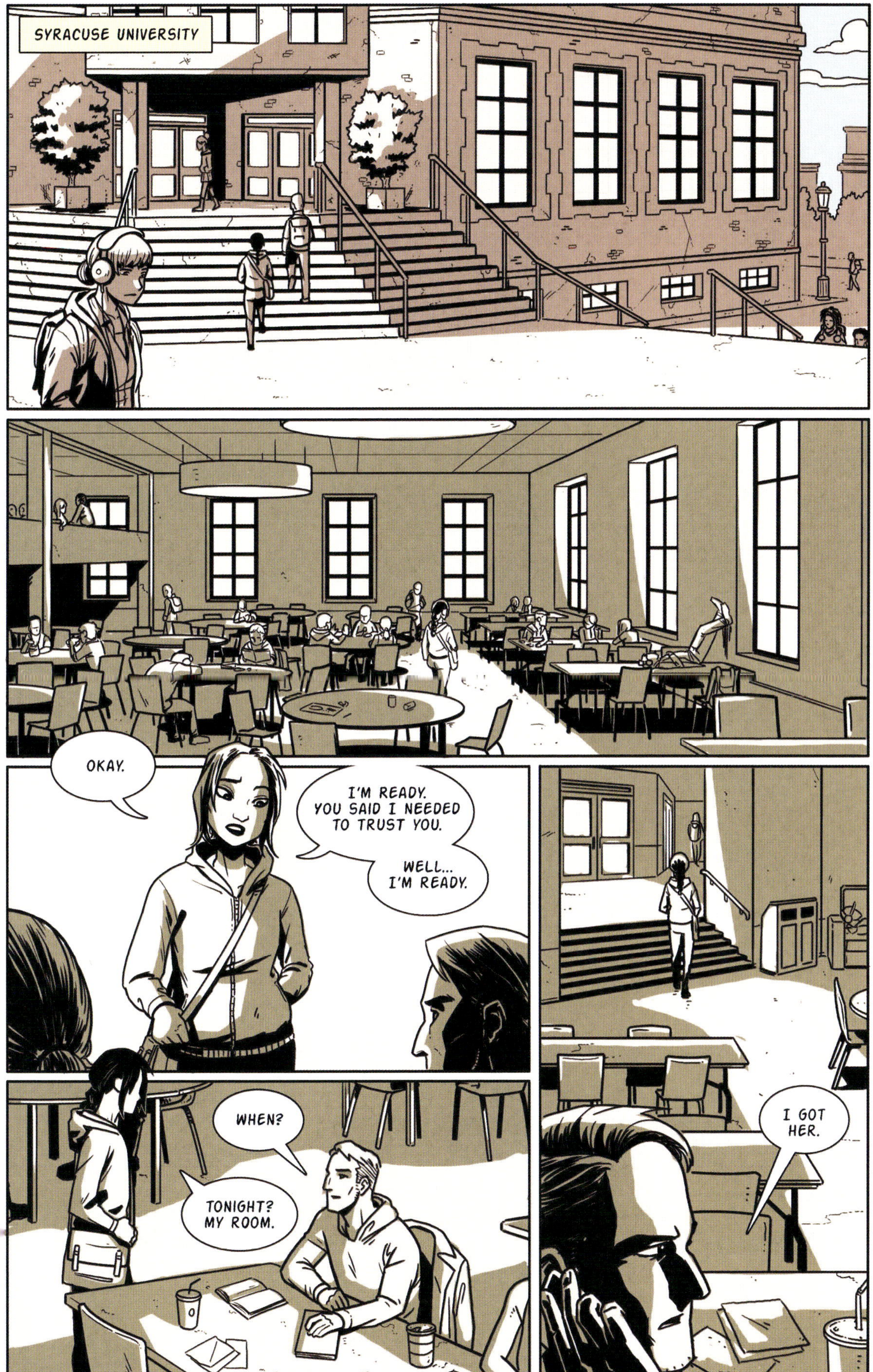
SYRACUSE UNIVERSITY
OKAY.
I'M READY. YOU SAID I NEEDED TO TRUST YOU.
WELL... I'M READY.
WHEN?
TONIGHT? MY ROOM.
I GOT HER.

BOO!

DAMN IT, ETHAN!

WHAT ARE YOU DOING HERE?

NOT GONNA LET MY TWIN SISTER CELEBRATE OUR BIRTHDAY ALONE.

THEY LET YOU OUT?

ETHAN!

DEFINE "LET".

WHAT? I KNOW YOU, CARTER. WHAT DO YOU HAVE PLANNED, TWO STUDY GROUPS AND THEN LAUNDRY?

THIS IS COLLEGE, E, THAT'S WHAT YOU'RE SUPPOSED TO DO.

HOW ARE WE RELATED?!

YOUR GPA WILL SURVIVE, I PROMISE.

REALLY? 'CAUSE I JUST SAW A BUNCH OF GUYS TRYING TO WATER-SKI ACROSS A PARKING LOT USING A CAR, SOME ROPE AND DINING HALL TRAYS.

ETHAN.

CARTER.

I'M NOT DOING THIS.

TO GRAVE DIGGERS EVERYWHERE!
CAN I ASK YOU SOMETHING?
YOU MAY.
YOU EVER THINK ABOUT HER?
WHO?
MOM.
CARTER--
I DO, SOMETIMES. I WONDER IF SHE'D BE PROUD.
SHE WOULD... OF YOU.
I'M SERIOUS.
SO AM I.
AND DAD?
HE DID HIS BEST, E.
HIS BEST SUCKED.
YOU REALLY THINK THAT?
YOU DON'T?
I THINK HE NEVER FIGURED OUT HOW TO RECOVER FROM THE FACT HE LOST A LIFE HE THOUGHT HE WAS GOING TO HAVE.
SOUNDS LIKE A NICE WAY OF SAYING HIS BEST SUCKED.

AND YOU SHOULD STOP DEFENDING HIM.
YOU ALWAYS THINK-- I'M NOT.
BECAUSE YOU AND I, WE'RE THE ONLY ONES WHO WILL LOOK OUT FOR EACH OTHER. IT'S YOU AND ME, CARTER. THAT'S IT.
I'M SERIOUS, C.
NOW, YOU READY?
I'M NOT DOING IT.
YEAH, YOU ARE.
NO.
ONE TIME, FOR YOUR PSYCHO BROTHER.
ONE, TWO, THREE...
WONDER TWIN'S POWER ACTIVATE!
FORM OF... AN ICEBERG!

YOU... YOU'RE HERE FOR ME.
WHAT?
YOU THINK YOU'RE GONNA FIX ME, IS THAT IT?
NO... MAYBE. WOULD THAT BE SO BAD?
I GUESS NOT. BUT YA BETTER HURRY.
AND NOW... I GOTTA PEE.
OUT THE DOOR, MAKE A RIGHT, MIDWAY DOWN ON YOUR LEFT.
ANY GOOD LOOKING GIRLS ON THE WAY?
I LIKE IT HERE, ETHAN. DO NOT SPEAK TO ANYONE.

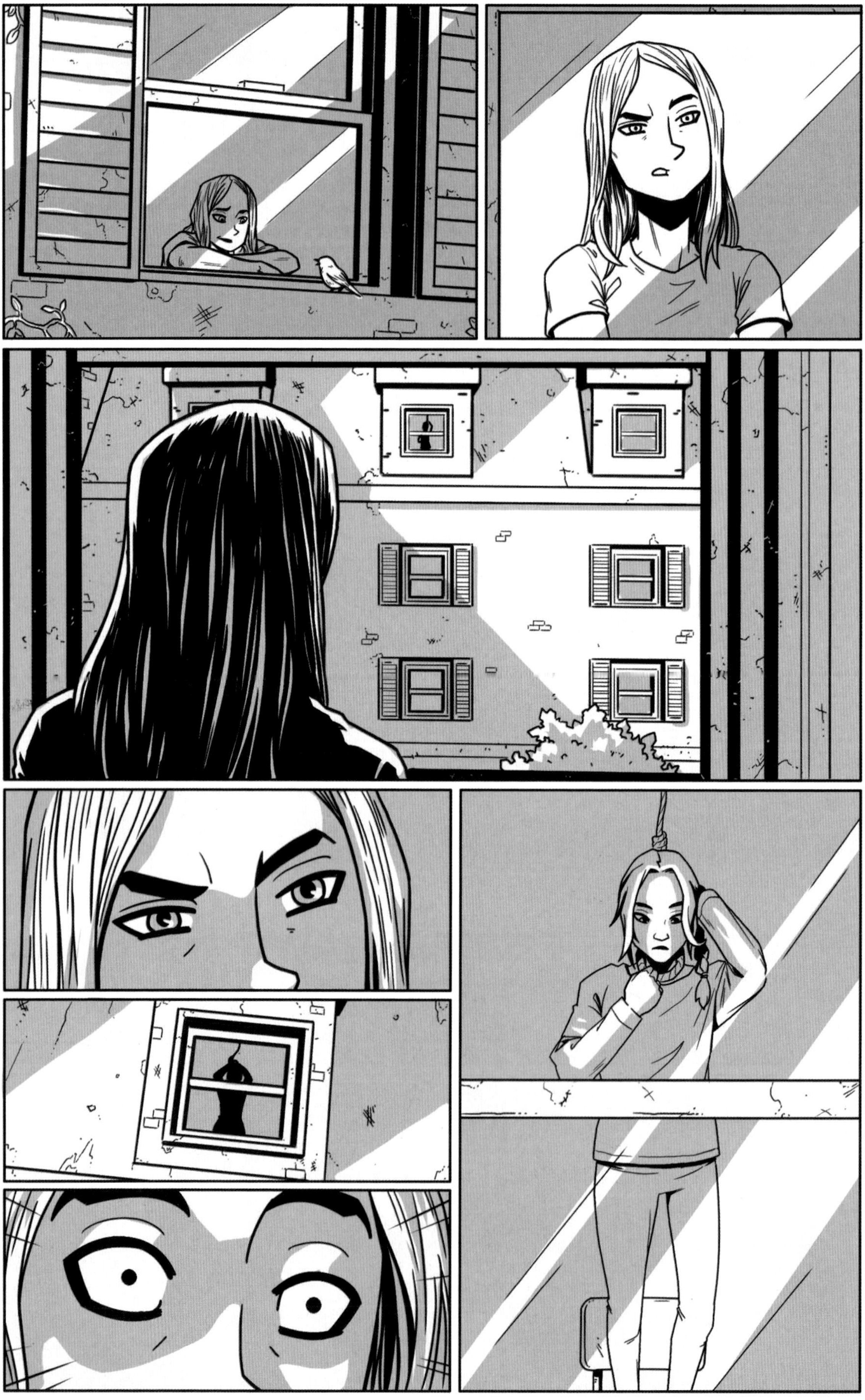

STAY HERE!

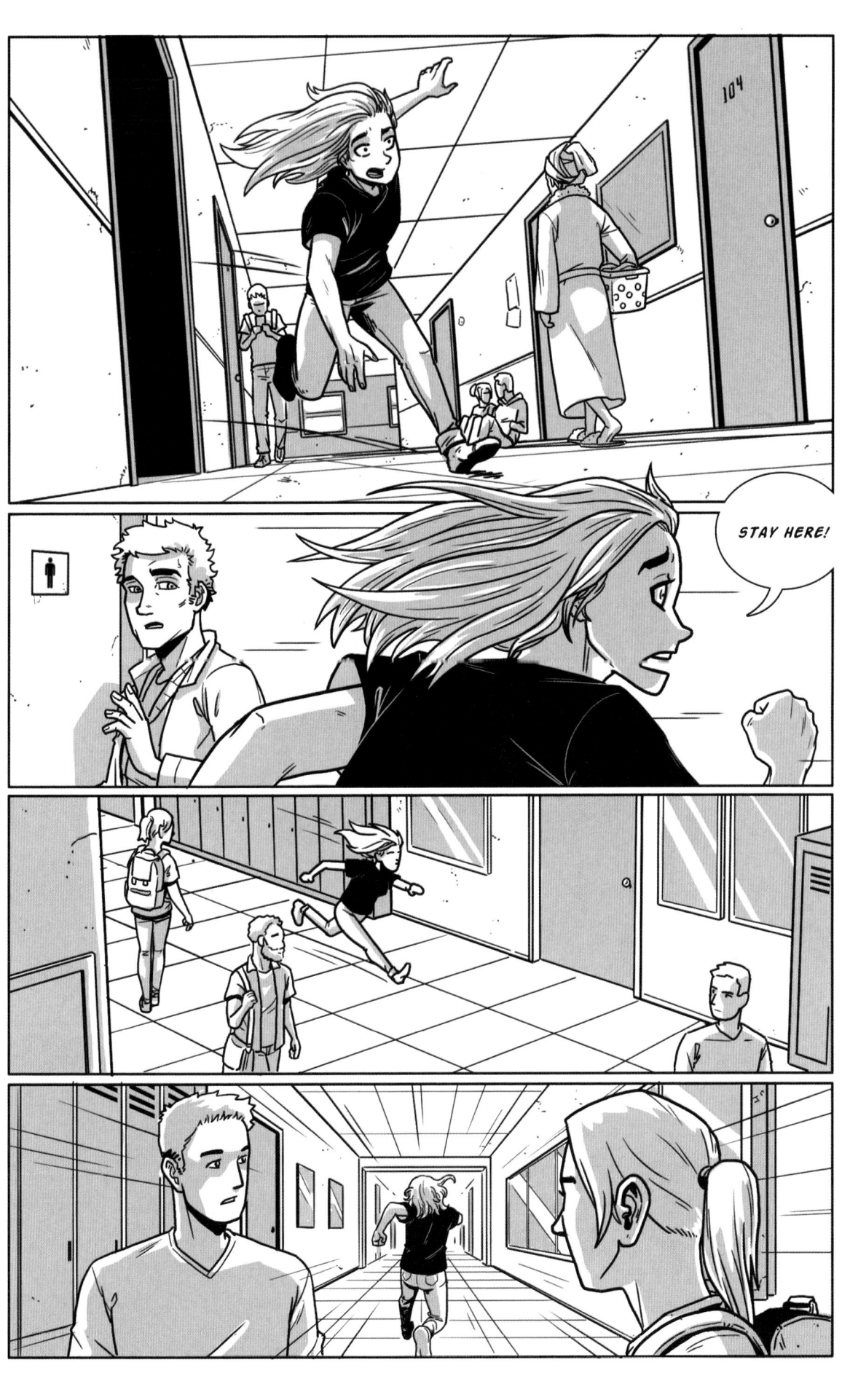

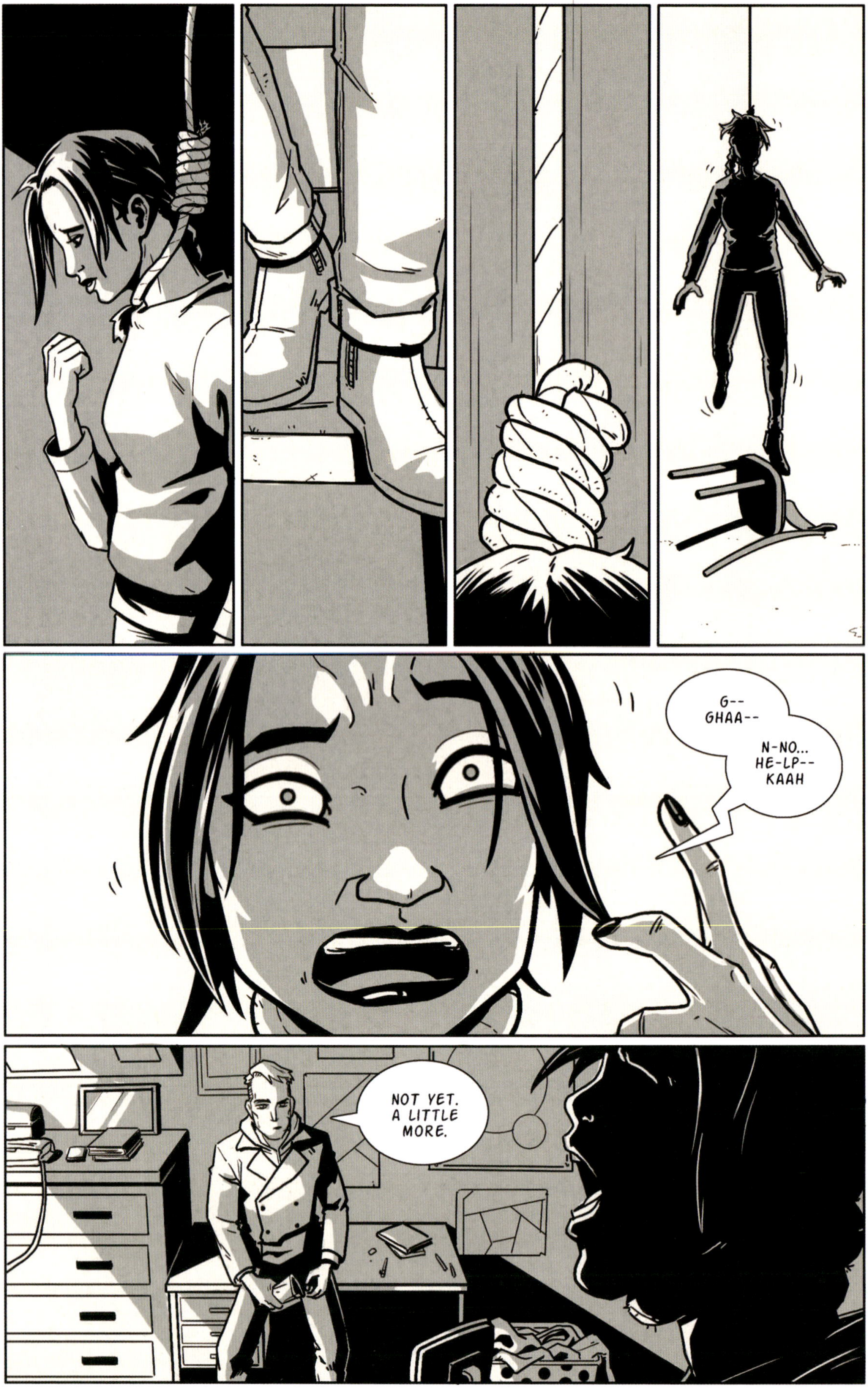
G--
GHAA--
N-NO...
HE-LP--
KAAH
NOT YET.
A LITTLE
MORE.

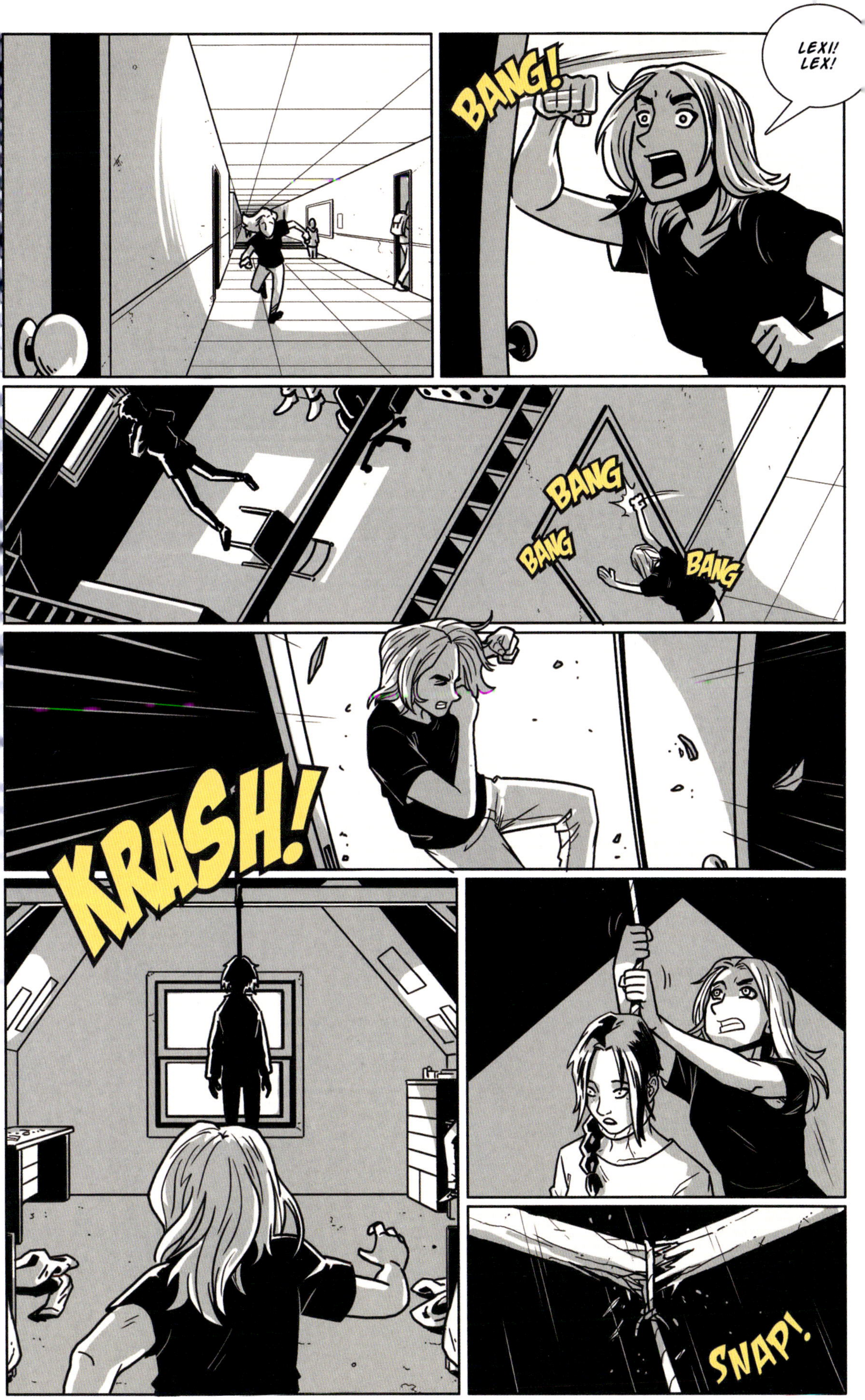

BANG!
LEXI! LEX!
BANG
BANG
BANG
KRASH!
SNAP!

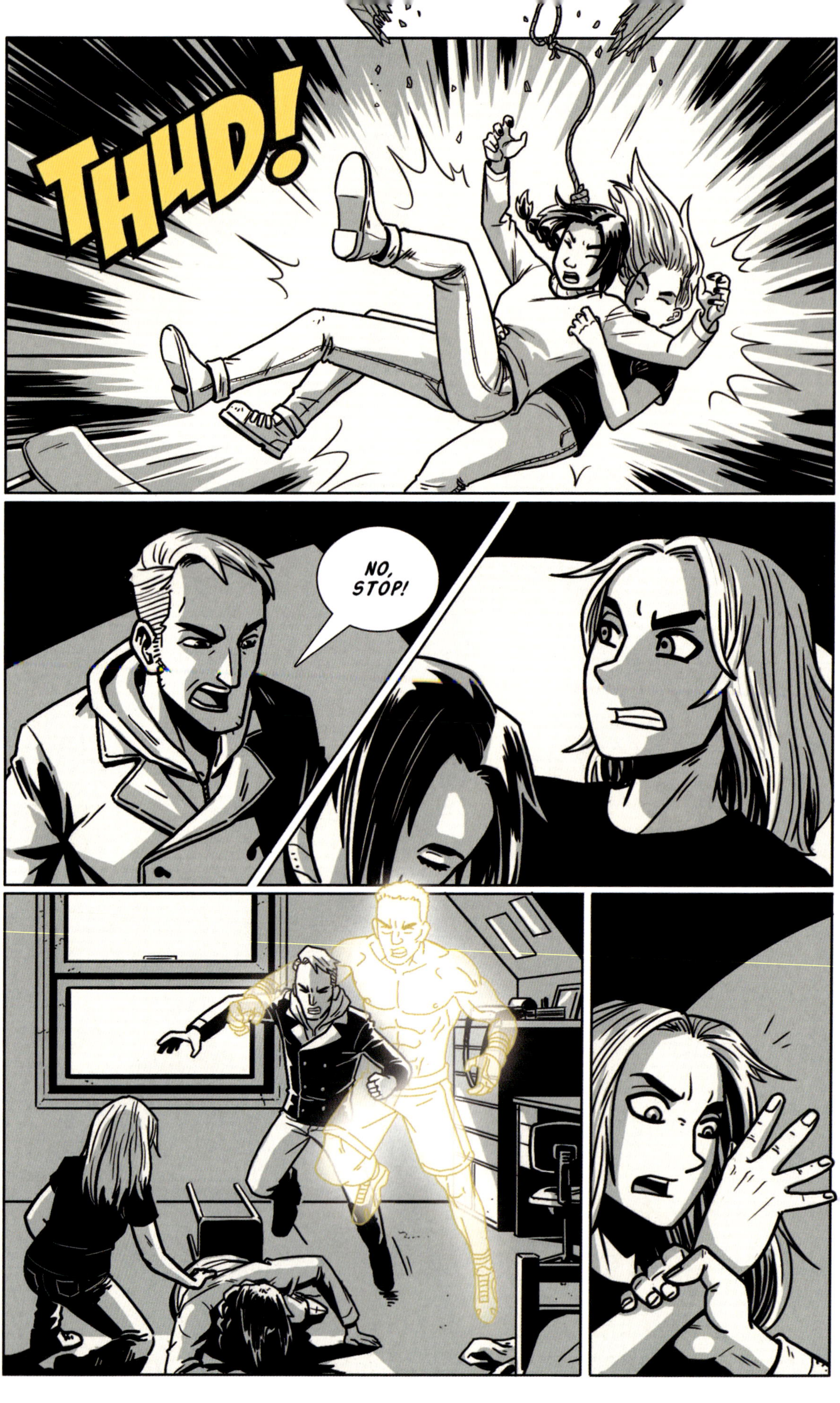
THUD!
NO, STOP!

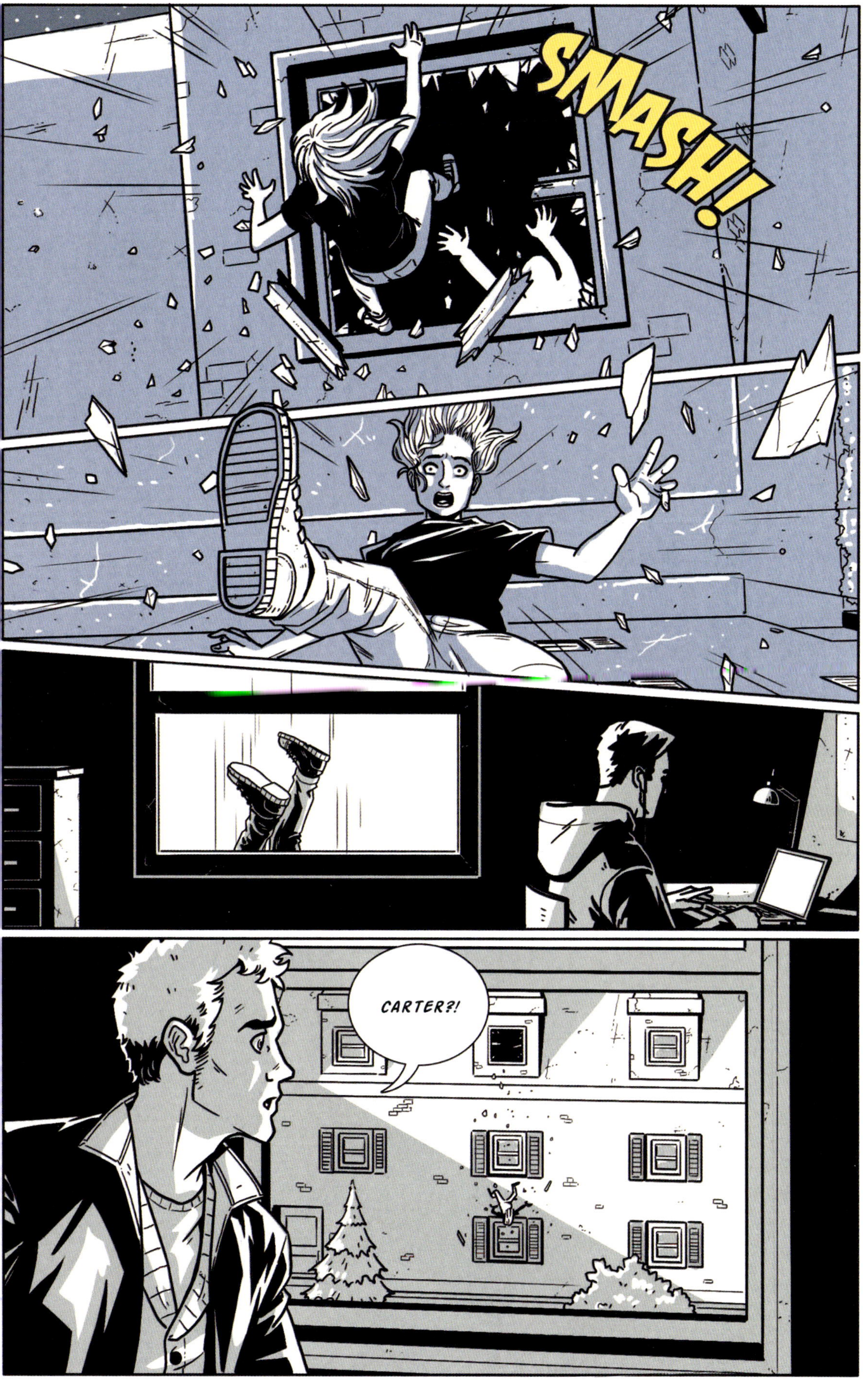
SMASH!
CARTER?!

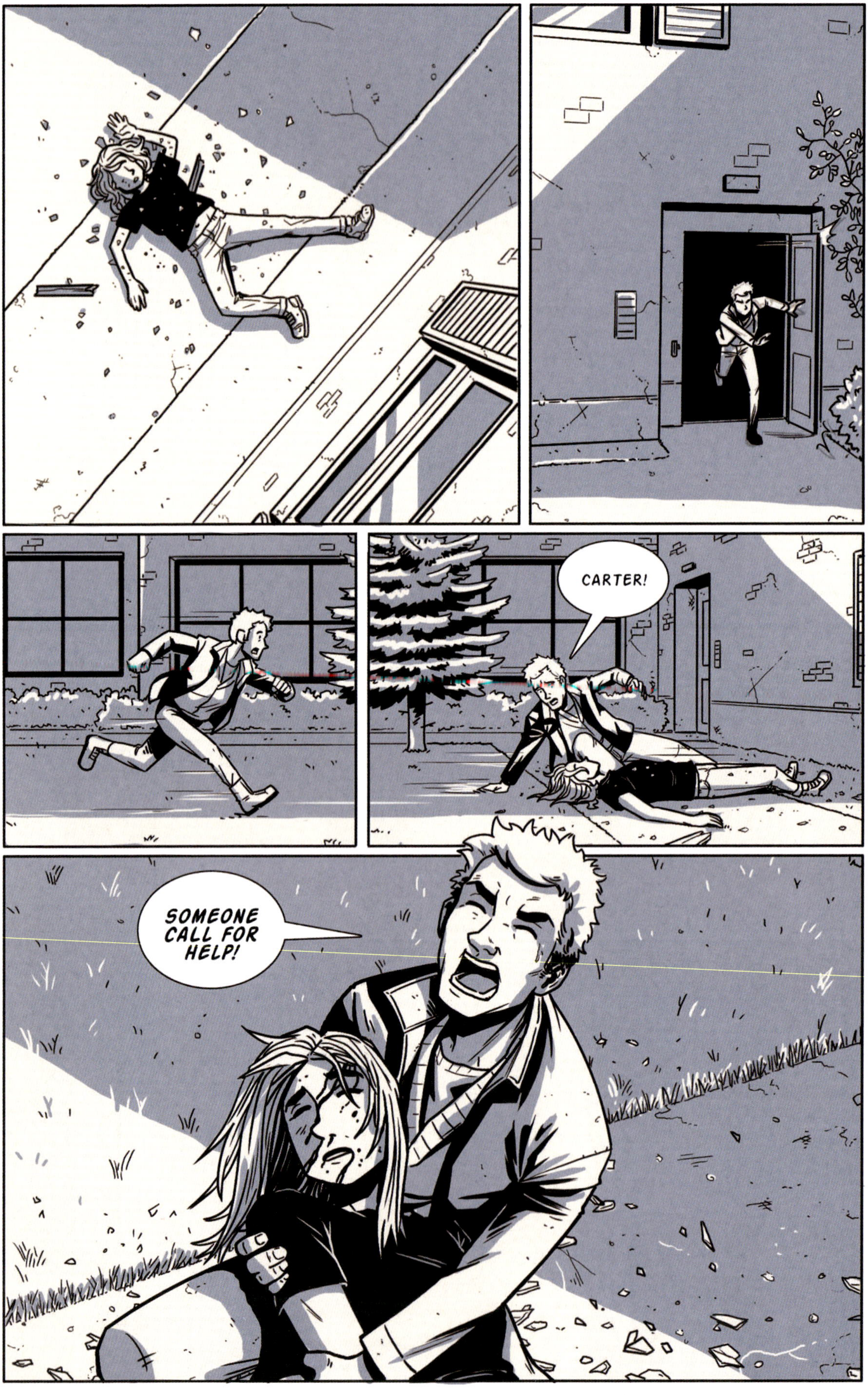
CARTER!
SOMEONE CALL FOR HELP!

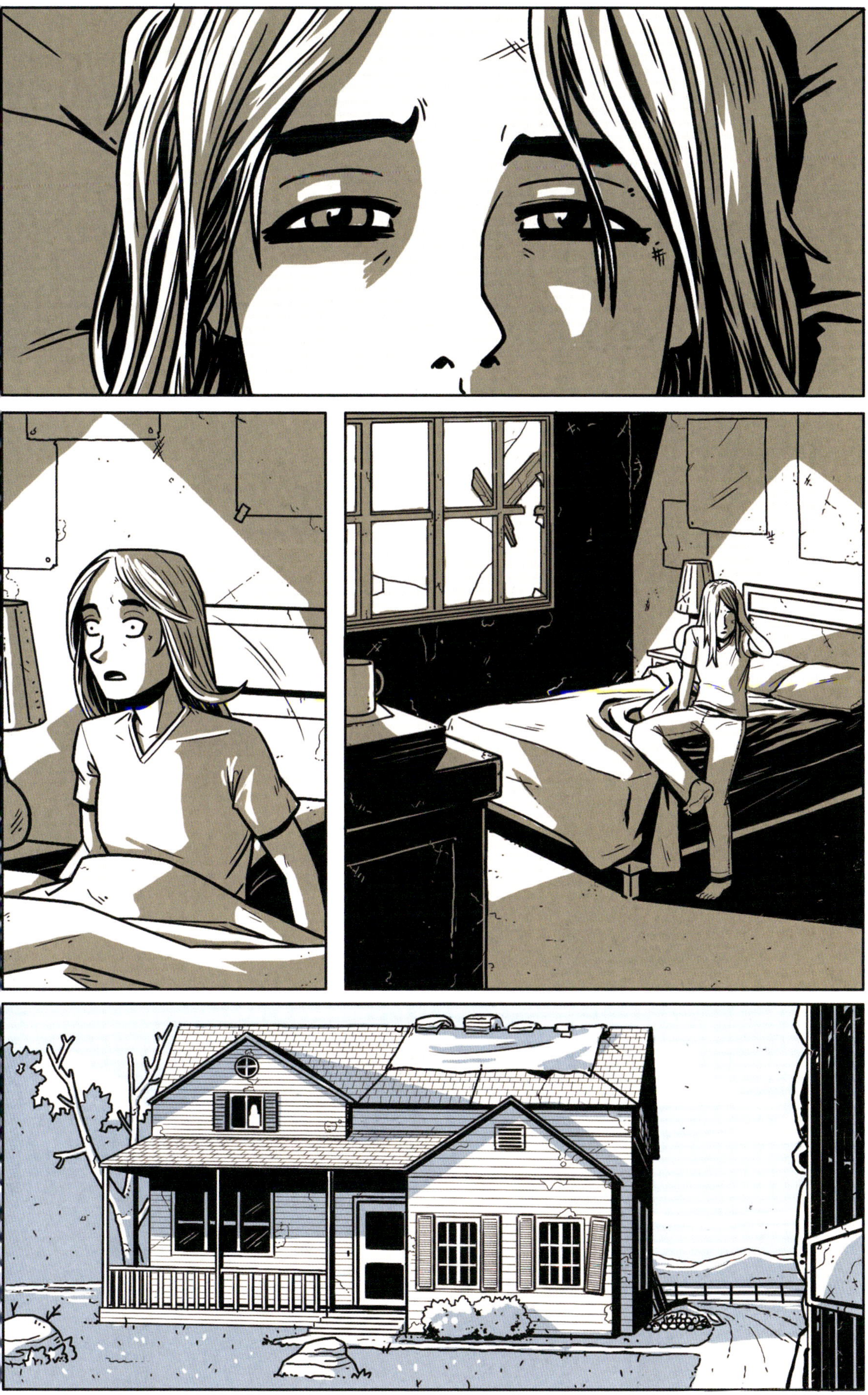

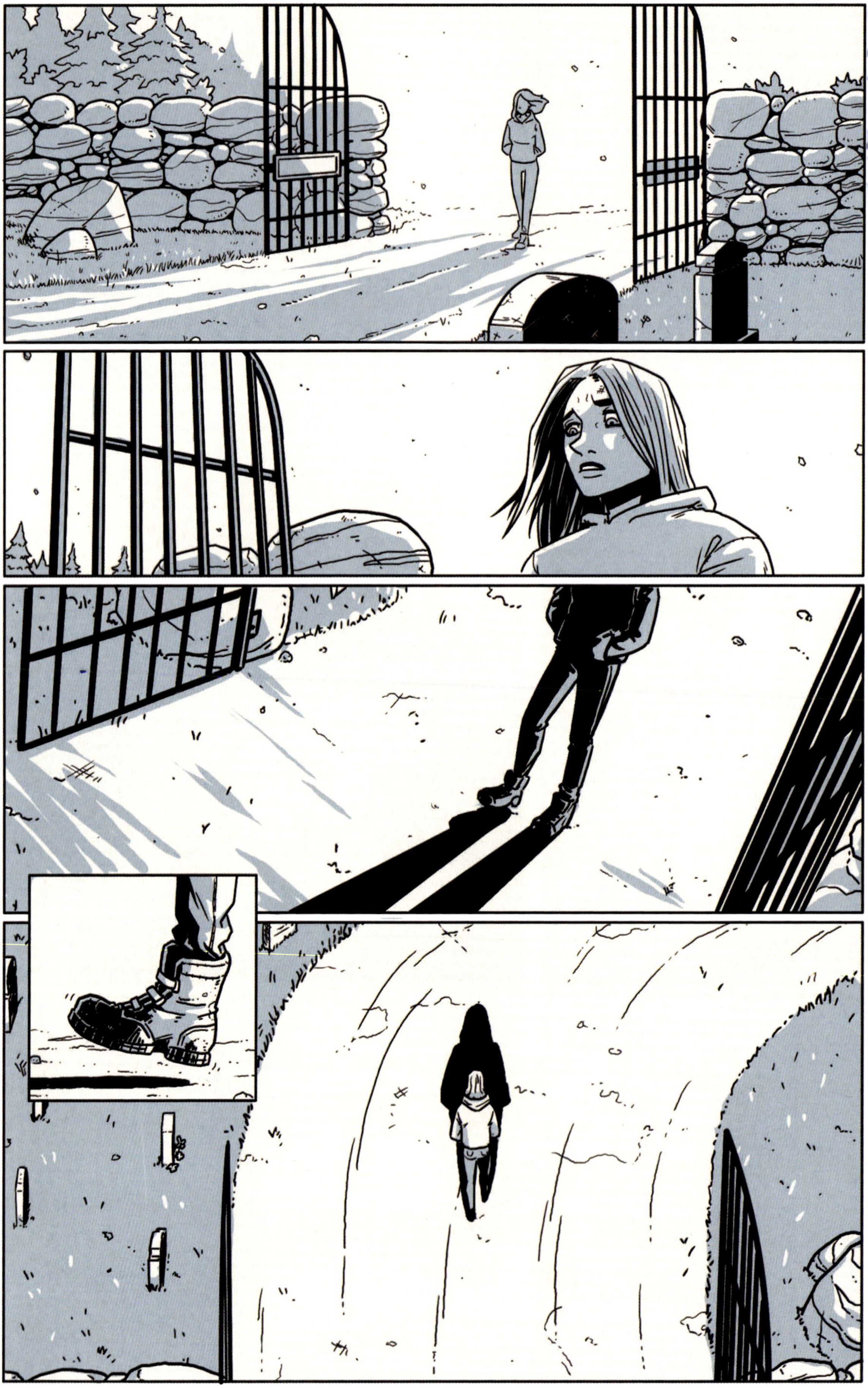

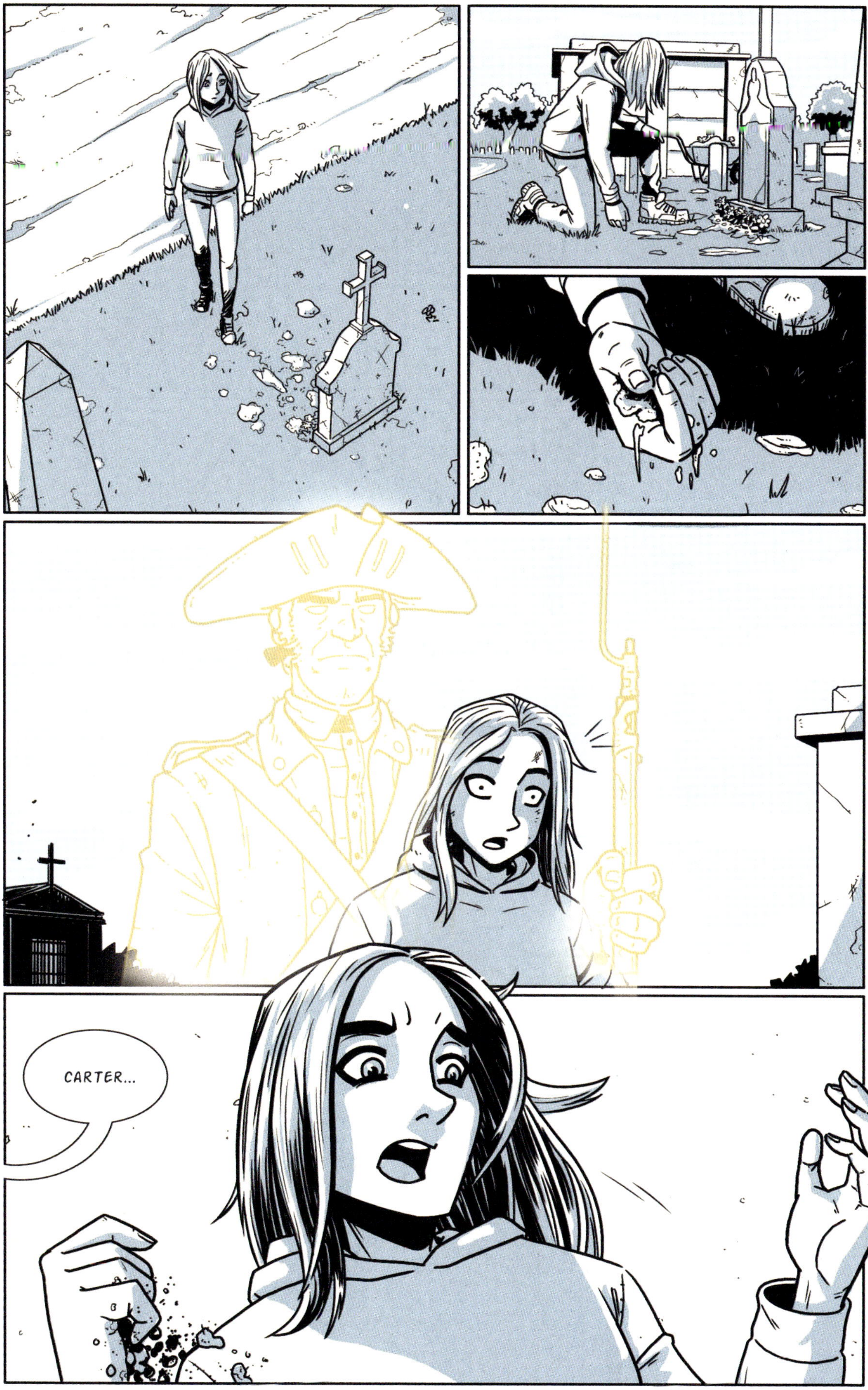
CARTER...

YOU OKAY?
I DON'T-- HOW LONG HAVE I BEEN HERE?
A FEW DAYS.
WHAT HAPPENED?
WHAT DO YOU REMEMBER?
A FRIEND... TRYING TO-- TO HURT HERSELF AND RUNNING AND THEN JUST...
THAT'S IT. WHAT HAPPENED?
YOU DIED, CARTER.
WH-- WAIT... WHAT?!
?!
YOU FELL OUT A WINDOW AND DROPPED ABOUT THIRTY FEET.
YOU DIED.

I DIED?
TECHNICALLY. FOR ABOUT A MINUTE AND A HALF, YES.
I-- I FELT SOMETHING.
YOU'VE BEEN THROUGH A LOT.
NO. I MEAN, I JUST FELT SOMETHING. NOW.
LIKE WHAT?
LIKE SOMETHING... SOMEONE... WAS INSIDE OF ME.
YOU SHOULD COME INSIDE.
WHY?
BECAUSE WE HAVE A LOT TO DISCUSS.
ABOUT WHAT? WHY? WHAT'S HAPPENED?
CARTER.

WHAT HAPPENED TO ME?!
IT'S THE DIRT.
YOU FELT IT WHEN YOU PICKED UP THE DIRT, RIGHT?
HOW... HOW DID YOU KNOW THAT?
IT'S WHAT WE CALL A SOUL SKILL.
WHAT?
CARTER, THIS IS GONNA SOUND COMPLETELY--
USUALLY THERE'S A BARRIER THAT SEPARATES THE WORLD OF THE LIVING FROM THE ONE OF THE DEAD.
USUALLY?
SOMETIMES SOMETHING HAPPENS AND A BREACH FORMS IN THE BARRIER THAT ALLOWS FOR A CERTAIN AMOUNT OF... MOVEMENT BETWEEN WORLDS.

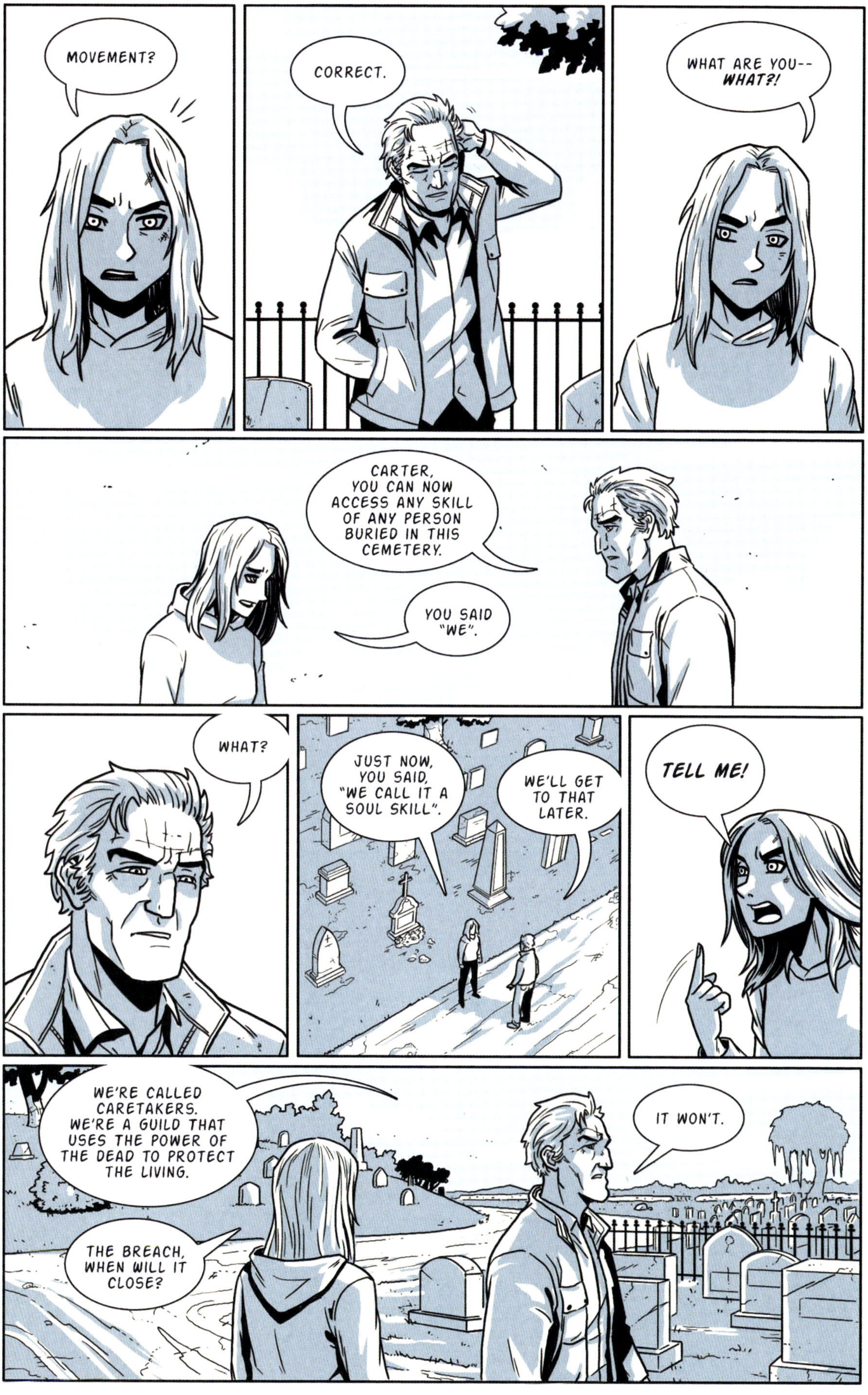
MOVEMENT?
CORRECT.
WHAT ARE YOU-- WHAT?!
CARTER, YOU CAN NOW ACCESS ANY SKILL OF ANY PERSON BURIED IN THIS CEMETERY.
YOU SAID "WE".
WHAT?
JUST NOW, YOU SAID, "WE CALL IT A SOUL SKILL".
WE'LL GET TO THAT LATER.
TELL ME!
WE'RE CALLED CARETAKERS. WE'RE A GUILD THAT USES THE POWER OF THE DEAD TO PROTECT THE LIVING.
THE BREACH, WHEN WILL IT CLOSE?
IT WON'T.

NO...
WHAT?
ETHAN.
TELL ME.
CARTER--
THIS WHOLE TIME?! THIS IS WHAT ETHAN FELT, RIGHT?!
HE'S NOT CRA--
CARTER--
YOU KNEW?! THIS WHOLE TIME YOU KNEW AND YOU STILL PUT HIM IN THERE?!
IT'S NOT AS SIMPLE AS YOU THINK.
NOTHING EVER IS WITH YOU!

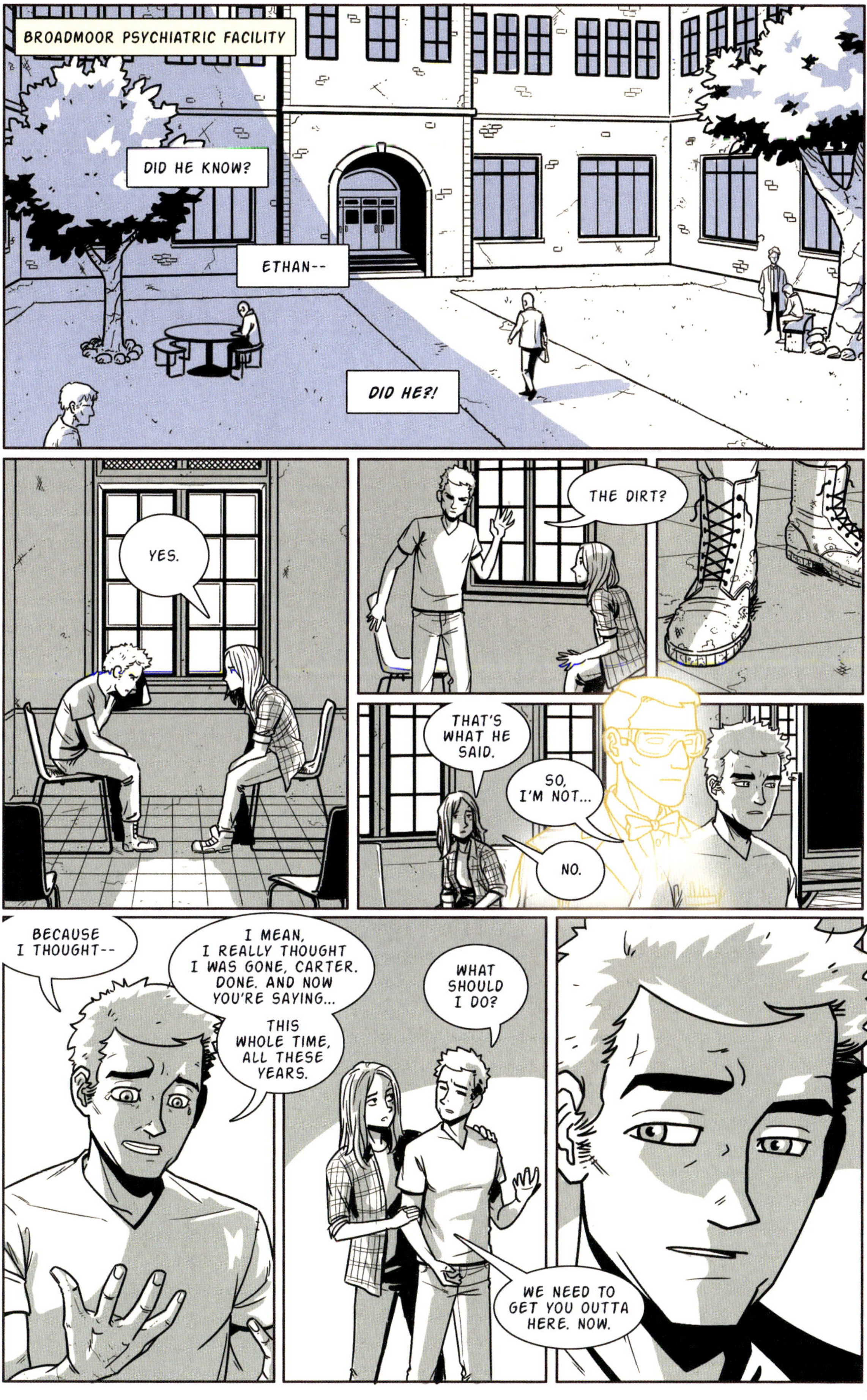

BROADMOOR PSYCHIATRIC FACILITY
DID HE KNOW?
ETHAN--
DID HE?!
YES.
THE DIRT?
THAT'S WHAT HE SAID.
SO, I'M NOT...
NO.
BECAUSE I THOUGHT--
I MEAN, I REALLY THOUGHT I WAS GONE, CARTER. DONE. AND NOW YOU'RE SAYING...
THIS WHOLE TIME, ALL THESE YEARS.
WHAT SHOULD I DO?
WE NEED TO GET YOU OUTTA HERE. NOW.

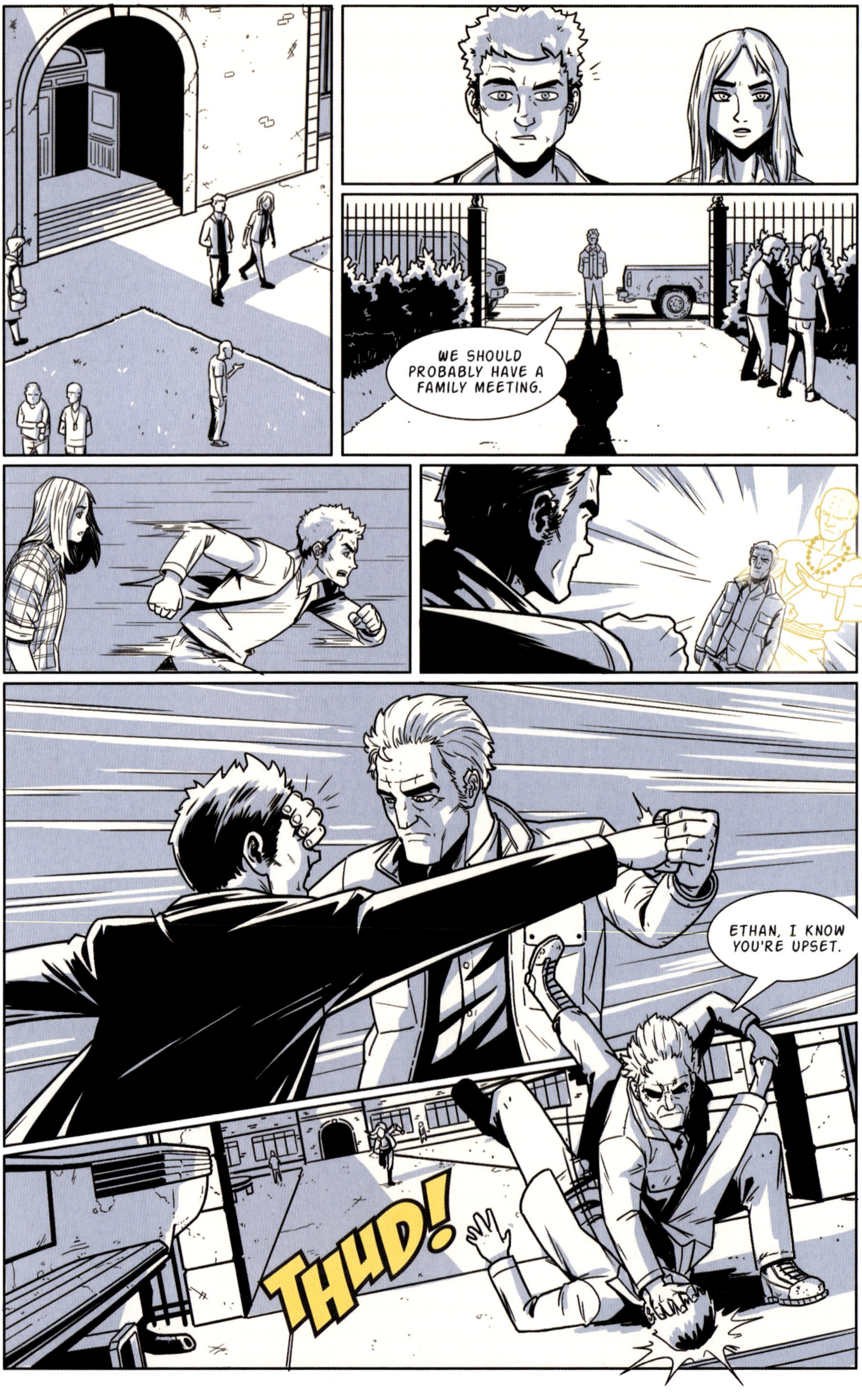
WE SHOULD PROBABLY HAVE A FAMILY MEETING.
ETHAN, I KNOW YOU'RE UPSET.
THUD!

AND I KNOW I MESSED UP. BUT TRUST ME, WE GOTTA GET PAST THIS.
"TRUST YOU?" ARE YOU SERIOUS?!
YOU LIED! AND NOT JUST ABOUT WHY I WAS HERE... ABOUT EVERYTHING!
TO ME! TO CARTER! YOU'VE BEEN LYING TO US OUR WHOLE LIVES!
THAT'S PART OF THE JOB.
WHAT?
LYING. IF IT MEANT KEEPING YOU SAFE, THEN YEAH, I LIED.
I LIED BECAUSE THAT'S WHAT SHE WANTED!
WHO?

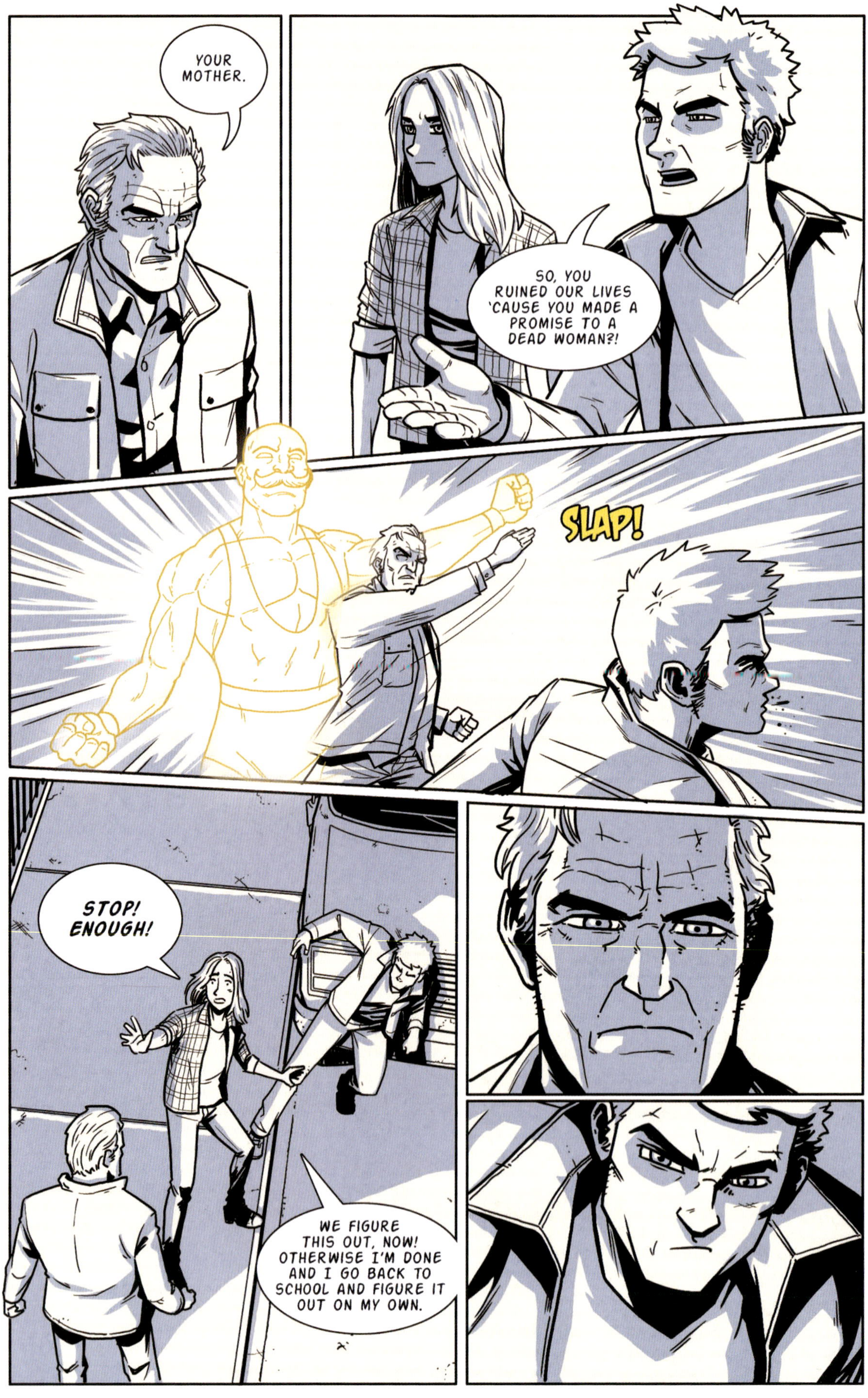
YOUR MOTHER.
SO, YOU RUINED OUR LIVES 'CAUSE YOU MADE A PROMISE TO A DEAD WOMAN?!
SLAP!
STOP! ENOUGH!
WE FIGURE THIS OUT, NOW! OTHERWISE I'M DONE AND I GO BACK TO SCHOOL AND FIGURE IT OUT ON MY OWN.

DINER
OPEN
IT ALL STARTS WITH THE SOUL SKILL. WE ACCESS THE SOUL IN ORDER TO USE IT'S SKILL.
A SKILL?
YEAH.
OF A SOUL?
CORRECT.
AND JUST TO BE, LIKE, TOTALLY CLEAR, YOU MEAN A HUMAN SOUL?
YES.
AFTER A PERSON DIES WE CAN TAP INTO THE SKILLS THAT PERSON HAD WHEN THEY WERE ALIVE.
ANY SKILL SOMEONE HAD WHILE ALIVE WE CAN ACCESS ONCE THEY'RE DEAD.
...WHAT?

USING THAT?
IT'S CALLED SAFE SOIL.
I'LL MAKE IT WORTH YOUR WHILE, PROMISE.
PICK A CARD.
REALLY, CARD TRICKS?
JUST PICK.
SHOW IT TO ME.
PUT IT BACK.
NOW THROW 'EM.
WHAT?
THROW THEM. ALL OF 'EM. UP IN THE AIR.

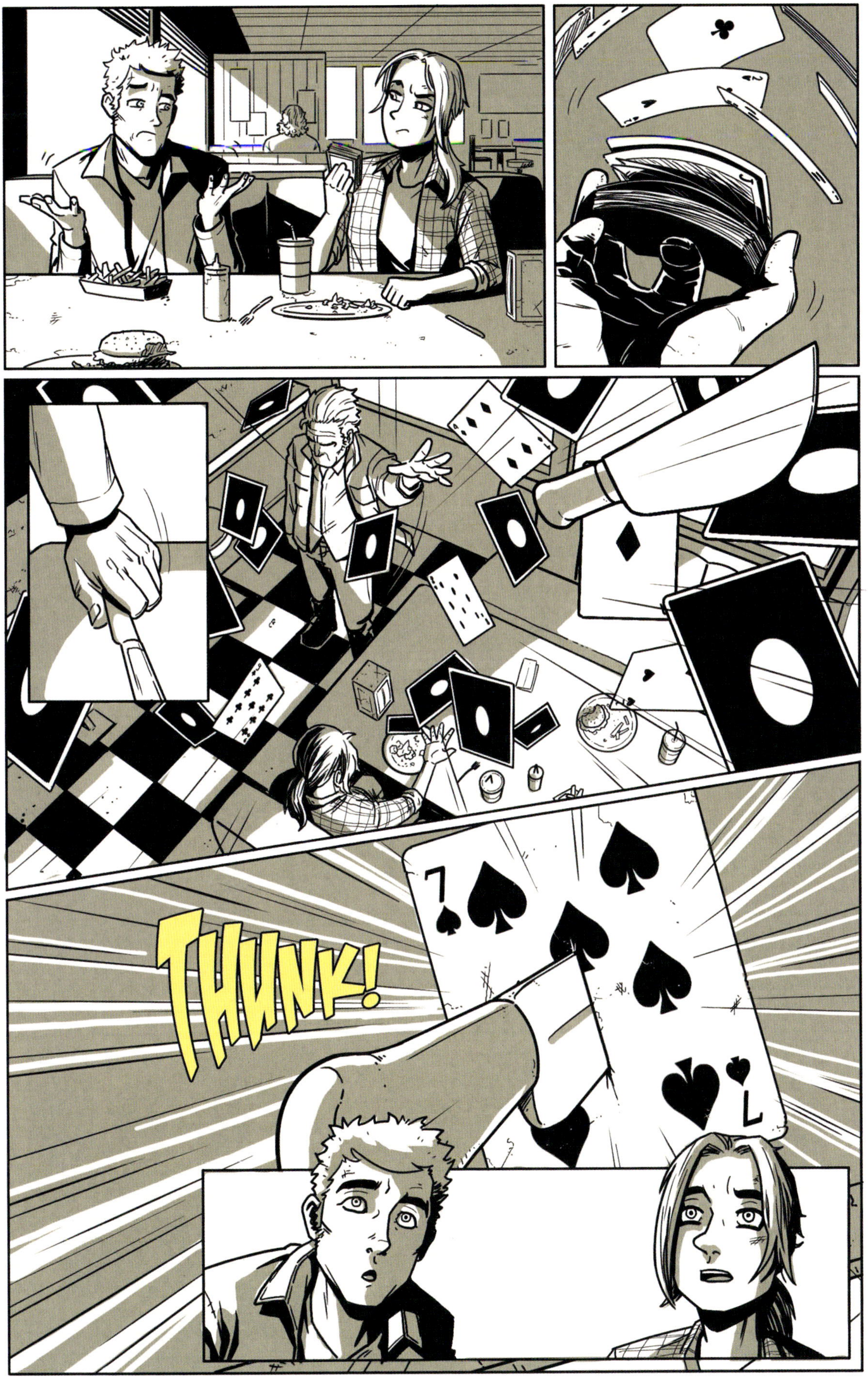
THUNK!

IT'S NOT ME. IT'S THE SOUL SKILL.
THIS IS TOTALLY INSANE.
SO, WHAT, NEXT STOP VEGAS?
THE ABILITY COMES WITH A CERTAIN AMOUNT OF...
...PRESSURE.
BUT THE ONLY THING YOU NEED TO REMEMBER IS THIS; WE USE THE POWER OF THE DEAD TO PROTECT THE LIVING.
PROTECT? FROM WHO?
THEY'RE CALLED, DARK HEARTS.

LIKE US THEY CAN ACCESS SKILLS, ONLY THE SOULS THEY EXPLOIT ARE THE WORLD'S WORST; PSYCHOPATHS, KILLERS, CRIMINALS, WHITE COLLAR EMBEZZLERS.
I KNOW THE AMOUNT OF GOOD ADVICE I'VE GIVEN EITHER ONE OF YOU COULD FIT INTO A FORTUNE COOKIE BUT IF YOU WANT THE TRUTH THEN HERE IT IS; YOU SHOULD RUN.
WHAT?!
AS FAR AND AS FAST AS YOU CAN.
THIS LIFE IS NOT--
ARE YOU-- YOU DROP THIS ON US AND THEN TELL US TO JUST RUN AWAY?! ARE YOU SERIOUS?!

THIS LIFE TAKES EVERYTHING FROM YOU. IT'S HARD AND VICIOUS AND THE SOULS WE CARRY GET HEAVY AND IT RUINED THIS FAMILY.
SO THINK LONG AND HARD BEFORE YOU WANT TO THROW AWAY WHATEVER IT IS YOU ENVISIONED FOR YOURSELF IN THE FUTURE.
I DON'T-- WHERE WOULD WE GO?
ANYWHERE. AWAY. BACK TO SCHOOL. FRIENDS. YOU HAVE FAMILY IN AKRON.
AKRON?! YOU WANT US TO GO TO AKRON?
I'M JUST TRYING TO HELP.
BULL! YOU'RE TRYING TO GET OUT FROM UNDER THIS. YOU'RE TOO *LAZY* TO TRY AND HELP!
E, C'MON.
OKAY, WHEN WE GET TO AKRON, WHAT IS IT WE TELL EVERYONE? OUR FATHER WAS PART OF SOME SECRET CULT WHO WERE PROTECTING THE WORLD FROM EVIL.
THE WORD CULT MIGHT FREAK SOME PEOPLE OUT BUT... SURE, WHY NOT.
WHY DIDN'T YOU TELL US BEFORE?
BECAUSE YOUR MOM WANTED MORE THAN THIS FOR YOU TWO.
MOM WAS A CARETAKER?
ONE OF THE BEST.

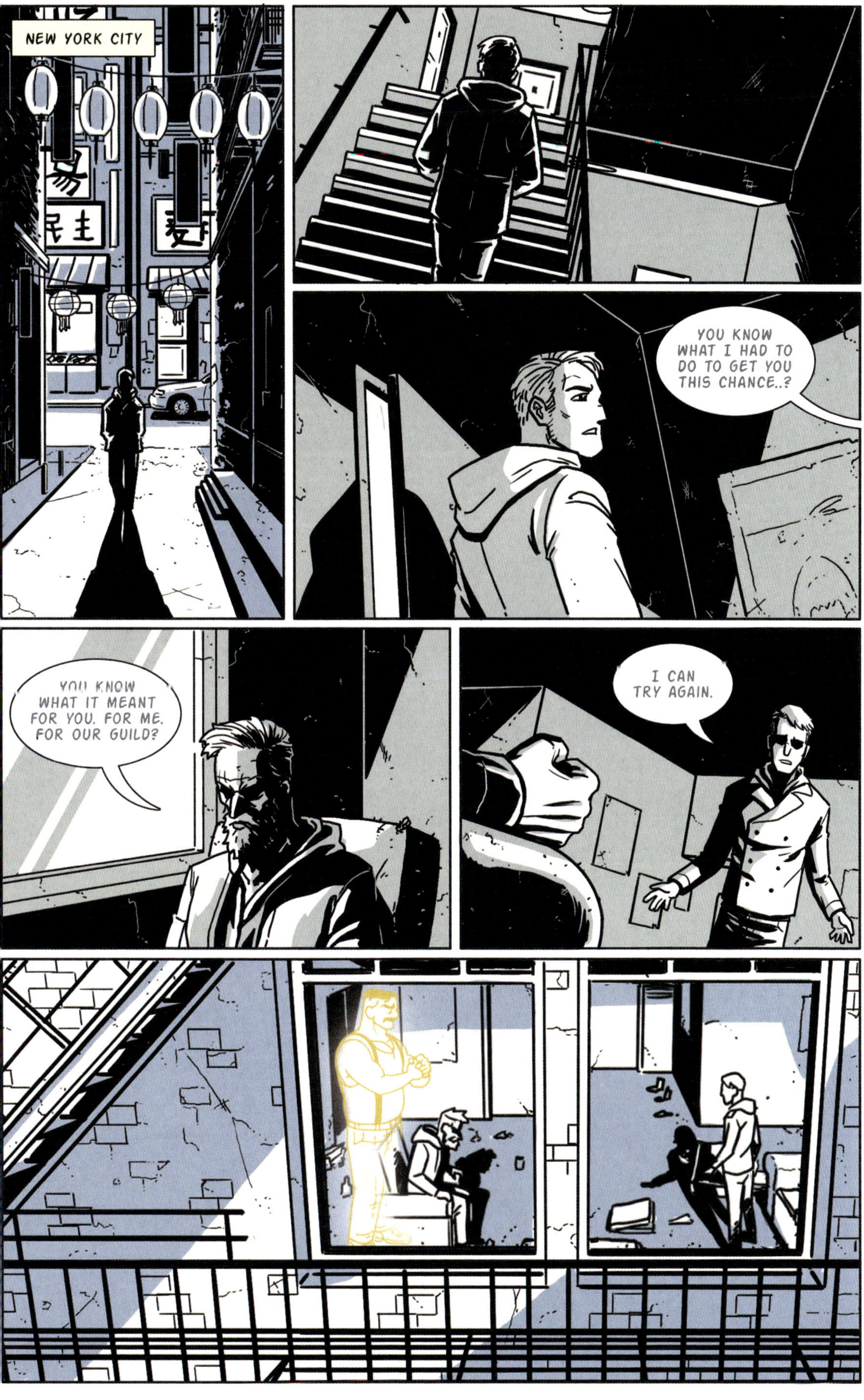
NEW YORK CITY
YOU KNOW WHAT I HAD TO DO TO GET YOU THIS CHANCE..?
YOU KNOW WHAT IT MEANT FOR YOU. FOR ME. FOR OUR GUILD?
I CAN TRY AGAIN.

ETHAN!

ETHAN, WAKE UP!

WAKE UP!

WH-- WHAT?

I... I THINK WE MAY HAVE A PROBLEM.

WITH WHAT?

YESTERDAY DAD SAID SOMETHING ABOUT THIS OTHER GUILD, RIGHT? THE DARK HEARTS.

WHO WAS IT?
SOME GUY LEXI MET AT A BAR.
OKAY. SO, DO YOU KNOW HIM?
NO, THEY JUST MET. HE WAS A TRANSFER STUDENT.
AND HE WAS IN THE ROOM WHEN YOU GOT THERE. WAS HE PASSED OUT OR...
NO, HE WAS-- I THINK HE WAS WATCHING.
OR HELPING.
I SAW HIM TOO. AFTER CARTER WENT OUT THE WINDOW.
AND YOU TWO DIDN'T THINK TO SAY ANYTHING?!
ABOUT WHAT?! TWO DAYS AGO WE DIDN'T KNOW ANYTHING!

OKAY! FINE. RELAX. THIS GIRL, LEXI, WHO IS SHE?
A FRIEND. YOU MET HER LAST YEAR WHEN YOU DROPPED ME--
AND HER FAMILY?
HER DAD JUST DIED. THAT'S WHY I THOUGHT SHE WAS TRYING TO HURT--
WAIT... HER FATHER DIED? WHEN? WHAT DID HE DO?
A FEW WEEKS AGO. I THINK HE RAN A PRETTY BIG INTERNATIONAL COMPANY THAT--
WE GOTTA GO. NOW!
WHAT?
CARTER, THIS KID YOU FOUND IN THE ROOM... HE DIDN'T JUST SHOW UP. LEXI WAS TARGETED.
WHY WOULD THEY WANT LEXI?
THEY DON'T. THEY WANT HER FATHER.

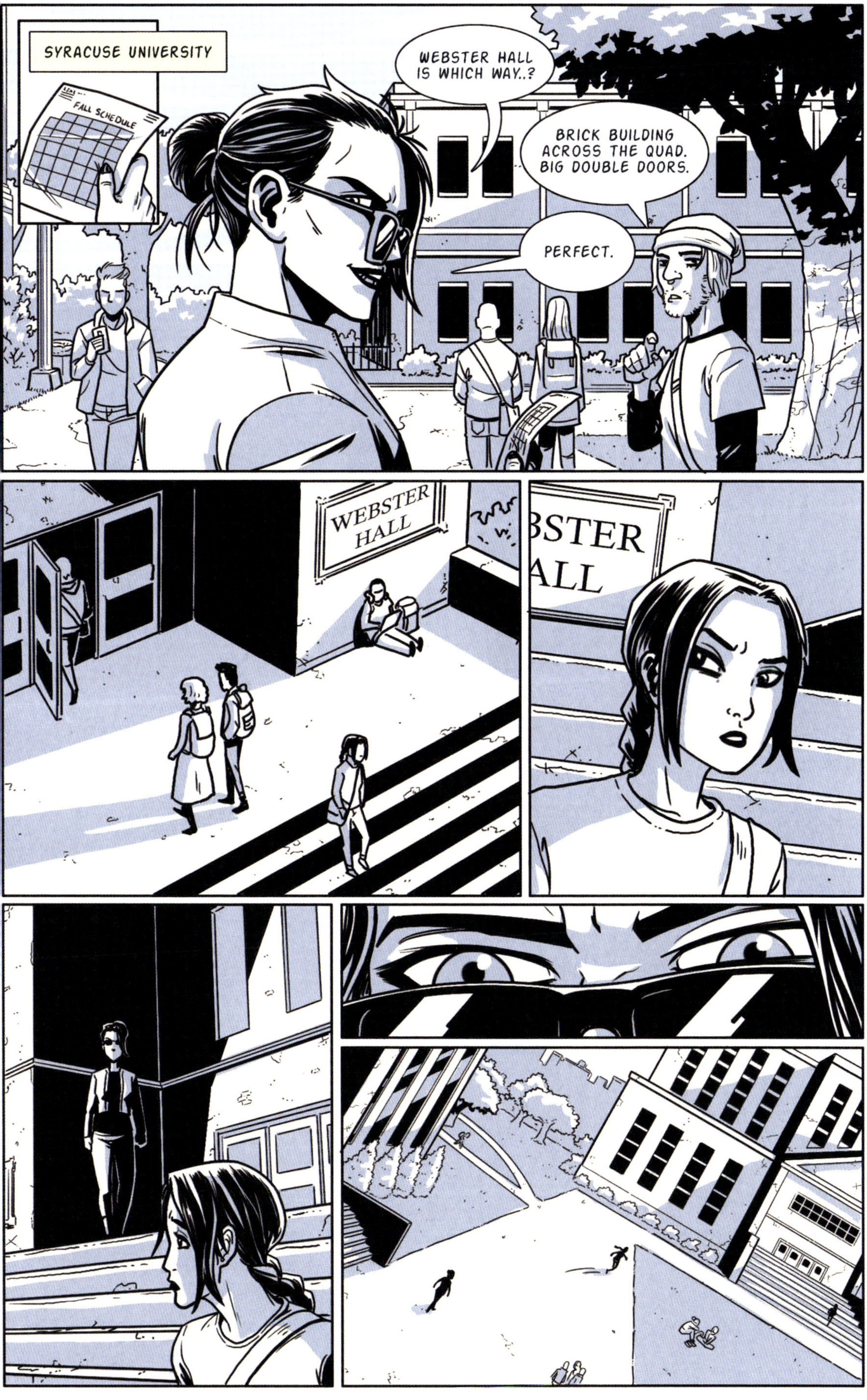
SYRACUSE UNIVERSITY
FALL SCHEDULE
WEBSTER HALL IS WHICH WAY..?
BRICK BUILDING ACROSS THE QUAD. BIG DOUBLE DOORS.
PERFECT.
WEBSTER HALL

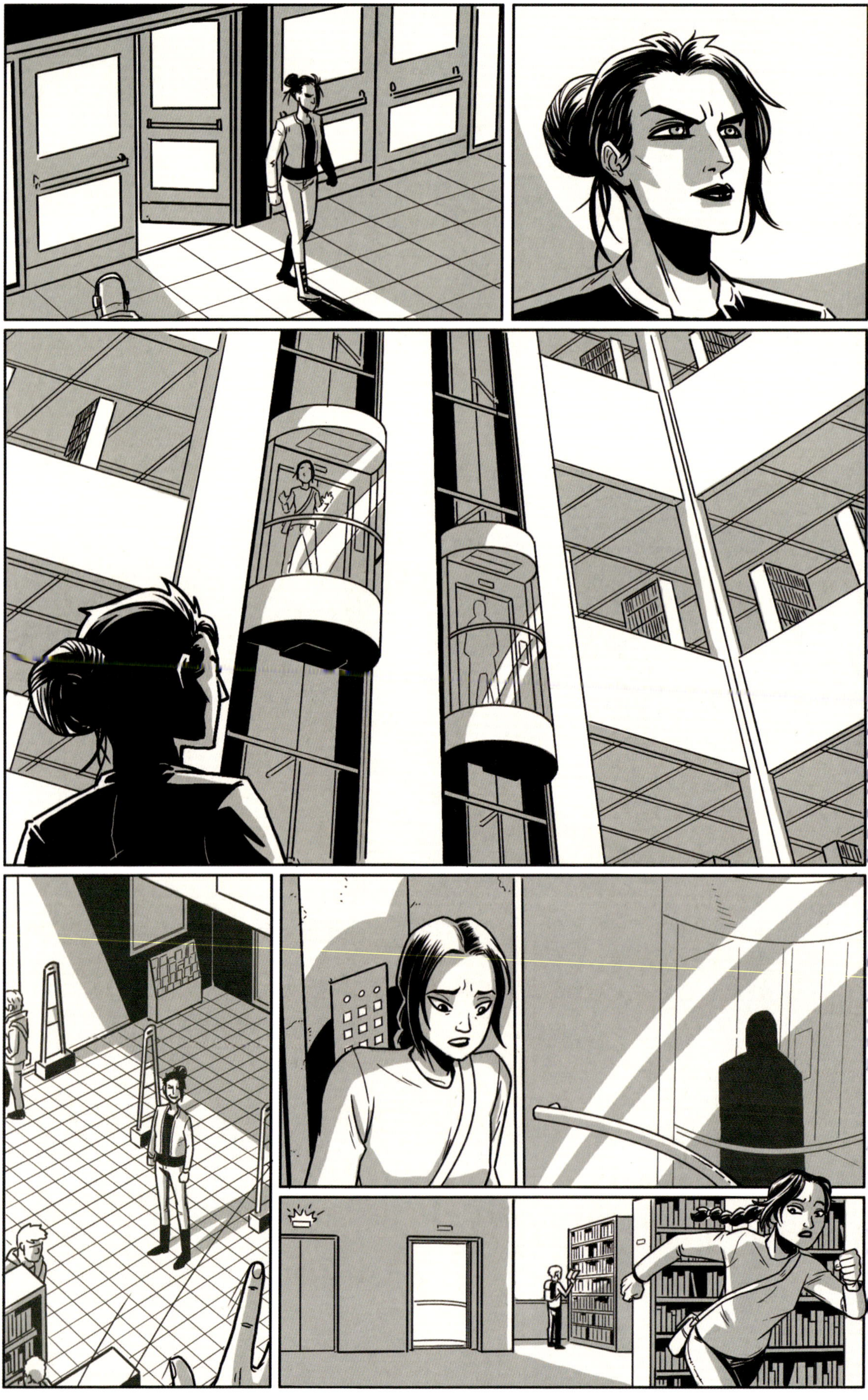

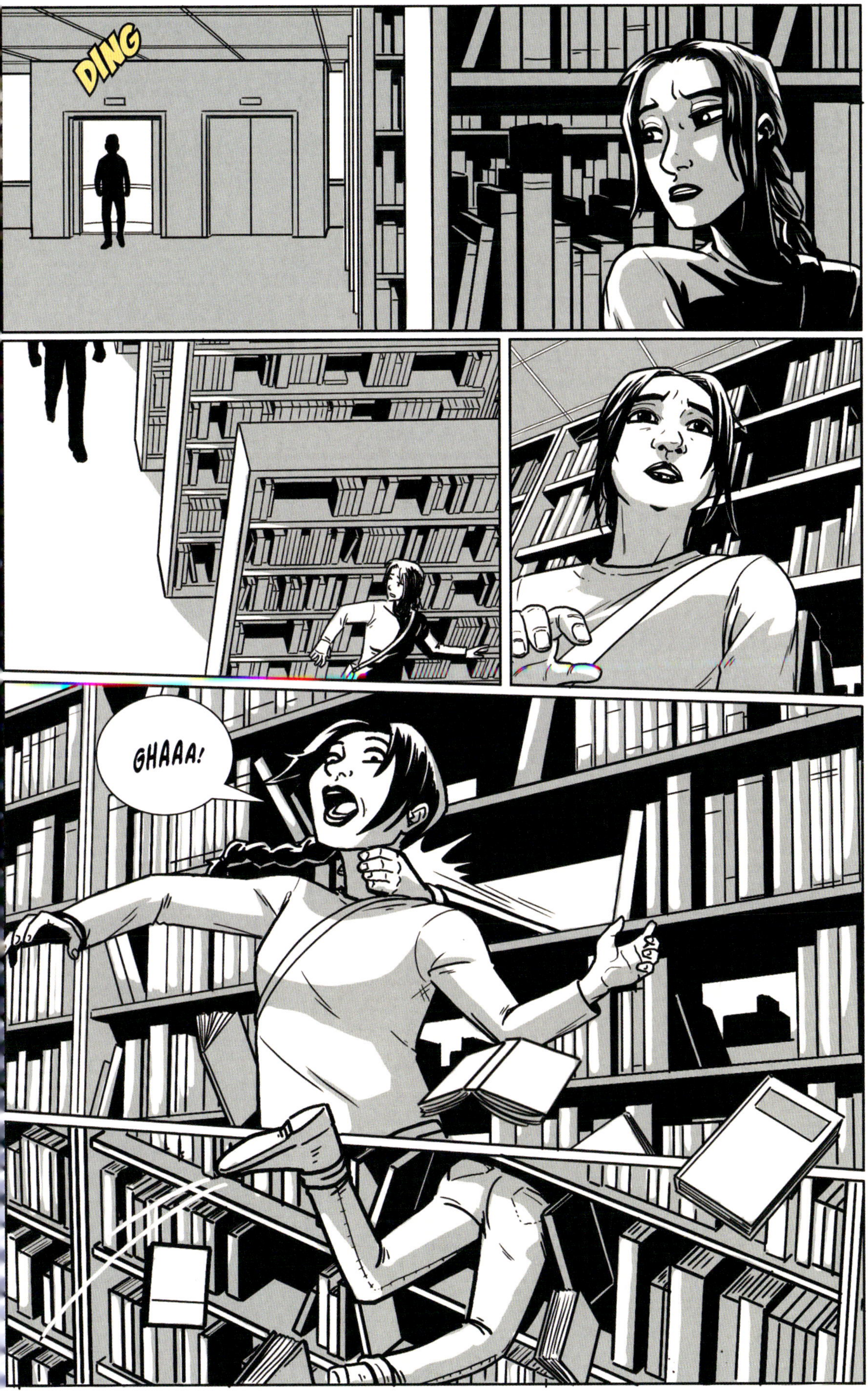
DING
GHAAA!

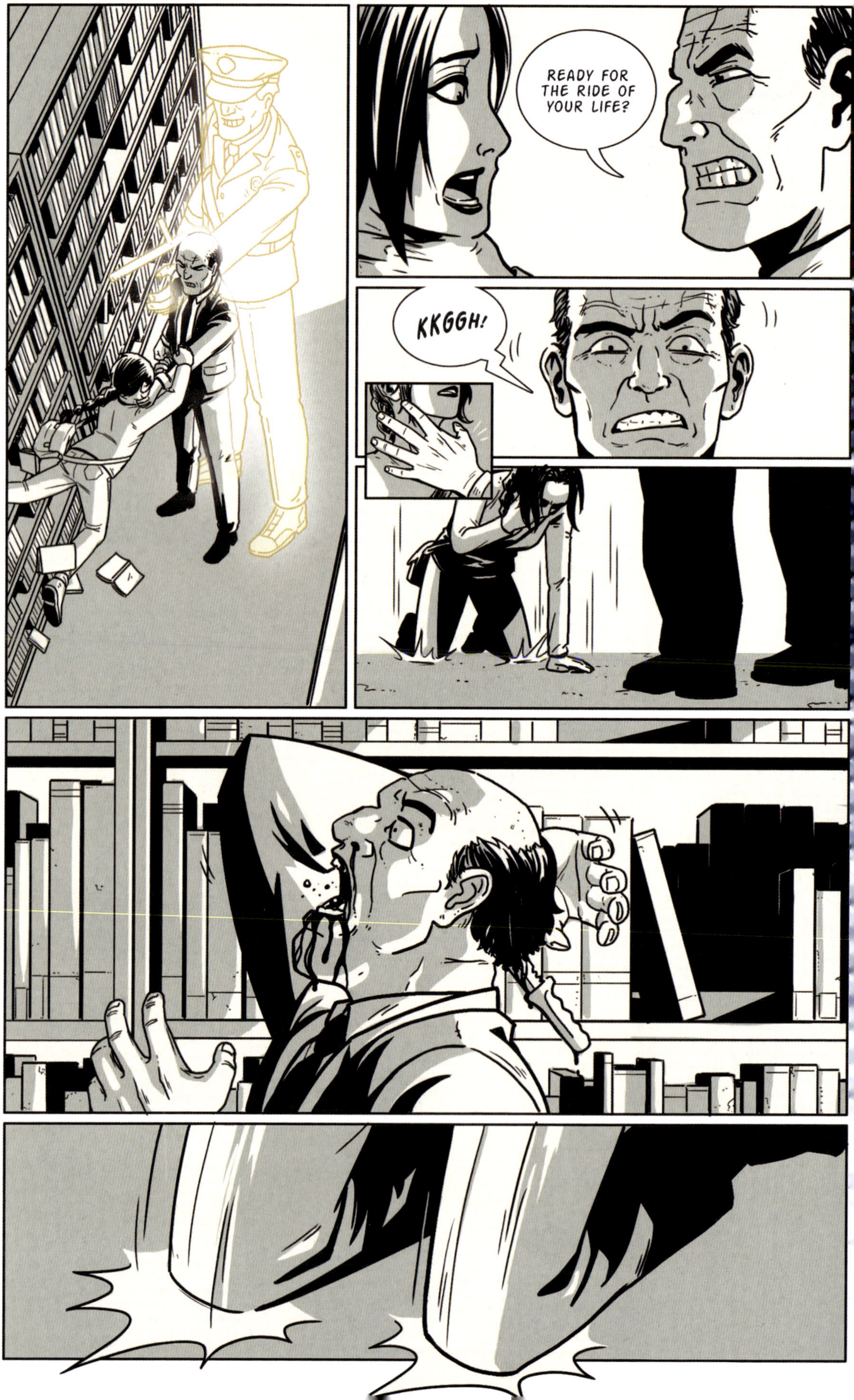
READY FOR THE RIDE OF YOUR LIFE?
KKGGH!

LEXI, IT'S ALRIGHT.
WH-- WHO ARE YOU?
CARTER'S DAD.
I DON'T-- YOU JUST KILLED THAT GUY.
YEAH.
ARE YOU GONNA KILL ME?
WHAT?! NO!
LEXI!
I SAID TO STAY DOWNSTAIRS AND WATCH THE DOORS.
YOU SAID NO ONE WOULD GET HURT!
HE TOTALLY JUST KILLED THAT GUY!
STOP KILLING PEOPLE, I LIKE GOING TO SCHOOL HERE!
HE WAS GOING TO--
HEY!

WE GOTTA BOLT!
I SAID STAY-- DOES NO ONE LISTEN?!
WHOSE THAT?
NICE. THIS LEXI?
DAD KILLED HIM.
YEAH.
HEY! WE DONE?
NOT YET, CARETAKER.
D- DADDY..?
GIVE ME THE GIRL AND WE'RE ALL GOOD. WE LEAVE, NO ONE ELSE HAS TO--

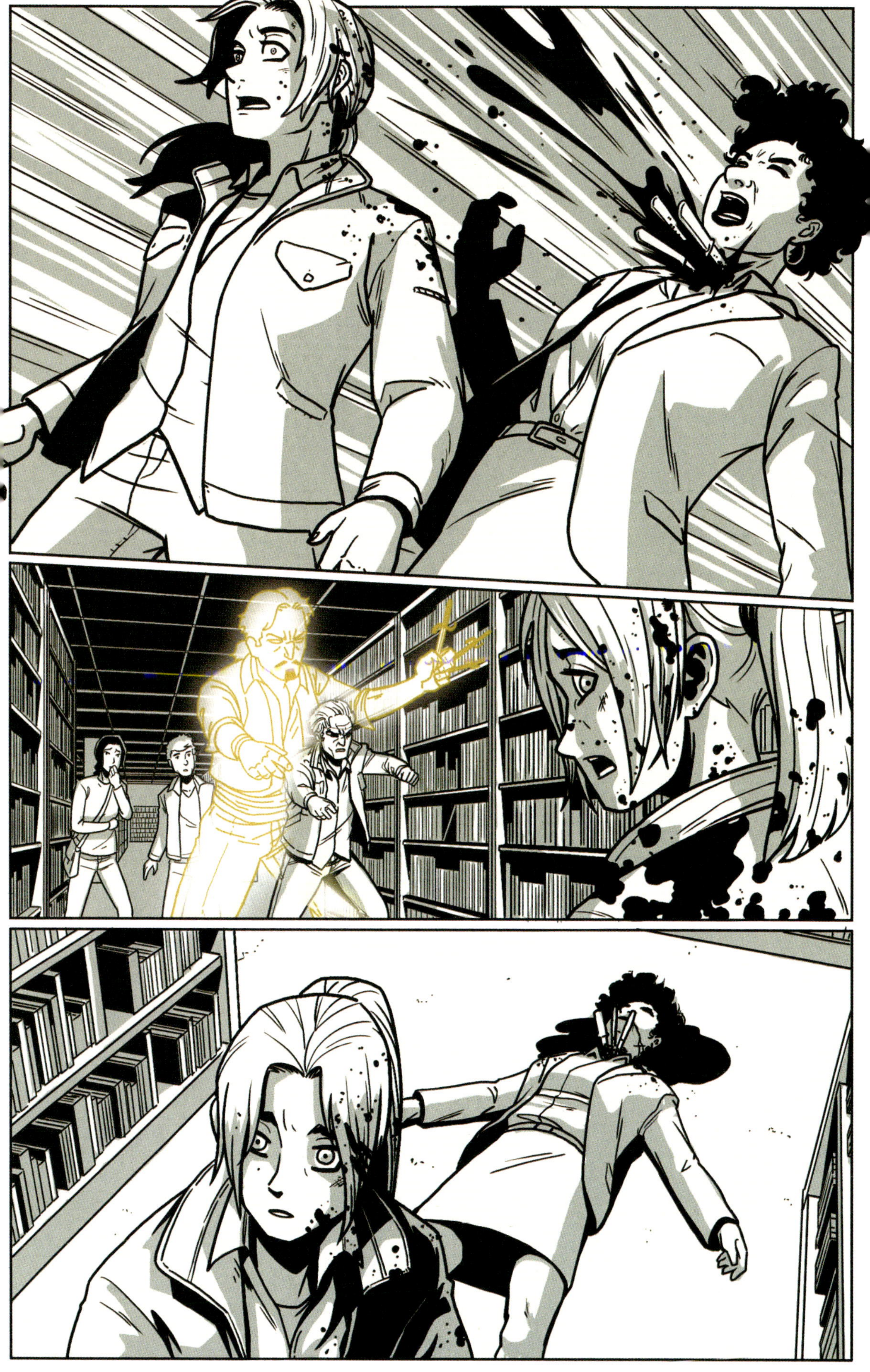

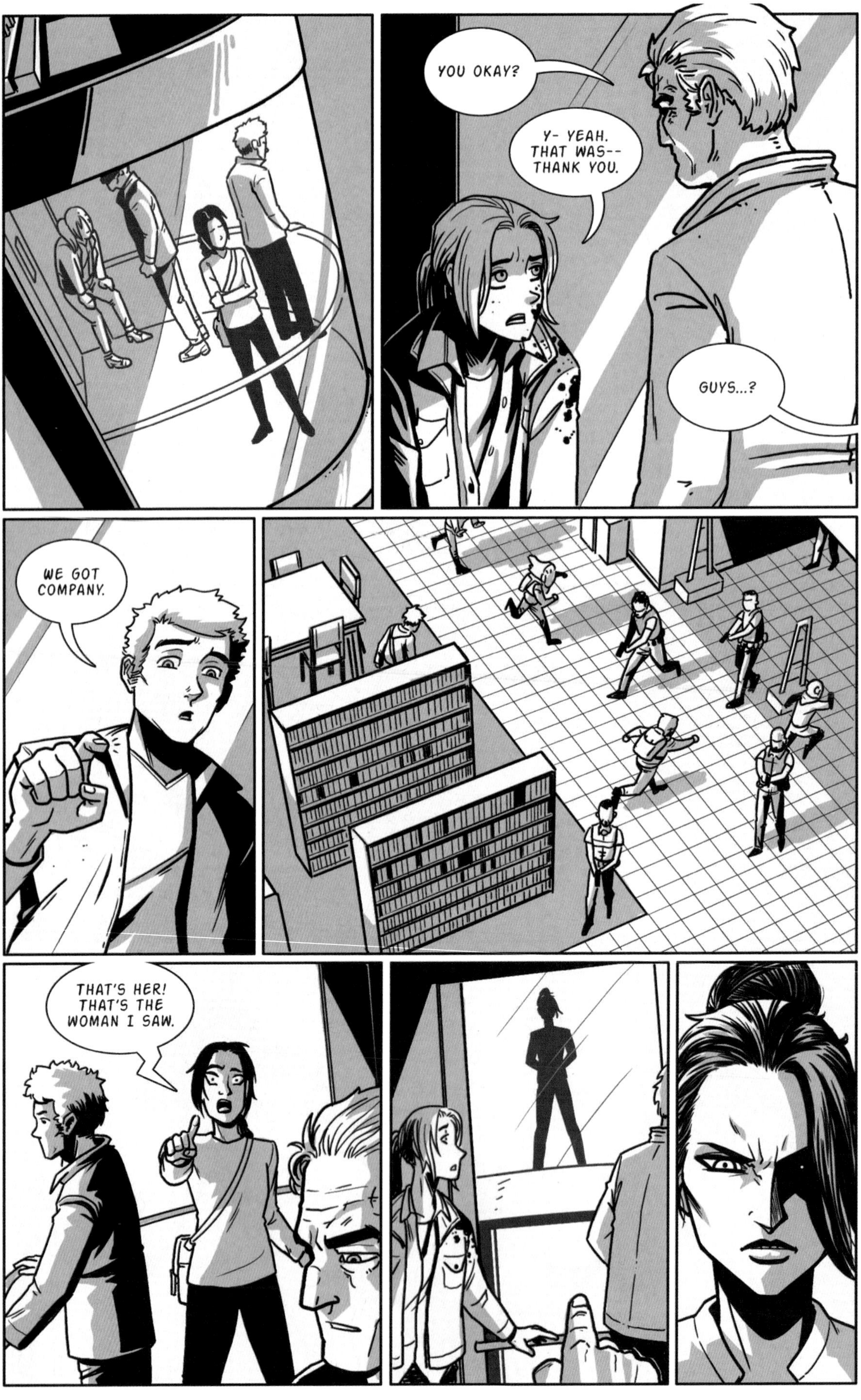
YOU OKAY?
Y- YEAH. THAT WAS-- THANK YOU.
GUYS...?
WE GOT COMPANY.
THAT'S HER! THAT'S THE WOMAN I SAW.

IS SHE--
YES.
DING
OFFICER?! THERE'S A WOMAN WITH A GUN OR SOMETHING. SHE'S COMING DOWN.

DOBBS FERRY, NY

"HEY, CARTER..."

"YOU SAID LEXI'S FATHER WAS KILLED. HOW?"

"CAR ACCIDENT. WHY?"

"I JUST THOUGHT-- IT'S NOTHING."

"YOU GUYS SHOULD GET SOME REST. WE CAN TALK TOMORROW."

"LINCOLN, I NEED A FAVOR."

"YEAH, WHAT ABOUT HIM?"

"THE GUY THAT WENT UP IN FLAMES WITH THE SUV? THE ONE ON THE MOUNTAIN ROAD--"

"I NEED YOU TO FIND OUT EVERYTHING YOU CAN ON HIM. FAST."

I SEE NOTHING'S CHANGED.
IS SOMEONE GONNA TELL ME WHAT IS GOING ON?
YOU DON'T WANNA KNOW.
UHH, YEAH, I DO, SINCE I DON'T THINK I'M GONNA GET BACK TO SCHOOL ANY TIME SOON.
LOOK, LEX, THIS IS NEW TO US TOO. ALL WE KNOW IS THAT SOME HOW YOU'VE BEEN TARGETED BY A GROUP OF PEOPLE WHO NEED YOU TO CONTACT YOUR FATHER.
CONTACT MY *DEAD* FATHER?
TOLD YOU, YOU DIDN'T WANT TO KNOW.
HOW CAN THEY--
THE SOUL IS CAPABLE OF ASTOUNDING THINGS, LEXI.
THEY NEED YOUR DAD BECAUSE OF SOMETHING HE KNEW.

?
SO THEY CAN ACCESS THE SKILLS OF DEAD PEOPLE. IF WE ALL HAVE SOULS WHY CAN'T I?
'CAUSE YOU'VE NEVER DIED.
THAT WHAT I LOOKED LIKE?
FOR MOST, A NEAR DEATH EXPERIENCE RESULTS IN AN OPENING OF THE BARRIER BETWEEN THIS WORLD AND THE NEXT BUT ULTIMATELY BECOMES RESEALED.
BUT FOR US THE BARRIER REMAINS OPEN, FLUID, ALLOWING US TO ACCESS SKILLS FROM THE OTHER SIDE.
GRADUALLY IT BECOMES BEARABLE UNTIL YOU START TO... FUNCTION. THRIVE.
AND YOU AND YOUR BROTHER CAN DO THIS?
YEAH.
AND YOU TOO?
YES.
HOW DID IT HAPPEN FOR YOU?
SWIMMING. WITH FRIENDS IN A GORGE. THERE WAS AN OLD CAR AT THE BOTTOM.

AND YOU?
I-- I DON'T KNOW.
IT WAS THE NIGHT YOUR MOTHER DIED.
THE CAR ACCIDENT?
YES.
IT WAS SNOWING, THE ROADS WERE ICY AND... ETHAN WAS THROWN FROM THE CAR. EVENTUALLY I REALIZED HIS BREACH WAS OPEN AND CARTER WAS--
NORMAL?
I WANTED TO TELL YOU, E, I DID.
BUT...?
BUT I ALSO WANTED TO KEEP YOU SAFE.
SO YOU LET ME THINK I WAS INSANE?
IT WAS THE ONLY WAY I THOUGHT I COULD KEEP YOU SAFE AND KEEP MY PROMISE.

NEW YORK CITY
BEEP BEEP
WHAT?
SCARLET, OTAMENDI WANTS TO SEE YOU.
18:26:52:4
NO MATCH FOUND
18:32:08:54
OUTGOING C
18:33:53:11
896-742-9999
896-511-1134
896-242-1111
896-752-9425
126-242-6543
896-756-5436
896-372-3289
896-977-5559
896-224-9458
896-544-2222
896-345-2349
896-066-6664
833-672-9457
896-877-9453
896-454-3477
876-141-8547
896-744-4737
896-668-3622
BROADMOOR
PSYCHIATRIC FACILITY
TELL HIM I'M BUSY.
CLICK
PATIENT HISTORY
NOBLE, ETHAN

STUDENT ID: 30124483
NOBLE, CARTER
896-325-3134
896-252-3647
134-533-2223
532-655-5234
722-657-3462
812-373-6643
532-385-7634
896-668-3622
896-433-2567
896-322-4562
896-976-2355
896-457-2132
896-477-5696
896-435-5678
344-866-4533
896-532-3735
896-643-5553
18:33:53:11

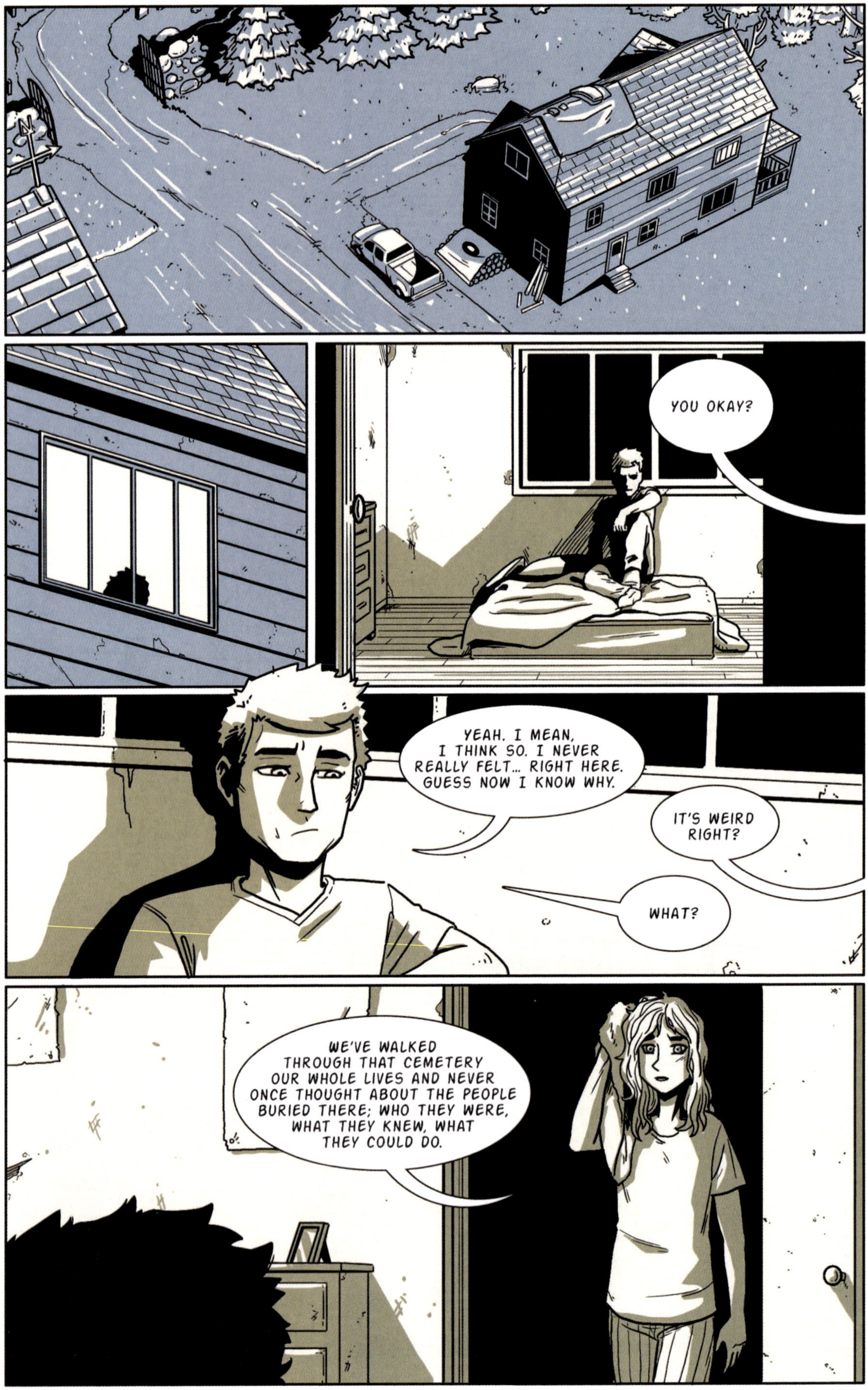
YOU OKAY?
YEAH. I MEAN, I THINK SO. I NEVER REALLY FELT... RIGHT HERE. GUESS NOW I KNOW WHY.
IT'S WEIRD RIGHT?
WHAT?
WE'VE WALKED THROUGH THAT CEMETERY OUR WHOLE LIVES AND NEVER ONCE THOUGHT ABOUT THE PEOPLE BURIED THERE; WHO THEY WERE, WHAT THEY KNEW, WHAT THEY COULD DO.

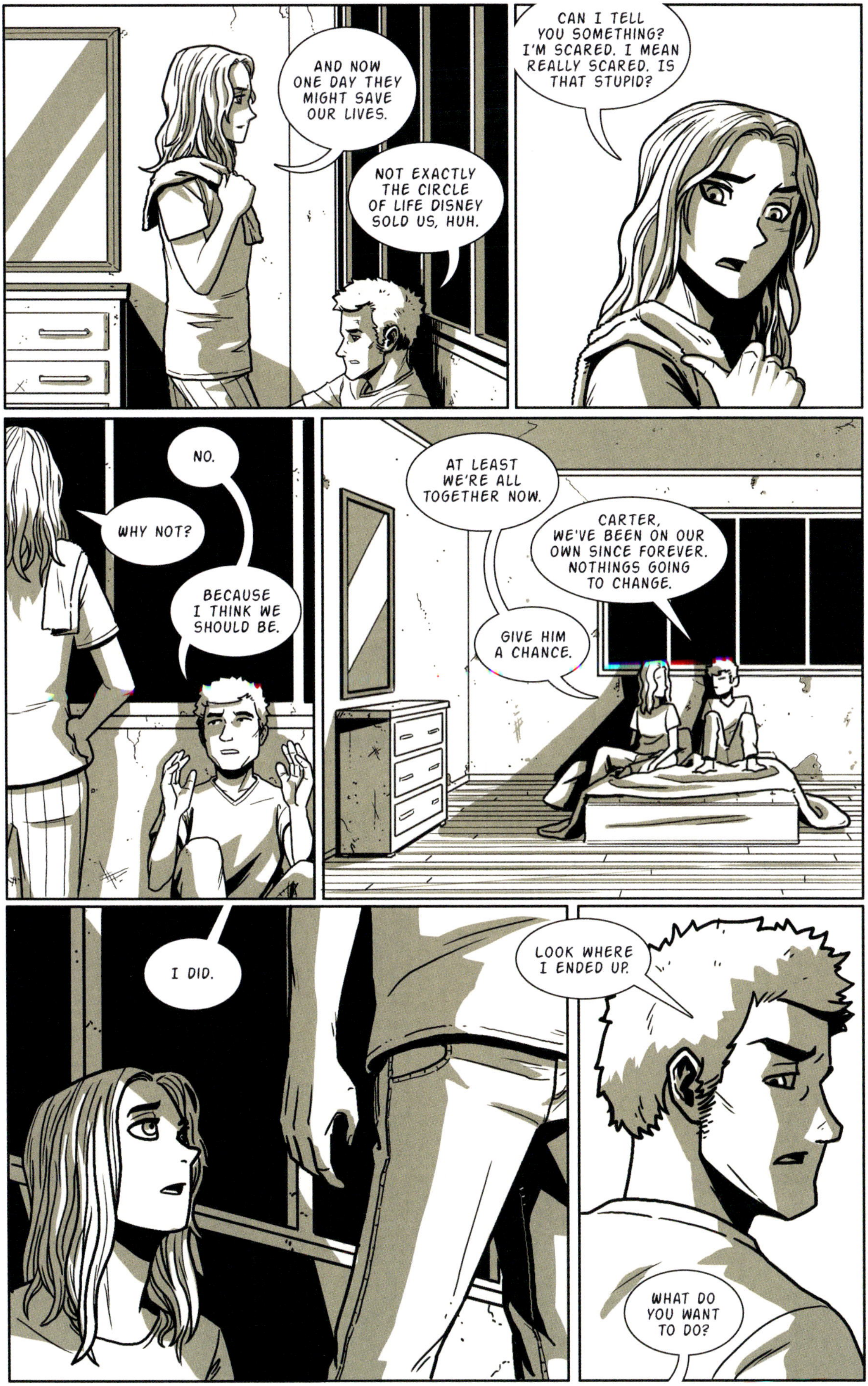
AND NOW ONE DAY THEY MIGHT SAVE OUR LIVES.
NOT EXACTLY THE CIRCLE OF LIFE DISNEY SOLD US, HUH.
CAN I TELL YOU SOMETHING? I'M SCARED. I MEAN REALLY SCARED. IS THAT STUPID?
NO.
WHY NOT?
BECAUSE I THINK WE SHOULD BE.
AT LEAST WE'RE ALL TOGETHER NOW.
CARTER, WE'VE BEEN ON OUR OWN SINCE FOREVER. NOTHINGS GOING TO CHANGE.
GIVE HIM A CHANCE.
I DID.
LOOK WHERE I ENDED UP.
WHAT DO YOU WANT TO DO?

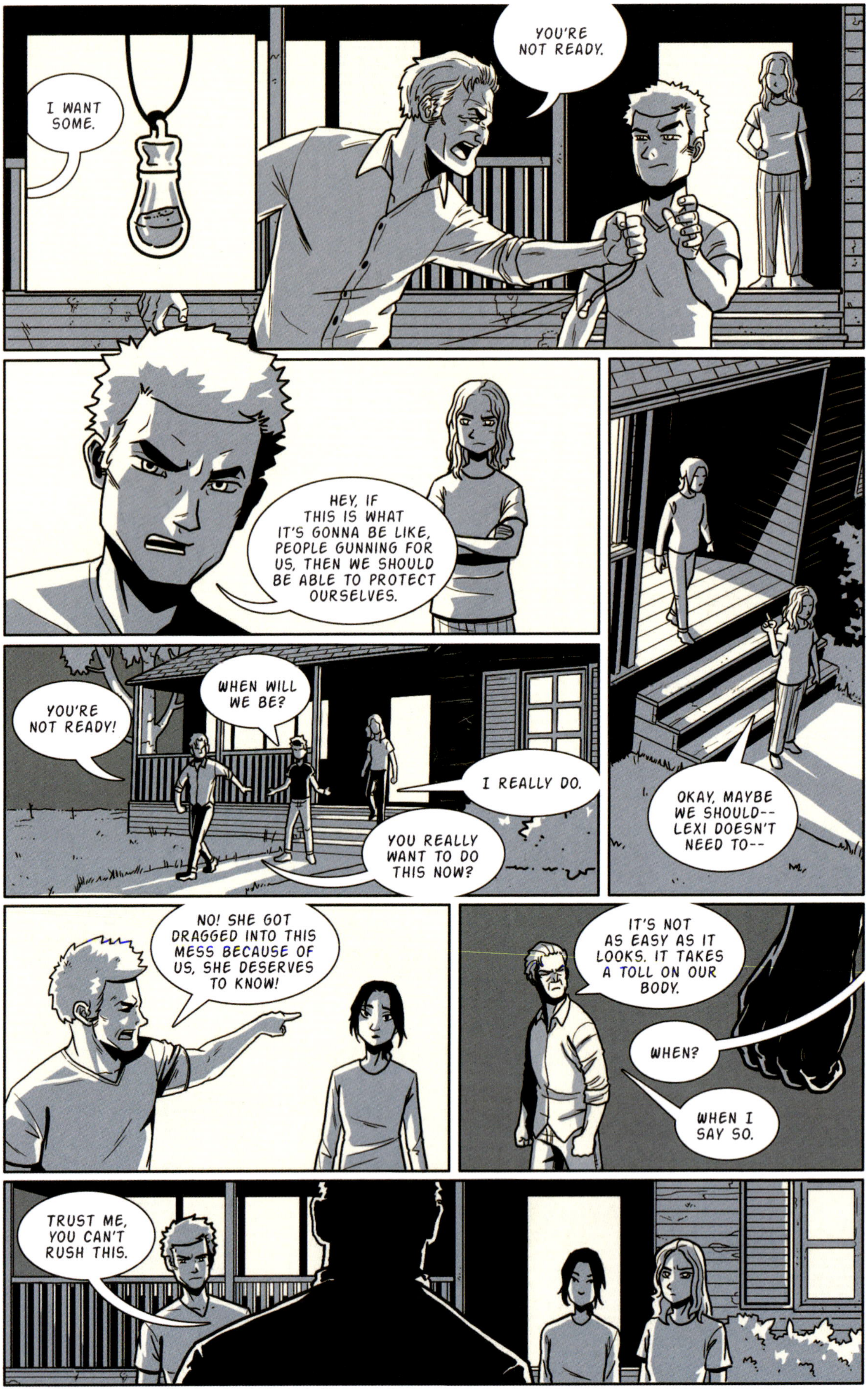
I WANT SOME.
YOU'RE NOT READY.
HEY, IF THIS IS WHAT IT'S GONNA BE LIKE, PEOPLE GUNNING FOR US, THEN WE SHOULD BE ABLE TO PROTECT OURSELVES.
YOU'RE NOT READY!
WHEN WILL WE BE?
I REALLY DO.
YOU REALLY WANT TO DO THIS NOW?
OKAY, MAYBE WE SHOULD-- LEXI DOESN'T NEED TO--
NO! SHE GOT DRAGGED INTO THIS MESS BECAUSE OF US, SHE DESERVES TO KNOW!
IT'S NOT AS EASY AS IT LOOKS. IT TAKES A TOLL ON OUR BODY.
WHEN?
WHEN I SAY SO.
TRUST ME, YOU CAN'T RUSH THIS.

AGAIN WITH THE TRUST! WHY SHOULD WE?!
'CAUSE YOU'RE GONNA END UP DEAD IF YOU DON'T.
ETHAN, THIS ISN'T JUST A PHYSICAL THING. THAT'S THE EASY PART. IT'S THE MENTAL YOU NEED TO WORRY ABOUT.
ABSORBING AN ENTIRE LIFE INSIDE YOURS BUT HAVING TO KEEP THEM FROM OVER LAPPING, TAKING OVER...
JUGGLING SOMEONE ELSE'S MEMORIES, EXPERIENCES, JOY, HEARTBREAKS ALL WHILE SOMEONE'S TRYING TO KILL YOU?
YOU'RE NOT READY. NOT EVEN CLOSE.
THEN GET US READY. TRAIN US.
SERIOUSLY?
YEAH.
RING
RING
WHAT?
YOU HAVE PROBLEMS. I'M COMING OUT.

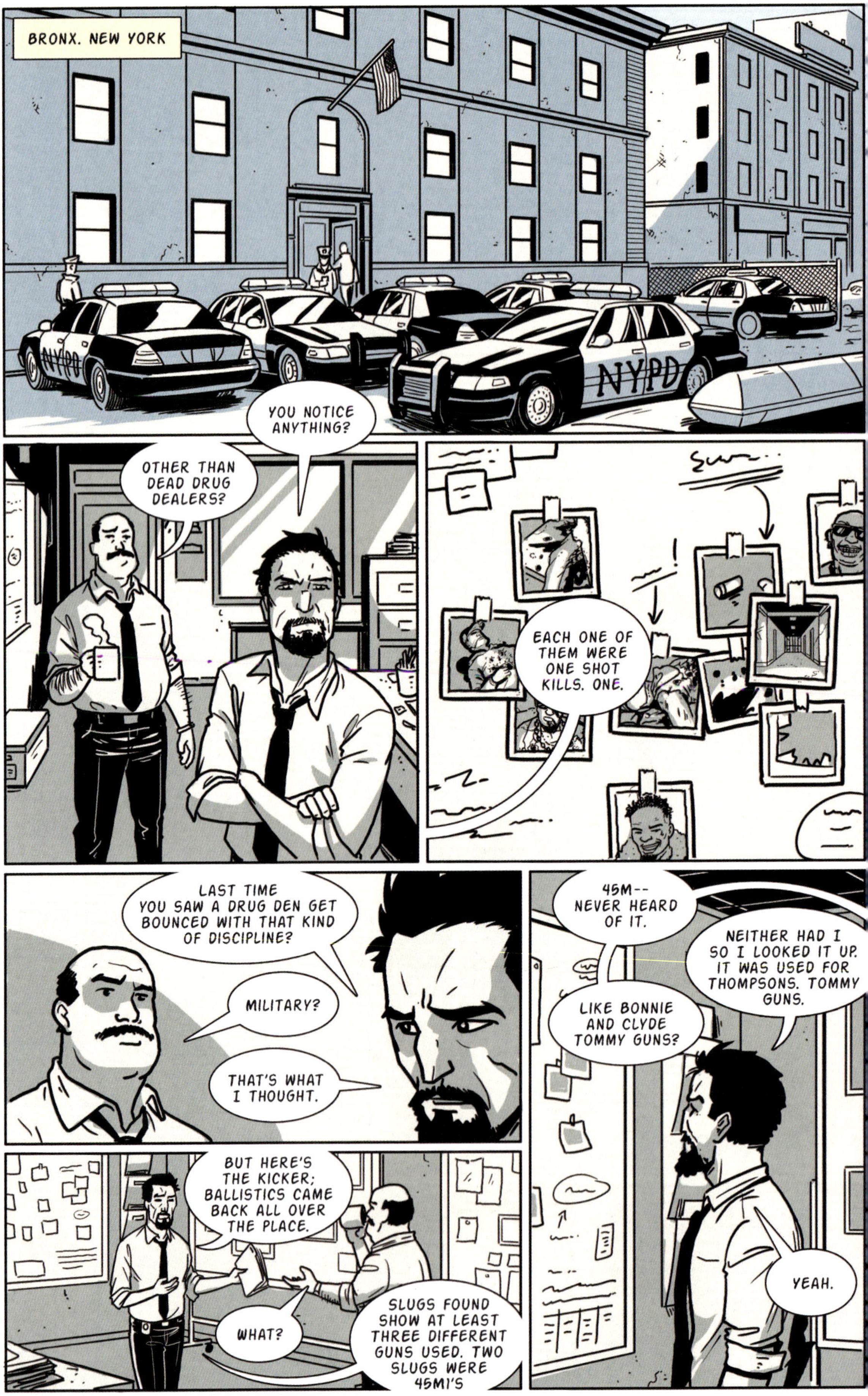
BRONX. NEW YORK
NYPD
NYPD
YOU NOTICE ANYTHING?
OTHER THAN DEAD DRUG DEALERS?
EACH ONE OF THEM WERE ONE SHOT KILLS. ONE.
LAST TIME YOU SAW A DRUG DEN GET BOUNCED WITH THAT KIND OF DISCIPLINE?
MILITARY?
THAT'S WHAT I THOUGHT.
BUT HERE'S THE KICKER; BALLISTICS CAME BACK ALL OVER THE PLACE.
WHAT?
SLUGS FOUND SHOW AT LEAST THREE DIFFERENT GUNS USED. TWO SLUGS WERE 45MI'S
45M-- NEVER HEARD OF IT.
NEITHER HAD I SO I LOOKED IT UP. IT WAS USED FOR THOMPSONS. TOMMY GUNS.
LIKE BONNIE AND CLYDE TOMMY GUNS?
YEAH.

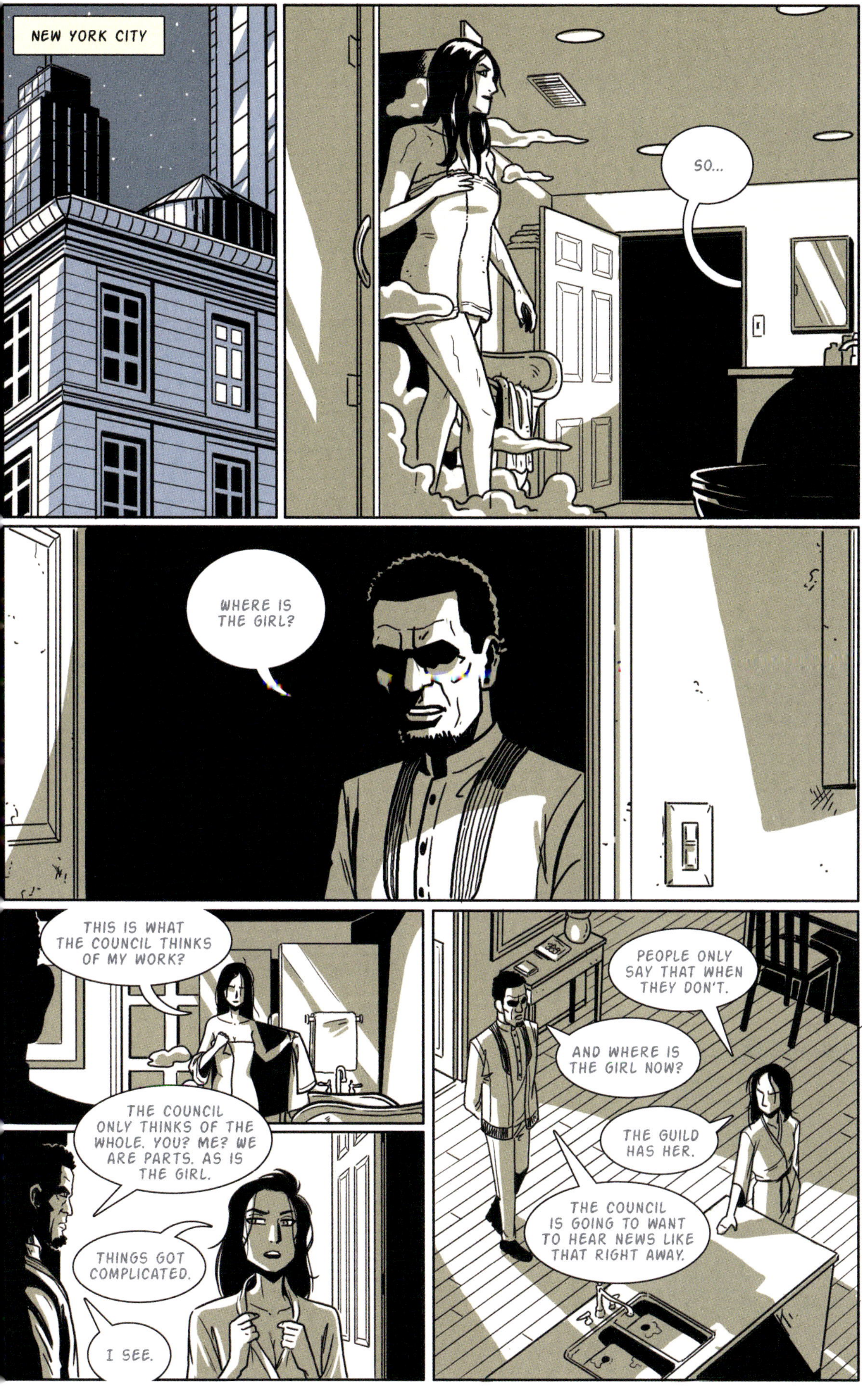
NEW YORK CITY
SO...
WHERE IS THE GIRL?
THIS IS WHAT THE COUNCIL THINKS OF MY WORK?
THE COUNCIL ONLY THINKS OF THE WHOLE. YOU? ME? WE ARE PARTS. AS IS THE GIRL.
THINGS GOT COMPLICATED.
I SEE.
PEOPLE ONLY SAY THAT WHEN THEY DON'T.
AND WHERE IS THE GIRL NOW?
THE GUILD HAS HER.
THE COUNCIL IS GOING TO WANT TO HEAR NEWS LIKE THAT RIGHT AWAY.

GIVE ME TIME AND I'LL MAKE THIS WORK.
HOW DO YOU KNOW?
BECAUSE I KNOW THIS GIRL. SHE PUT A NOOSE AROUND HER NECK, ON HER OWN. SHE WANTS WHAT WE HAVE.
I'LL GET HER. IT'S JUST GOING TO TAKE MORE TIME.
VERY WELL.
OTAMENDI...
SO YOU KNOW, THE NEXT TIME YOU ENTER MY HOME UNINVITED I WILL KILL YOU.
AND TELL THE COUNCIL IF THEY'RE UNHAPPY WITH THE JOB I'M DOING THEY CAN HAVE IT.
THE NEXT TIME THE COUNCIL IS UNHAPPY WITH YOUR PERFORMANCE THEY'RE GOING TO TAKE MORE THEN YOUR JOB.

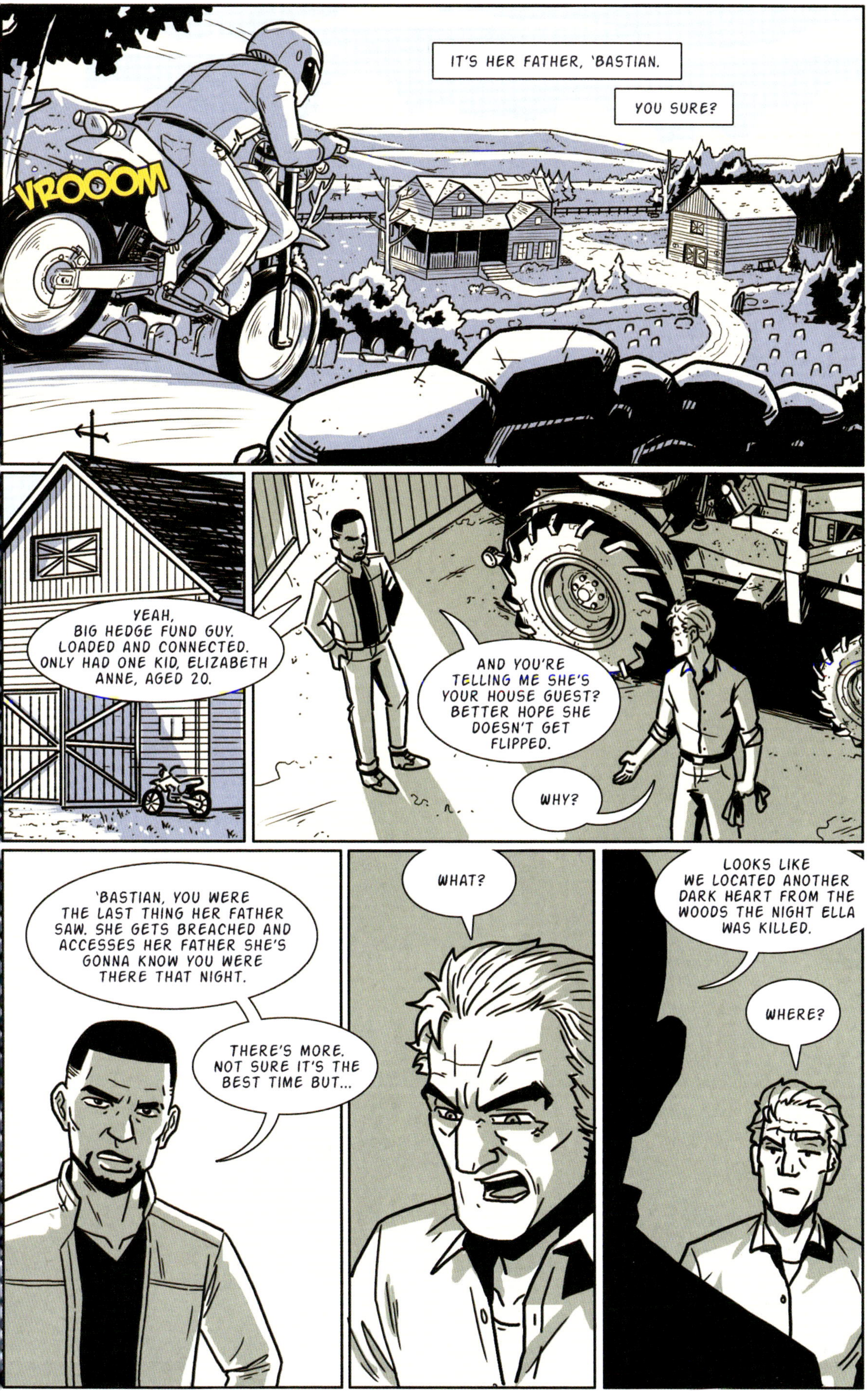
IT'S HER FATHER, 'BASTIAN.
YOU SURE?
VROOOM
YEAH, BIG HEDGE FUND GUY. LOADED AND CONNECTED. ONLY HAD ONE KID, ELIZABETH ANNE, AGED 20.
AND YOU'RE TELLING ME SHE'S YOUR HOUSE GUEST? BETTER HOPE SHE DOESN'T GET FLIPPED.
WHY?
'BASTIAN, YOU WERE THE LAST THING HER FATHER SAW. SHE GETS BREACHED AND ACCESSES HER FATHER SHE'S GONNA KNOW YOU WERE THERE THAT NIGHT.
THERE'S MORE. NOT SURE IT'S THE BEST TIME BUT...
WHAT?
LOOKS LIKE WE LOCATED ANOTHER DARK HEART FROM THE WOODS THE NIGHT ELLA WAS KILLED.
WHERE?

CHICAGO.
SECURITY UNIT OUT OF L.A GRABBED TWO IN SAN DIEGO. I CALLED IN A FAVOR. ONE OF THEM PLACED THIS GUY IN CHICAGO IN THE WOODS THE NIGHT ELLA WAS MURDERED.
OKAY, LET ME FIGURE THIS OUT AND I'LL GET THERE AS SOON AS I CAN.
FIGURE WHAT OUT?
N- NOTHING. I JUST HAVE A LOT TO JUGGLE. WHAT'S UP? WHERE'S LEXI?
INSIDE, RESTING.
WE WANT TO TALK.
ABOUT?
OUR SAFE SOIL.
THERE'S NOTHING TO-- YOU CRAWL THEN WALK. YOU TWO WANT TO GO RUN A MARATHON. YOU'RE NOT READY.
THEN GET US READY.
I CAN'T. I NEED TO GO TO CHICAGO.
IF WE NEED TRAINING, TRAIN US.
OKAY, YOU WANNA BE TRAINED? FINE. BUT DON'T SAY I DIDN'T WARN YOU.

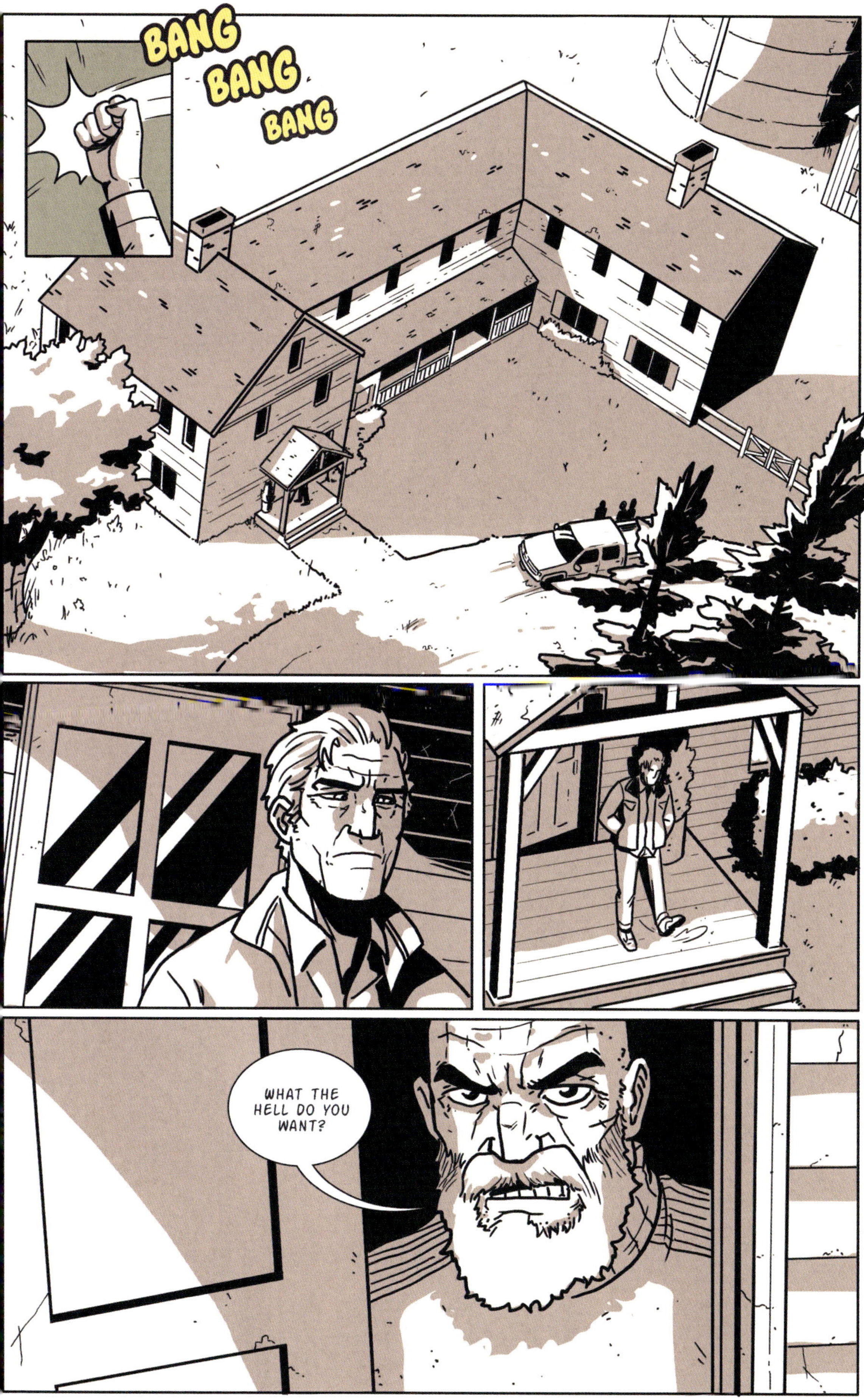
BANG
BANG
BANG
WHAT THE HELL DO YOU WANT?

WE NEED TO TALK.
GOOD TO SEE YOU TOO, FLOOD.
YOU LOOK LIKE CRAP. WE DONE?
SHUT UP.
I NEED YOUR HELP.
YOU NEED MY-- I NEED A UNICORN WHO CRAPS GOLD. ONE OF THOSE THINGS IS NEVER GONNA HAPPEN.
OKAY. *THEY* NEED YOUR HELP.
WHAT ARE THEY DOING HERE?
THEY KNOW. EVERYTHING.
WHAT DO YOU WANT, SEBASTIAN?
I WANT YOU TO TRAIN 'EM.
ARE YOU OUT OF YOUR-- FORGET IT.
IT'S NOT WHAT ELLA WANTED.
IT'S NOT WHAT I WANTED EITHER! NONE OF IT. AND YET ***HERE WE ARE!*** THEY KNOW AND I'M ***DONE*** RUNNING FROM THIS!

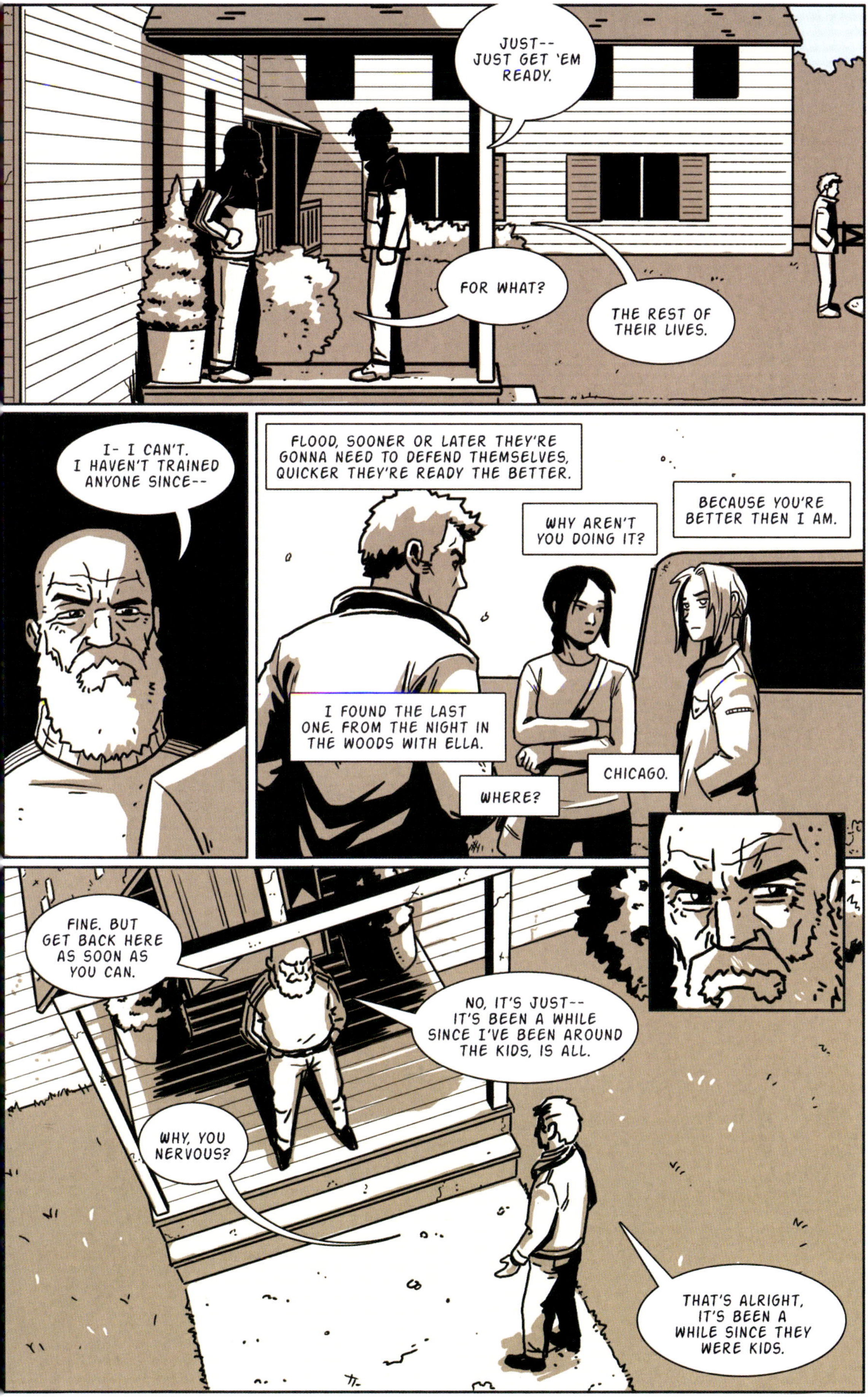
JUST-- JUST GET 'EM READY.
FOR WHAT?
THE REST OF THEIR LIVES.
I- I CAN'T. I HAVEN'T TRAINED ANYONE SINCE--
FLOOD, SOONER OR LATER THEY'RE GONNA NEED TO DEFEND THEMSELVES, QUICKER THEY'RE READY THE BETTER.
WHY AREN'T YOU DOING IT?
BECAUSE YOU'RE BETTER THEN I AM.
I FOUND THE LAST ONE. FROM THE NIGHT IN THE WOODS WITH ELLA.
WHERE?
CHICAGO.
FINE. BUT GET BACK HERE AS SOON AS YOU CAN.
NO, IT'S JUST-- IT'S BEEN A WHILE SINCE I'VE BEEN AROUND THE KIDS, IS ALL.
WHY, YOU NERVOUS?
THAT'S ALRIGHT, IT'S BEEN A WHILE SINCE THEY WERE KIDS.

Panel 1:
- HOW'D IT GO?
- HE'S A COMPLETE PRICK.
- WHO IS HE?
- YOUR GRANDFATHER.

Panel 2:
- WAIT... WHAT?!
- WHAT ARE WE DOING HERE?
- YOU WANTED YOUR OWN SAFE SOIL, RIGHT?
- YEAH.

Panel 3:
- WELL, WHEN HE SAYS YOUR READY YOU'LL GET IT.
- YOU'RE JUST GONNA LEAVE US HERE? WE DON'T EVEN KNOW HIM!
- HE'S YOUR GRANDFATHER.

Panel 4:
- YOU JUST SAID HE WAS A TOTAL DICK!
- HE IS.
- SERIOUSLY, HAVE YOU READ ANY PARENTING BOOKS?!

Panel 5:
- I DIG THE HOUSE.
- SEE! LEXI DIGS THE HOUSE. GOOD ATTITUDE, LEX!

Panel 6:
- WHY CAN'T YOU GET US READY?
- BECAUSE I'M NOT GOOD ENOUGH.

Panel 7:
- AND HOW DO WE KNOW HE IS?
- 'CAUSE HE TRAINED YOUR MOM AND SHE WAS ONE OF THE BEST CARETAKERS THE GUILD EVER HAD.

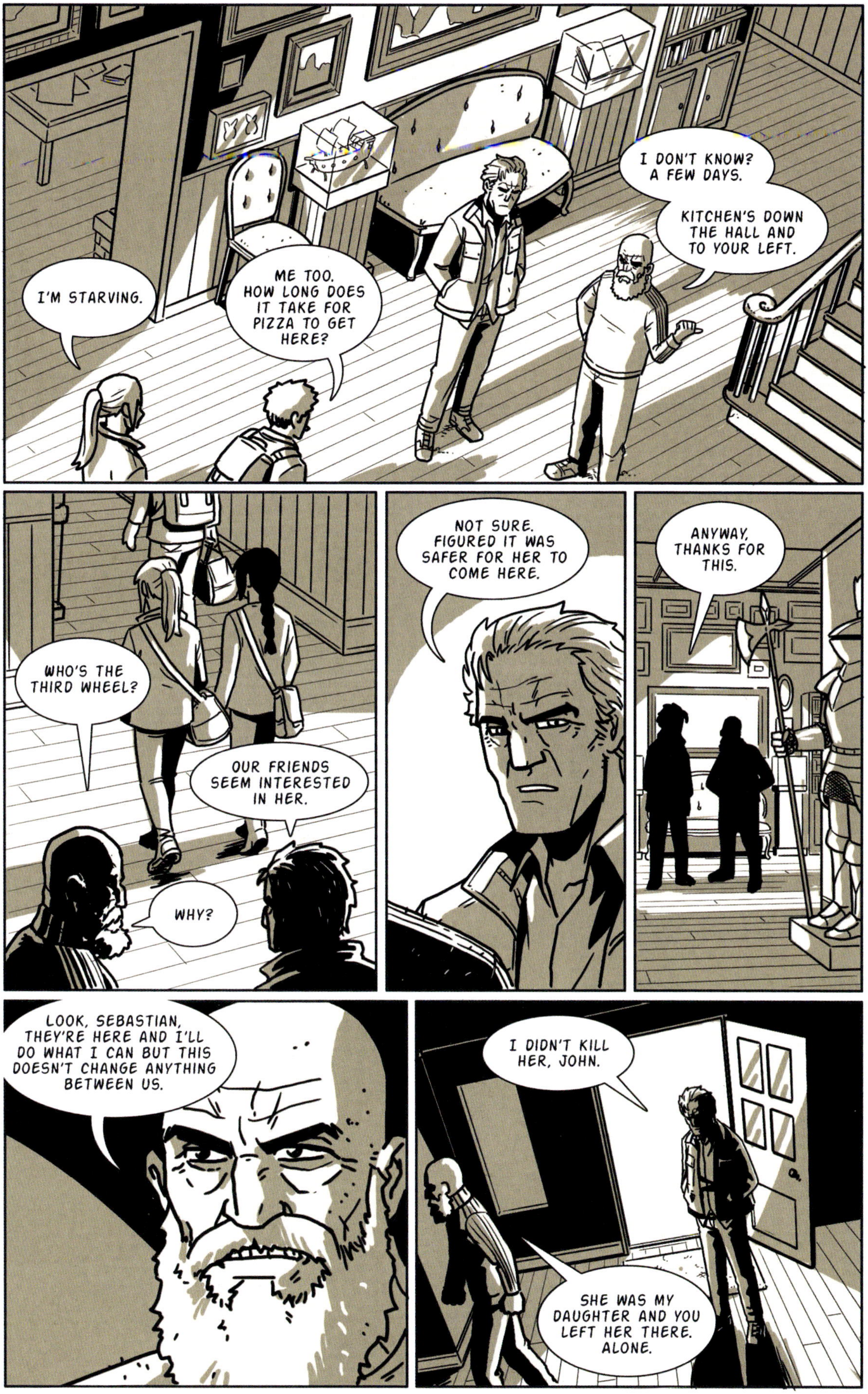
I'M STARVING.
ME TOO. HOW LONG DOES IT TAKE FOR PIZZA TO GET HERE?
I DON'T KNOW? A FEW DAYS.
KITCHEN'S DOWN THE HALL AND TO YOUR LEFT.
WHO'S THE THIRD WHEEL?
OUR FRIENDS SEEM INTERESTED IN HER.
WHY?
NOT SURE. FIGURED IT WAS SAFER FOR HER TO COME HERE.
ANYWAY, THANKS FOR THIS.
LOOK, SEBASTIAN, THEY'RE HERE AND I'LL DO WHAT I CAN BUT THIS DOESN'T CHANGE ANYTHING BETWEEN US.
I DIDN'T KILL HER, JOHN.
SHE WAS MY DAUGHTER AND YOU LEFT HER THERE. ALONE.

WHAT WAS IT LIKE BEING IN THAT PLACE?
THE SHRINK FARM?
IT WAS... BIZARRE. AND FUNNY AND DEPRESSING.
DID YOU EVER THINK ABOUT IT?
ABOUT WHAT?
KILLING YOURSELF.
AT THE BEGINNING, I DID. WHEN I COULDN'T FIGURE OUT WHAT WAS HAPPENING.
WHY DIDN'T YOU?
KILL MYSELF? CARTER, I GUESS. I JUST DIDN'T WANT HER TO BE... DISAPPOINTED IN ME.
WHAT MADE YOU PUT THE NOOSE ON?
M- MY MOTHER DIED WHEN I WAS SIX AND FOR A LONG TIME IT WAS JUST ME AND MY DAD.
EVERY NIGHT BEFORE BED HE'D READ ME A STORY. EVERY NIGHT. WE STARTED WITH HARRY POTTER AND JUST-- IT BECAME THIS THING... OUR THING.
AND SOMEHOW, I DON'T KNOW WHY, IT KEPT GOING.
HIGH SCHOOL. COLLEGE. VACATIONS. SPRING BREAK. EVERY NIGHT, NO MATTER WHERE HE WAS, HE'D CALL AND READ ME SOMETHING.
WHAT IF YOU COULDN'T ANSWER OR YOU HAD CLASS OR--
HE'D LEAVE IT ON MY VOICE-MAIL.
IT WAS SOMETHING WE DID TOGETHER, JUST US. AND NO MATTER WHAT, IT WAS ALWAYS THE BEST PART OF MY DAY. ALWAYS.
I PUT THE NOOSE AROUND MY NECK BECAUSE I WANTED TO FEEL THAT AGAIN.
I WISH I HAD WHAT YOU AND CARTER HAVE.

THIS WAS YOUR MOM'S ROOM.

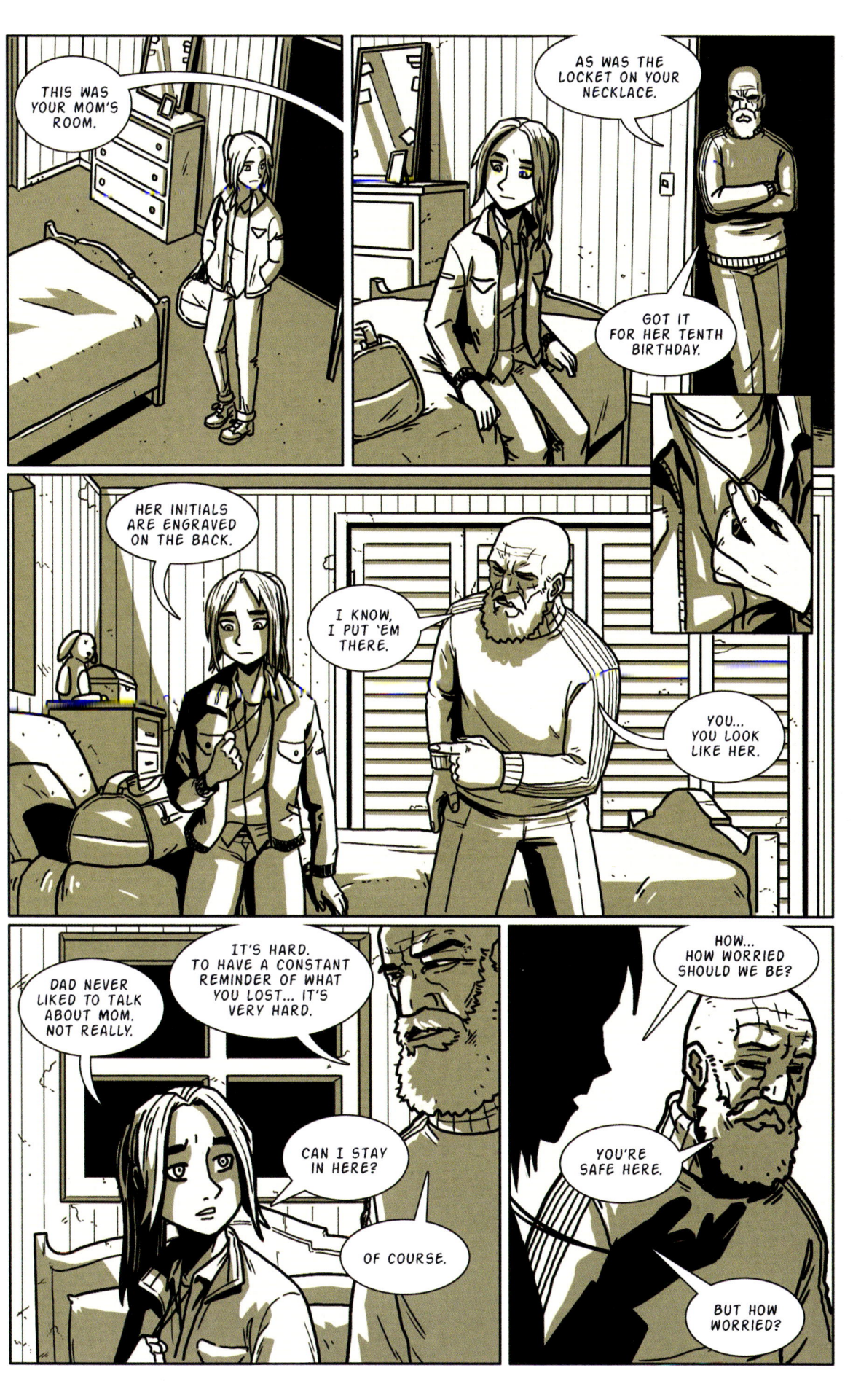

AS WAS THE LOCKET ON YOUR NECKLACE.

GOT IT FOR HER TENTH BIRTHDAY.

HER INITIALS ARE ENGRAVED ON THE BACK.

I KNOW, I PUT 'EM THERE.

YOU... YOU LOOK LIKE HER.

DAD NEVER LIKED TO TALK ABOUT MOM. NOT REALLY.

IT'S HARD. TO HAVE A CONSTANT REMINDER OF WHAT YOU LOST... IT'S VERY HARD.

CAN I STAY IN HERE?

OF COURSE.

HOW... HOW WORRIED SHOULD WE BE?

YOU'RE SAFE HERE.

BUT HOW WORRIED?

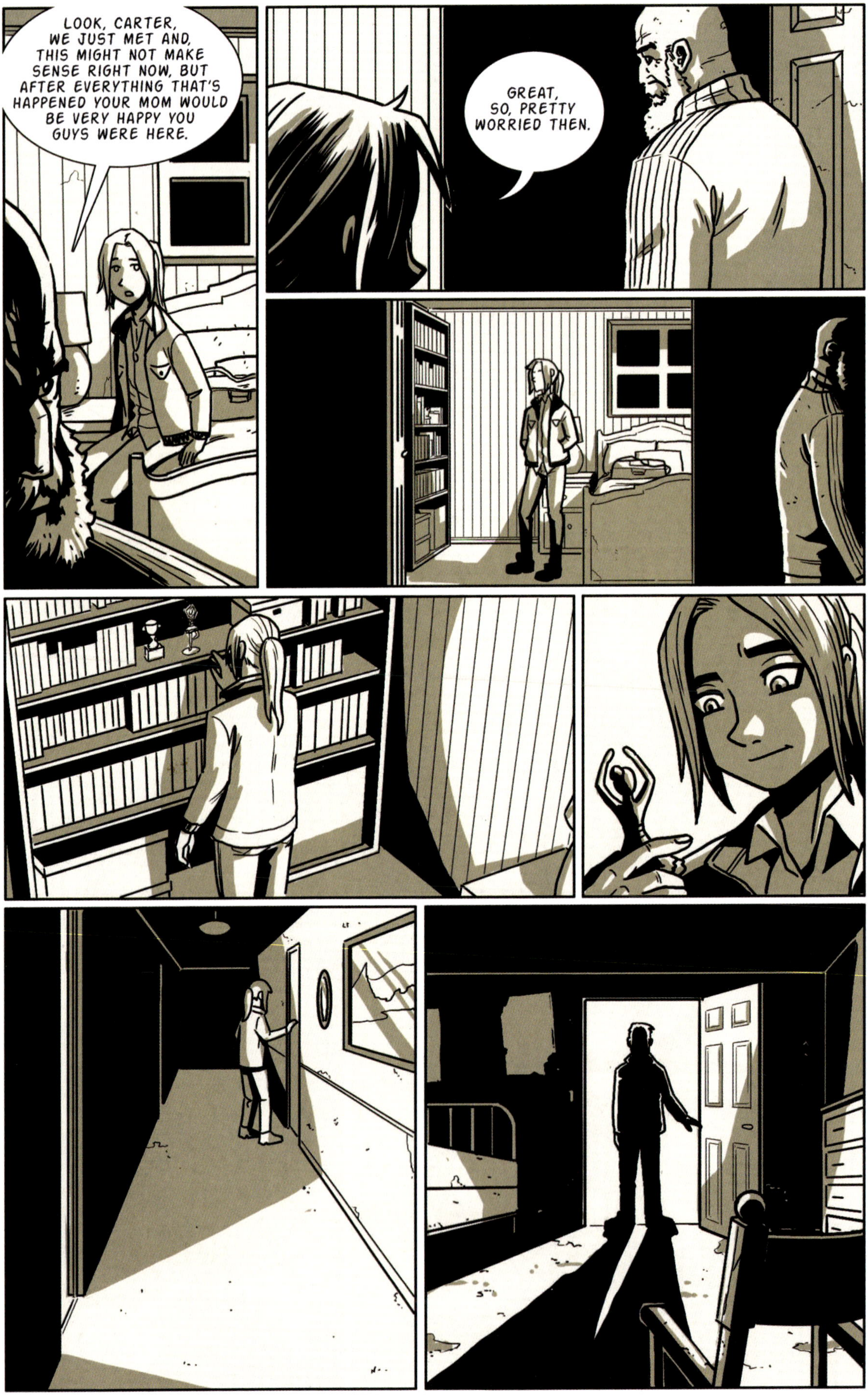
LOOK, CARTER, WE JUST MET AND, THIS MIGHT NOT MAKE SENSE RIGHT NOW, BUT AFTER EVERYTHING THAT'S HAPPENED YOUR MOM WOULD BE VERY HAPPY YOU GUYS WERE HERE.
GREAT, SO, PRETTY WORRIED THEN.

LET'S GO! C'MON! WAKE UP!
WHAT IS THIS?
FIRST THINGS FIRST. WE GOTTA CLEAN UP THE CEMETERY.
CEMETERY?
I DIDN'T SEE A CEMETERY.
IT'S BEEN A WHILE SINCE I CUT THE GRASS.
OKAY, WELL... GOOD LUCK.
NOT SO FAST. IF YOU'RE HERE, YOU'RE HELPING.

BRONX, NEW YORK
HANG OUT?
YES.
I DON'T-- WHAT DOES THAT MEAN? HANG OUT?
I JUST WANNA CHILL. MAYBE GO BACK TO SLEEP.
SO... STAY HERE WITHOUT ME?
I DON'T HAVE A SHIFT TODAY. IS THIS A PROBLEM? YOU DON'T WANT ME HERE?
NO, NO. IT JUST FEELS LIKE THAT'S KINDA... LEVEL TWO STUFF.
LEVEL TWO? AND WHAT LEVEL DO YOU CONSIDER LAST NIGHT?!
RING RING
YEAH..?
WE GOT A HIT.

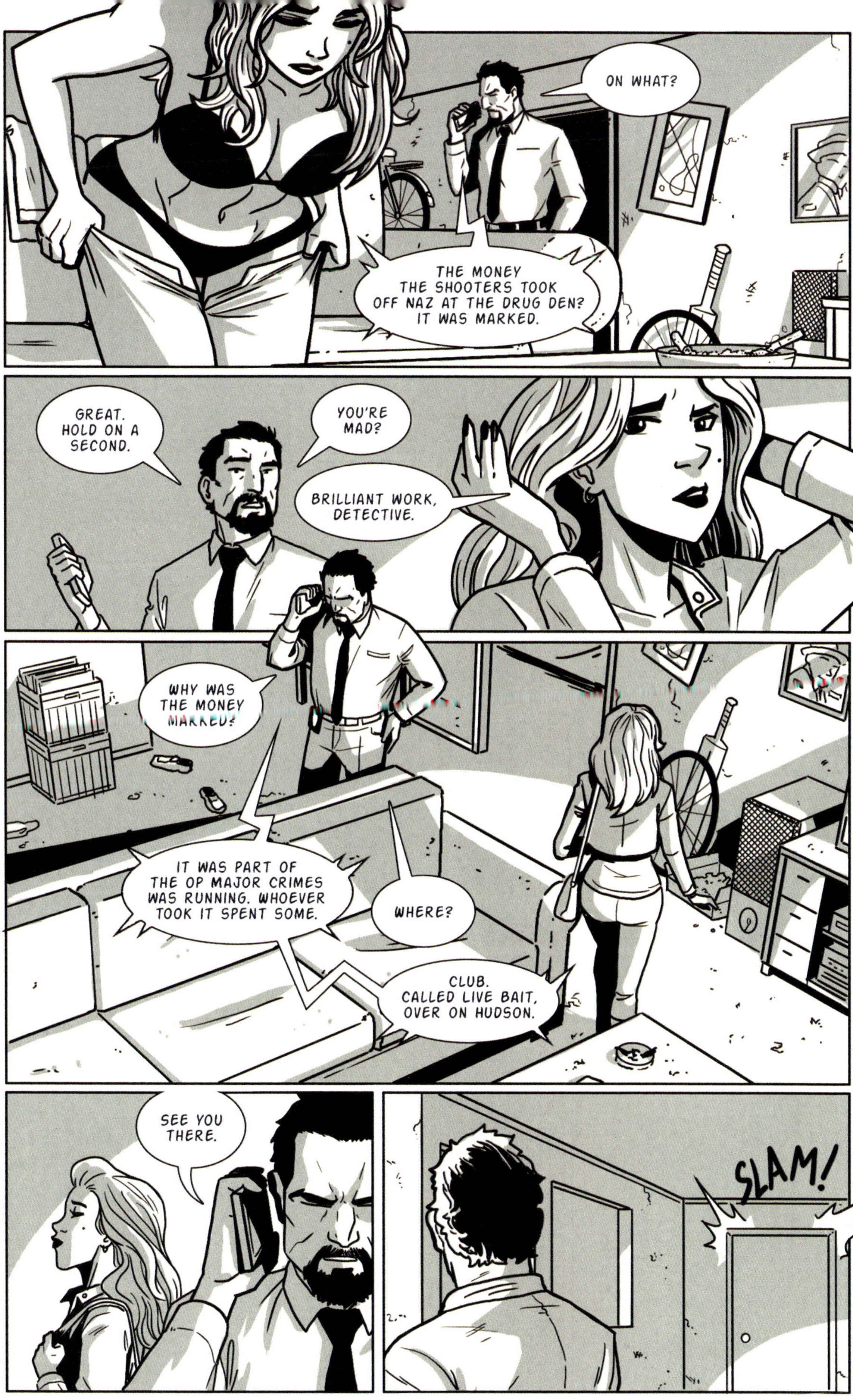
ON WHAT?
THE MONEY THE SHOOTERS TOOK OFF NAZ AT THE DRUG DEN? IT WAS MARKED.
GREAT. HOLD ON A SECOND.
YOU'RE MAD?
BRILLIANT WORK, DETECTIVE.
WHY WAS THE MONEY MARKED?
IT WAS PART OF THE OP MAJOR CRIMES WAS RUNNING. WHOEVER TOOK IT SPENT SOME.
WHERE?
CLUB. CALLED LIVE BAIT, OVER ON HUDSON.
SEE YOU THERE.
SLAM!

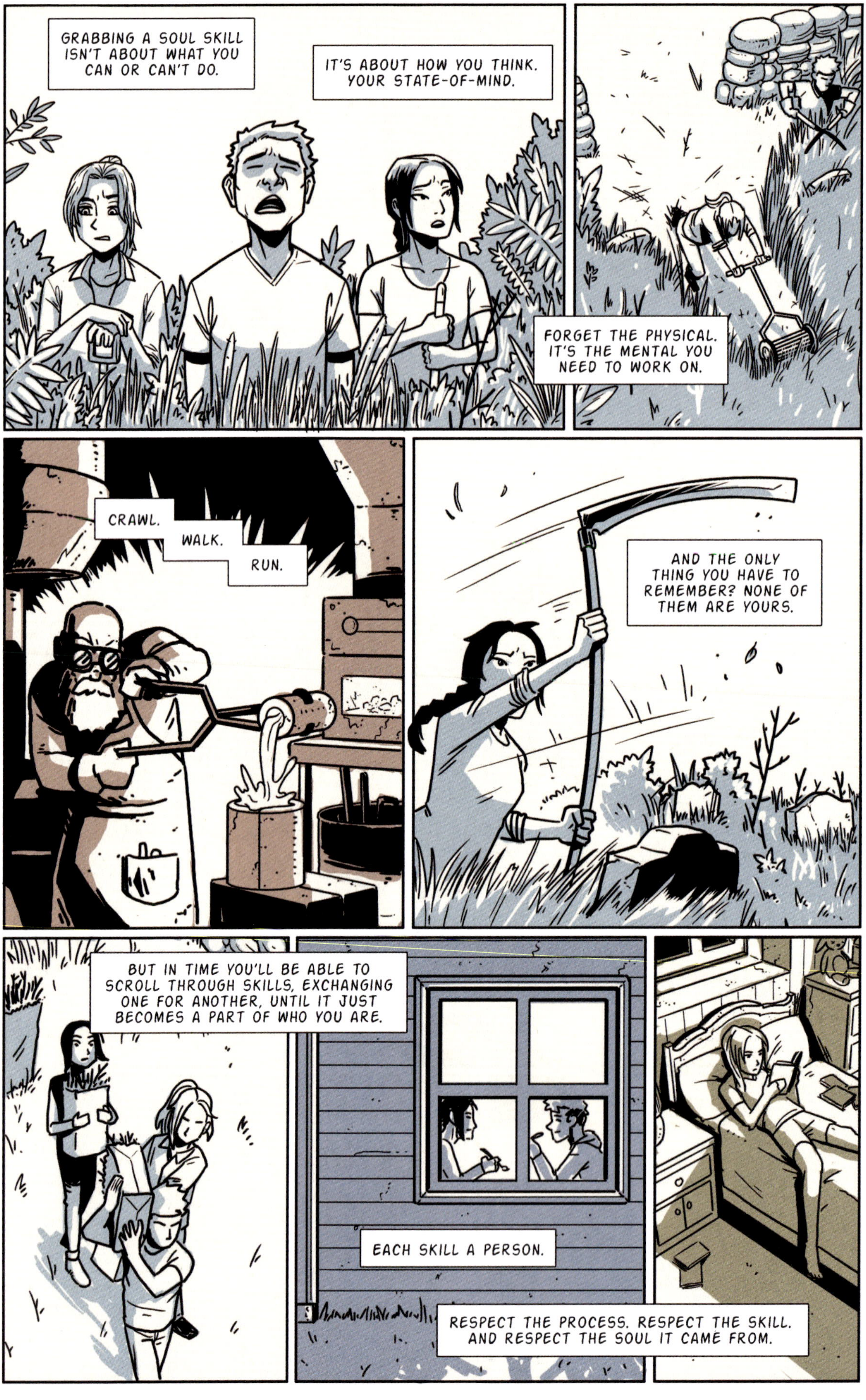
GRABBING A SOUL SKILL ISN'T ABOUT WHAT YOU CAN OR CAN'T DO.
IT'S ABOUT HOW YOU THINK. YOUR STATE-OF-MIND.
FORGET THE PHYSICAL. IT'S THE MENTAL YOU NEED TO WORK ON.
CRAWL.
WALK.
RUN.
AND THE ONLY THING YOU HAVE TO REMEMBER? NONE OF THEM ARE YOURS.
BUT IN TIME YOU'LL BE ABLE TO SCROLL THROUGH SKILLS, EXCHANGING ONE FOR ANOTHER, UNTIL IT JUST BECOMES A PART OF WHO YOU ARE.
EACH SKILL A PERSON.
RESPECT THE PROCESS. RESPECT THE SKILL. AND RESPECT THE SOUL IT CAME FROM.

THE LESS CLUTTERED YOU'RE HEAD, THE FASTER YOU CAN GRAB A SKILL.

IT'S AN ABILITY. ONE YOU CAN HONE.

YOU DIDN'T EARN THEM. YOU JUST BORROW THEM.

AT FIRST YOU'LL GRAB ONE AND YOU'LL HOLD ON TO IT WITH ALL YOUR MIGHT AND EVEN THEN IT WON'T STICK. YOU'LL FEEL IT SLIP AWAY.

BECAUSE AT THE END OF THE DAY WE'RE JUST CUSTODIANS...

GUARDIANS...

...CARETAKERS.

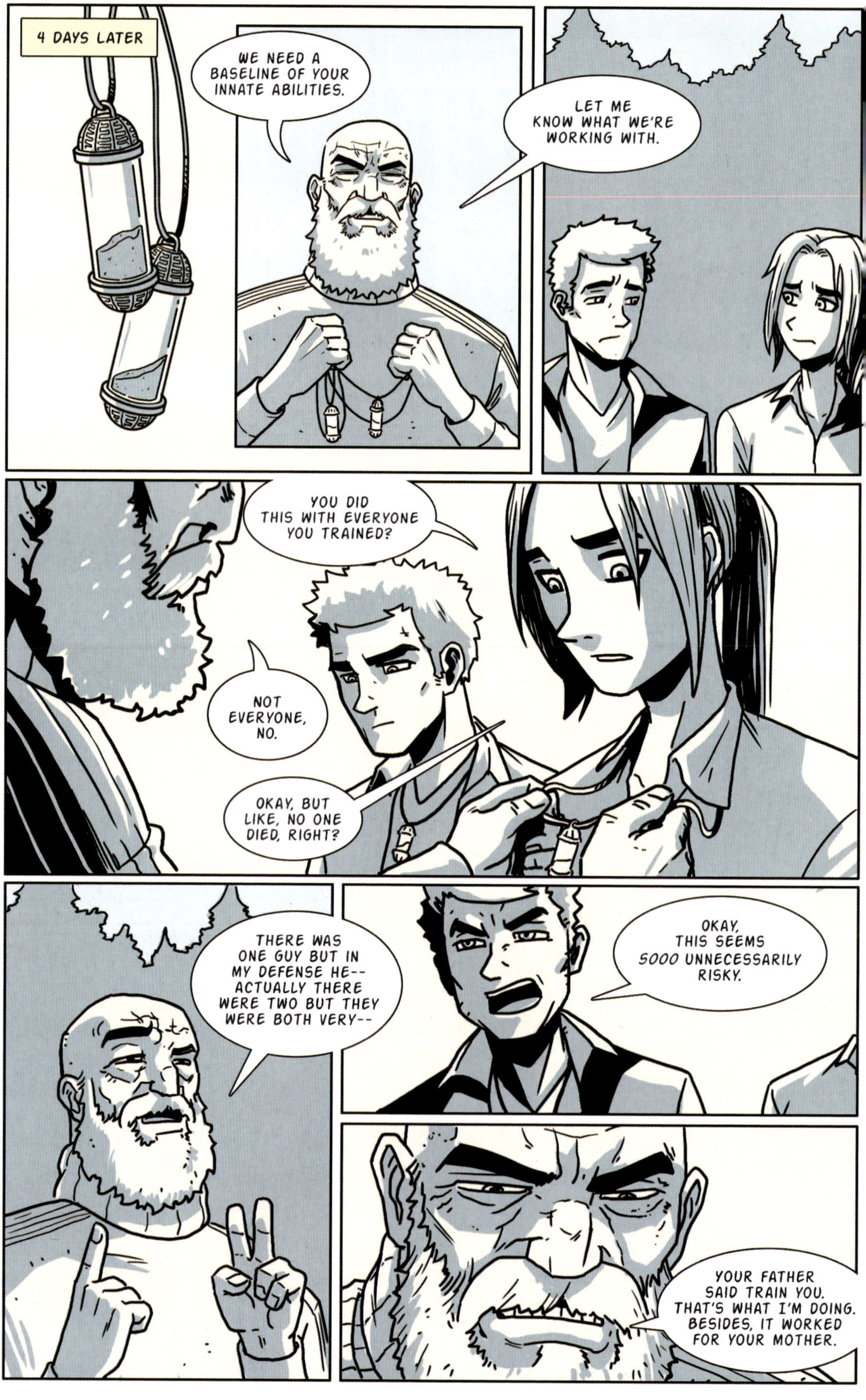
4 DAYS LATER
WE NEED A BASELINE OF YOUR INNATE ABILITIES.
LET ME KNOW WHAT WE'RE WORKING WITH.
YOU DID THIS WITH EVERYONE YOU TRAINED?
NOT EVERYONE, NO.
OKAY, BUT LIKE, NO ONE DIED, RIGHT?
THERE WAS ONE GUY BUT IN MY DEFENSE HE-- ACTUALLY THERE WERE TWO BUT THEY WERE BOTH VERY--
OKAY, THIS SEEMS *SOOO* UNNECESSARILY RISKY.
YOUR FATHER SAID TRAIN YOU. THAT'S WHAT I'M DOING. BESIDES, IT WORKED FOR YOUR MOTHER.

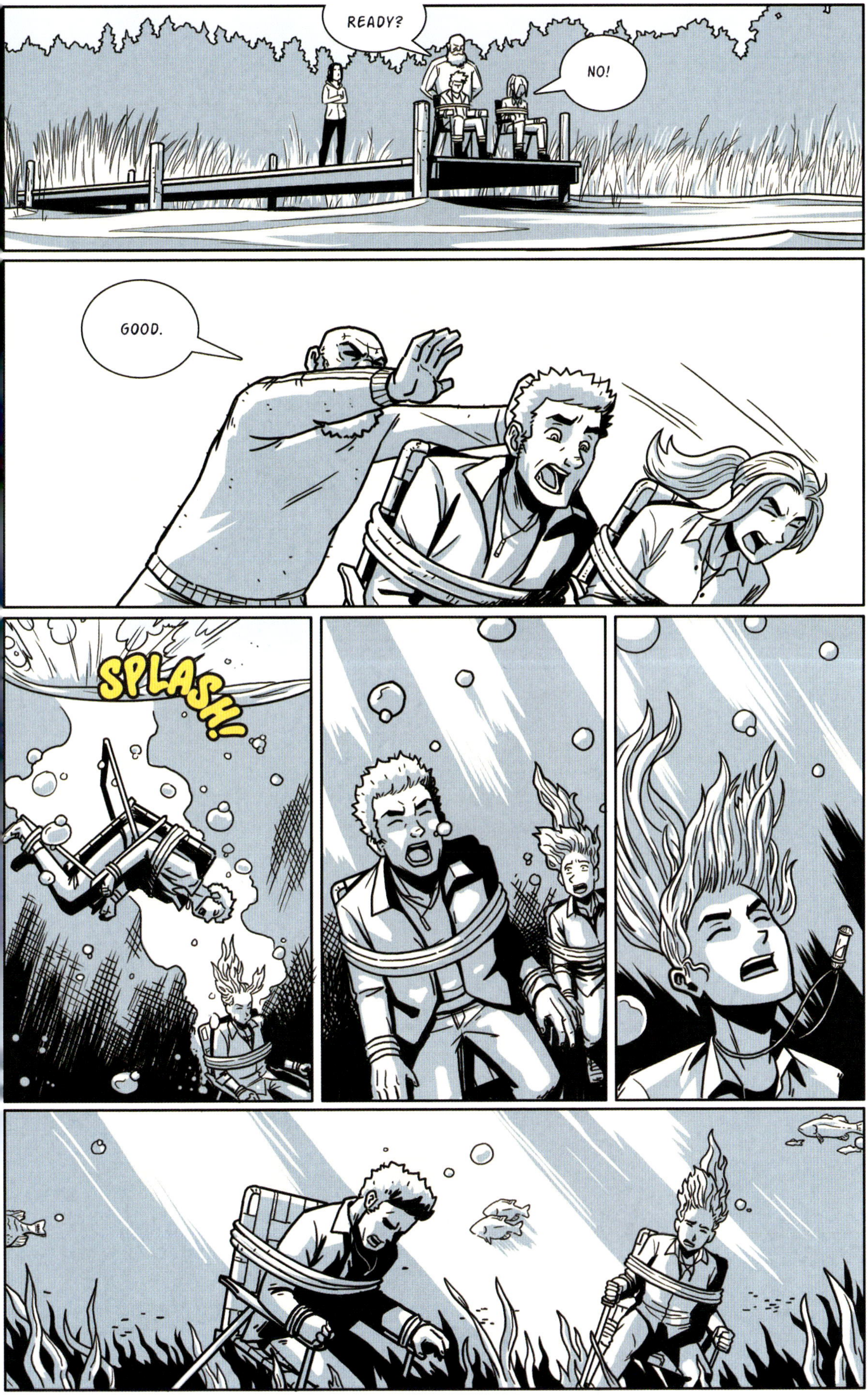
READY?
NO!
GOOD.
SPLASH!

THIS SAFE?
THEORETICALLY. IF THEY'RE ANY GOOD.
AND IF THEY AREN'T?
SPLASH!

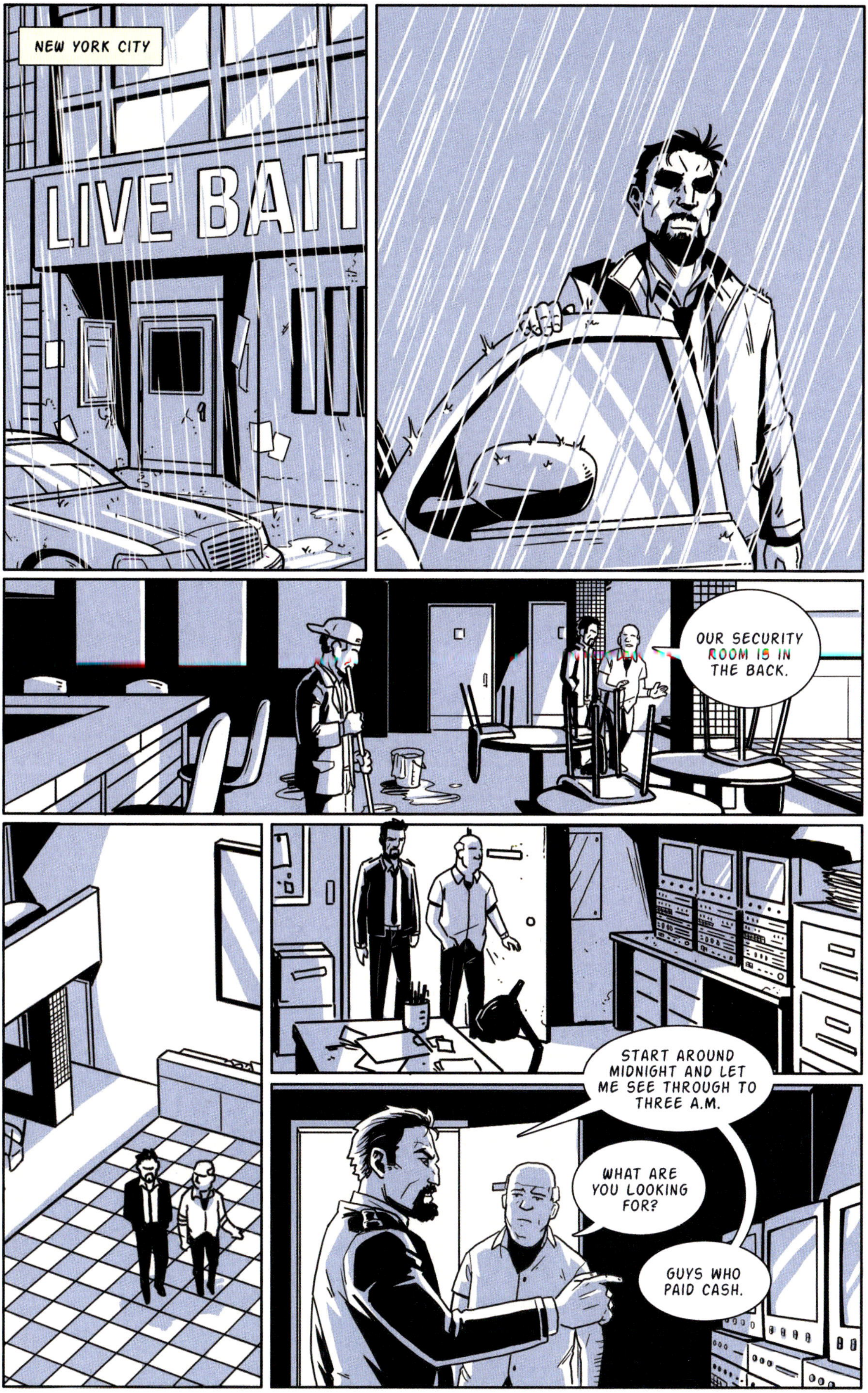

NEW YORK CITY
LIVE BAIT
OUR SECURITY ROOM IS IN THE BACK.
START AROUND MIDNIGHT AND LET ME SEE THROUGH TO THREE A.M.
WHAT ARE YOU LOOKING FOR?
GUYS WHO PAID CASH.

CHICAGO, ILLINOIS.

LET ME HAVE IT.

SAFE SOIL OFF THE GUY WE GRABBED IN SAN DIEGO.

IT'S HIM. HE'S THE ONE WHO SHOT ELLA.

TWO EGGS EACH. I HEAR AS MUCH AS A PEEP FROM ONE OF THOSE BIRD'S AN' YOU START AGAIN.
BUK BUK
SQUAK!
SQUAK!
SQUAK!
UGH... THEY'RE NEAR USELESS.
MAYBE START SMALLER?
DON'T GET MUCH SMALLER THAN TWO STUPID EGGS!

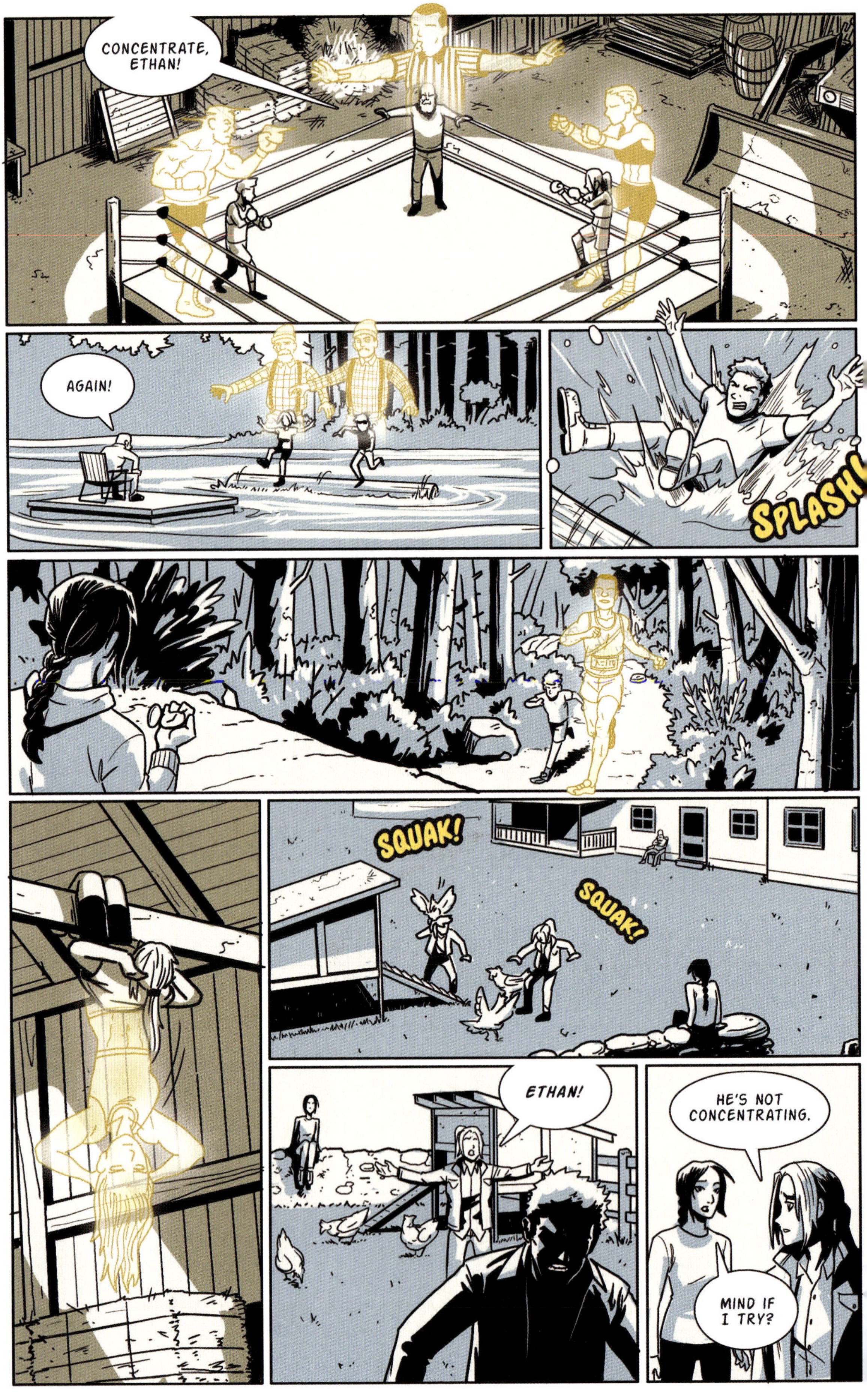
CONCENTRATE, ETHAN!
AGAIN!
SPLASH!
SQUAK!
SQUAK!
ETHAN!
HE'S NOT CONCENTRATING.
MIND IF I TRY?

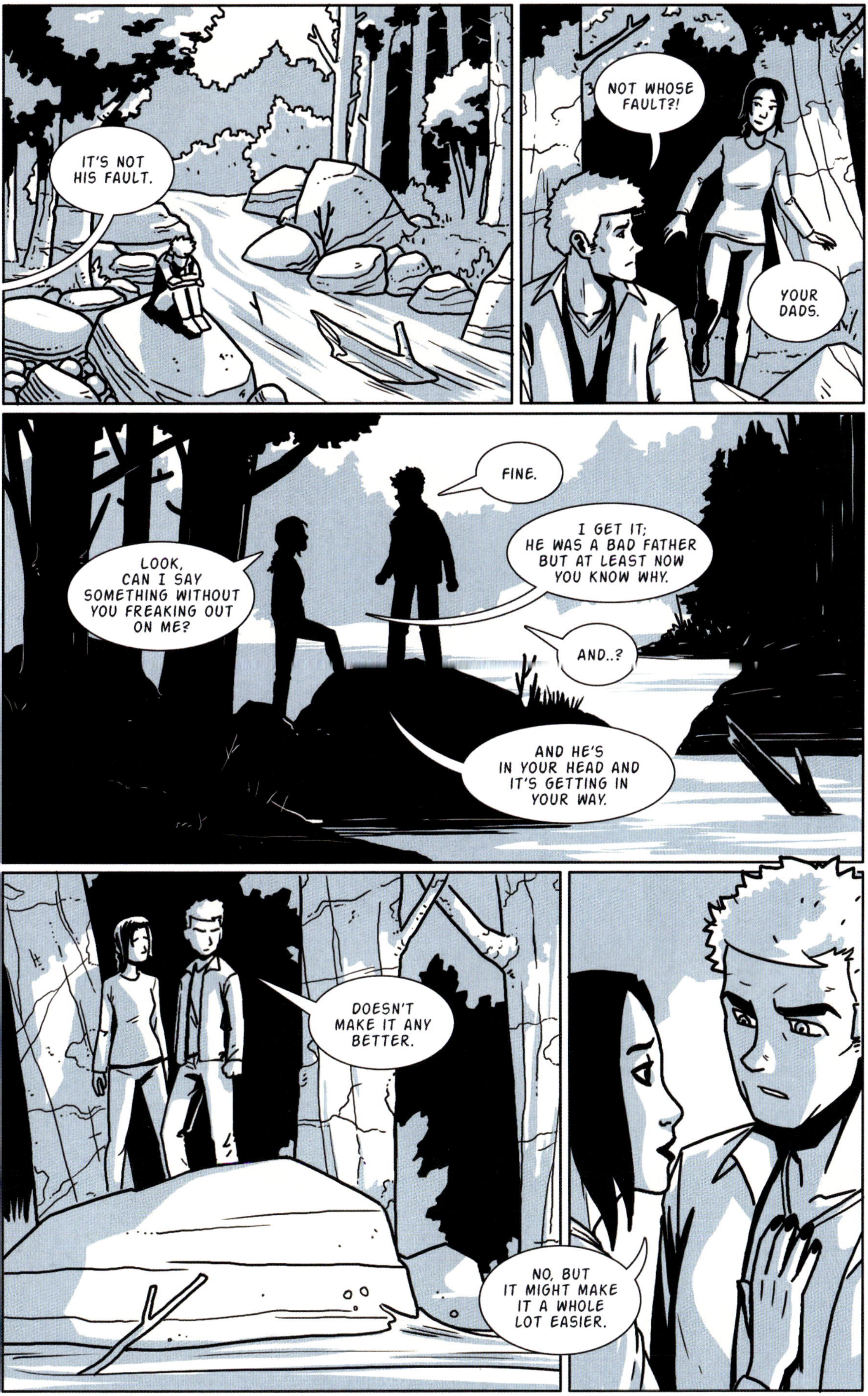
IT'S NOT HIS FAULT.
NOT WHOSE FAULT?!
YOUR DADS.
LOOK, CAN I SAY SOMETHING WITHOUT YOU FREAKING OUT ON ME?
FINE.
I GET IT; HE WAS A BAD FATHER BUT AT LEAST NOW YOU KNOW WHY.
AND..?
AND HE'S IN YOUR HEAD AND IT'S GETTING IN YOUR WAY.
DOESN'T MAKE IT ANY BETTER.
NO, BUT IT MIGHT MAKE IT A WHOLE LOT EASIER.

CHICAGO, ILLINOIS
HE'S MOVING NOW...
SOMETHING'S HAPPENED.
WHERE IS HE?
I DON'T KN-- HE'S GONE.

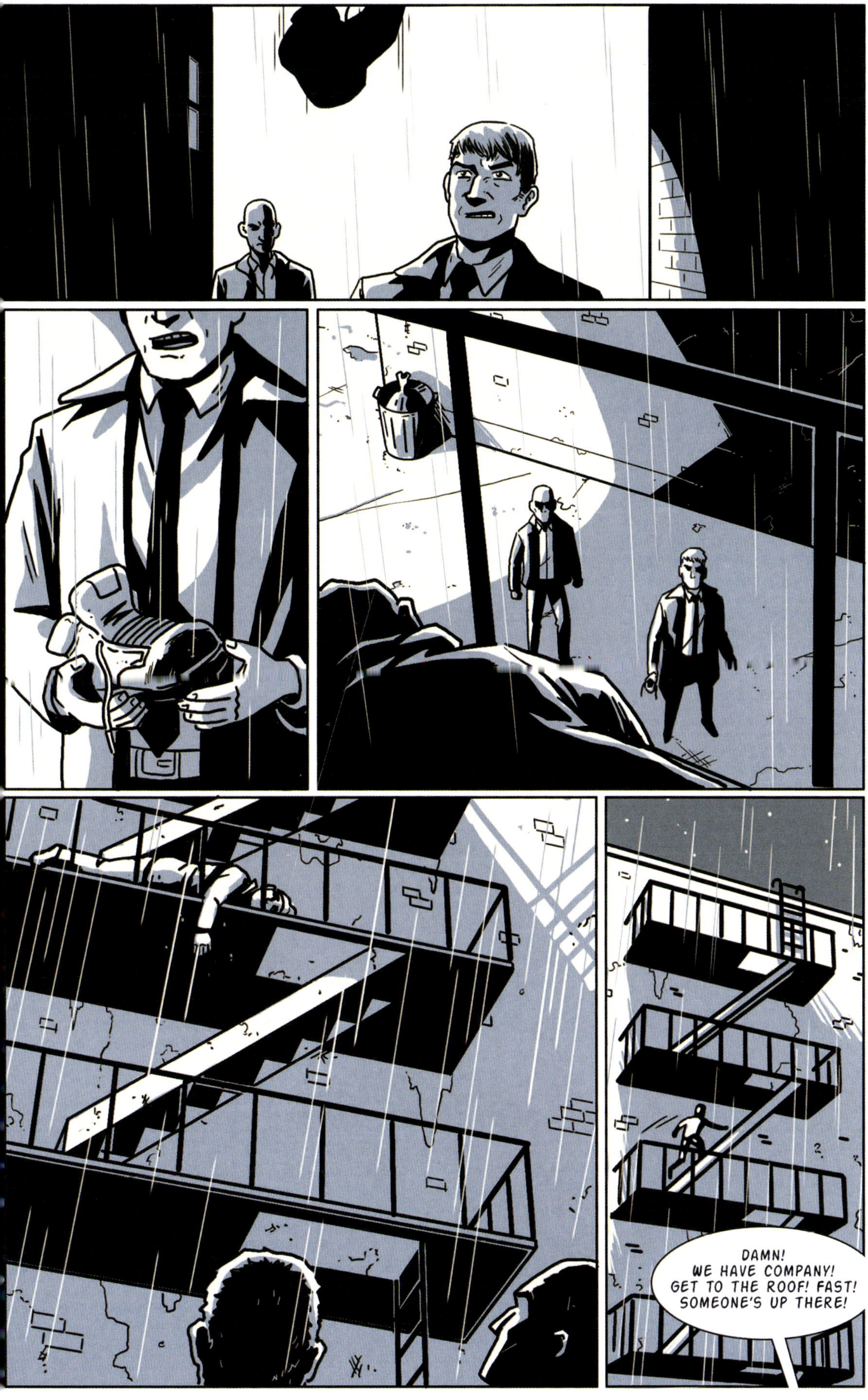
DAMN!
WE HAVE COMPANY!
GET TO THE ROOF! FAST!
SOMEONE'S UP THERE!

NOBLE, YOU BASTARD!

DO YOU HAVE ANY IDEA WHAT YOU JUST DID?

SEEMS LIKE AN ODD TIME TO START PLAYING TWENTY QUESTIONS, WALCOT.

WHAAAAP!
WH- WHAT DO YOU WANT?
A YEAR AND HALF!
WE'VE BEEN WORKING TO FLIP THIS GUY FOR A YEAR AND HALF!
HE KILLED ELLA!
AN ASSET INSIDE THE DARK HEARTS GONE BECAUSE YOU STILL CAN'T--
I DON'T CARE!
WELL, GUESS WHAT? I DO!

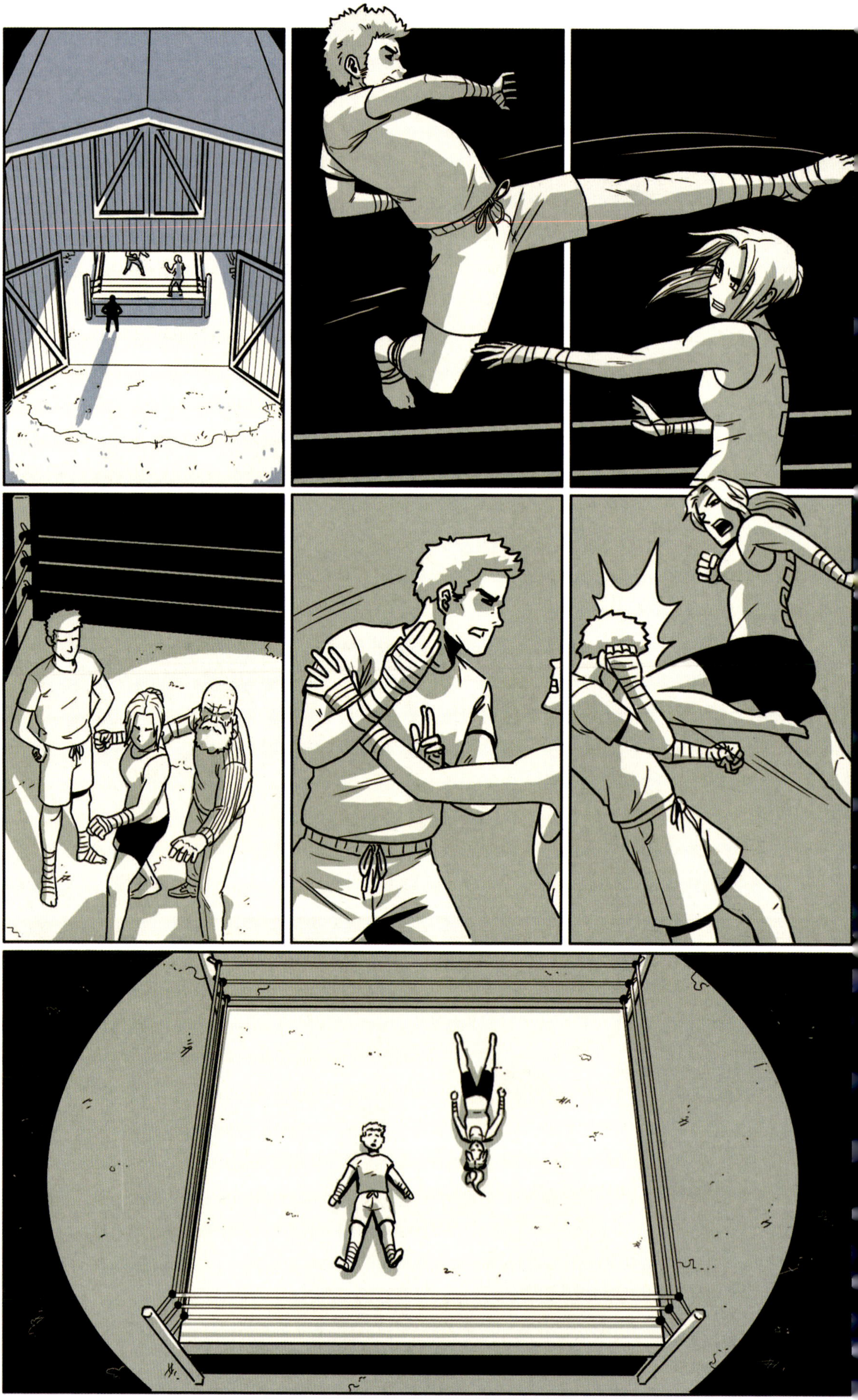

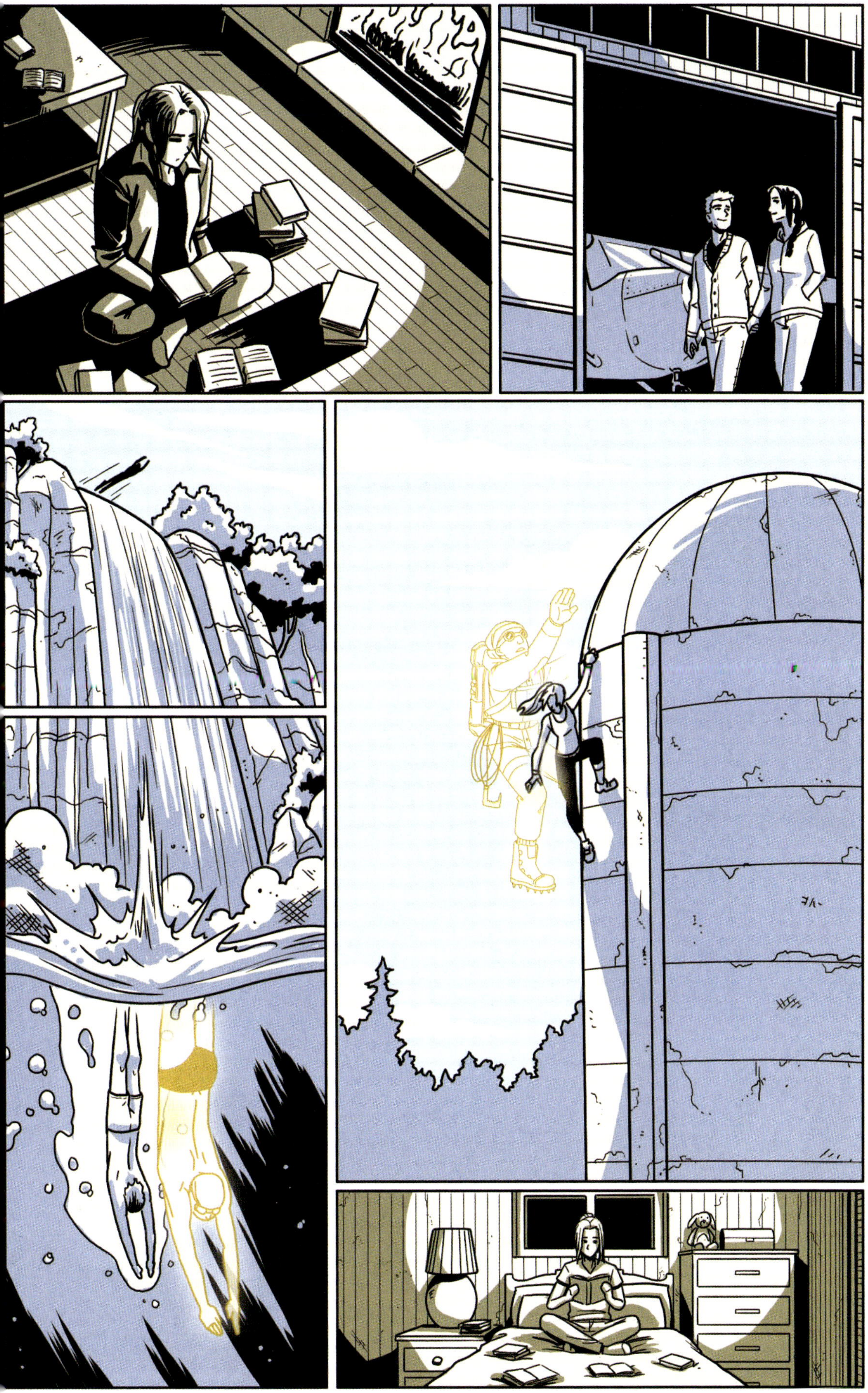

WHAT'S IT FEEL LIKE?
WHAT?
WHEN YOU'RE GHOSTED, WHAT'S IT FEEL LIKE?
IT'S... WEIRD. IT'S LIKE I'VE SWALLOWED THIS WHOLE OTHER LIFE THAT I INSTANTLY KNOW IN EVERY DETAIL. AS IF I LIVED IT MYSELF...
AND YET I KNOW IT'S NOT--
I WANT TO TRY AGAIN.
WHAT?!
I WANT TO SEE WHAT IT'S LIKE. FOR MYSELF.
LEX, IT ISN'T SOMETHING YOU JUST PLAN.
AND IF YOU COULD JUST PLAN IT?
YOU NEVER KNEW YOUR MOTHER AND NOW TWENTY YEARS AFTER SHE DIED YOU CAN, IN SOME WAY, KNOW HOW SHE FELT ABOUT YOU, ABOUT CARTER. YOU CAN KNOW THINGS SHE KNEW.
I KNEW MY FATHER MY WHOLE LIFE AND I DON'T WANT TO LET HIM GO.
LEX, THERE'S NO GUARANTEE IT EVEN WORKS. AND IF IT GOES SOUTH THAT MEANS YOU'LL BE DEAD.
JUST THINK ABOUT IT. FOR ME. US.

HOW DID IT HAPPEN FOR MY MOM?

FLOOD...

THERE WAS AN ACCIDENT. A DRUNK DRIVER. YOUR GRANDMOTHER DIED. ME AND YOUR MOM CAME BACK.

DAD SAID SHE DIED IN THE WOODS. THAT THE D.H'S HAD SURPRISED THEM.

THAT IS... TRUE.

BUT NOT THE WHOLE TRUTH.

CARTER--

FLOOD, YOU'RE TRAINING US FOR A REASON, RIGHT?

I'M TRAINING YOU SO YOU CAN PREPARE YOURSELF FOR THE REST OF YOUR LIFE.

THE REST OF OUR LIVES DOESN'T START UNTIL WE FIGURE THIS OUT.

LOOK, MY DAD'S BEEN CHASING SOMETHING SINCE WE WERE BORN. WHATEVER IT IS DON'T YOU THINK WE DESERVE TO KNOW?

CARTER, I CAN'T-- YOU HAVE TO ASK HIM. I'M SORRY.

HE'S NOT HERE... AS USUAL.
YOUR MOTHER WAS WORKING ON AN ANTIDOTE.
FOR WHAT?
THE BREACH.
THE THOUGHT WAS IF THERE WAS SOME WAY, SOMETHING, TO REVERSE A PERSON'S BREACH, WE COULD PREVENT THEM FROM BEING ABLE TO GRAB A SOUL SKILL. THEY'D RETURN TO NORMAL.
A CURE. TO USE ON THE DARK HEARTS.
YES.
THE GUILD HAD BEEN TRYING FOR YEARS BUT OVER THAT TIME A LOT OF GOOD CARETAKERS WERE KILLED TRYING TO FIGURE IT OUT.
BUT WHY SO SECRET?
CARTER, IN A WORLD WHERE THE SECRETS SOMEONE TAKES TO THE GRAVE ARE NO LONGER SAFE, IT'S *THAT* MUCH MORE IMPORTANT THAT SOMEONE STEP UP AND PROTECT THAT INFORMATION.
YOU AND ETHAN HAVE TO UNDERSTAND. THIS IS A WAR. AND WARS ARE FOUGHT BY ANY MEANS NECESSARY.
THAT'S WHAT YOUR MOM WAS TRYING TO DO.

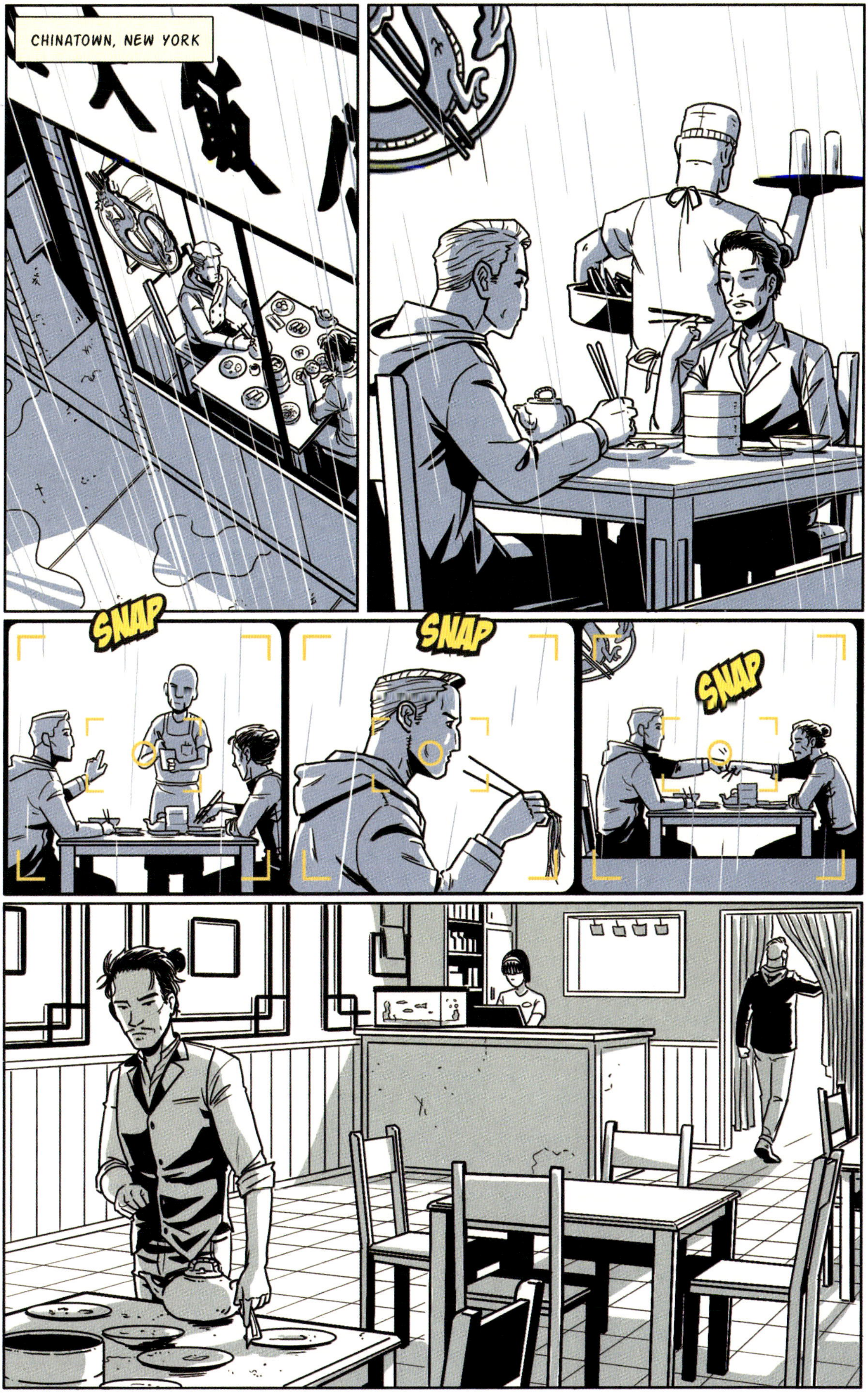
CHINATOWN, NEW YORK
SNAP
SNAP
SNAP

DO NOT MOVE.
PUT YOUR HANDS BEHIND YOUR HEAD.
I DO SOMETHING WRONG OFFICER?
MOVE TO THE WALL. NOW!
FEET APART. WIDER.
DETECTIVE, I THINK YOU HAVE ME MISTAKEN FOR SOMEONE ELSE.

THE MONEY YOU STOLE WAS MARKED, GENIUS.
BUT WANNA KNOW WHAT I CAN'T FIGURE? HOW YOU GOT IN.
SAID PRETTY PLEASE.
TRY AGAIN. NAZ'S PLACE WAS FORT KNOX. NO WAY YOU TALKED YOUR WAY IN 'CAUSE NAZ DIDN'T TRUST ANYONE.
AND NO WAY YOU CONNED HIM CAUSE NAZ NEVER GOT CONNED IN HIS LIFE. SO... HOW'D YOU GET IN?
I WENT THROUGH THE WINDOW.
REALLY?
FLOORS UP.
BADGE NUMBER 2653, NOLITO, OVER.
DETECTIVE.
CRUNCH!

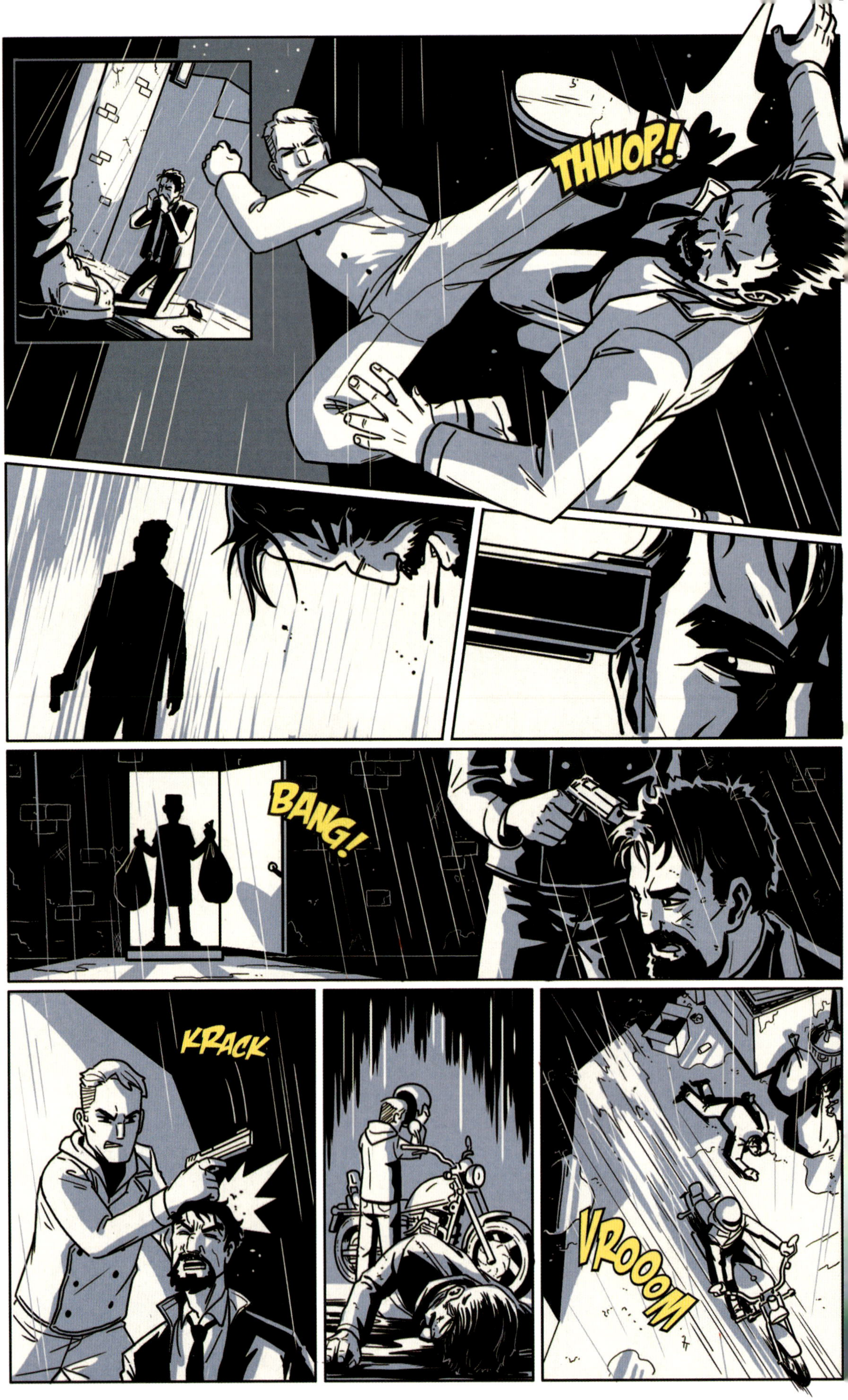
THWOP!
BANG!
KRACK
VROOOM

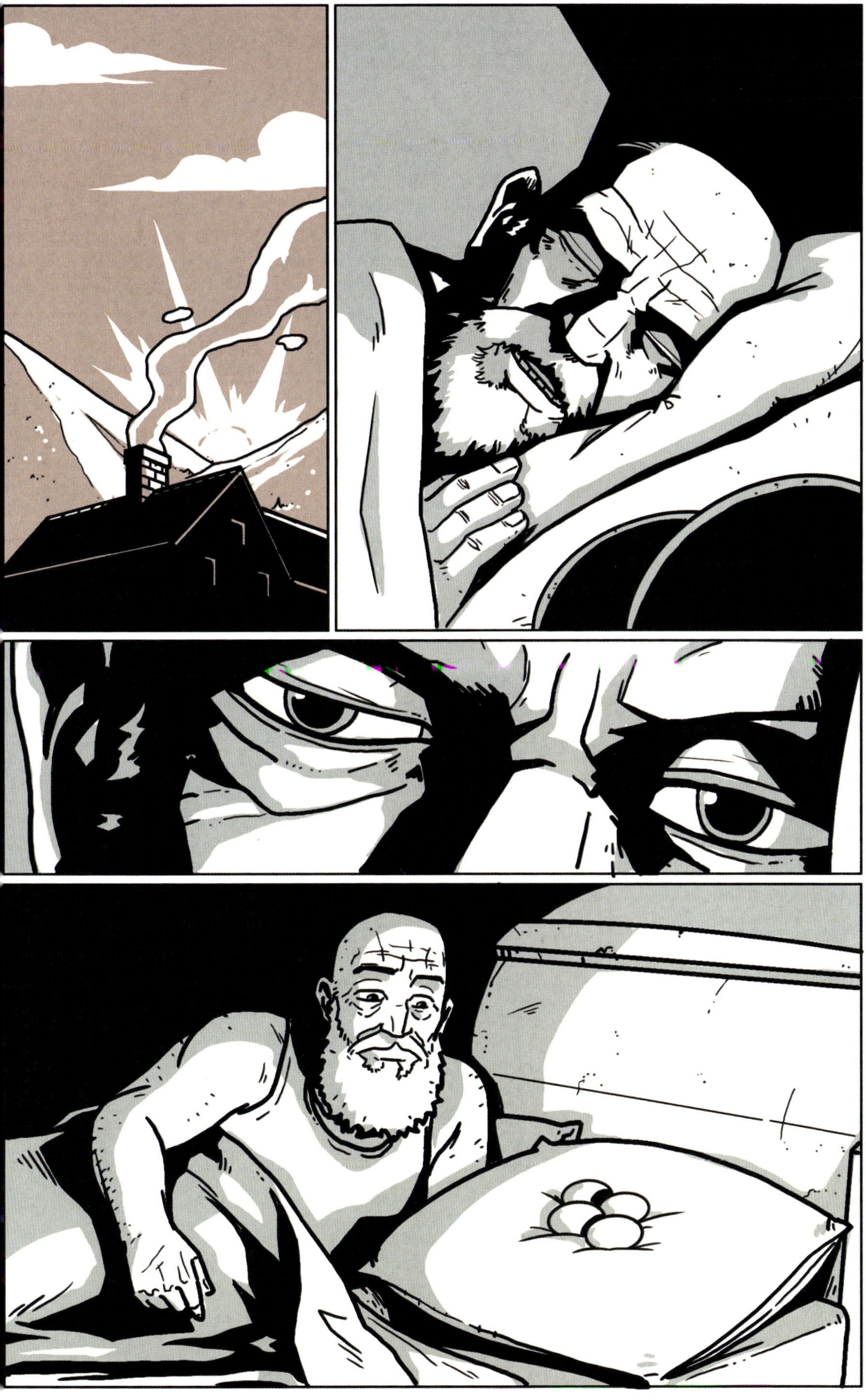

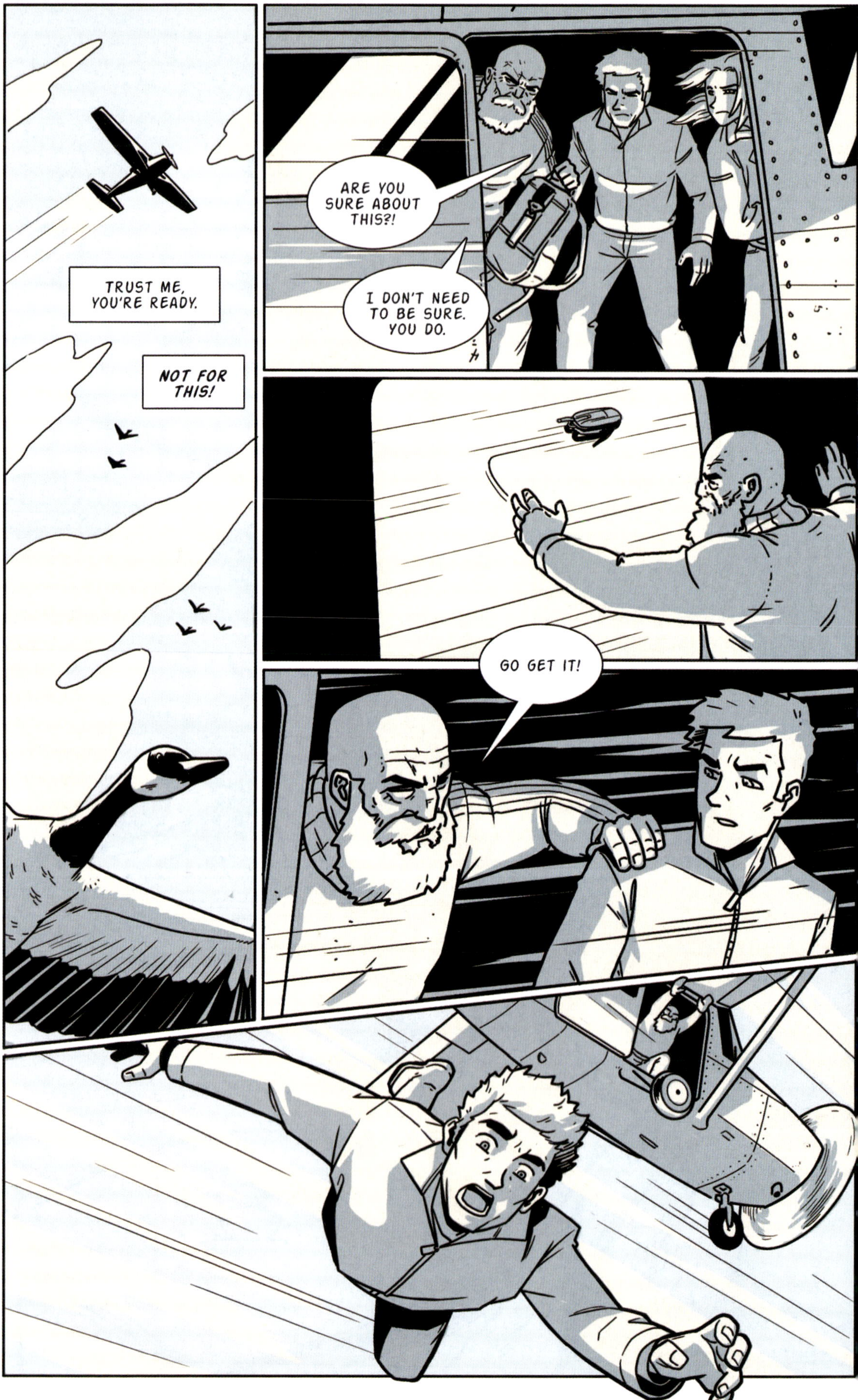
TRUST ME, YOU'RE READY.
NOT FOR THIS!
ARE YOU SURE ABOUT THIS?!
I DON'T NEED TO BE SURE. YOU DO.
GO GET IT!

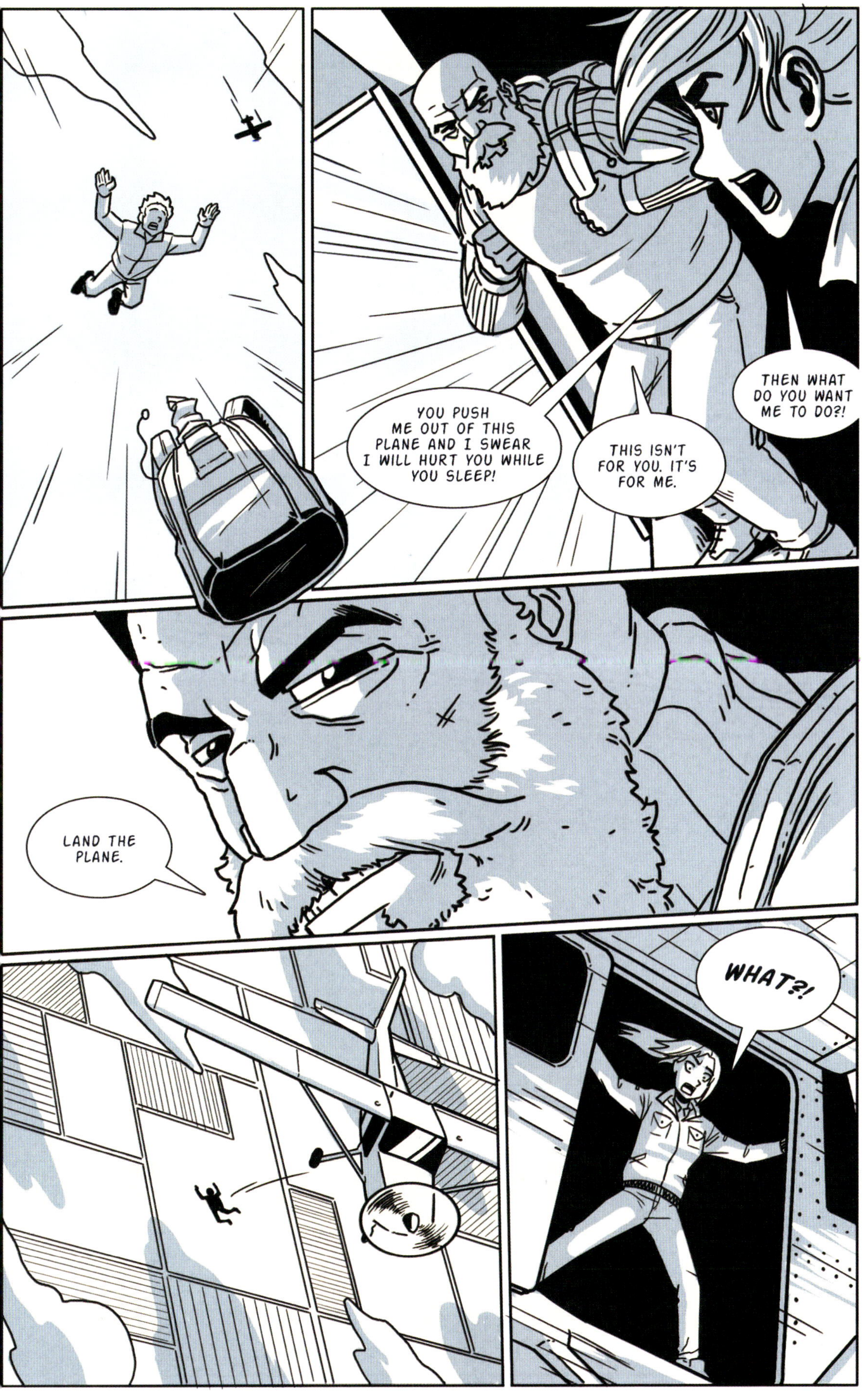
YOU PUSH ME OUT OF THIS PLANE AND I SWEAR I WILL HURT YOU WHILE YOU SLEEP!
THIS ISN'T FOR YOU. IT'S FOR ME.
THEN WHAT DO YOU WANT ME TO DO?!
LAND THE PLANE.
WHAT?!

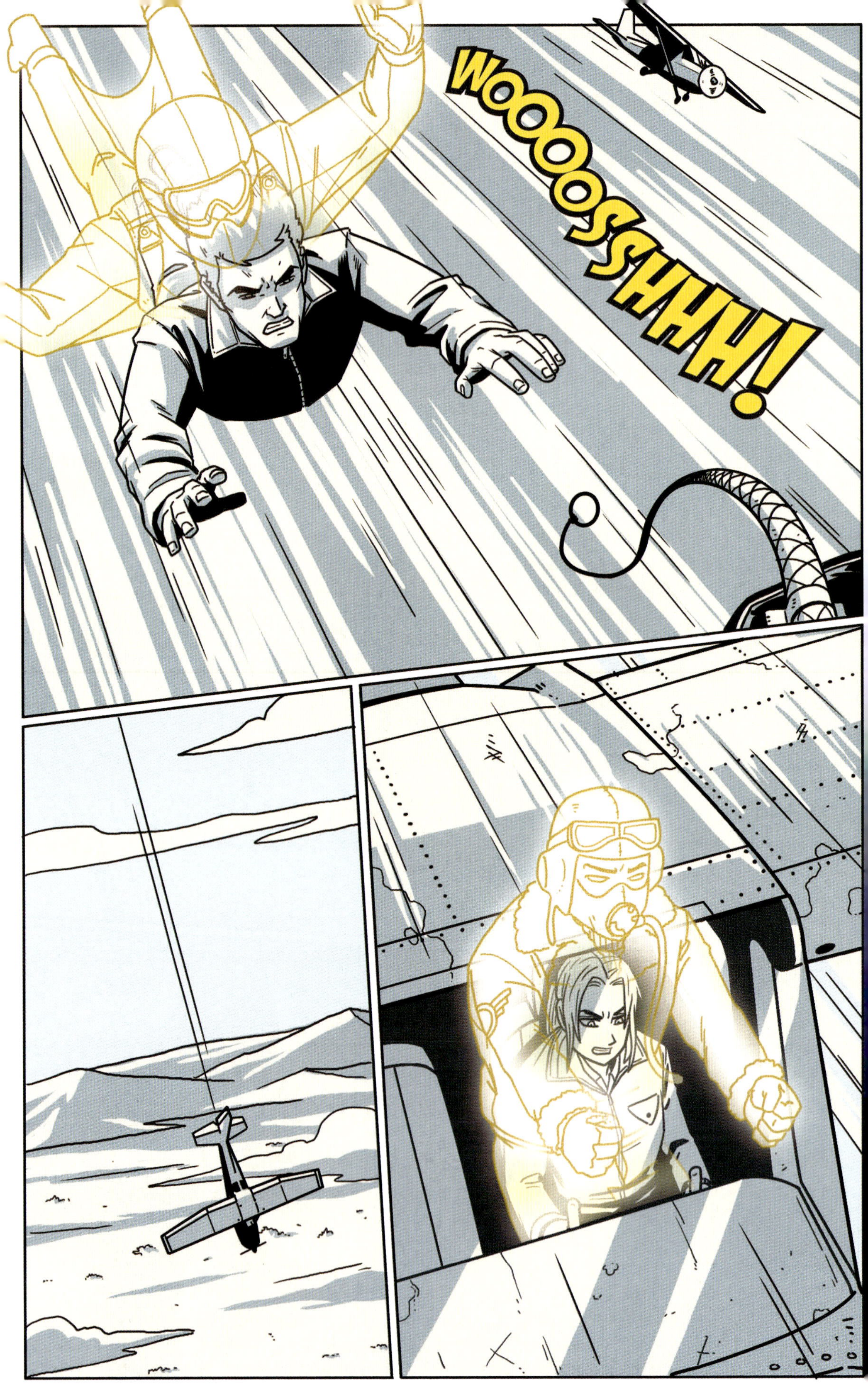
WOOOOSSHHH!

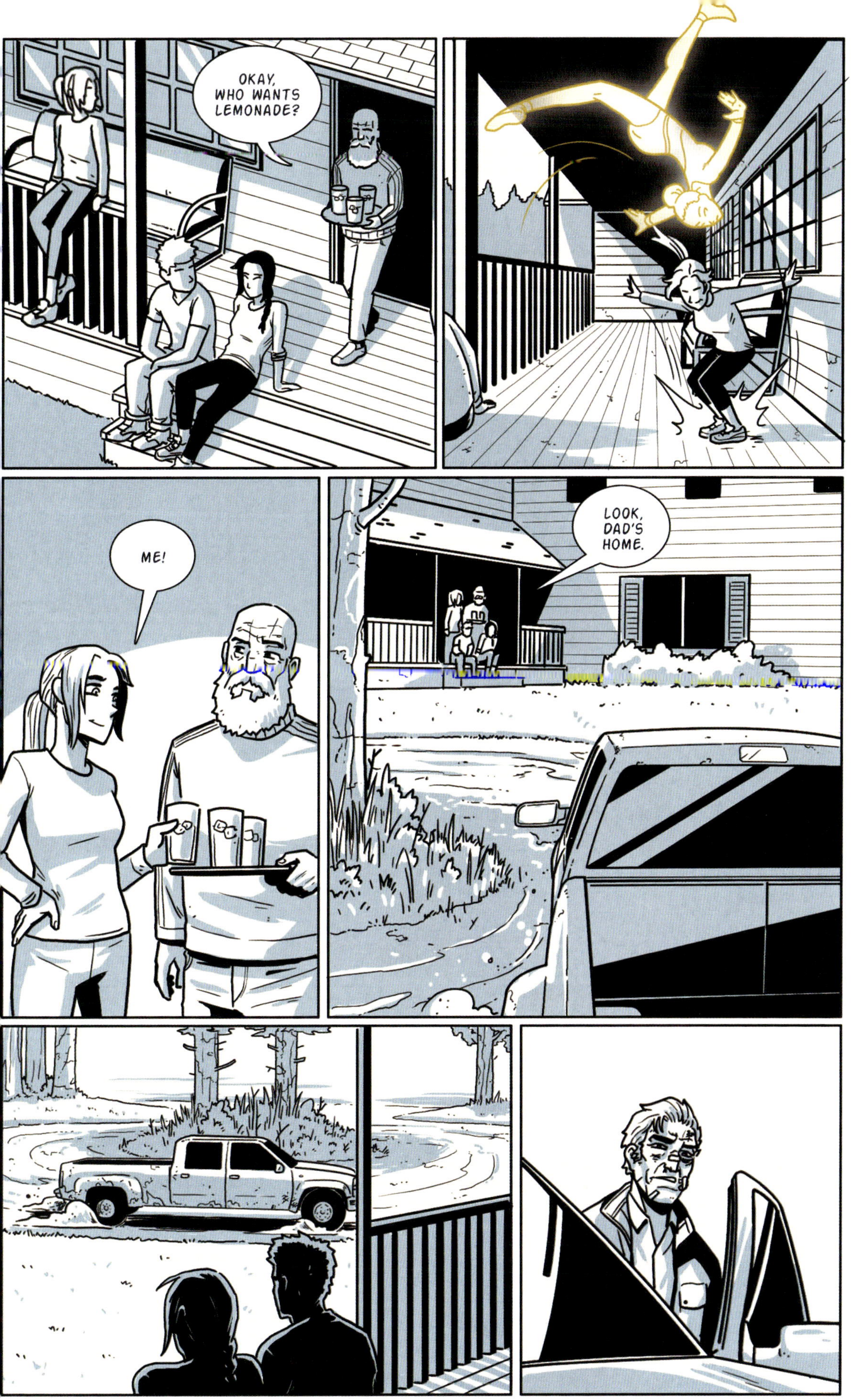
OKAY, WHO WANTS LEMONADE?
ME!
LOOK, DAD'S HOME.

WHAT THE HELL HAPPENED?
THIS WAS FROM OUR FRIENDS IN GUILD SECURITY.
WHAT?
THEY HAD THE GUY I WANTED UNDER SURVEILLANCE. THEY WERE TRYING TO FLIP HIM.
SEBASTIAN, THE COMMITTEE IS NOT GOING TO BE--
I KNOW.
NO, YOU DON'T. THIS ISN'T ALL ABOUT YOU ANY MORE.
CARTER, ETHAN, THEY'RE IN IT NOW. THE FALLOUT FOR WHAT YOU DO, THE PEOPLE YOU PISS OFF, LANDS ON THEM.
ARE THEY READY?
THEY WILL BE.
BOTH OF THEM?
HOW'S HE DOING?
YOU CAN'T RUSH THIS, YOU KNOW THAT. HE JUST NEEDS MORE TIME.
HE DOESN'T HAVE MORE TIME.
'BASTIAN, YOU PUSH HIM TOO FAR TOO FAST AND ALL YOU'LL DO IS SEND HIM BACK TO THAT FACILITY.
IF HE CAN BE BROKEN THAT EASILY THEN HE'S NO GOOD TO ME ANYWAY.
NO GOOD TO YOU? WHAT DOES THAT MEAN?
N- NOTHING. IT'S JUST-- I WANT TO SEE WHAT THEY CAN DO.
SEBASTIAN--
FLOOD, I'M PUSHING HIM BECAUSE OF WHERE HE JUST CAME FROM.
HAVE 'EM READY TO GO TOMORROW MORNING.

THE NEXT MORNING

US AGAINST YOU?

OKAY, LET'S GO.

CHRISTMAS COMES EARLY.

I'M OLD, TIRED AND I GOT BEAT UP THE OTHER NIGHT. AT LEAST TWO OF THOSE ARE IN YOUR FAVOR.

THIS IS SO NOT GONNA END WELL, IS IT?

NOPE.

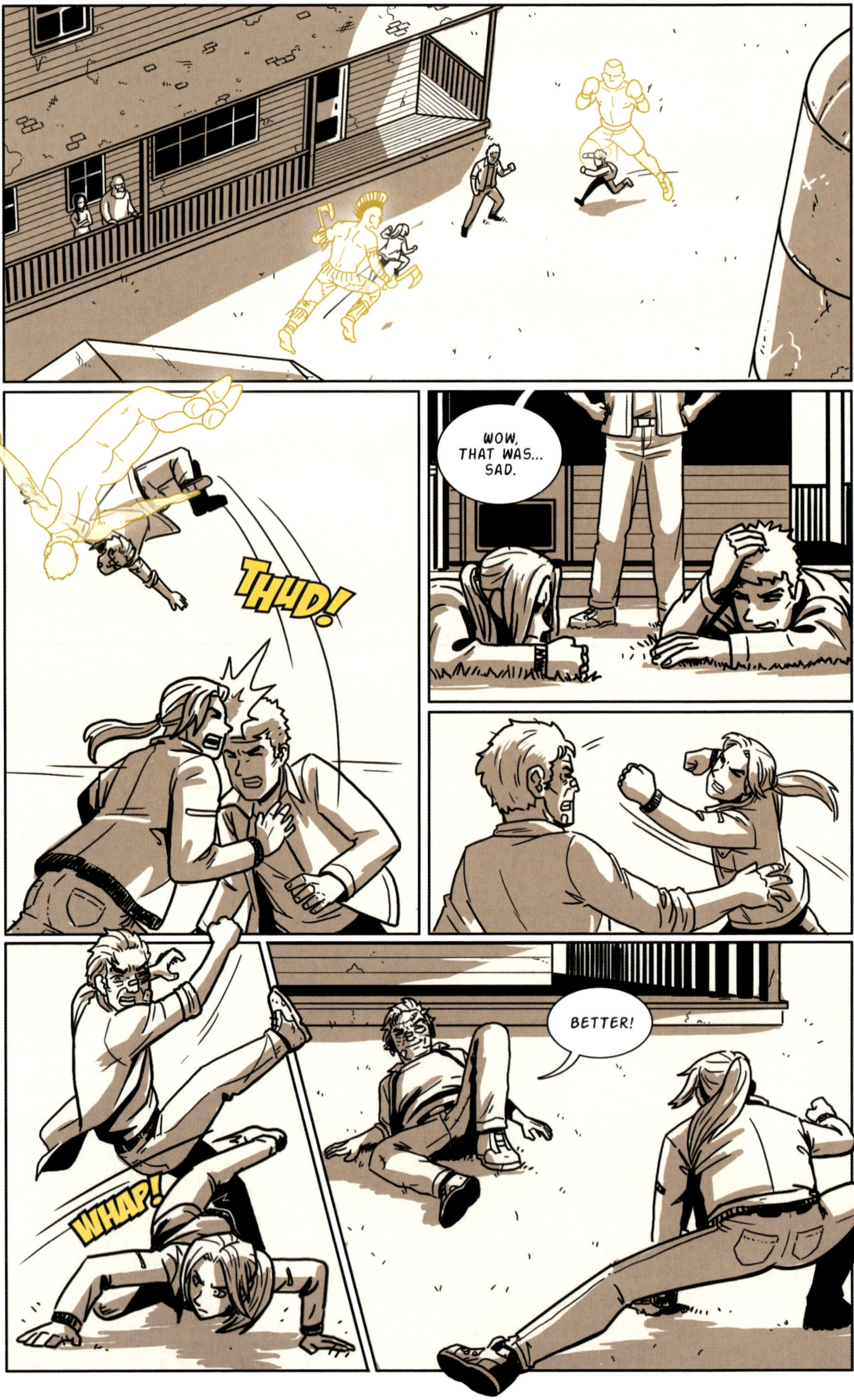
THUD!
WOW, THAT WAS... SAD.
WHAP!
BETTER!

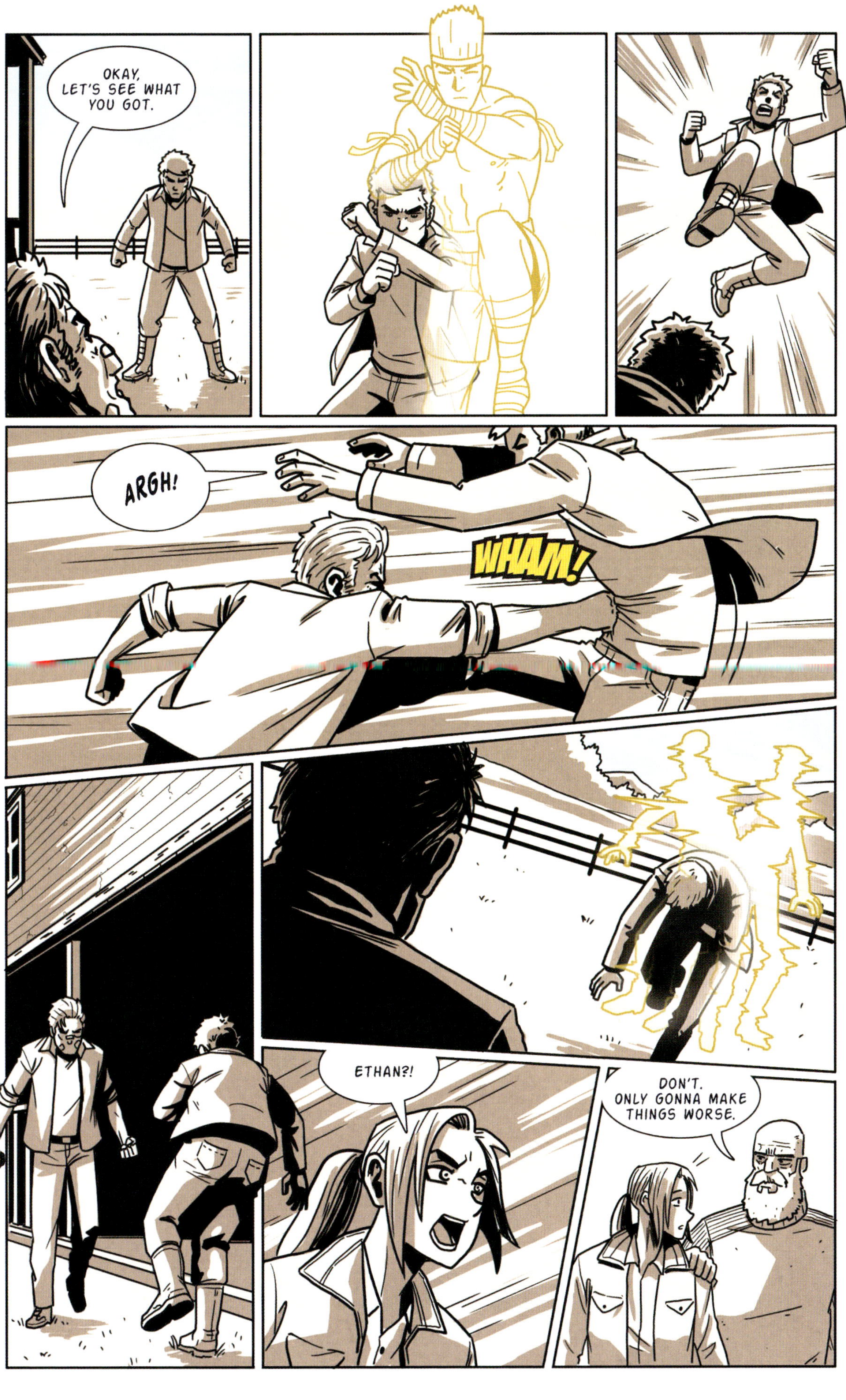
OKAY, LET'S SEE WHAT YOU GOT.
ARGH!
WHAM!
ETHAN?!
DON'T. ONLY GONNA MAKE THINGS WORSE.

E, GRABBING A SKILL IS ONE THING BUT IF YOU CAN'T HOLD ONTO IT THEN YOU'RE SCREWED.
A FEW WEEKS AND ALREADY YOU HAVE ME PEGGED AS A FAILURE?
YOU'RE NOT READY.
WHACK
HE'S NOT READY.
HE WAS NERVOUS.
NERVOUS?!
AND WHAT HAPPENS WHEN HE'S IN FRONT OF A DARK HEART WHO'S TRYING TO KILL HIM?
YOU WANTED THE RESPONSIBILITY OF YOUR OWN SAFE SOIL WELL, THIS IS WHAT IT FEELS LIKE.
GET OFF MY BACK!
I'M NOT ON YOUR BACK, I'M IN YOUR HEAD!
IF YOU CAN'T DEAL WITH THAT, THEN WE GOT BIGGER PROBLEMS.
ENOUGH!
CLAP
CLAP

CLAP
CLAP
CLAP
I SEE SOME THINGS NEVER CHANGE.
GOOD TO KNOW THE NOBLES ARE STILL AS MESSED UP AS I REMEMBER.
WHAT DO YOU WANT, WALCOTT?
THE THREE WISE MEN WANT THE PLEASURE OF YOUR COMPANY DOWN AT THE STORE.
WHY?
BECAUSE HE'S VINDICTIVE, A SECURITY RISK, SELF-SERVING AND DOESN'T PLAY WELL WITH OTHERS.
AND BY ALL MEANS DON'T SHOW UP, I'D LOVE TO GO ANOTHER ROUND.
DAMN IT!
THE STORE? WHAT DID HE MEAN? WHAT IS THAT?
GUILD HEADQUARTERS.
YOU REALLY THINK THEY NEED TO GET INVOLVED WITH THIS?
CONSIDER IT PART OF THEIR TRAINING.
OKAY BUT BEFORE WE GO I WANNA DO ONE THING FIRST.

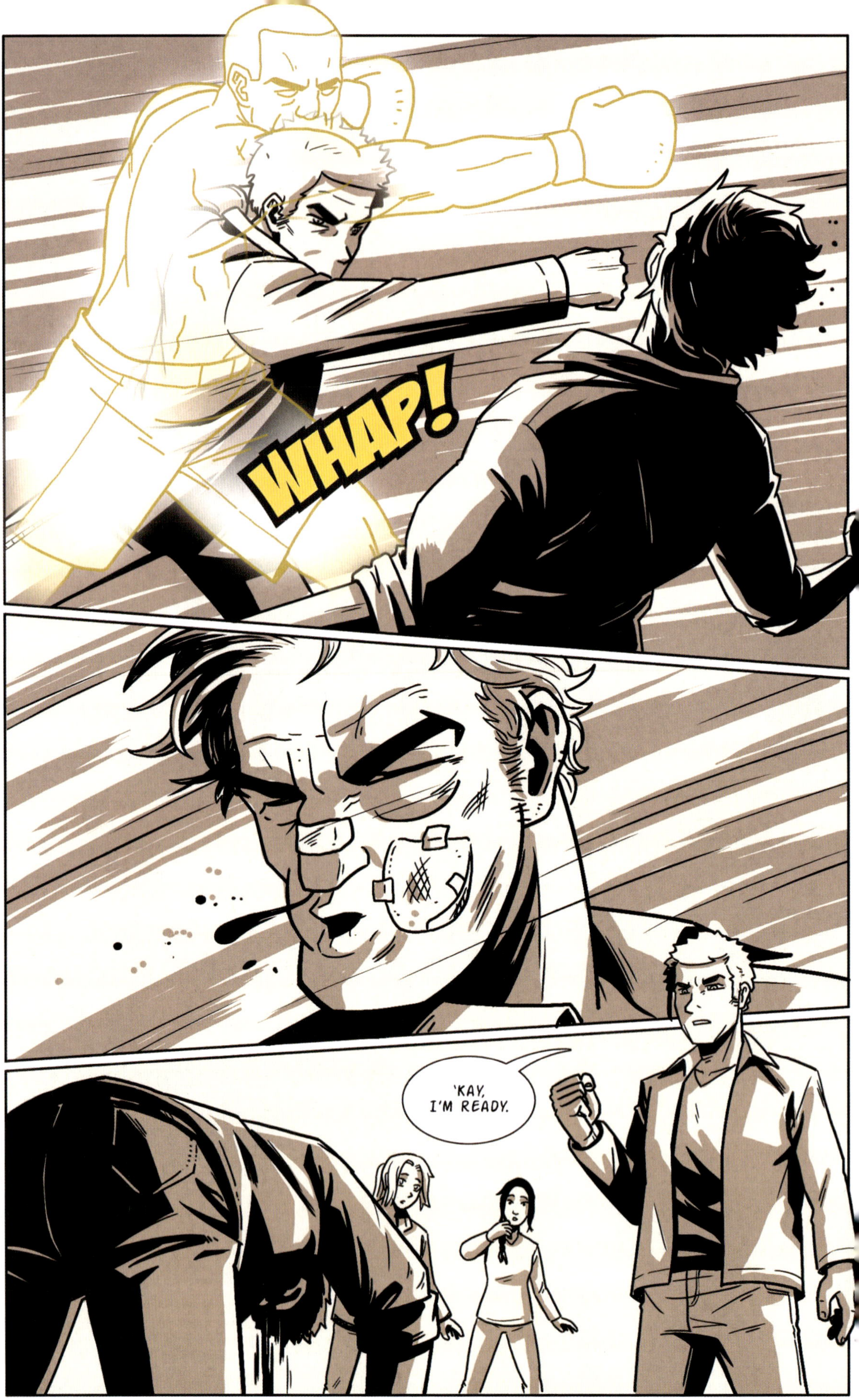
WHAP!
'KAY, I'M READY.

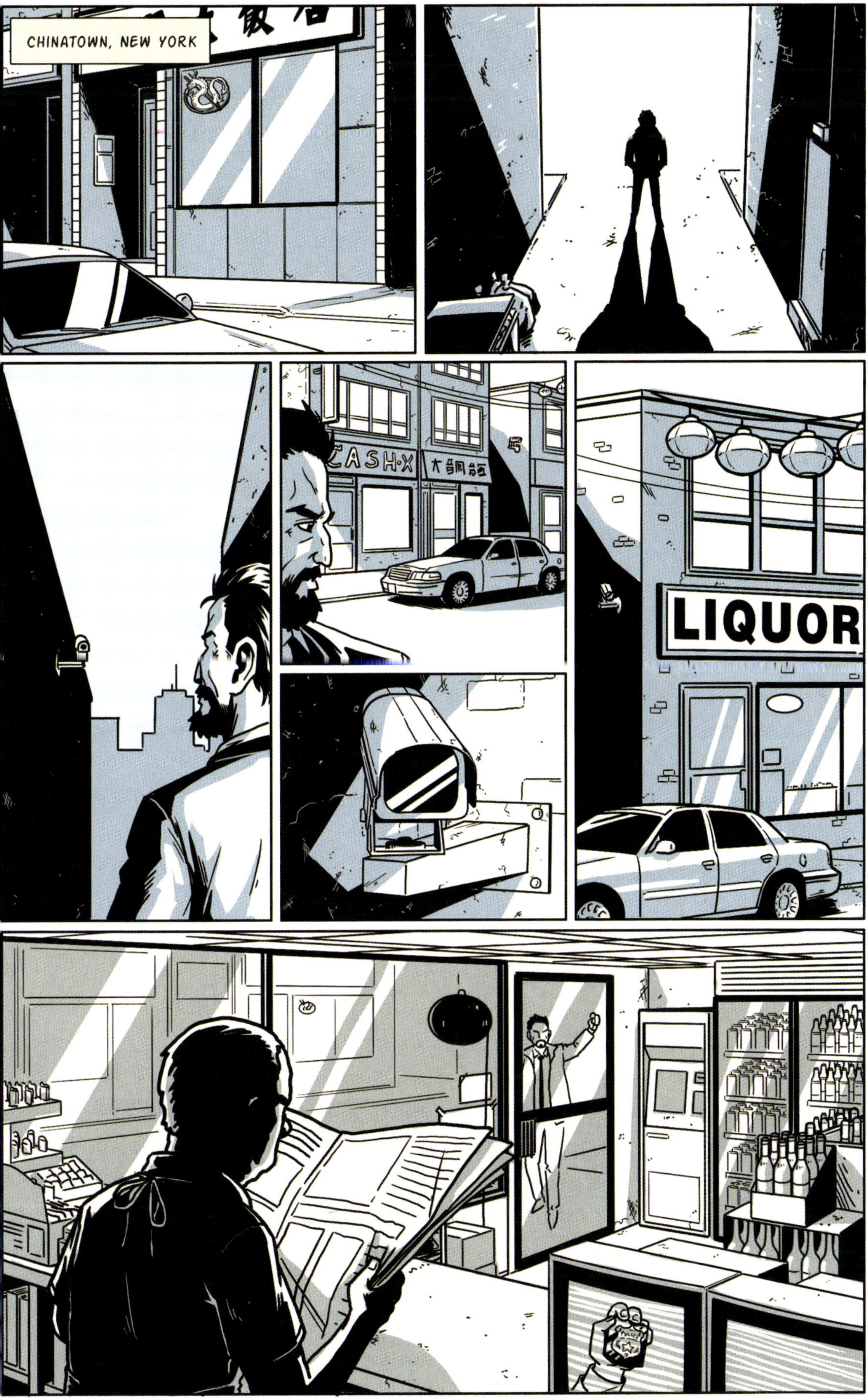
CHINATOWN, NEW YORK
CASH·X
LIQUOR

YOU OKAY?
NOTHING BRUISED BUT MY EGO.
TELL YOU THE TRUTH, KINDA GLAD HE DID IT.
TELL YOU THE TRUTH, SO AM I.
JUST SAYIN'.
WHY DON'T YOU EVER TALK ABOUT MOM?
CARTER--
IT'S TRUE.
I DON'T KNOW WHAT YOU WANT, CARTER. I FIGURED IF I DIDN'T DRAG YOU DOWN INTO WHATEVER I WAS GOING THROUGH, YOU TWO WOULD JUST... MOVE ON.
SHE WAS OUR MOTHER.
WHAT DID YOU WANT TO KNOW? HOW MUCH SHE LOVED YOU? HOW SHE WAS MURDERED. HOW I LEFT HER IN THE WOODS TO DIE.

CARTER, THE HARDEST THING I'VE EVER DONE IN MY LIFE WAS LEAVE YOUR MOM IN THAT TRUCK.
WHY DIDN'T YOU TELL US ABOUT THE ANTIDOTE?
CARTER--
WHY SHOULD WE TRUST YOU IF YOU DON'T TRUST US?
I KNEW SHE WAS WORKING ON AN ANTIDOTE AND I KNEW THEY ALL FAILED.
DID SHE KNOW?
YEAH.
AND THE ANTIDOTE?
GUILD GAVE UP ON IT. TOO MANY CARETAKERS DIED TRYING TO FIGURE IT OUT.
WELL, MOM DIDN'T WORK ALONE DID SHE? WHY NOT START OVER AND--
THE GUY SHE WORKED WITH IS DEAD.
DARK HEARTS?
NO, THE GUILD. HE WAS THE ONE WHO SET YOUR MOM UP.
DID YOU KILL HIM?
NO. WANTED TO BUT GUILD SECURITY GOT TO HIM FIRST. YOU'LL MEET HIM TONIGHT.
HE'S STILL HEAD OF GUILD SECURITY?
NO. HE'S THE HEAD OF THE GUILD.

COUNTY MORGUE
COUNTY MORGUE
ARE YOU JOKING?
WHERE'S TECH SUPPORT, A FUNERAL HOME?
ACTUALLY...
SERIOUSLY?
YEAH. NOW PUT YOUR HANDS UP.
WHAT? WHY?
MORGUE
HOW BAD IS THIS GONNA BE FOR YOU?
PRETTY BAD.

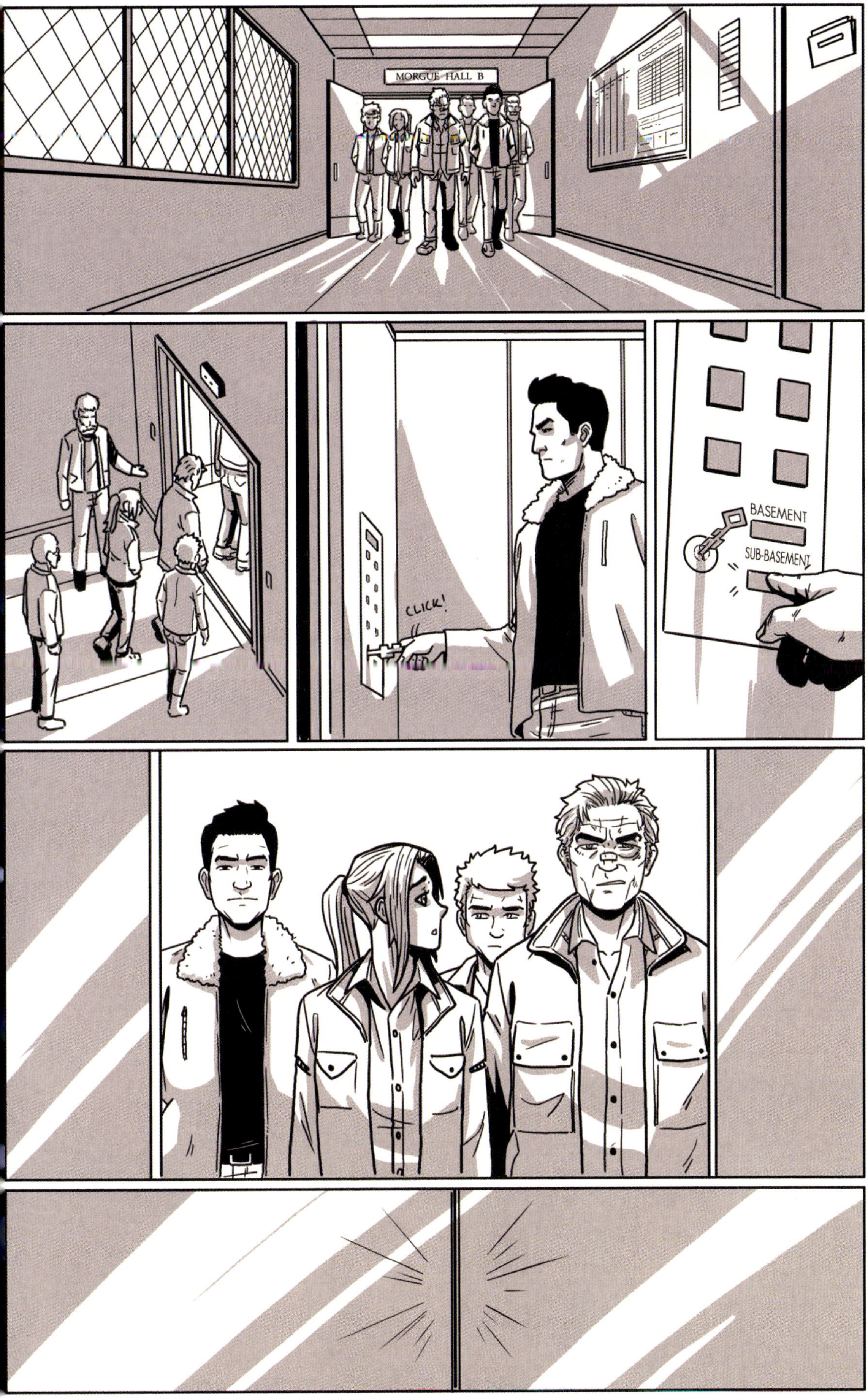
MORGUE HALL B
CLICK!
BASEMENT
SUB-BASEMENT

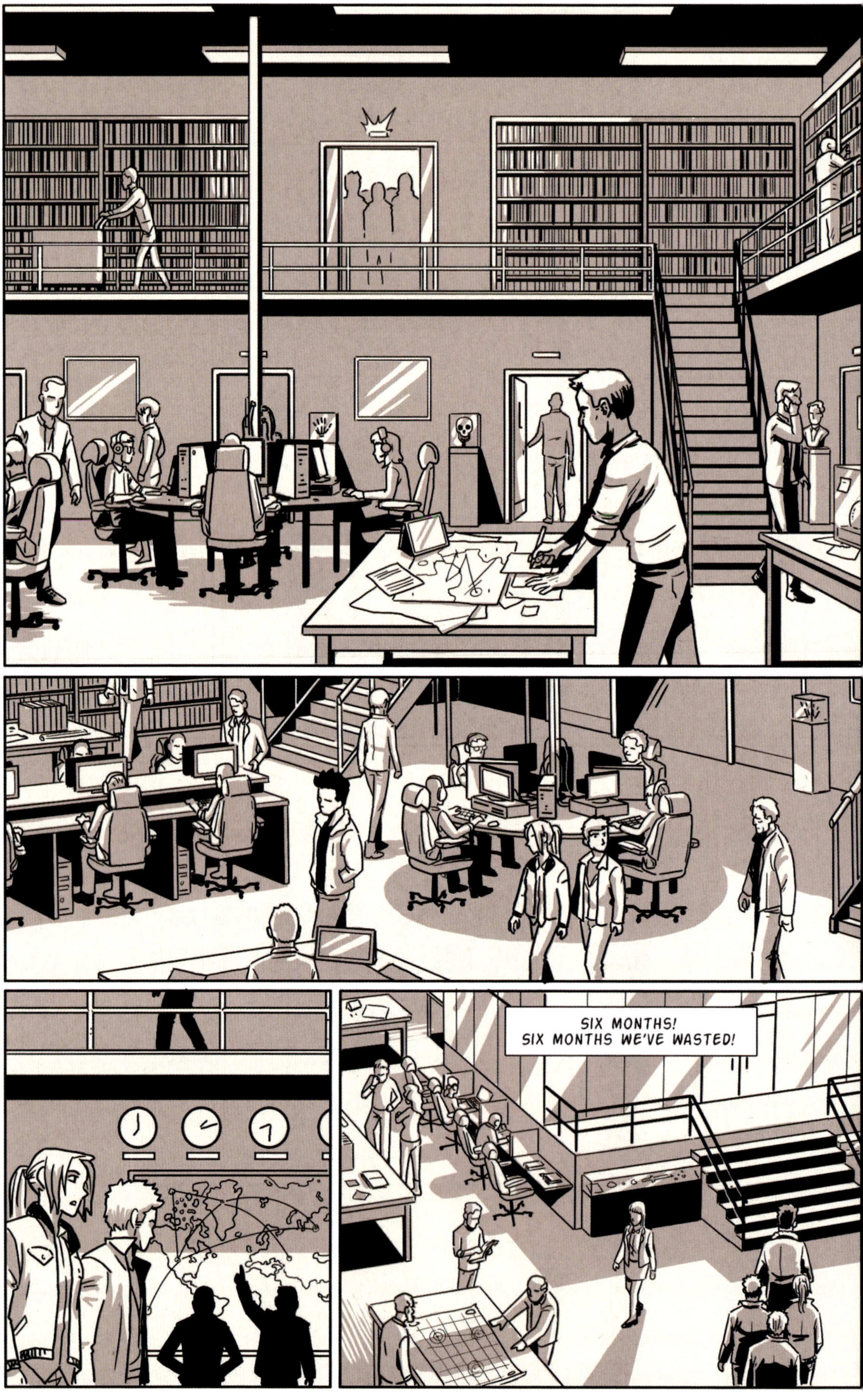
SIX MONTHS!
SIX MONTHS WE'VE WASTED!

AND FOR WHAT?!
KEATES, I TOLD YOU A LONG TIME AGO, I WAS GOING TO FIND 'EM ALL.
YOU THINK YOU'RE THE ONLY ONE WHOSE SACRIFICED, SEBASTIAN? WE'VE ALL LOST PEOPLE WE LOVE.
YOU PUT YOURSELF ABOVE THIS GUILD. AGAIN.
WE'RE TRYING VERY HARD TO FIND REASONS NOT TO TERMINATE YOU, SEBASTIAN.
DON'T DO ME ANY FAVORS.
WE'RE NOT.
WE'RE DOING IT FOR ELLA. BUT OUR PATIENCE HAS LIMITS.
THIS VENDETTA, NO MATTER HOW JUSTIFIED, ONLY DISTRACTS US FROM WHERE OUR FOCUS NEEDS TO BE.
AND MY GRIEF DOESN'T.
MY FOCUS IS MY FAMILY.
THAT WHY YOU PUT YOUR SON IN A NUT HOUSE?
RRAAAHH!

SETTLE DOWN. BOTH OF YOU.
THIS CONCERNS YOU TOO. IT'S YOUR LIFE. EITHER OF YOU HAVE ANY OPINIONS?
OUR MOTHER DIED FOR THIS GUILD. SOONER WE DECIDE IF WE WILL TOO THE BETTER.
VERY WELL. IF YOU EVER NEED ANYTHING, DON'T HESITATE TO ASK. DESPITE WHAT YOUR FATHER MIGHT HAVE TOLD YOU, WE'RE NOT THE ENEMY.
OKAY, WE'RE DONE.
SEBASTIAN.
YOU'VE BEEN CHASING ELLA'S GHOST FOR TWENTY YEARS AND YOU'RE STILL NO CLOSER TO PUTTING IT BEHIND YOU.
YOU'RE WRONG, SINCLAIR. COUNTING THE GUY IN CHICAGO, I'M EXACTLY EIGHT PEOPLE CLOSER.

— CAN'T SLEEP?

— GUESS I'M BEGINNING TO UNDERSTAND WHY MY MOTHER WANTED US AS FAR AWAY FROM ALL THIS AS POSSIBLE.

— HOW'D IT GO?

— WELL, THEY HATE MY FATHER. A LOT.

— YOU HATE YOUR FATHER A LOT.

— LOOK, LEX, I THINK YOU MIGHT BE RIGHT.

— ABOUT WHAT?

— TRYING AGAIN. OPENING YOUR BREACH.

— SERIOUSLY?

— THE GUILD DOESN'T TRUST MY DAD AND HE DOESN'T SEEM TO CARE. HE'S LIVING OFF THE FUMES OF WHATEVER GOODWILL MY MOTHER EARNED.

FLOOD IS OLD. AND CARTER IS GONNA NEED SOMEONE SHE CAN TRUST. SOMEONE, WHO UNDERSTANDS WHAT IT'S LIKE.

— WHAT ABOUT YOU?

— WHAT?

— YOU SAID CARTER WOULD NEED SOMEONE TO TRUST.

— AND ME, YEAH. BOTH OF US. I JUST THINK THINGS ARE GONNA GET CRAZY.

— OKAY, SO, HOW ARE WE GONNA DO IT?

— DO WHAT?

— KILL ME.

LOWER MANHATTAN
HE STOPS. OR WE STOP HIM.
TWENTY YEARS LATER?
HE WASN'T A RISK AT THE START OF THIS, WAS HE?
WHAT WAS HE?
MOTIVATED.
AND NOW?
HE KILLED A CIVILIAN UPSTATE AND A HIGH LEVEL ASSET IN CHICAGO.
NOW HE'S A PROBLEM.
HOW MANY MORE DARK HEARTS ARE LEFT FROM THE NIGHT ELLA WAS KILLED?
TWO. THREE, MAYBE. THERE'S AN END IN SIGHT.
YOU TRUST HIM TO STOP?
WHY WOULDN'T HE? SEBASTIAN NOBLE WAS ONCE A VALUED AGENT FOR THIS GUILD. MAYBE HE STILL CAN BE.
YOU ALWAYS WERE NAIVE, JOHN. IT'S WHAT I LIKED MOST ABOUT YOU.
KEATES, THIS GUILD NEEDS ALL THE HELP IT CAN GET.
SEBASTIAN NOBLE HAS NO INTEREST IN HELPING US AND HE'S NOT JUST GOING TO STOP.
YOU SOUND PARANOID.
MY SOLE RESPONSIBILITY IS TO PROTECT THIS GUILD. BEING PARANOID IS PART OF THE JOB.
HOW CAN YOU BE SO SURE HE WON'T?
BECAUSE IT WOULDN'T BE THE FIRST TIME SOMEONE IN THAT FAMILY BETRAYED THIS GUILD.

NO. NOPE. NEXT.

WHAT? WE FILL IT UP, PLUG IT IN, AND KINDA JUST... DIP IT.

NO. WAY.

BEEN THERE, DONE THAT.

I CAN'T EVEN SWALLOW ASPIRIN. BESIDES THERE'S NO REAL GUARANTEE IT'D WORK, RIGHT..?

YOU DRIVE, ME SHOTGUN, NO SEAT BELT.

NOOO. NOPE. NO. CARTER WOULD KILL ME. FOR REAL.

I'M NOT SHOOTING YOU, LEX. I CAN'T.

WHAT ELSE IS LEFT?

WHAT HAPPENS IF I HIT SOMETHING IMPORTANT?

GRAB A SHARPSHOOTER AND DON'T.

AND IF I CAN'T BRING YOU BACK?

ETHAN, LOOK AT ME.

I WANT YOU TO DO THIS. I NEED YOU TO DO THIS.
PLEASE.
I- I CAN'T.
E, YOU WERE PUT IN THAT FACILITY BECAUSE OF WHAT YOU DIDN'T KNOW.
AND I FEEL LIKE I'M GONNA END UP THERE BECAUSE OF WHAT I DO KNOW.
I-- I CAN'T DO IT.
THEN... MAYBE I KNOW SOMEONE WHO MIGHT.

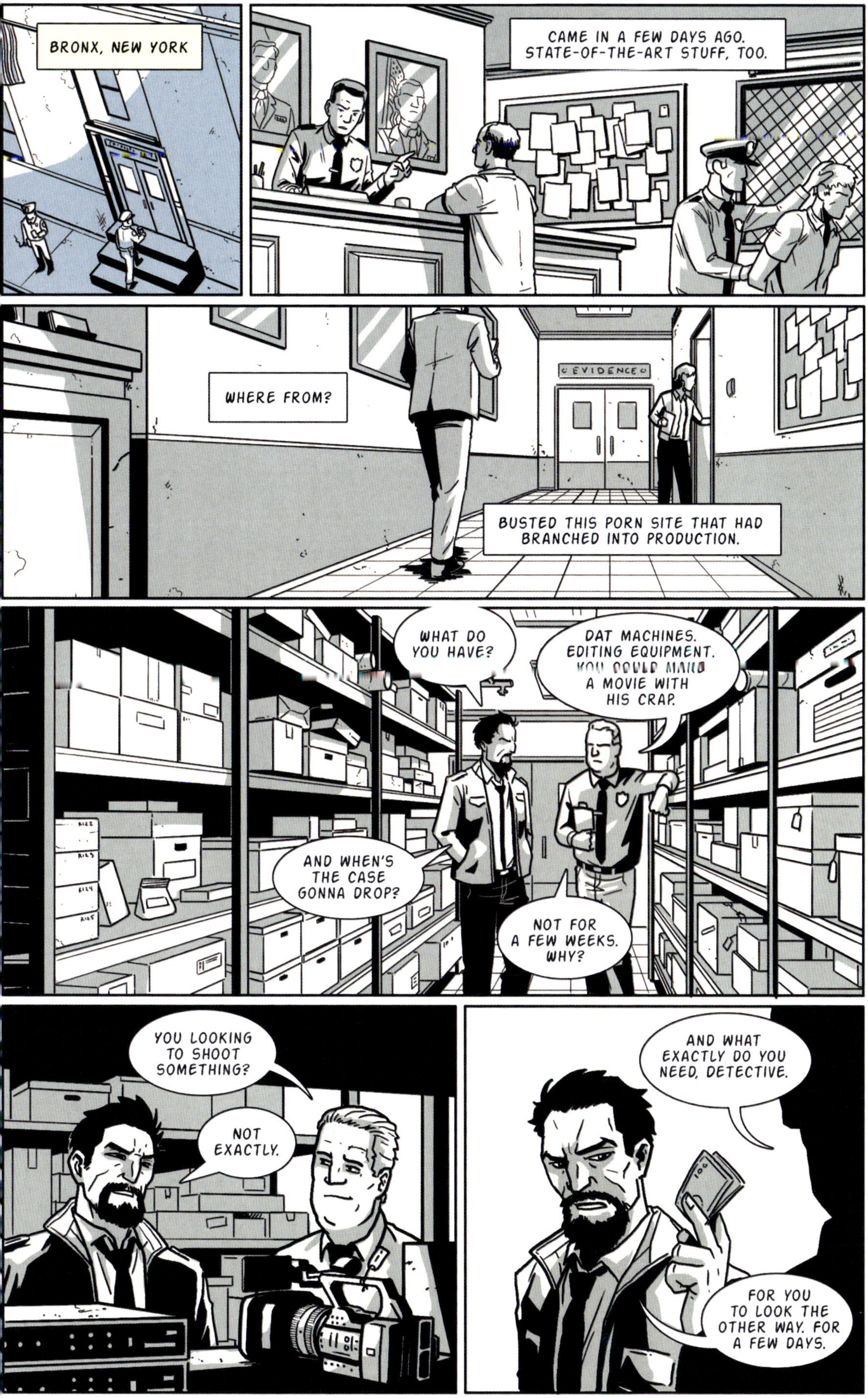
BRONX, NEW YORK
CAME IN A FEW DAYS AGO. STATE-OF-THE-ART STUFF, TOO.
WHERE FROM?
EVIDENCE
BUSTED THIS PORN SITE THAT HAD BRANCHED INTO PRODUCTION.
WHAT DO YOU HAVE?
DAT MACHINES. EDITING EQUIPMENT. YOU COULD MAKE A MOVIE WITH HIS CRAP.
AND WHEN'S THE CASE GONNA DROP?
NOT FOR A FEW WEEKS. WHY?
YOU LOOKING TO SHOOT SOMETHING?
NOT EXACTLY.
AND WHAT EXACTLY DO YOU NEED, DETECTIVE.
FOR YOU TO LOOK THE OTHER WAY. FOR A FEW DAYS.

KRASH!
GREAT.
DAD? DADDY...
DON'T-- DON'T GO.
HOW LONG HAVE YOU BEEN USING IT?

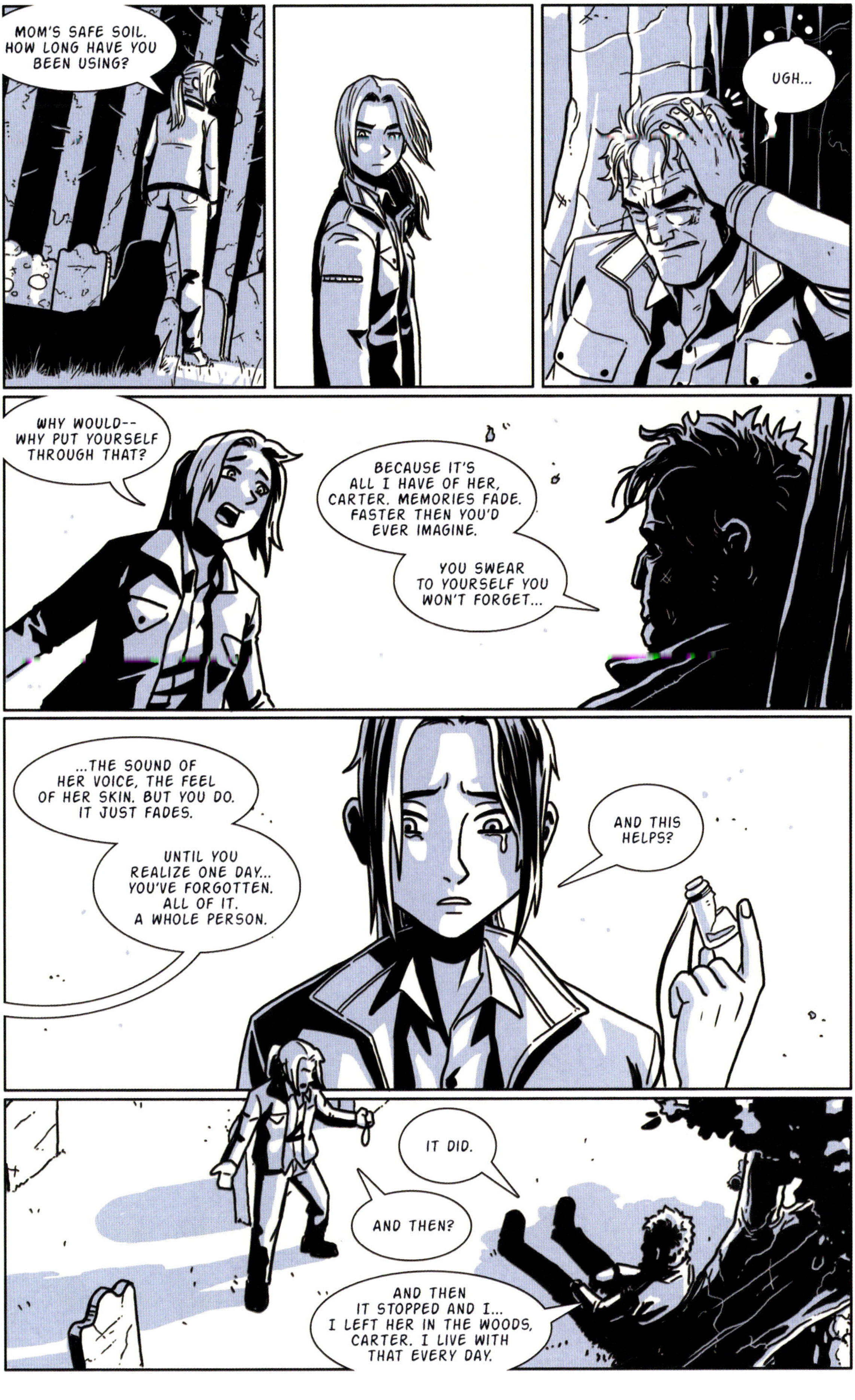
MOM'S SAFE SOIL. HOW LONG HAVE YOU BEEN USING?
UGH...
WHY WOULD-- WHY PUT YOURSELF THROUGH THAT?
BECAUSE IT'S ALL I HAVE OF HER, CARTER. MEMORIES FADE. FASTER THEN YOU'D EVER IMAGINE.
YOU SWEAR TO YOURSELF YOU WON'T FORGET...
...THE SOUND OF HER VOICE, THE FEEL OF HER SKIN. BUT YOU DO. IT JUST FADES.
UNTIL YOU REALIZE ONE DAY... YOU'VE FORGOTTEN. ALL OF IT. A WHOLE PERSON.
AND THIS HELPS?
IT DID.
AND THEN?
AND THEN IT STOPPED AND I... I LEFT HER IN THE WOODS, CARTER. I LIVE WITH THAT EVERY DAY.

BECAUSE YOU RE-LIVE IT EVERY DAY!
DON'T YOU UNDERSTAND?! I DESERVE THE GUILT! THE PAIN!
NO, YOU DON'T.
I LEFT HER THERE!
YOU DID WHAT YOU THOUGHT WAS BEST. WHY CAN'T YOU FORGIVE YOURSELF?
I- I DON'T KNOW.
AND YOU NEVER FOUND ANYTHING IN HER SAFE SOIL THAT MIGHT HAVE HELPED?
I WASN'T LOOKING FOR HELP, CARTER.
HOW MANY MORE ARE THERE?
HOW MANY MORE WHAT?
DARK HEARTS THAT WERE THERE THE NIGHT MOM WAS KILLED?
THREE. WHY?
BECAUSE I WANT TO BE THERE FOR THE REST OF THEM.

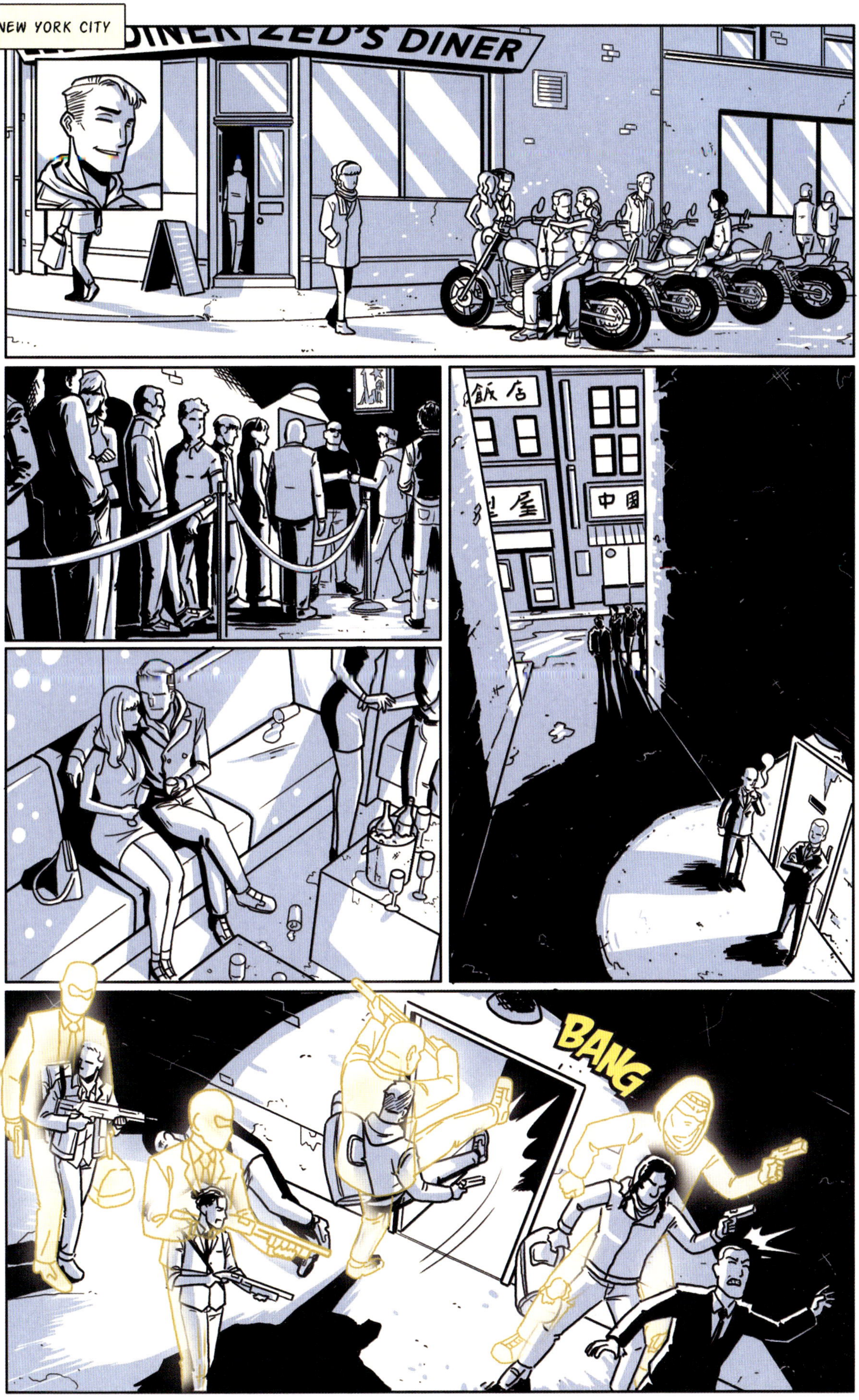
NEW YORK CITY
ZED'S DINER
飯店
中国
BANG

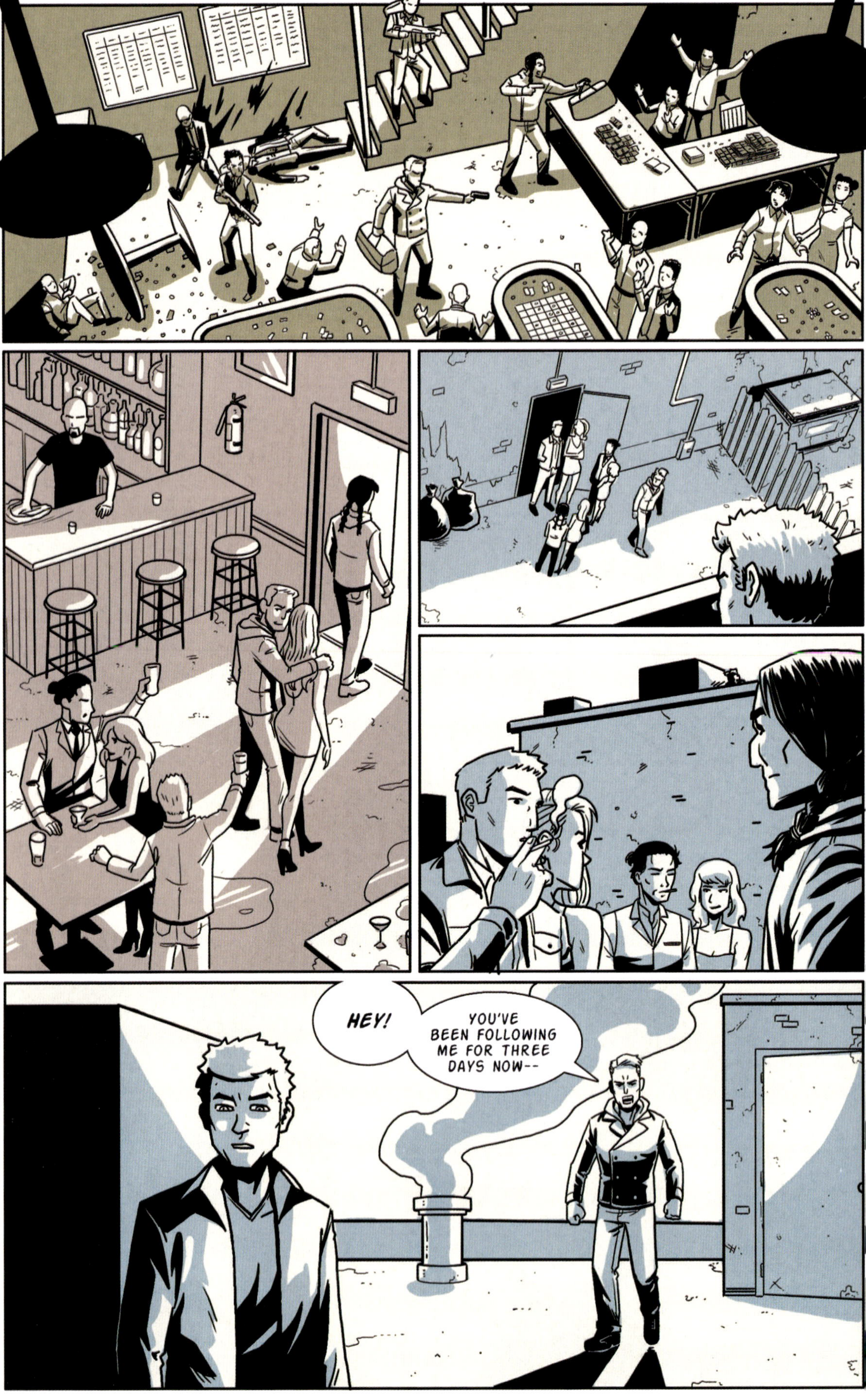
HEY!
YOU'VE BEEN FOLLOWING ME FOR THREE DAYS NOW--

WHAT DO YOU WANT?
I DO YOU'RE GIRLFRIEND OR SOMETHING?!
NO, BUT YOU DID TRY HANGING HER.
THE DORM ROOM. YOU WERE THERE THAT NIGHT.
WHAT'S YOUR NAME?
ETHAN.
NOBLE.
I SHOULD KILL YOU HERE AND NOW!
GO AHEAD, DEATH WOULD SOLVE A LOT OF PROBLEMS FOR ME.

BUT YOU WERE IN HER DORM ROOM FOR A REASON AND I'M PRETTY SURE YOU'D WANT ANOTHER CHANCE AT IT.
WHAT DO YOU WANT?
SHE WANTS TO TRY AGAIN.
AND YOU CAME TO ME?
I CAN'T-- I TRIED, BUT--
YOU CAN'T BREACH HER.
THIN LINE BETWEEN WHAT WE HAVE AND WHO WE GET IT FROM.
I KNOW WHO YOUR FATHER IS, ETHAN. AND I KNOW YOU KNOW I'M NOT IN YOUR GUILD.
I JUST GOT HERE, NOT SURE IT'S MY GUILD.
I'M GONNA ASK AGAIN AND IF I DON'T LIKE YOUR ANSWER I WILL KILL YOU. WHY ARE YOU HERE?
BECAUSE I LOVE HER.
WHY DIDN'T YOU GO TO YOUR FATHER?
HE WON'T DO IT.
WHY?
HE'S GOT CERTAIN... OPINIONS ABOUT THINGS LIKE THIS. THAT WHAT WE HAVE IS A--
PRIVILEGE?
I SEE YOU'VE MET.
YOU KNOW WHAT THEY DON'T GET? WE DIDN'T HAVE A SAY IN ANY OF THIS.

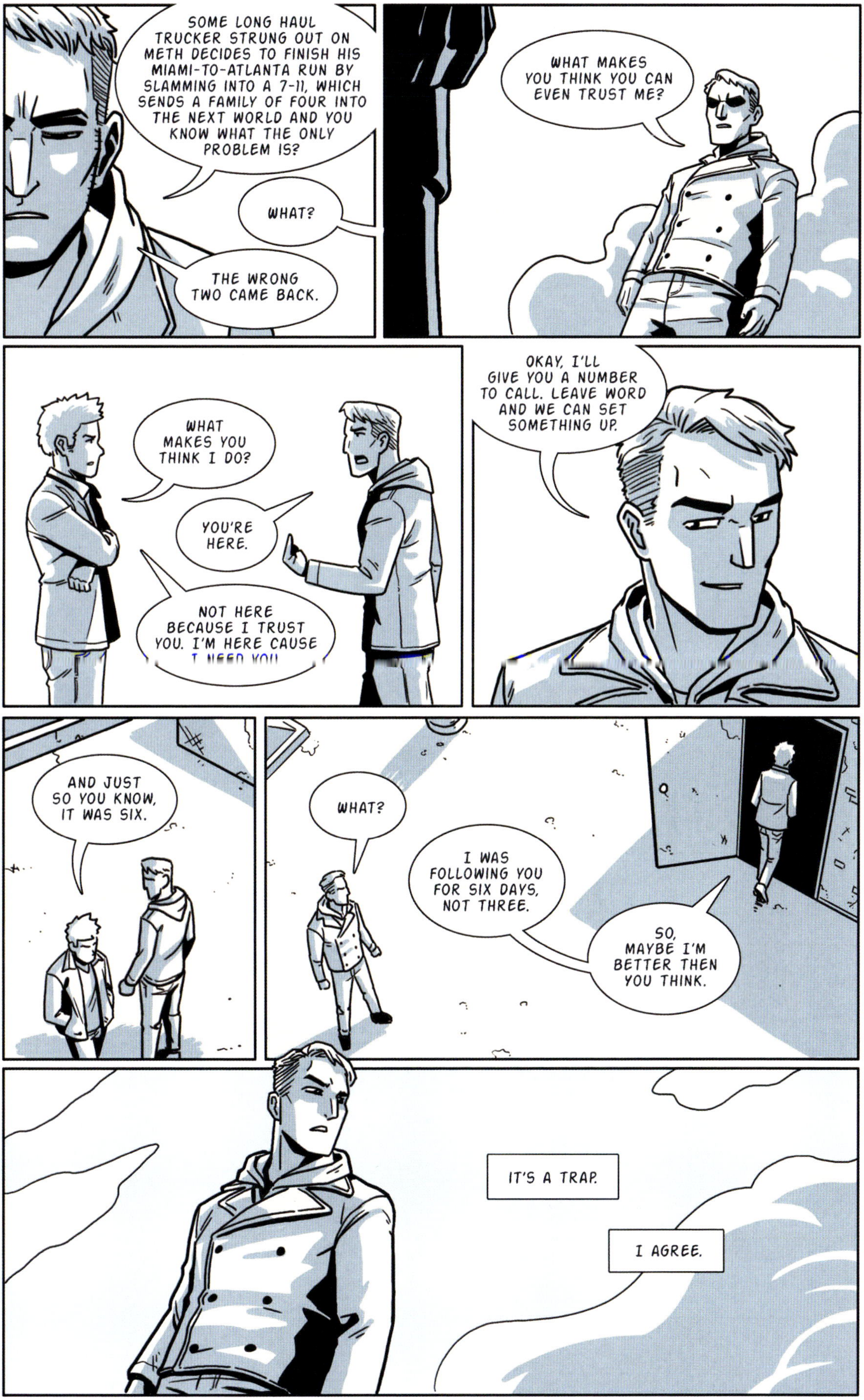
SOME LONG HAUL TRUCKER STRUNG OUT ON METH DECIDES TO FINISH HIS MIAMI-TO-ATLANTA RUN BY SLAMMING INTO A 7-11, WHICH SENDS A FAMILY OF FOUR INTO THE NEXT WORLD AND YOU KNOW WHAT THE ONLY PROBLEM IS?
WHAT?
THE WRONG TWO CAME BACK.
WHAT MAKES YOU THINK YOU CAN EVEN TRUST ME?
WHAT MAKES YOU THINK I DO?
YOU'RE HERE.
NOT HERE BECAUSE I TRUST YOU. I'M HERE CAUSE
OKAY, I'LL GIVE YOU A NUMBER TO CALL. LEAVE WORD AND WE CAN SET SOMETHING UP.
AND JUST SO YOU KNOW, IT WAS SIX.
WHAT?
I WAS FOLLOWING YOU FOR SIX DAYS, NOT THREE.
SO, MAYBE I'M BETTER THEN YOU THINK.
IT'S A TRAP.
I AGREE.

I DON'T.

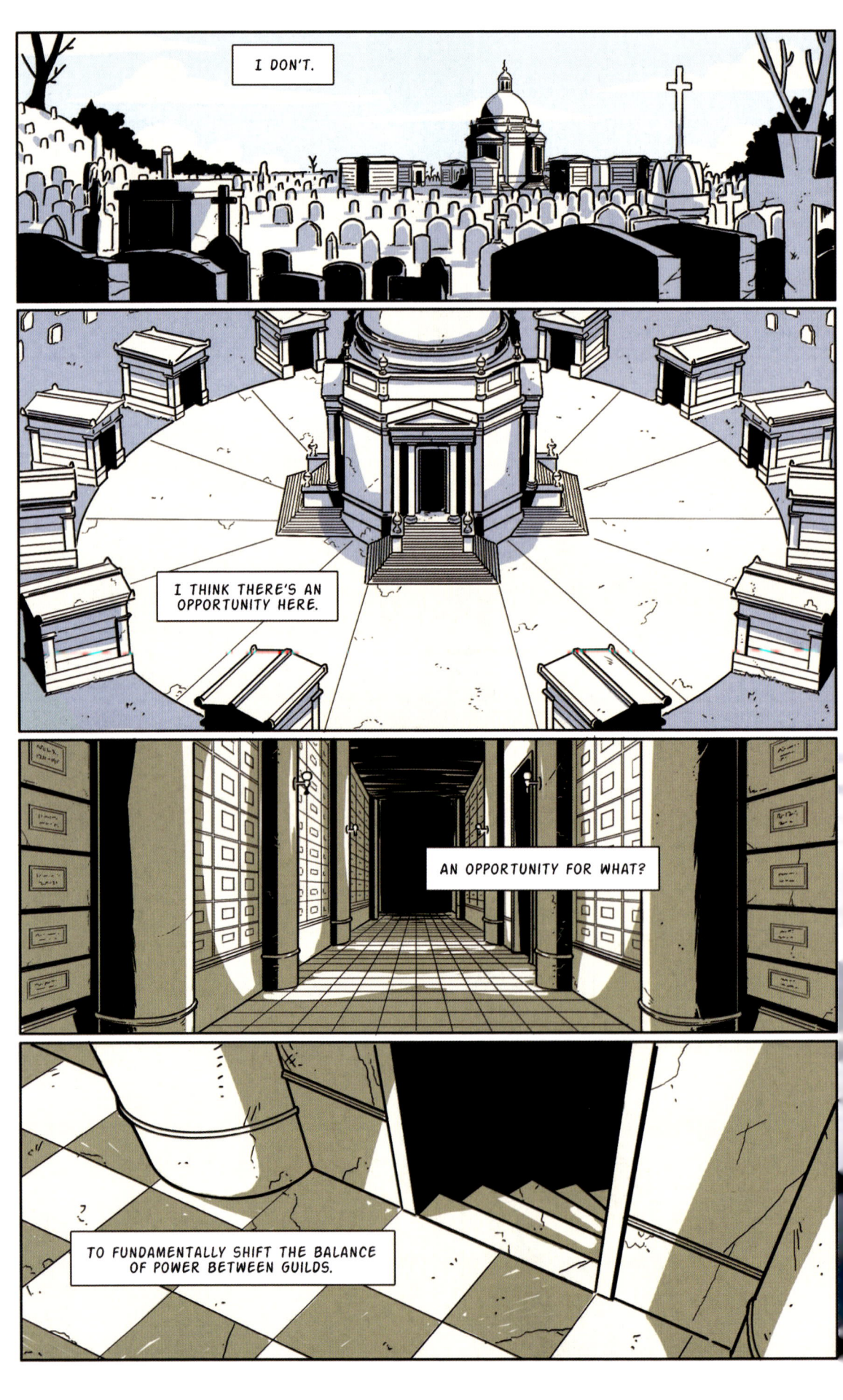

I THINK THERE'S AN OPPORTUNITY HERE.

AN OPPORTUNITY FOR WHAT?

TO FUNDAMENTALLY SHIFT THE BALANCE OF POWER BETWEEN GUILDS.

SEBASTIAN NOBLE'S SON DOESN'T NEED TO COME TO ONE OF US TO HELP HIM OPEN A BREACH.
UNLESS, OF COURSE, SEBASTIAN NOBLE'S SON CAN'T ASK HIM FOR HELP.
THEN WHY NOT WAIT TILL HE CAN DO IT HIMSELF?
AND IF HE GET'S IT WRONG? THE GIRL DIES. IT'S NOT LIKE YOU CAN PRACTICE TAKING SOMEONE THROUGH A NEAR DEATH EXPERIENCE.
SO SET UP ANOTHER MEETING. YOUR FATHER OR SCARLET CAN--
HE WON'T DO IT. IT'S ME OR NO ONE.
WHY DOES HE TRUST YOU?
HE DOESN'T. THE GIRL DOES.
I STILL DON'T-- WHY NOT JUST ASK HIS FATHER?
BECAUSE HE DOESN'T TRUST HIS FATHER.
HOW DO YOU KNOW?
BECAUSE OF THIS.
WHAT IS THAT?
UP UNTIL A FEW WEEKS AGO THIS WAS ETHAN NOBLE'S HOME FOR THE LAST TWO YEARS. ANYONE WANT TO GUESS WHY?
HE DIDN'T KNOW.

NO, HE DID NOT.
HIS BREACH WAS OPEN BUT HIS FATHER NEVER TOLD HIM WHAT HE WAS. WHAT HE COULD DO. WHY HE COULD DO IT.
ARE WE SURE IT'S OPEN.
IT'S OPEN. AND HE'S GOT SKILLS.
SEBASTIAN NOBLE CHOSE TO ALLOW HIS SON TO ROT IN SOME HELL HOLE.
AND AS TERRIBLE AS THAT IS, IT'S NOT HALF AS BAD AS LEARNING THAT YOUR FATHER HAD AN EXPLANATION FOR EVERY-THING YOU THOUGHT WAS WRONG WITH YOURSELF THE WHOLE TIME.
AND YOU KNOW WHAT THAT MAKES HIM?
VULNERABLE.
AND A KID LIKE ETHAN DOESN'T JUST PUT THAT BEHIND HIM.
THE GUILD IS BOTH BIGGER AND STRONGER THAN WE ARE. WE'RE LOSING GROUND EVERYWHERE.
NO CHEATING. EITHER ONE OF YOU.
NEVER.

"HE GREW UP HOPING THERE WAS A PILL OR A VACCINE THAT HE COULD TAKE TO MAKE HIM NORMAL."

"AND THEN ONE DAY HE WOKE UP AND FOUND OUT HE WAS NORMAL."

"I KNOW THAT KID BECAUSE I WAS THAT KID. AND MAYBE SOME OF YOU WERE TOO."

"AND YOU KNOW WHERE KIDS LIKE THAT END UP?"

"A PLACE JUST LIKE THIS."

"TRUST ME, WHEN IT'S LATE AT NIGHT AND ETHAN NOBLE CAN'T SLEEP DO YOU WANT TO KNOW WHAT HE DOES...?"

"WH- WHAT?"

"BLAME THE PERSON WHO MADE HIM FEEL THAT WAY."

"YOU ASKED IF WE CAN GET ETHAN NOBLE?"

"WE WON'T HAVE TO."

"HE'S COMING TO US."

"AND HE'LL BRING THE GIRL WE NEED WITH HIM."

I WANT TO GO AGAIN.
YOU AND ME. ONE MORE ROUND.
I WASN'T JOKING, YOU'RE NOT READY.
THUD!

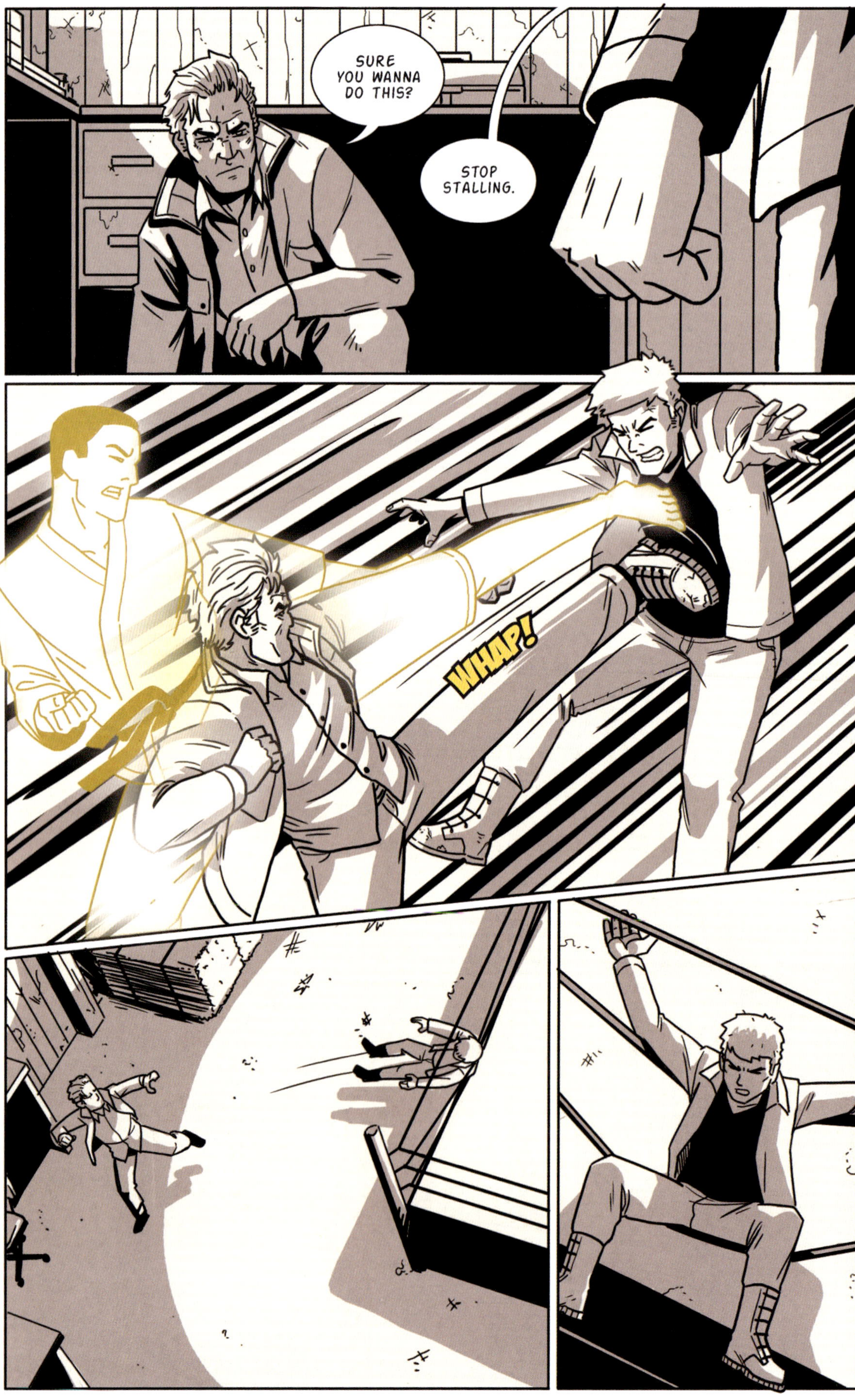
SURE YOU WANNA DO THIS?
STOP STALLING.
WHAP!

I DON'T WANT TO HURT YOU, E.
A LITTLE LATE FOR THAT, POP.
I DIDN'T PUT YOU IN THERE BECAUSE I DIDN'T LOVE YOU.
I PUT YOU IN THERE BECAUSE I DID.

"YOU MISSED THE POINT. ALWAYS DID."

"OKAY, THEN. WHAT'S YOU'RE POINT?"

"THAT YOU PUT ME IN THERE AT ALL."

"YOU LITTLE SH-- SHE WANTED ME TO GO!"

GO HEAD BLAME ME!
BUT IF I HADN'T GONE, YOU AND YOUR SISTER WOULD'VE BEEN DEAD!
YOU DON'T KNOW THAT!
YOU WEREN'T THERE!
I WAS! I WAS THERE AND I'VE BEEN PAYING FOR IT EVER SINCE!

CAN'T SLEEP?
BAD DREAM.
MOM?
YOU TOO, HUH?
EVER SINCE THE BREACH.
CAN I SAY SOMETHING WITHOUT YOU--
JUST SAY IT, CARTER.
THIS THING WITH DAD, YOU GOTTA LET IT GO. I DON'T BLAME YOU. YOU HAVE EVERY RIGHT TO HATE HIM. GOD KNOWS I WOULD TOO.
THEN WHY DOES IT FEEL LIKE YOU'RE ALWAYS DEFENDING HIM?
MAYBE I AM.
WHY?
MAYBE... MAYBE 'CAUSE NOW THAT I KNOW EVERYTHING I THINK HE MADE WHAT HE THOUGHT WAS THE BEST DECISION FOR YOU.
YOU REALLY BELIEVE THAT?
I KNOW IT WAS HARD FOR YOU, E. I KNOW I HAD IT FAR EASIER AND I KNOW IT'S NOT FAIR.
BUT...
IT COULDN'T HAVE BEEN EASY FOR HIM EITHER, NOT THE WAY IT HAPPENED,
NOT WITH WHAT HE HAD TO DO.
THEN WHY DID YOU HAVE ME LIFT MOM'S SAFE SOIL?

WHEN YOU HUGGED HIM, RIGHT?
YEAH.
IT'S NOT WHAT YOU THINK.
I THINK YOU DON'T TRUST HIM.
THAT'S NOT--
YOU WANNA KNOW WHY HE'S A MESS?
'CAUSE HE'S BEEN USING MOM'S SAFE SOIL TO HOLD ON TO WHATEVER HE CAN OF WHAT'S LEFT OF HER. HE'S DROWNING IN HER MEMORIES, E.
HE SHOULD MOVE ON.
HE CAN'T!
CAN'T OR WON'T? HE'S HAD THIS FOR TWENTY YEARS, CARTER. YOU DON'T THINK HE'S SIFTED THROUGH EVERY MEMORY IN HERE?
THAT'S WHAT I'M TRYING TO TELL YOU! HE HASN'T BEEN LOOKING FOR ANSWERS HE'S BEEN PUNISHING HIMSELF!
SO WE SUFFERED BECAUSE HE SPENT HIS LIFE CHASING GHOSTS?!
YES! BUT AT LEAST NOW WE CAN FIND OUT IF HE'S BEEN CHASING THE RIGHT ONES.
MOM'S MEMORIES ARE GONNA GUT YOU, CARTER. YOU'RE NOT READY. I'LL DO IT.
ETHAN--
YOU'VE READ TEXT BOOKS, C, BUT I'VE LIVED IT. YOU'RE NOT READY.
AND YOU ARE?
I'VE BEEN DEALING WITH THIS A LOT LONGER THAN YOU HAVE.
I'M ALREADY DAMAGED. WHERE I WAS, WHAT I'VE BEEN THROUGH, I'M ALREADY USED TO CERTAIN KIND OF PAIN.
LET ME DO THIS. LET ME HELP YOU.

I ALREADY HAVE HELP. YOU READ THINGS, YOU LEARN THINGS.
THE CARETAKERS WHO CAN DO IT CALL IT, SPLICING.
WITH ENOUGH PRACTICE THEY CAN ABSORB A SOUL SKILL WITHOUT INTEGRATING IT INTERNALLY.
IT ENABLES US TO BREAK DOWN THE SKILLS INTO INDIVIDUAL MEMORIES ALLOWING THOSE WHO CAN SPLICE TO BASICALLY SCAN THE MEMORIES LIKE FILES ON A COMPUTER.
YOU EVER DONE IT BEFORE?
ETHAN.
I JUST DID.
917-674-8923.
WHAT IS THAT?
THE PHONE NUMBER OF THE GUY MOM CALLED BEFORE SHE DIED.
CARTER, THAT WAS TWENTY YEARS-- IT'S A DEAD END.
YOU SHOULD KNOW BY NOW THAT BEING DEAD NO LONGER MATTERS.
OKAY, WHAT DO YOU NEED ME TO DO?
DIG. WE NEED AN ADDRESS.

NEXT MORNING
ETHAN...
YOU'VE BEEN HERE ALL NIGHT?
HUH? OH, YEAH.
WHAT ARE YOU LOOKING FOR?
MY SISTER GAVE ME PHONE NUMBER I NEEDED TO TRACK DOWN.
IT TOOK ALL NIGHT TO TRACK DOWN A CELL NUMBER?
NO, BUT I FOUND ANOTHER NUMBER LINKED TO THE ACCOUNT. A LAND LINE.
WHAT'S A LAND LINE?
AND THAT'S WHY IT TOOK ME ALL NIGHT.
GOOD THING ABOUT LAND LINES? ALL THAT OLD WIRING IS STILL IN PLACE. ONCE YOU KNOW WHAT TO LOOK FOR YOU CAN FOLLOW 'EM LIKE A MAP.
WHAT'S THAT?
THE ADDRESS TO THE PHONE NUMBER MY MOM CALLED THE DAY SHE DIED.
MAYBE CARTER WAS RIGHT.
MAYBE I GOT OUT OF THAT FACILITY FOR A REASON.

* TRANSLATED FROM RUSSIAN
BRIGHTON BEACH, BROOKLYN
SO YOU REMEMBER THE MAN? *
OH, YES. SPOKE SUCH GOOD RUSSIAN.
HE WAS RUSSIAN?
NO, NO- AMERICAN BUT COULD SPEAK RUSSIAN PERFECTLY. BETTER THAN MY TEACHERS BACK HOME.
AND IN ANY DIALECT. I TELL YOU THE TRUTH, ANY ONE. AMAZING MAN, AMAZING.
HE LIVED HERE?
YES AND OWNED THE WHOLE BUILDING. SO NICE HE WAS TO ME AND MY FAMILY.
WHAT HAPPENED?
JUST GONE. NO MORE. DISAPPEARED. AND NO ONE SINCE HAS LIVED THERE.

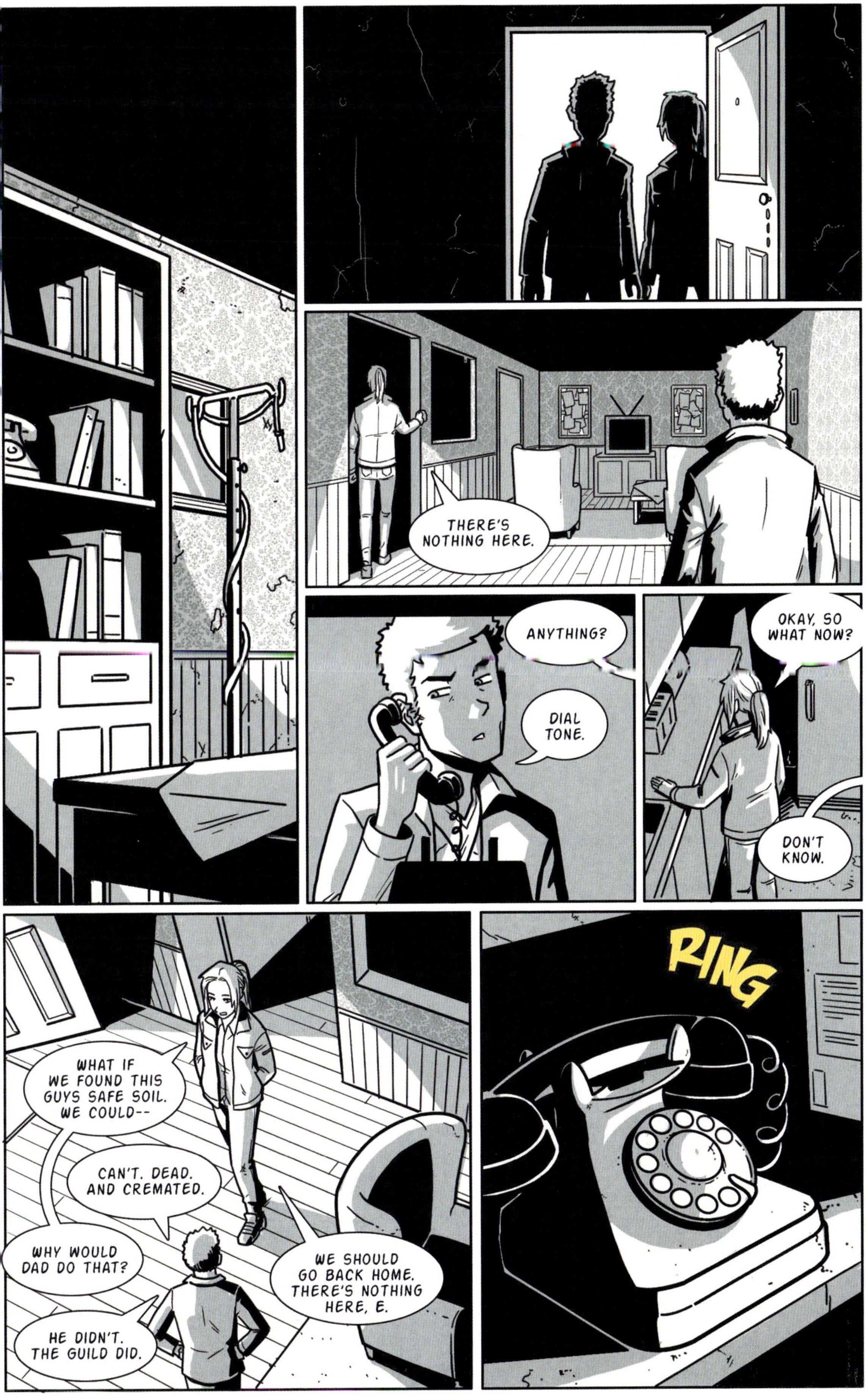
THERE'S NOTHING HERE.
ANYTHING?
DIAL TONE.
OKAY, SO WHAT NOW?
DON'T KNOW.
WHAT IF WE FOUND THIS GUYS SAFE SOIL. WE COULD--
CAN'T. DEAD. AND CREMATED.
WHY WOULD DAD DO THAT?
HE DIDN'T. THE GUILD DID.
WE SHOULD GO BACK HOME. THERE'S NOTHING HERE, E.
RING

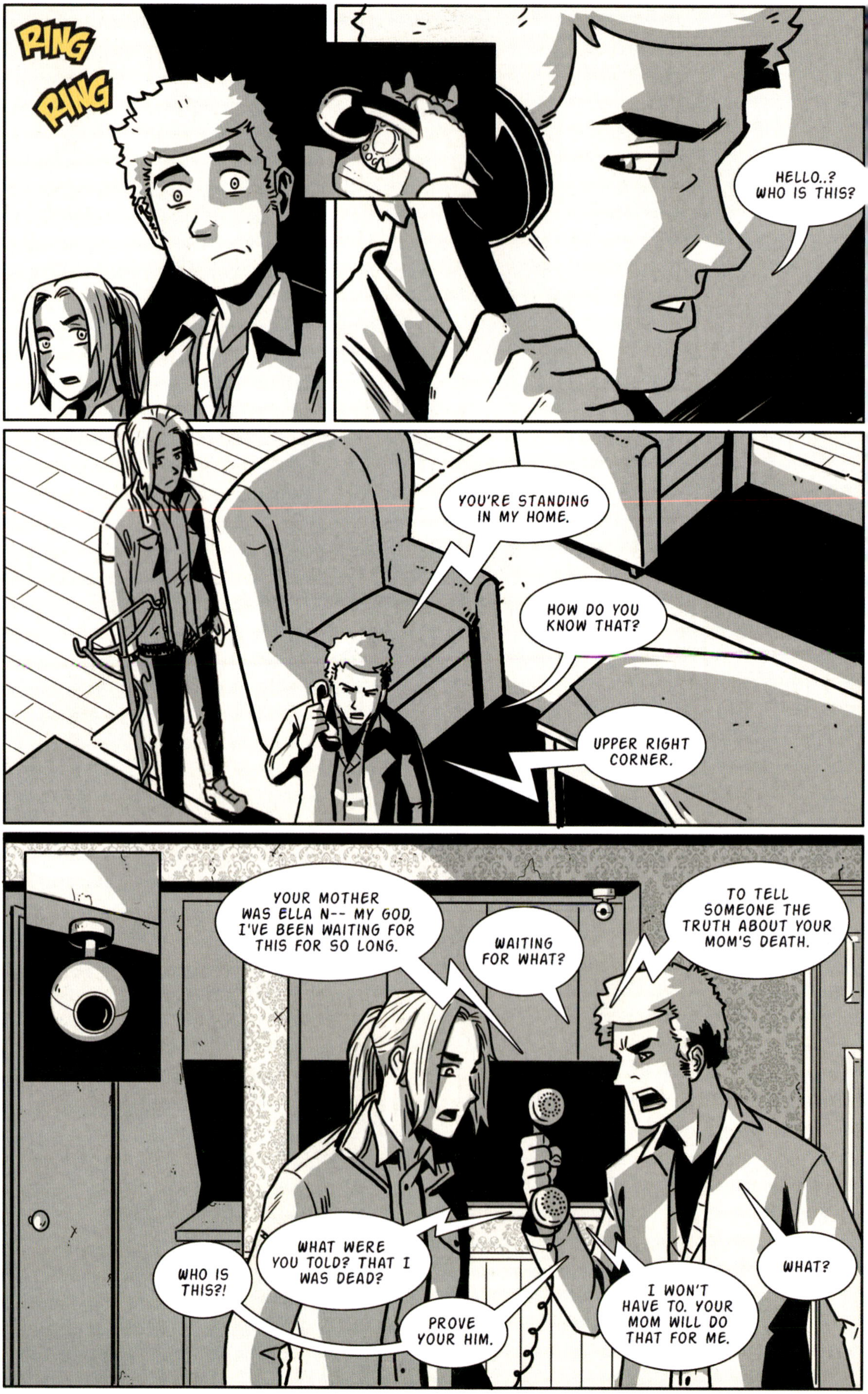
RING
RING
HELLO..? WHO IS THIS?
YOU'RE STANDING IN MY HOME.
HOW DO YOU KNOW THAT?
UPPER RIGHT CORNER.
YOUR MOTHER WAS ELLA N-- MY GOD, I'VE BEEN WAITING FOR THIS FOR SO LONG.
WAITING FOR WHAT?
TO TELL SOMEONE THE TRUTH ABOUT YOUR MOM'S DEATH.
WHAT?
WHAT WERE YOU TOLD? THAT I WAS DEAD?
WHO IS THIS?!
PROVE YOUR HIM.
I WON'T HAVE TO. YOUR MOM WILL DO THAT FOR ME.

THE ANTIDOTE WORKED, CARTER. YOUR MOM FOUND IT.
HOW DO-- HOW COULD YOU KNOW THAT?
BECAUSE SHE CURED ME.
BULL! I GHOSTED MY MOTHER. I KNOW WHAT SHE KNEW. THOSE TRIALS ALL CAME BACK NEGATIVE.
BECAUSE THAT'S WHAT I TOLD HER!
WHY?!
BECAUSE THAT'S WHAT THE GUILD WANTED ME TO TELL HER.
THE GUILD? ARE YOU SAYING THE GUILD HAD SOMETHING TO DO WITH--
YOU HAVE NO PROOF!
I *AM* THE PROOF!
ARE YOU SAYING THE GUILD HAD OUR MOM KILLED?
OR YOUR FATHER.
SHUT UP!
I DON'T BELIEVE YOU!
HE WAS THE ONLY ONE WHO KNEW WHERE SHE WAS WORKING.
I WOULDN'T EXPECT YOU TOO. BUT I HAVE QUESTIONS. AND SO SHOULD YOU.
LIKE WHAT?
HOW DID HE GET TO HER SO FAST? WHY DIDN'T HE COME LOOKING FOR ME?
HE WAS TOLD YOU WERE DEAD!
SO WERE YOU AND YET LOOK WHERE YOU'RE STANDING!
DAMN! YOU GOTTA GO!!
WHAT? WHY?
THEY FOLLOWED YOU.

WHO?
I DON'T KNOW. WHO KNOWS YOU'RE THERE?!
NO ONE!
WELL, SOMEONE KNOWS, LOOK OUTSIDE.
YOU SHOULD GO, ETHAN!
TELL ME WHERE YOU ARE FIRST!
NOT YET.
HE'S RIGHT.

BUT NOW THAT I KNOW YOU AND CARTER ARE SAFE I'LL FIND YOU. BUT YOU NEED TO GO. NOW!
THEY'RE COMING UP!
THERE'S A DOOR IN THE BACK. YOU HAVE ABOUT THIRTY SECONDS. MAKE A DECISION; LISTEN TO ME OR TAKE YOUR CHANCES WITH THEM.

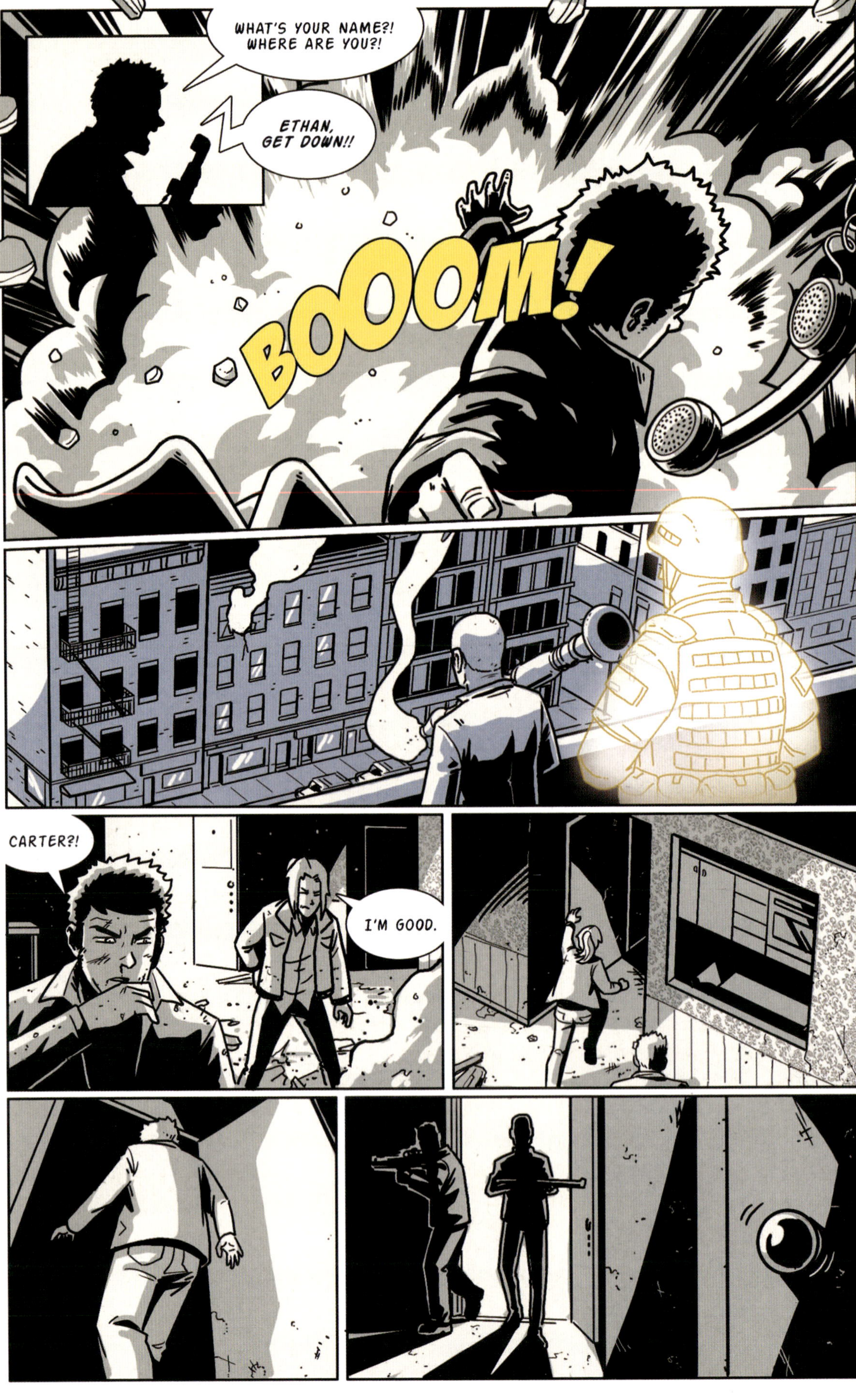
WHAT'S YOUR NAME?! WHERE ARE YOU?!
ETHAN, GET DOWN!!
BOOOM!
CARTER?!
I'M GOOD.

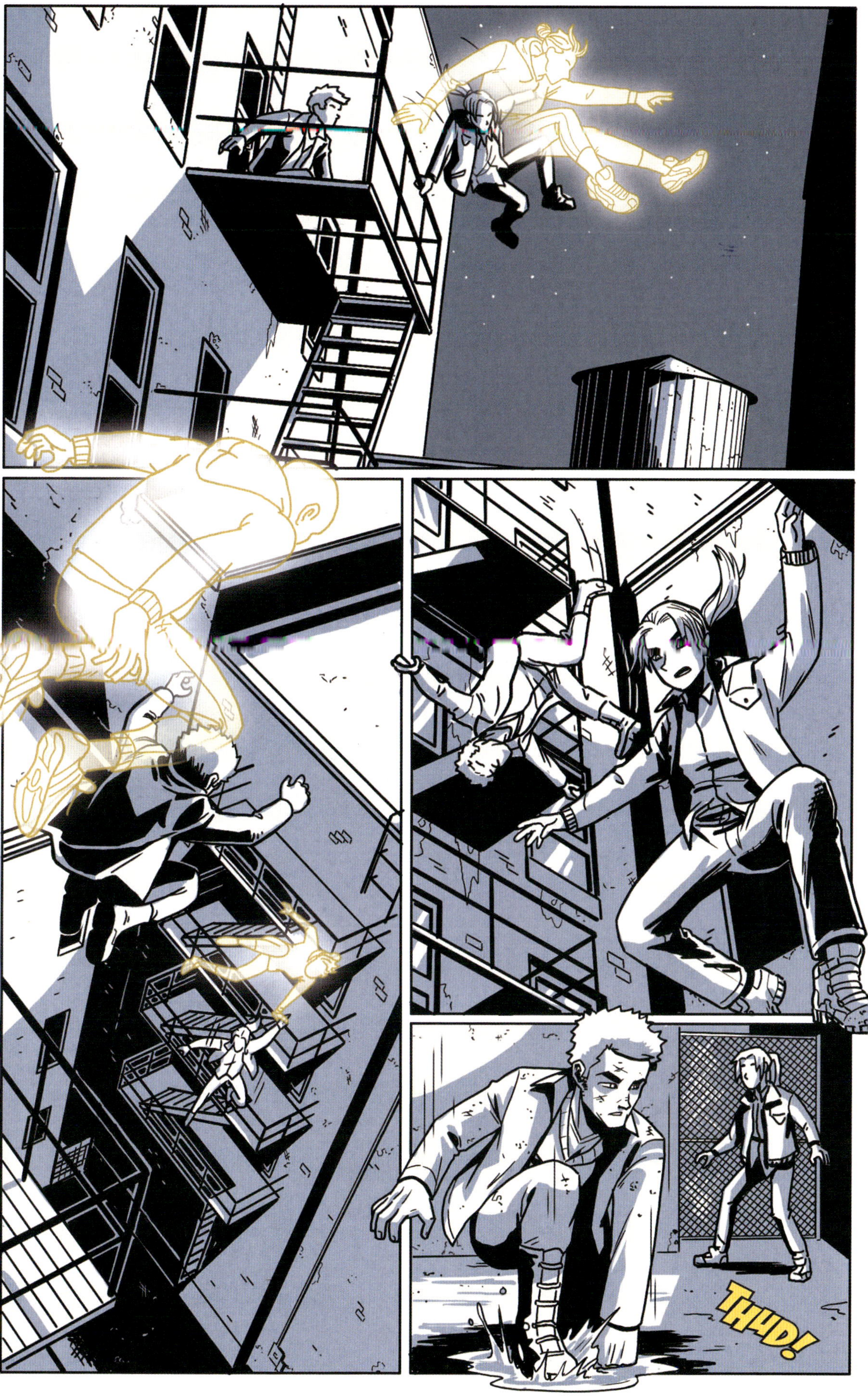
THUD!

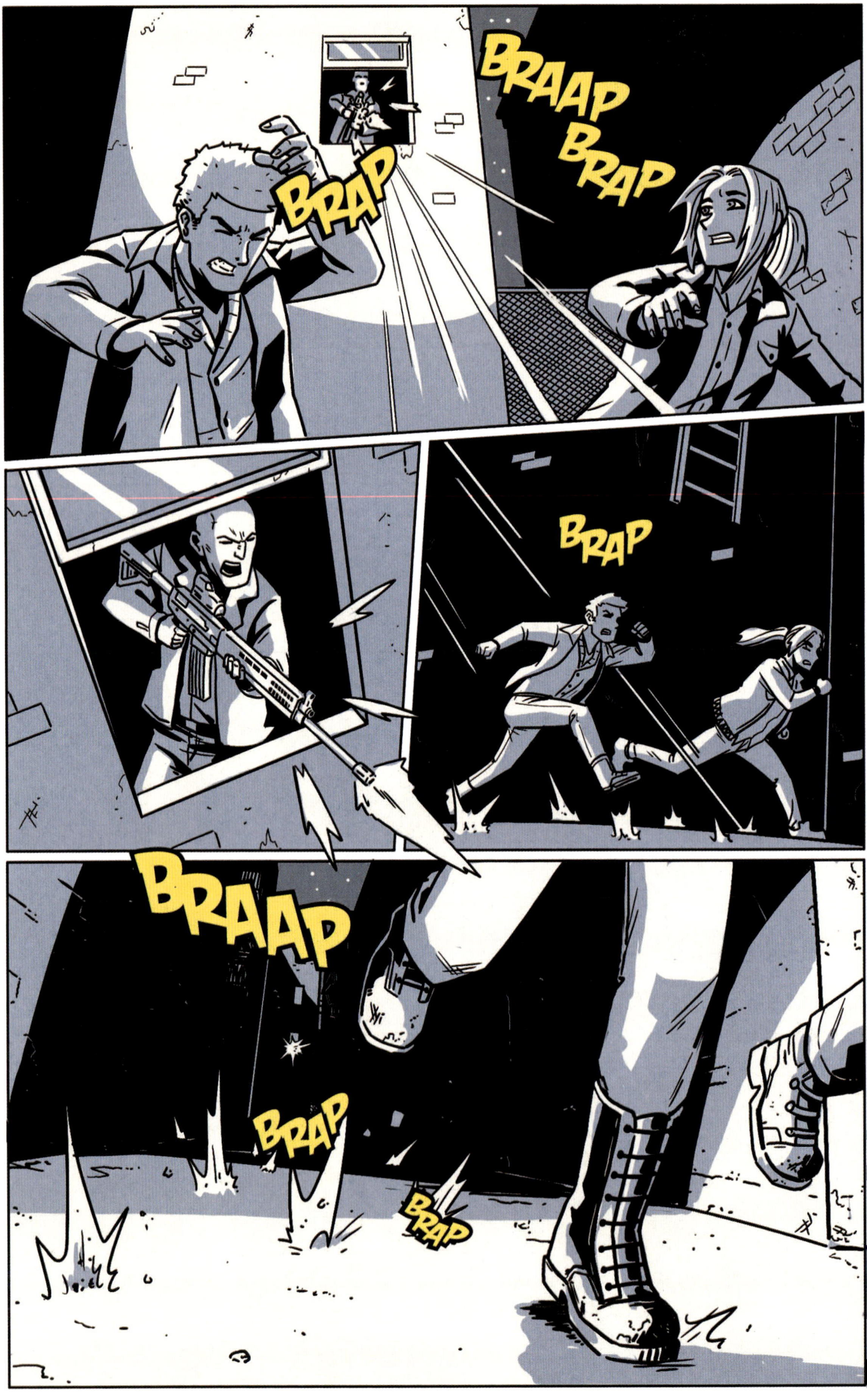
BRAAP
BRAP
BRAP
BRAP
BRAAP
BRAP
BRAP

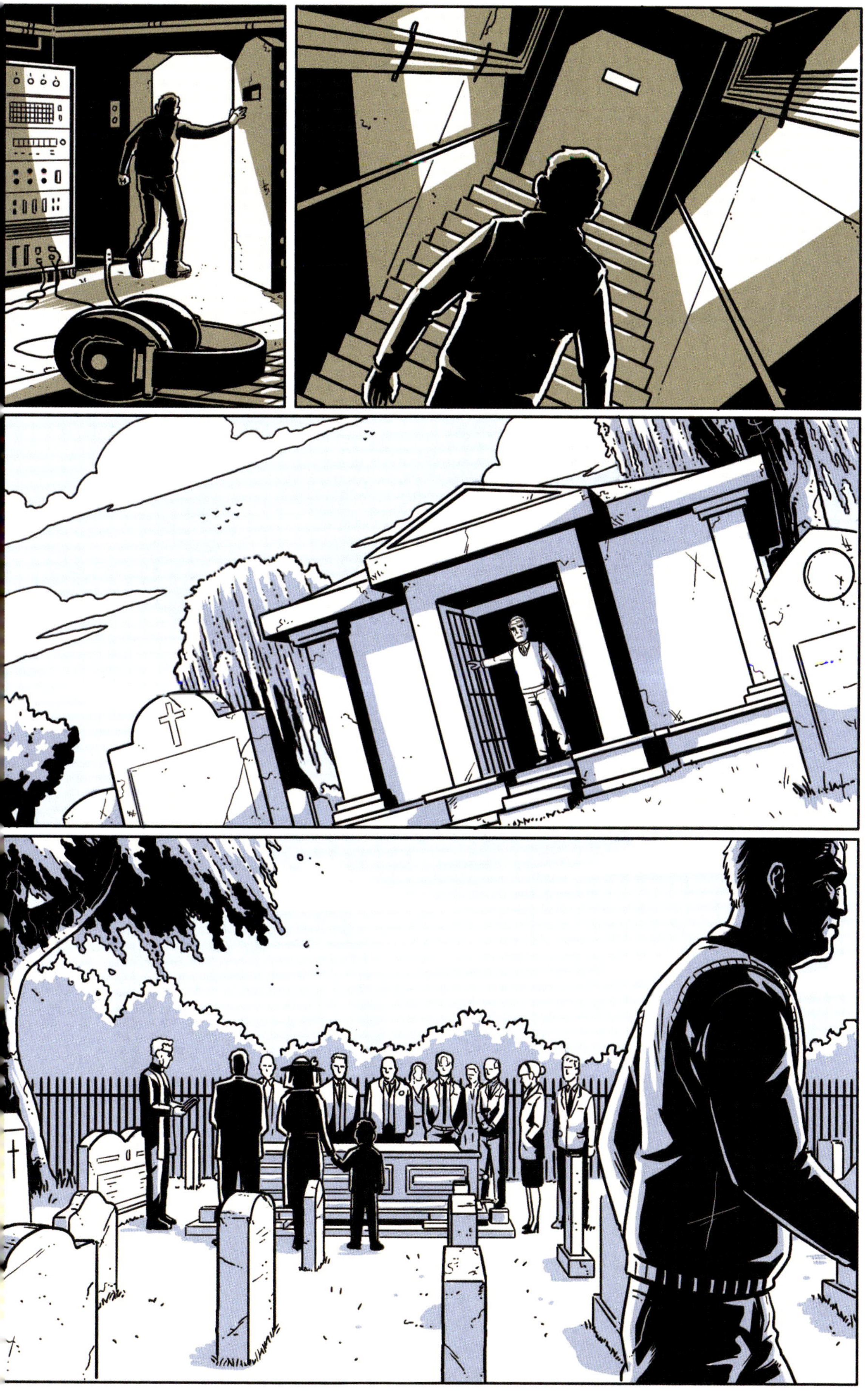

VROOM

YOU DON'T EVEN KNOW IF IT WAS REALLY HIM!

IT WAS HIM! I RECOGNIZED THE VOICE!

HOW COULD YOU--

MOM'S SAFE SOIL.

CARTER, THINK, NOW THAT WE KNOW MAYBE WE CAN DO WHAT DAD COULDN'T OR WOULDN'T.

WHICH IS WHAT?

FIND OUT THE TRUTH! YOU HEARD HIM, CARTER.

DAD DIDN'T DO IT!

BUT IT'S A POSSIBILITY! YOU WANT THE TRUTH, THEN YOU HAVE TO STOP MAKING EXCUSES FOR HIM.

DING

← LEXI

Where are you?

Be there soon.

K called. Wants 2 meet.

Wait for me.

Already left. Meet me ASAP.

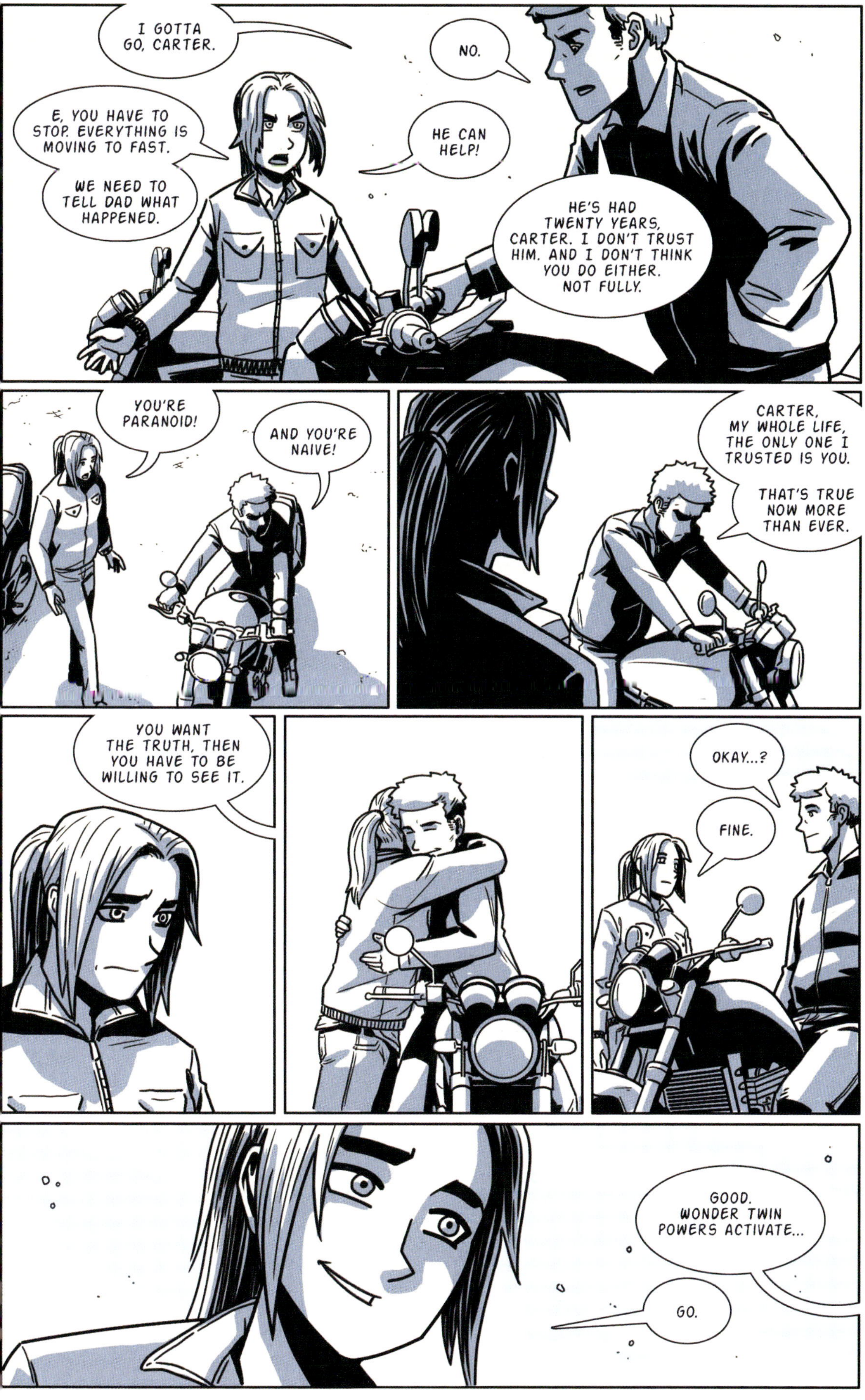
I GOTTA GO, CARTER.
NO.
E, YOU HAVE TO STOP. EVERYTHING IS MOVING TO FAST.
WE NEED TO TELL DAD WHAT HAPPENED.
HE CAN HELP!
HE'S HAD TWENTY YEARS, CARTER. I DON'T TRUST HIM. AND I DON'T THINK YOU DO EITHER. NOT FULLY.
YOU'RE PARANOID!
AND YOU'RE NAIVE!
CARTER, MY WHOLE LIFE, THE ONLY ONE I TRUSTED IS YOU.
THAT'S TRUE NOW MORE THAN EVER.
YOU WANT THE TRUTH, THEN YOU HAVE TO BE WILLING TO SEE IT.
OKAY...?
FINE.
GOOD. WONDER TWIN POWERS ACTIVATE...
GO.

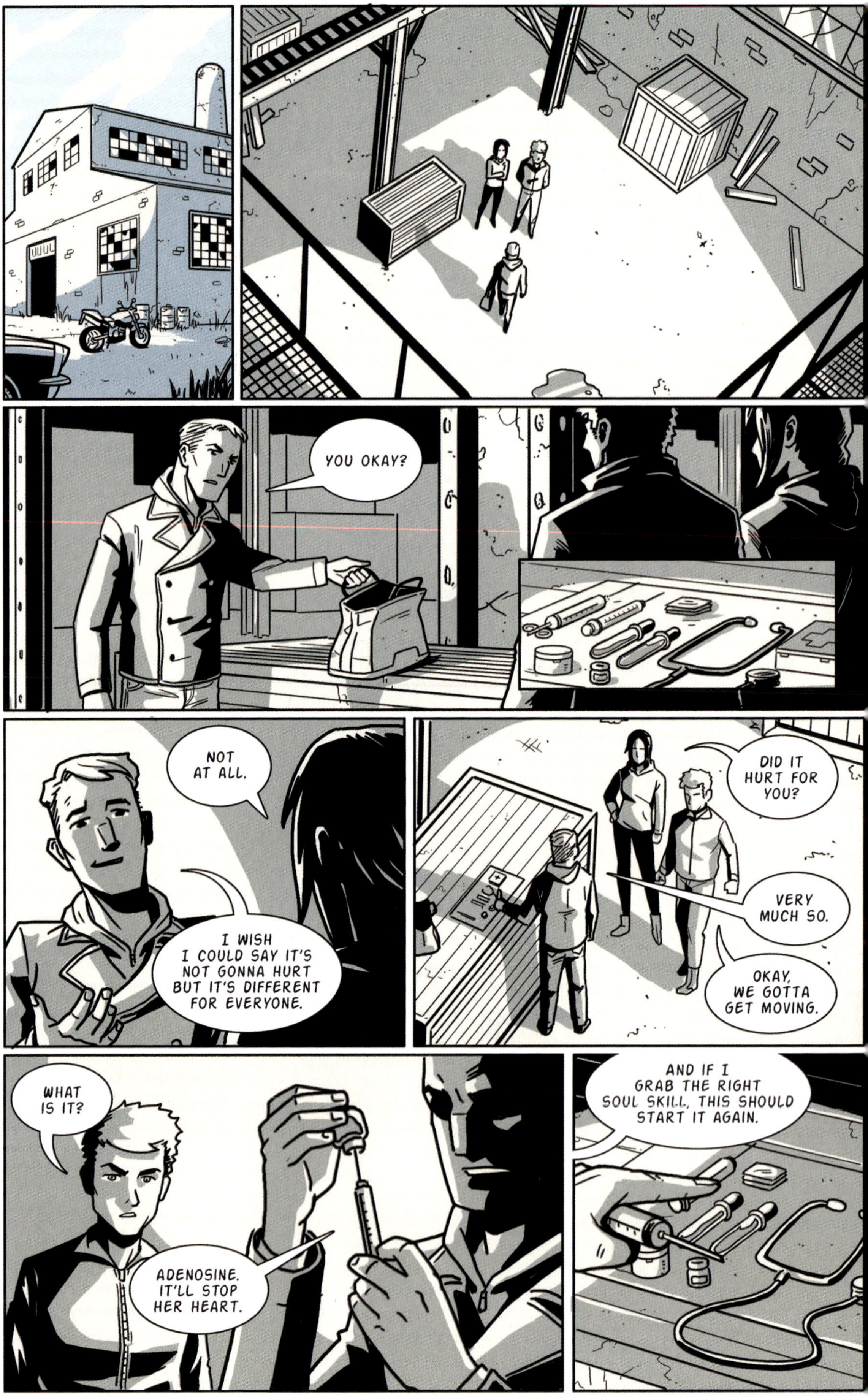
YOU OKAY?
NOT AT ALL.
I WISH I COULD SAY IT'S NOT GONNA HURT BUT IT'S DIFFERENT FOR EVERYONE.
DID IT HURT FOR YOU?
VERY MUCH SO.
OKAY, WE GOTTA GET MOVING.
WHAT IS IT?
ADENOSINE. IT'LL STOP HER HEART.
AND IF I GRAB THE RIGHT SOUL SKILL, THIS SHOULD START IT AGAIN.

I'LL BE RIGHT HERE WHEN YOU GET BACK.
ETHAN!
YOU CAN'T OPEN HER BREACH, ETHAN. THEY'LL JUST USE HER.
HOW DID YOU EVEN FIND--
...CARTER?!
I'M SORRY, ETHAN.
I TRUSTED YOU.

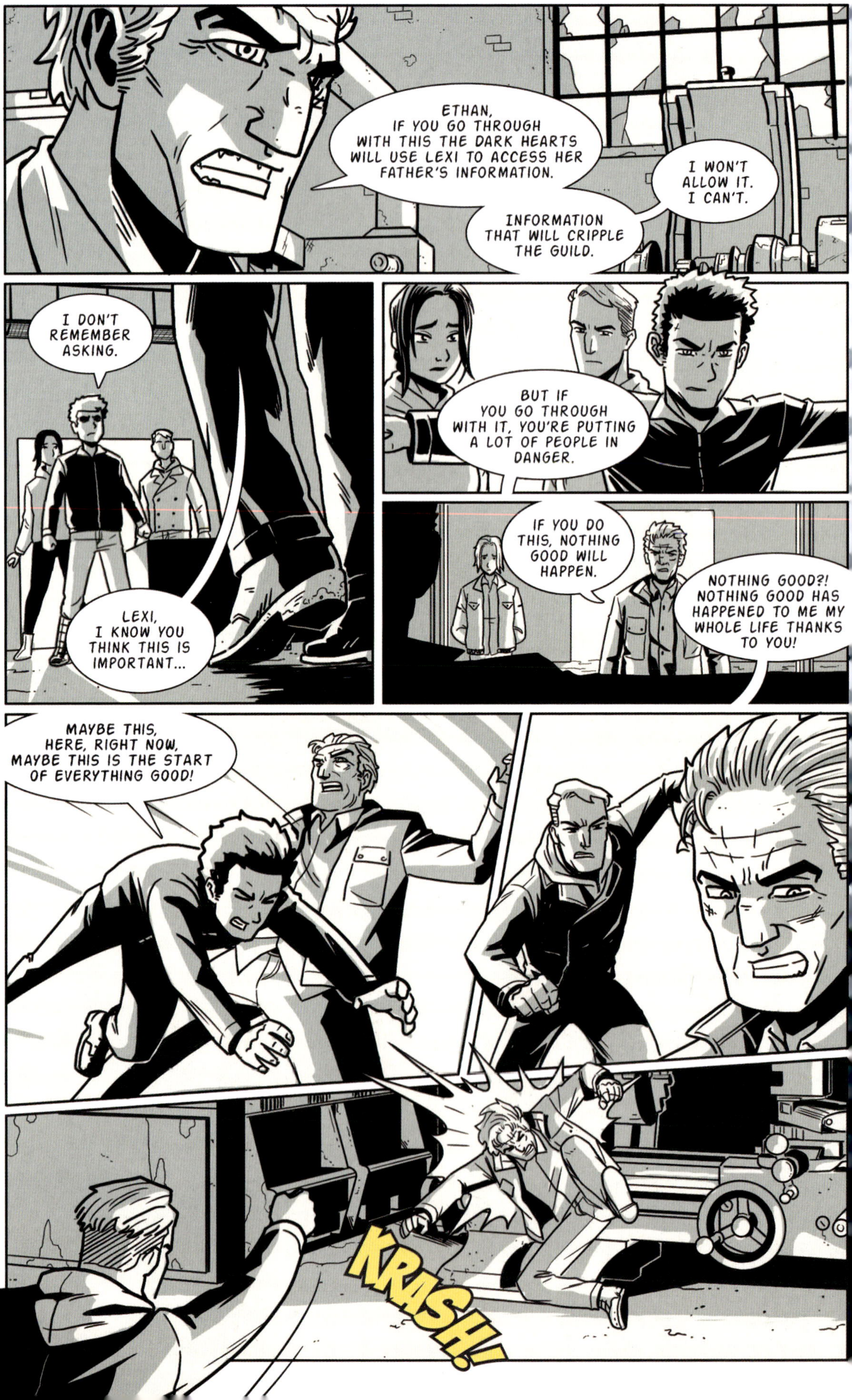
ETHAN, IF YOU GO THROUGH WITH THIS THE DARK HEARTS WILL USE LEXI TO ACCESS HER FATHER'S INFORMATION.
INFORMATION THAT WILL CRIPPLE THE GUILD.
I WON'T ALLOW IT. I CAN'T.
I DON'T REMEMBER ASKING.
LEXI, I KNOW YOU THINK THIS IS IMPORTANT...
BUT IF YOU GO THROUGH WITH IT, YOU'RE PUTTING A LOT OF PEOPLE IN DANGER.
IF YOU DO THIS, NOTHING GOOD WILL HAPPEN.
NOTHING GOOD?! NOTHING GOOD HAS HAPPENED TO ME MY WHOLE LIFE THANKS TO YOU!
MAYBE THIS, HERE, RIGHT NOW, MAYBE THIS IS THE START OF EVERYTHING GOOD!
KRASH!

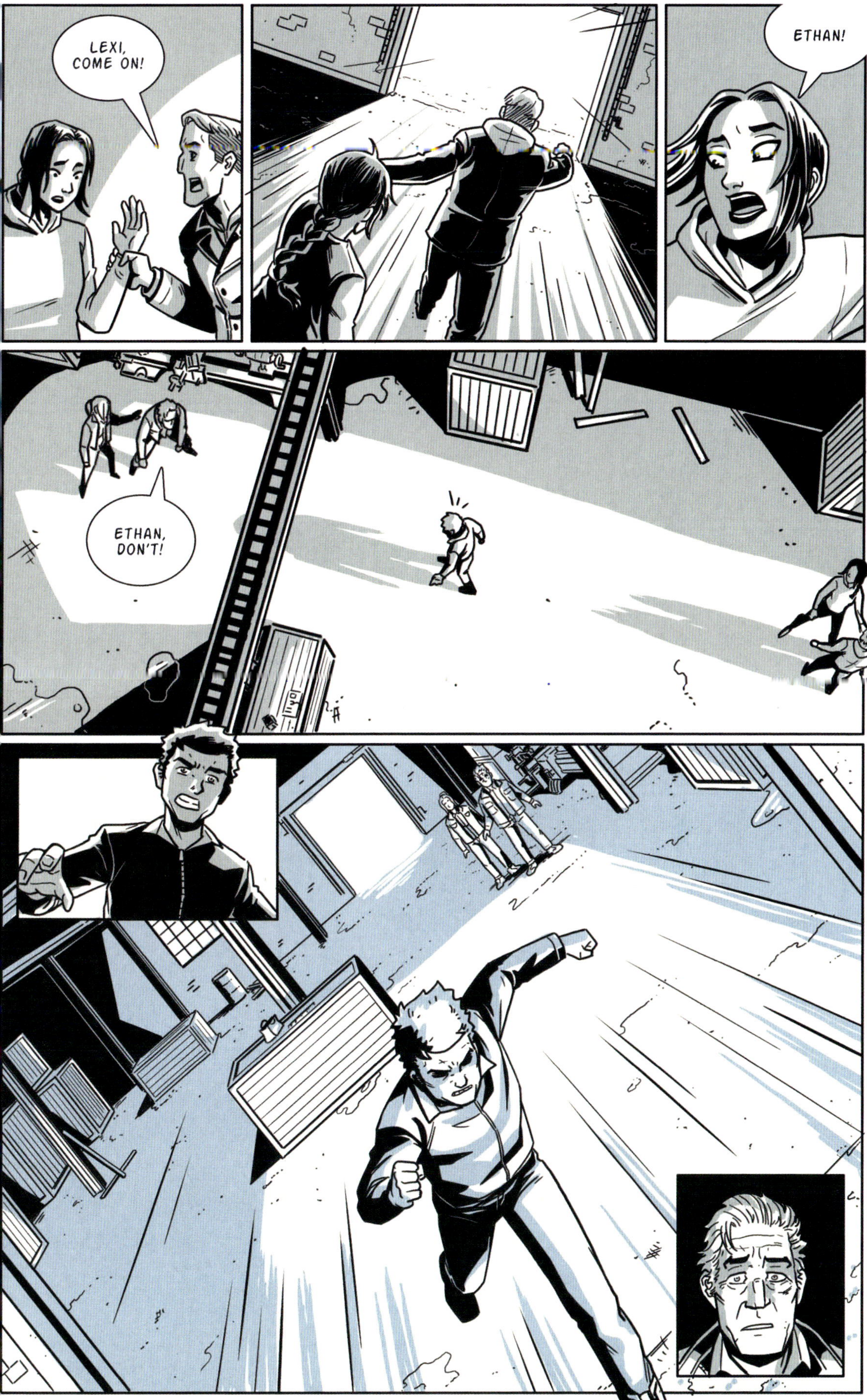
LEXI,
COME ON!
ETHAN!
ETHAN,
DON'T!

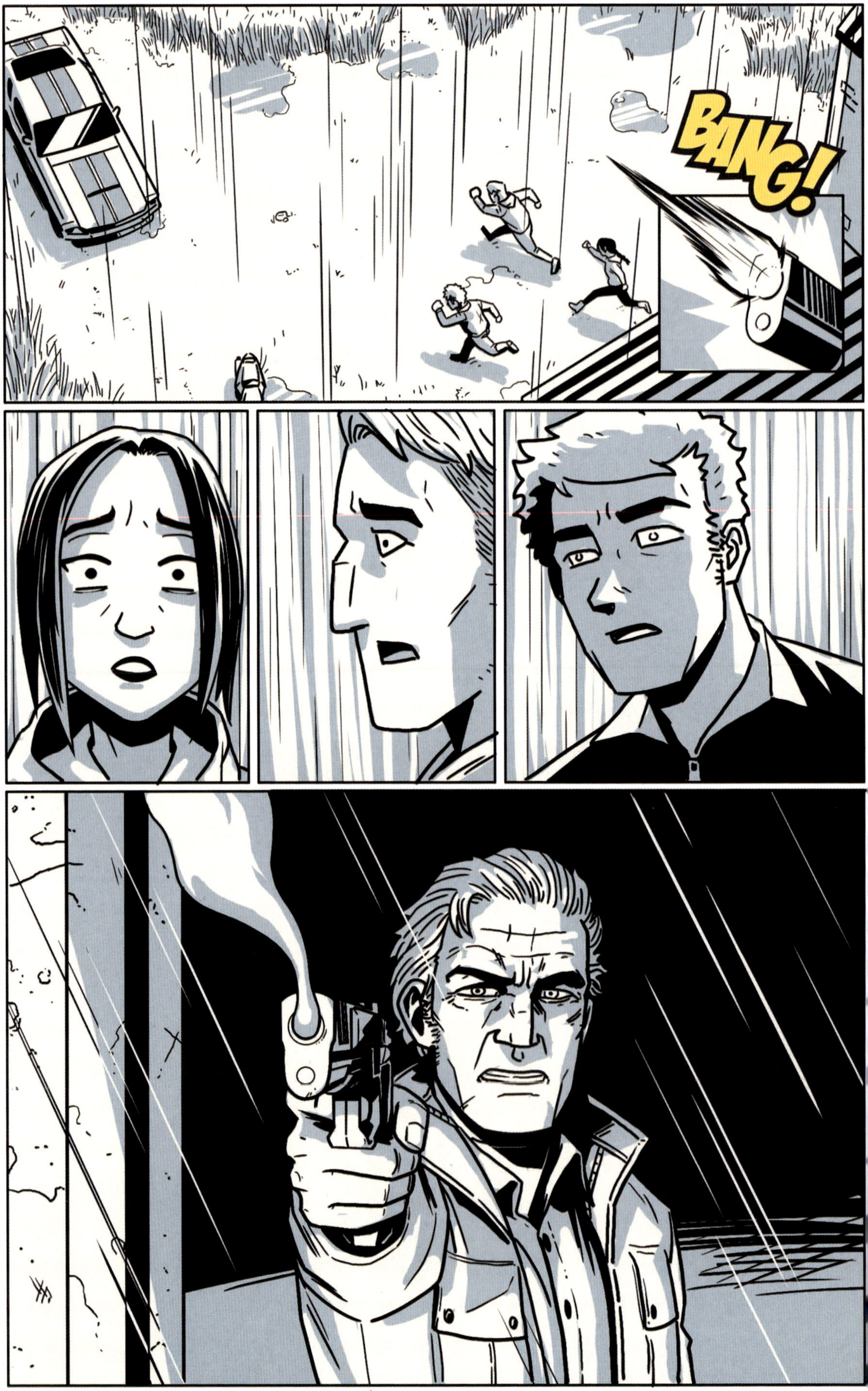
BANG!

LEXI?!
WH- WHAT DID YOU DO?
LEXI!
LEXI!
HELP HER!
ETHAN, WE GOTTA GO!
I DIDN'T--
SHE'S GONE, MAN!
WHAT DID YOU DO?!
BLAM!
BLAM
NO!
C'MON!

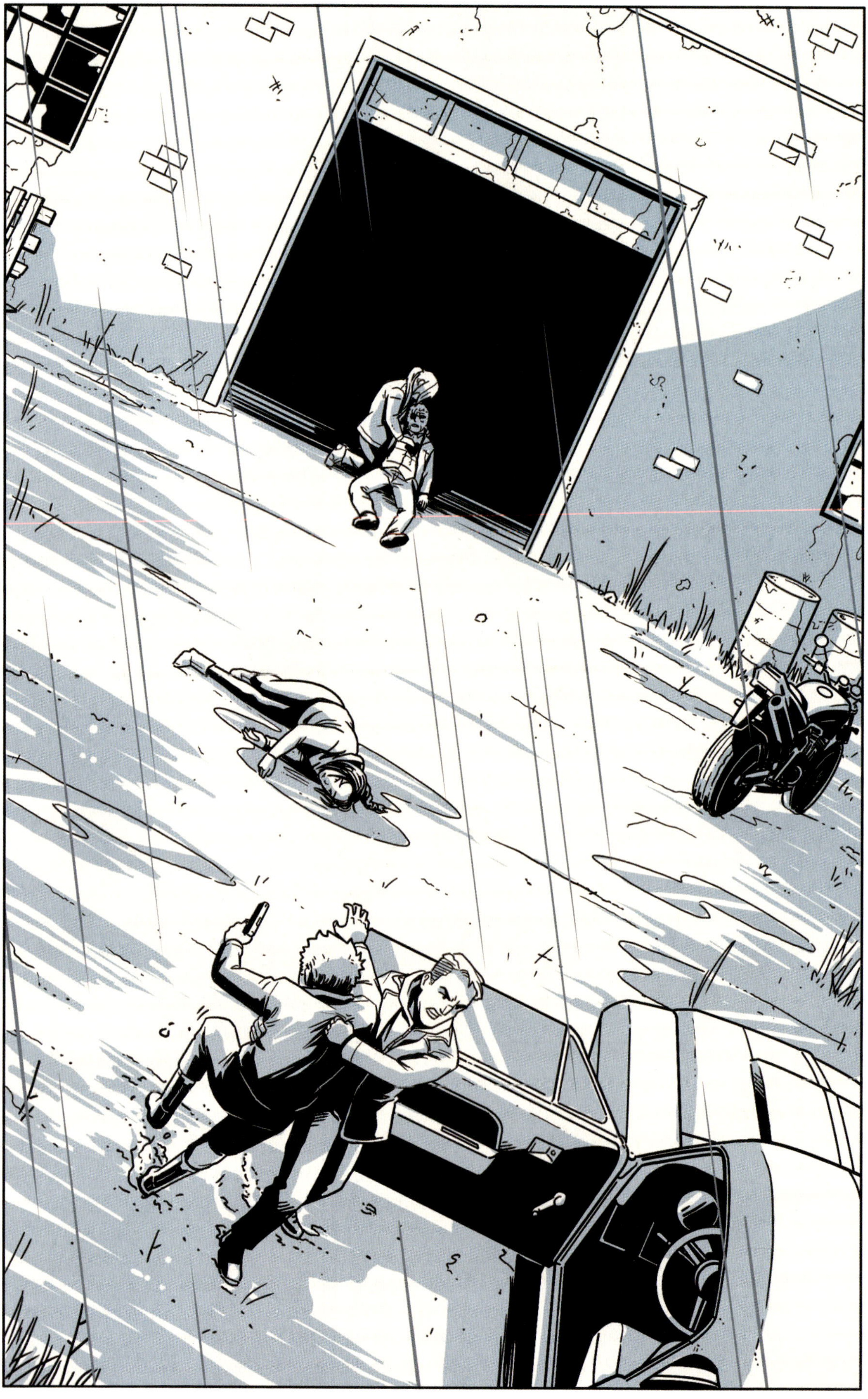

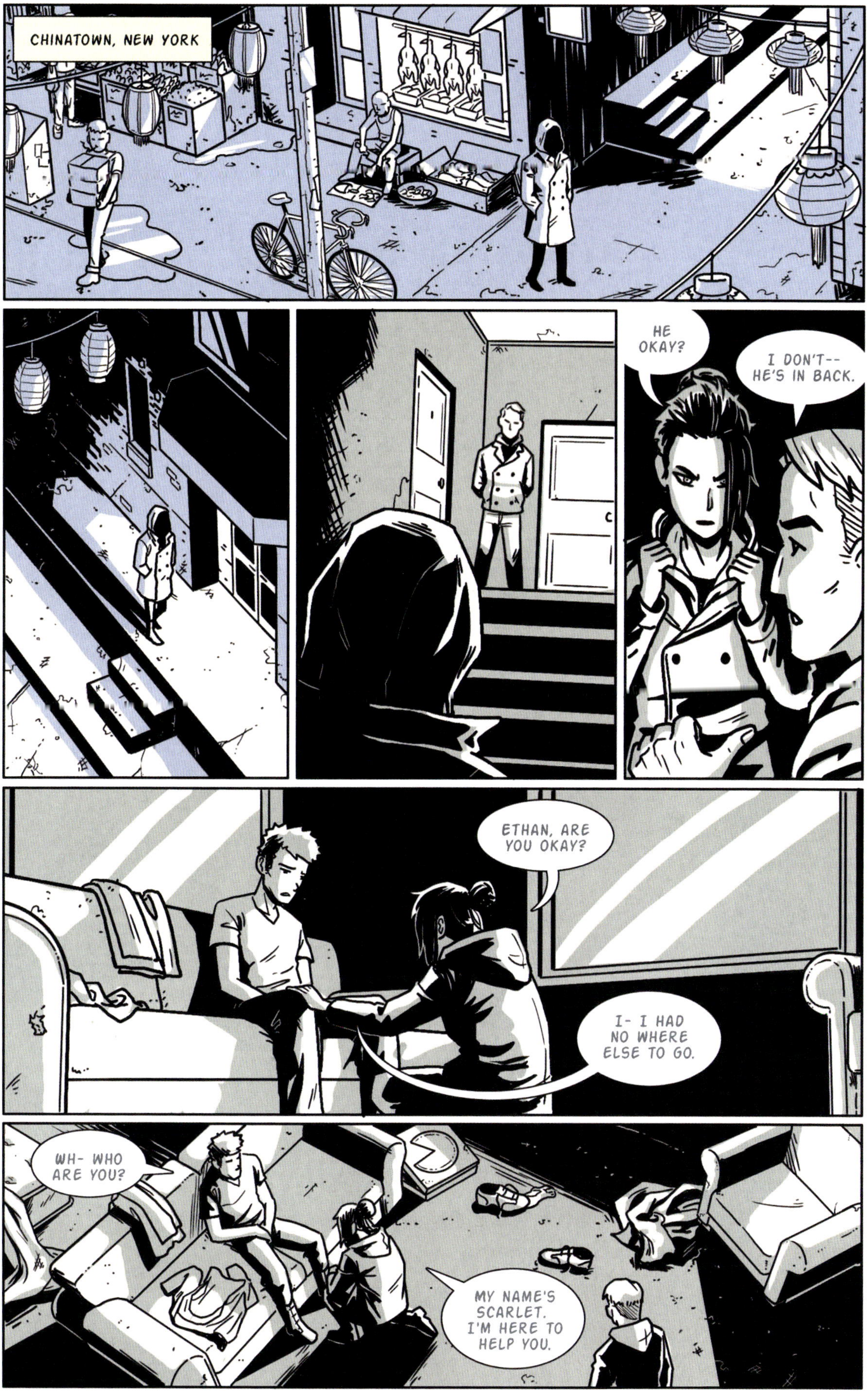
CHINATOWN, NEW YORK
HE OKAY?
I DON'T-- HE'S IN BACK.
ETHAN, ARE YOU OKAY?
I- I HAD NO WHERE ELSE TO GO.
WH- WHO ARE YOU?
MY NAME'S SCARLET. I'M HERE TO HELP YOU.

3 DAYS LATER

HOW DO YOU FEEL?

CARTER, I'M FINE. I HAD A GREAT DOCTOR.

VERY FUNNY.

HELL, EASIER THEN MED SCHOOL, RIGHT? YOU OKAY?

THESE BOOKS MADE IT SEEM SO SIMPLE. OR AT LEAST UNDERSTANDABLE.

I WAS NEVER GONNA BE ABLE TO HELP HIM, WAS I?

IT'S NOT YOUR FAULT. IT WAS MINE.

NONE OF THIS FEELS REAL.

IT WILL, SOONER OR LATER.

CAN I TELL YOU SOMETHING.

OF COURSE, ANYTHING.

I KNOW THINGS NOW. I'VE LEARNED MORE AND I... I NEED TO KNOW THE TRUTH.

ABOUT WHAT?

MOM.

OKAY, WHAT DO YOU WANT TO KNOW?

NOTHING, IT CAN WAIT.

YOU SURE? YEAH. IT'S LATE. I'M GONNA GO TO BED. YOU OKAY? NEED ANYTHING?

I'M GOOD.

CARTER...

I KNOW THIS IS HARD FOR YOU BUT EVERYTHING I'VE DONE IS BECAUSE I ONLY WANT WHAT'S BEST FOR YOU.

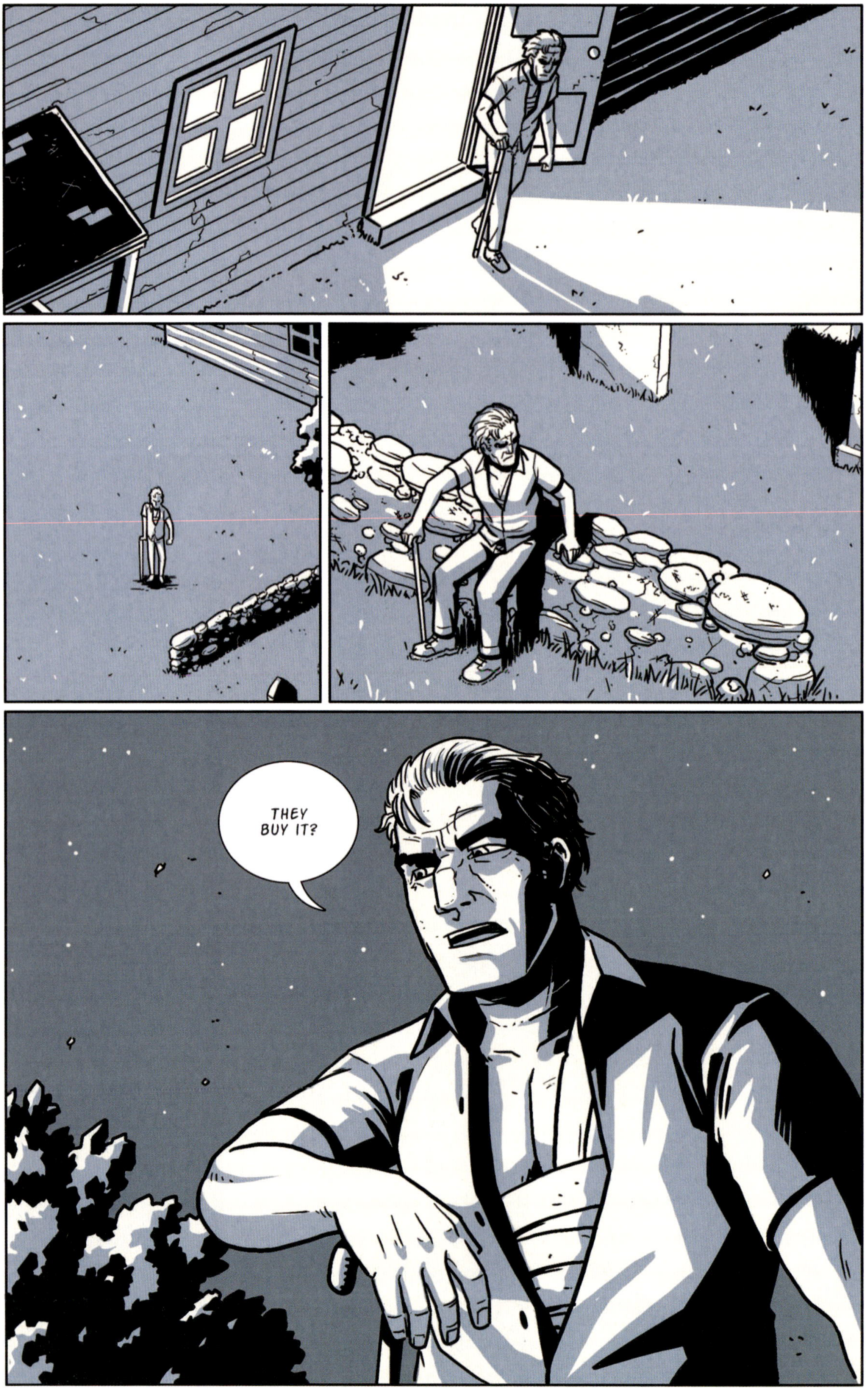
THEY BUY IT?

IS SHE DEAD?
ETHAN.
IS. LEXI. DEAD?
I DIDN'T-- IT WAS FOR YOUR OWN SAFETY, E.
ARE YOU SERIOUS?!
THAT'S WHAT YOU'RE GONNA GO WITH?!
YOU THINK I'D LET YOU RUIN TWO YEARS OF ALL YOUR WORK, OF ALL OUR PLANNING, FOR A GIRL YOU JUST MET?!
I LOVED HER!
LEXI WASN'T PART OF THE PLAN!
ETHAN, THEY NEEDED TO KNOW THEY COULD TRUST YOU. WITHOUT THAT TRUST ALL OUR WORK WOULD BE FOR NOTHING!
THE ONLY PLAN WE HAD WAS TO FIND OUT WHO KILLED YOUR MOTHER!
I- I TOLD HER SHE'D BE ALRIGHT. EVERYTHING WOULD BE FINE.
THIS IS THE LIFE, ETHAN. THIS IS WHAT WE DO.
I CAN'T DO IT.
YOU CAN. THE HARD PART'S OVER. YOU'RE IN. THE PAST TWO YEARS IN THE PSYCH WARD? IT WORKED.
I'M TELLING, CARTER.
YOU CAN'T.
YOU'LL PUT HER IN MORE DANGER, ETHAN.
SHE CAN'T KNOW.

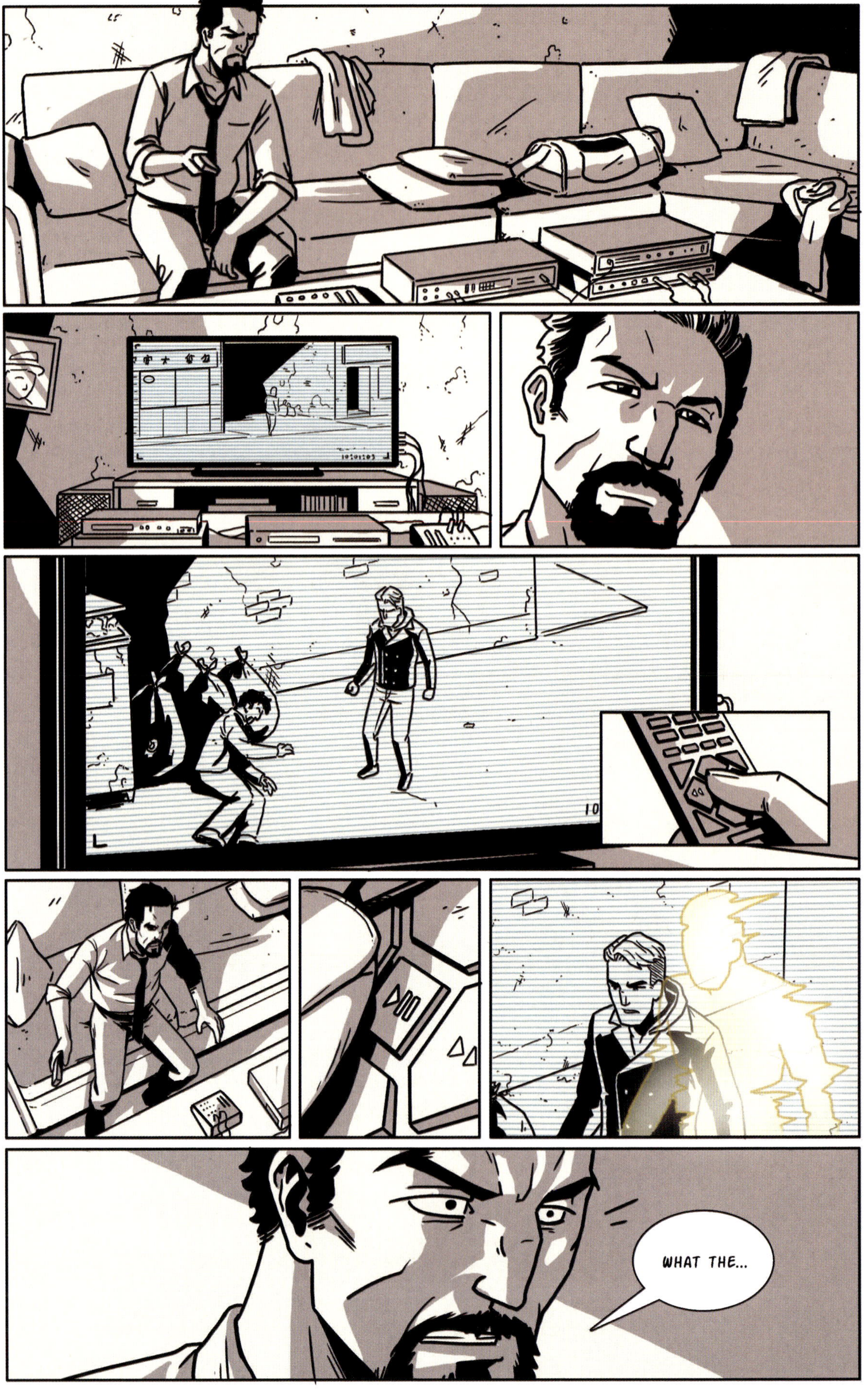
WHAT THE...

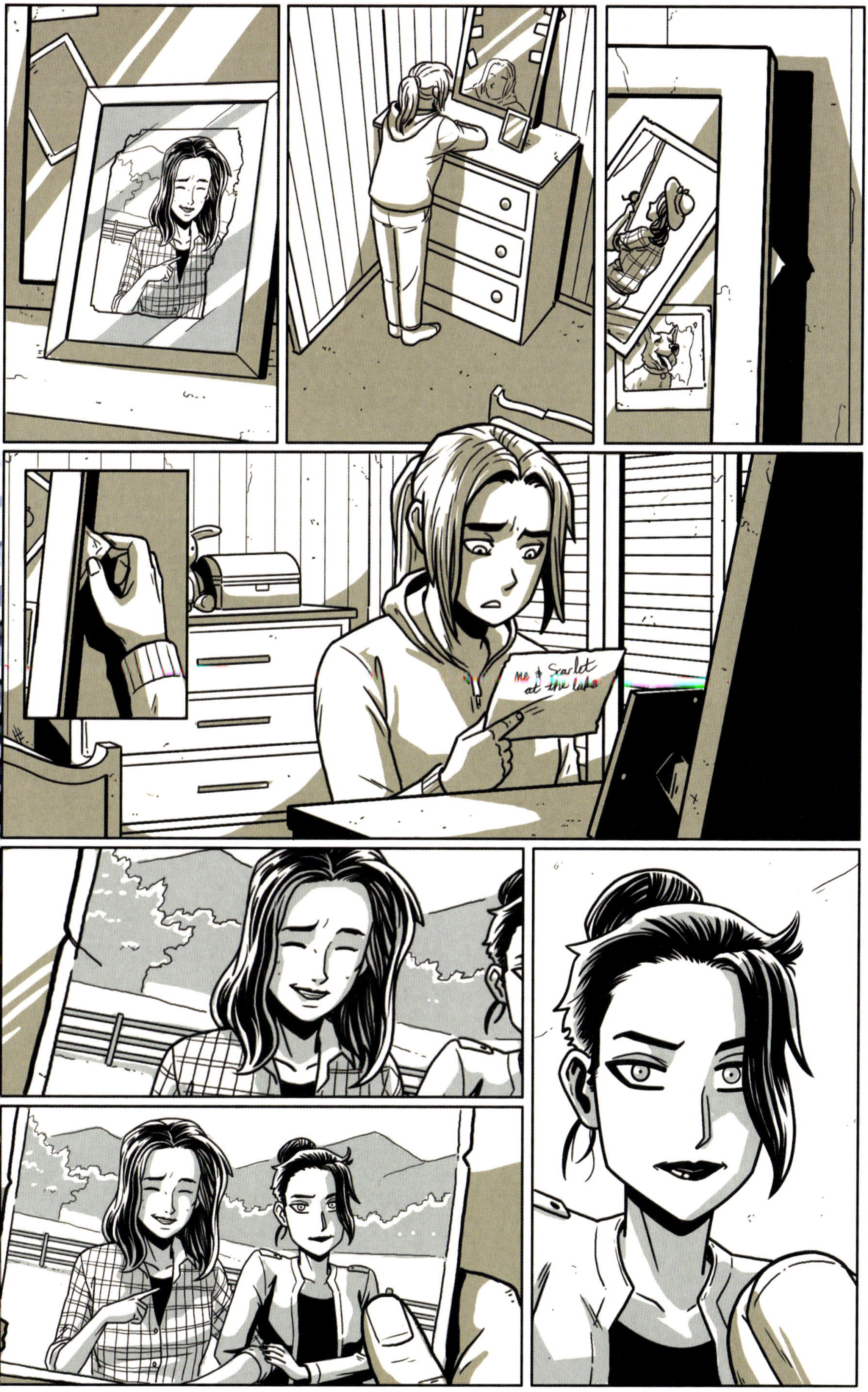
me & Scarlet
at the lake

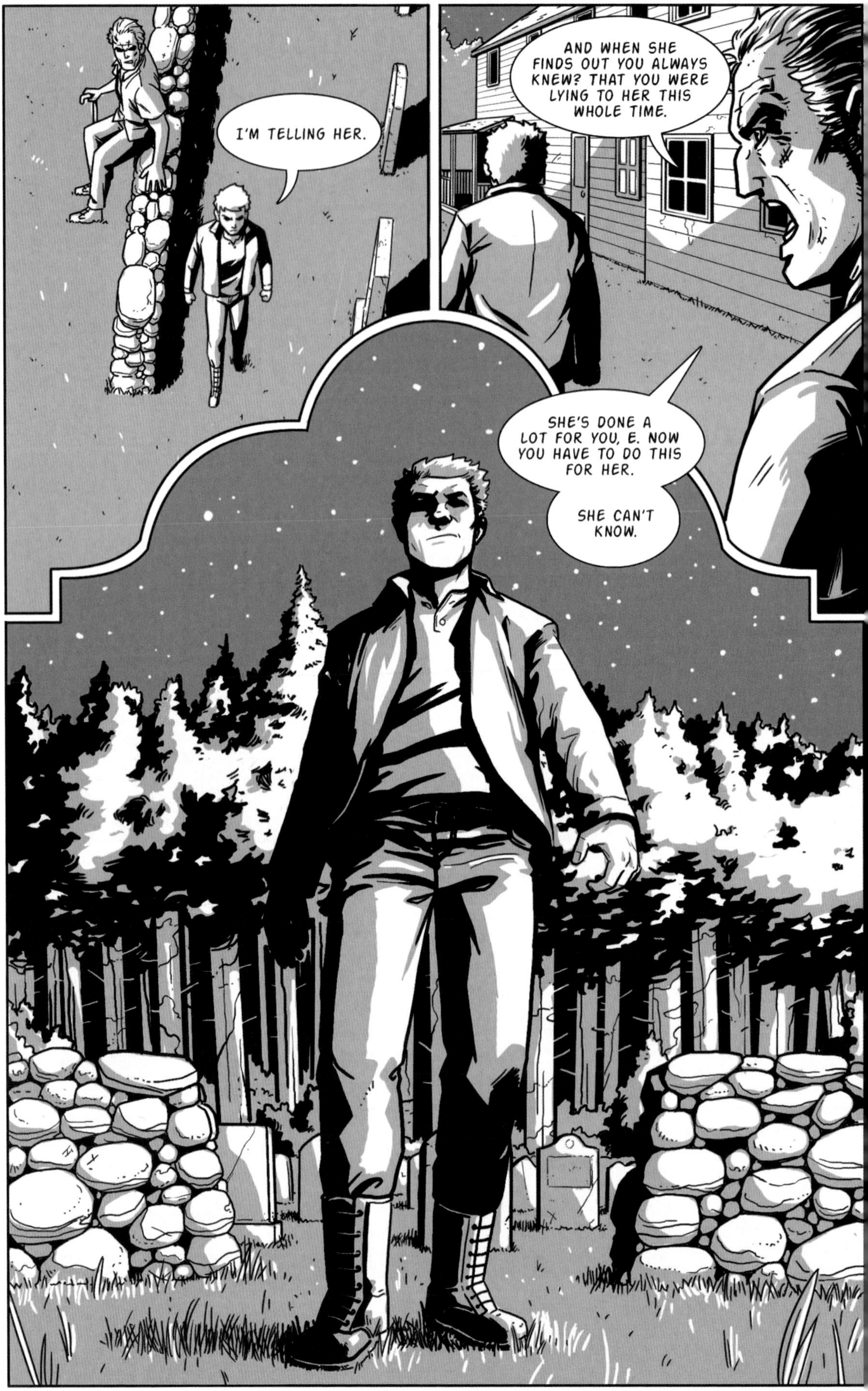

TO BE CONTINUED...

GraveYard Wars

BONUS MATERIAL

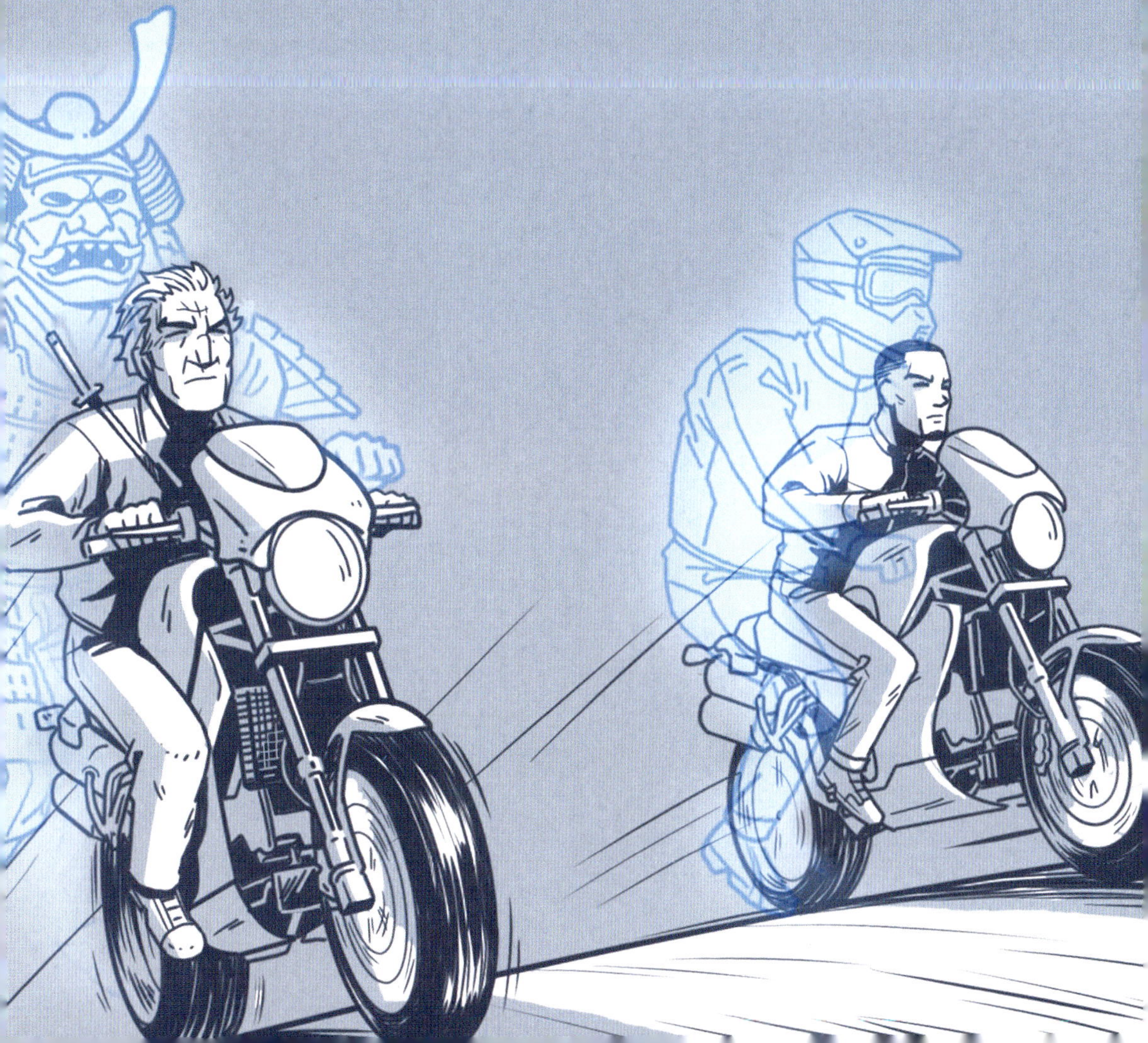

GraveYard Wars
SKETCHBOOK
Notes by AJ Lieberman

Carter

Andrew hit Carter pretty quick. It was really about finding her "look" more than her actual physical appearance.

The three original looks for Sebastian. I suggested that Andrew reference the actor, Jeff Bridges.

A   B   C

Sebastian Noble

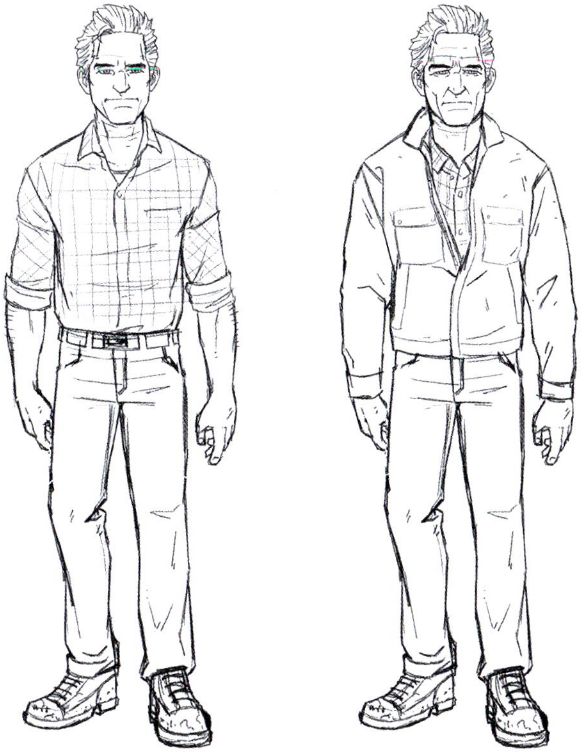

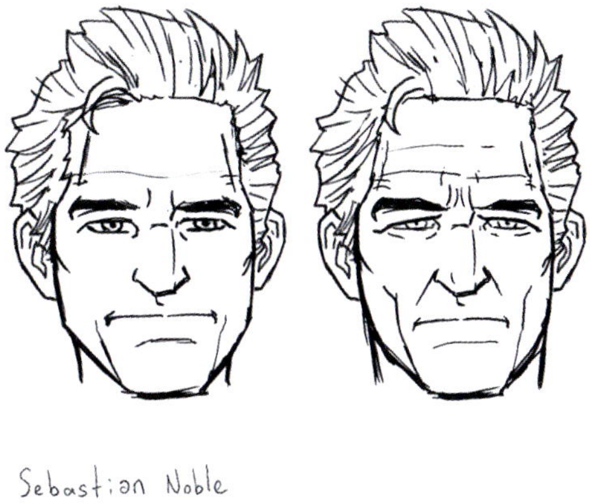
Sebastian Noble

Once we honed in on the version we liked, Andrew drilled down a little further.

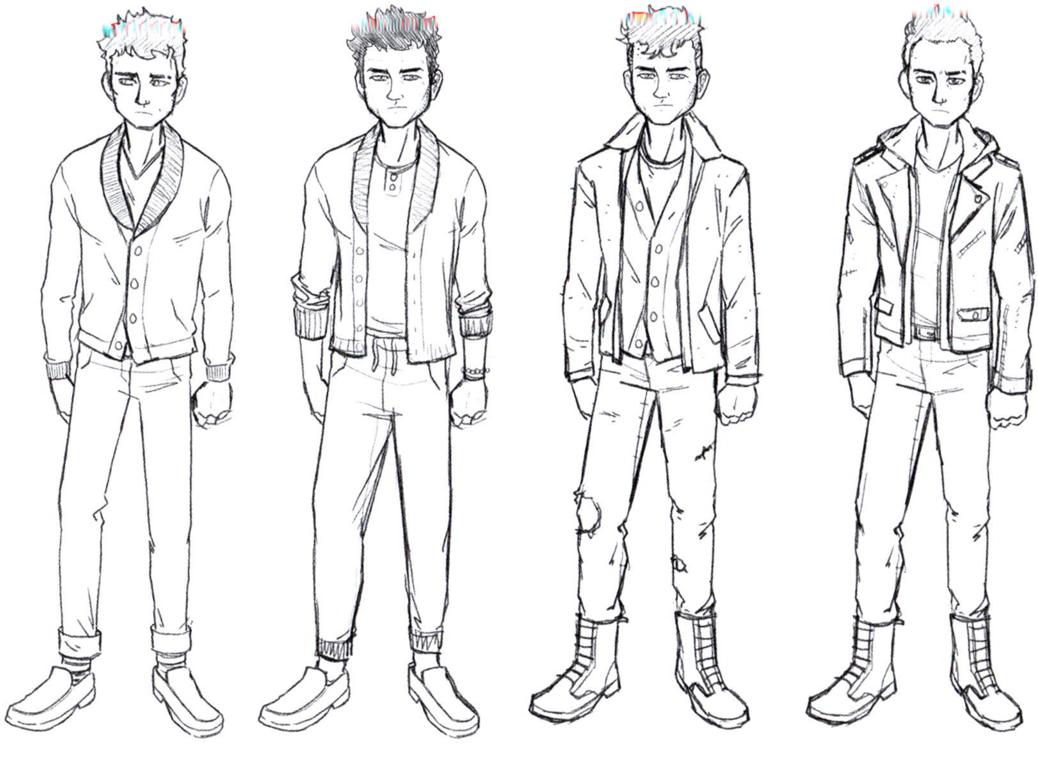
Ethan

Various designs of Ethan, just so Andrew knew what he looked like in different situations. My description for Ethan was skittish, unsure, and pissed off a lot. An actor I mentioned for reference was Alden Ehrenreich.

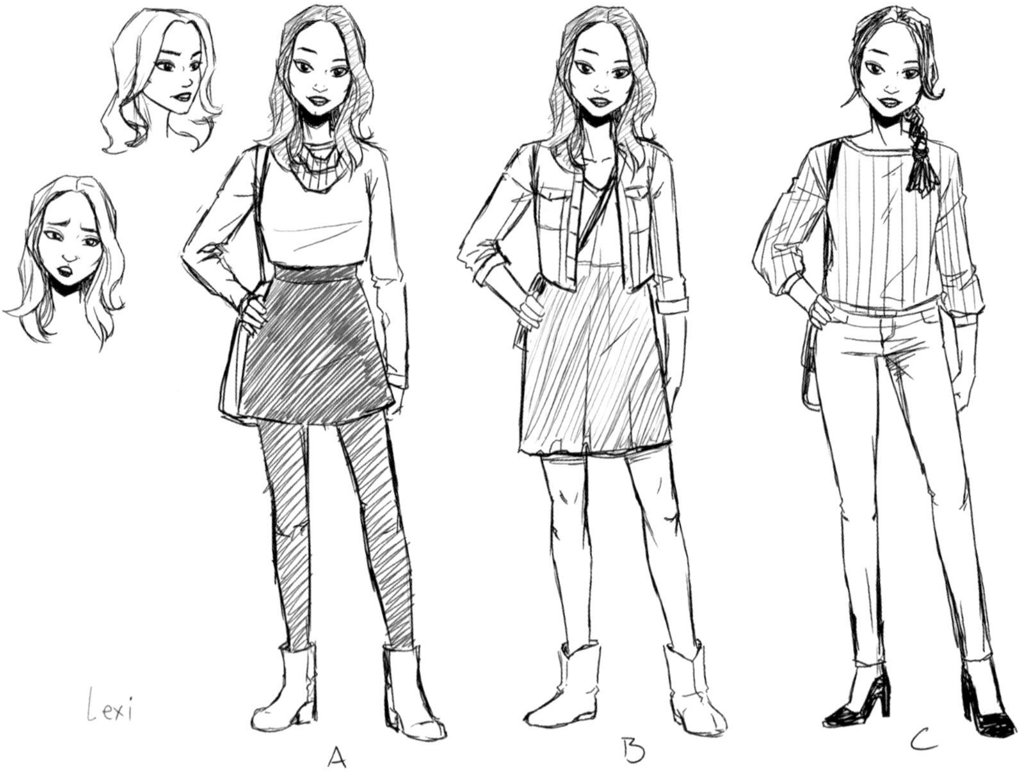
Lexi
A
B
C

She doesn't show up in the story right away but Lexi is a very important character. Again, Andrew was able to find her design pretty quickly and did a few costume variants.

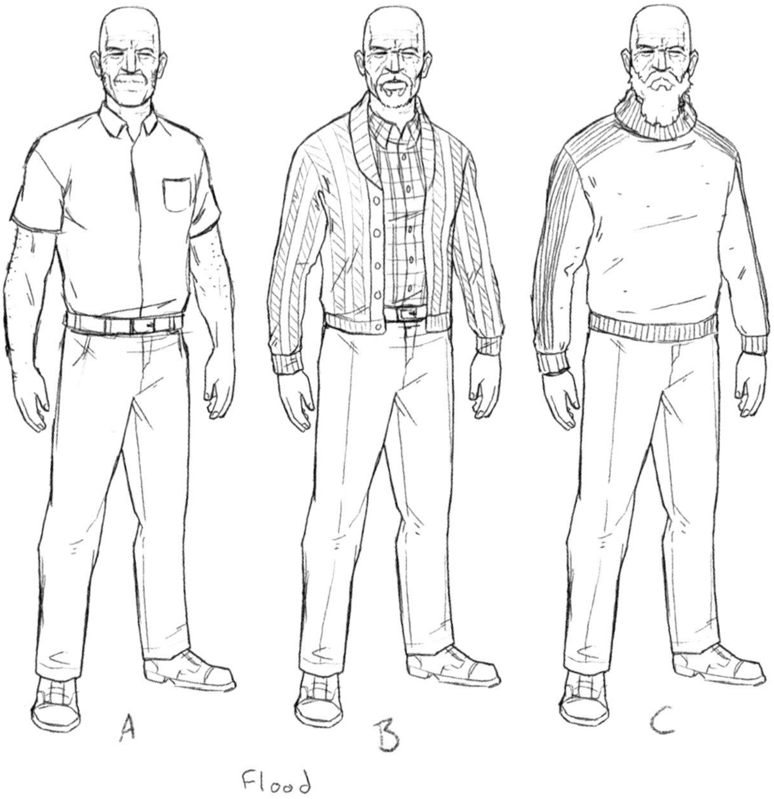
A
B
C
Flood

Three versions of Flood (all pretty similar) but even here you can feel the force behind this guy. I told Andrew to think of Bruce Willis after not shaving for a few weeks.

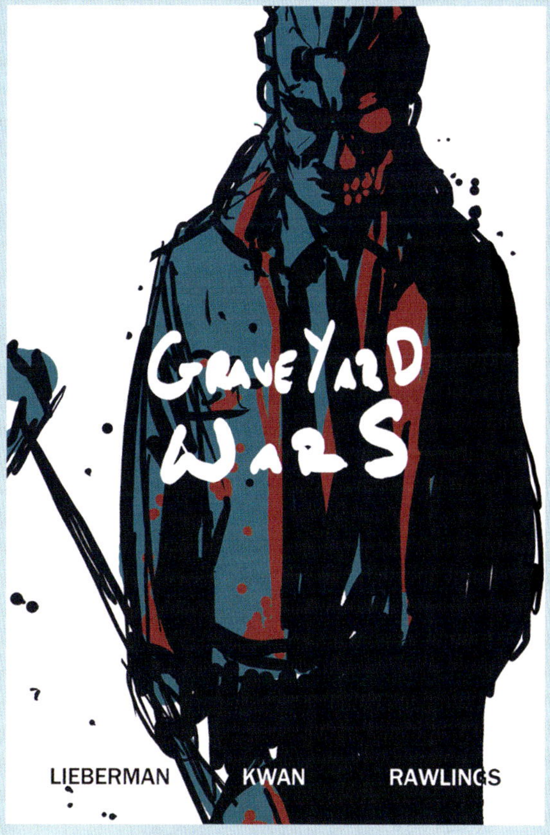
GRAVEYARD
WARS
LIEBERMAN
KWAN
RAWLINGS

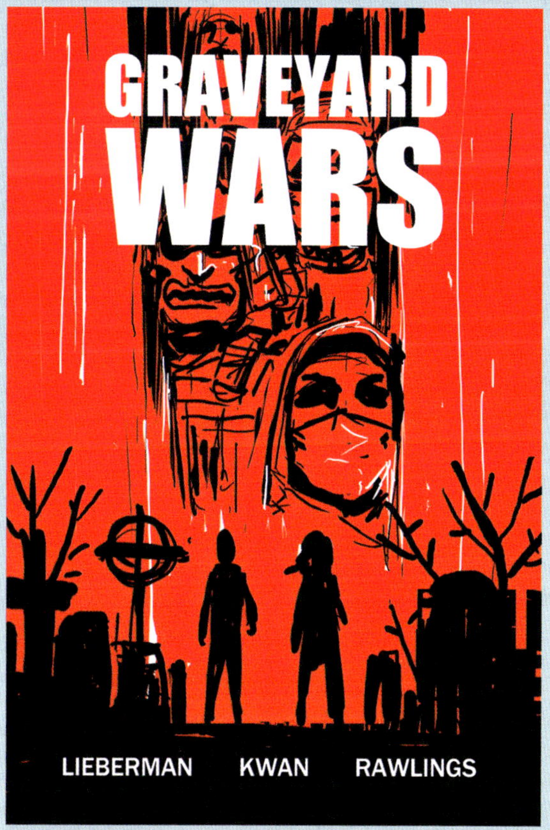
GRAVEYARD
WARS
LIEBERMAN
KWAN
RAWLINGS

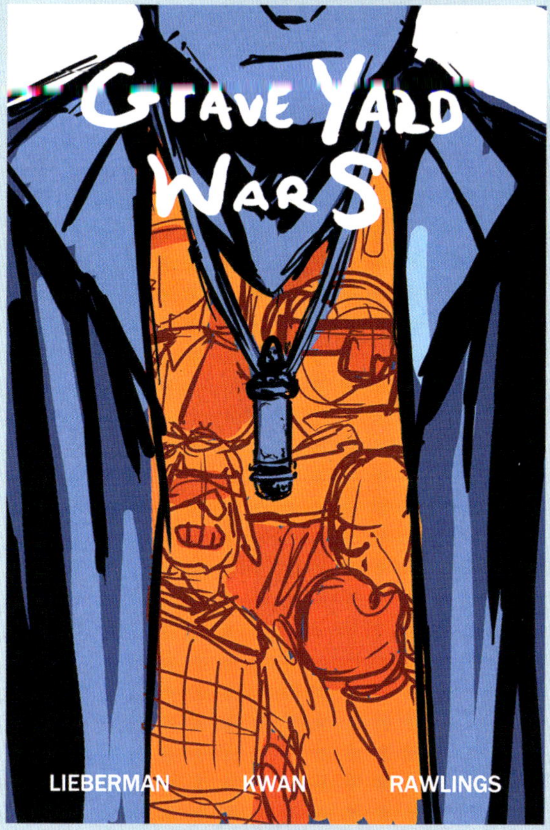
GRAVEYARD
WARS
LIEBERMAN
KWAN
RAWLINGS

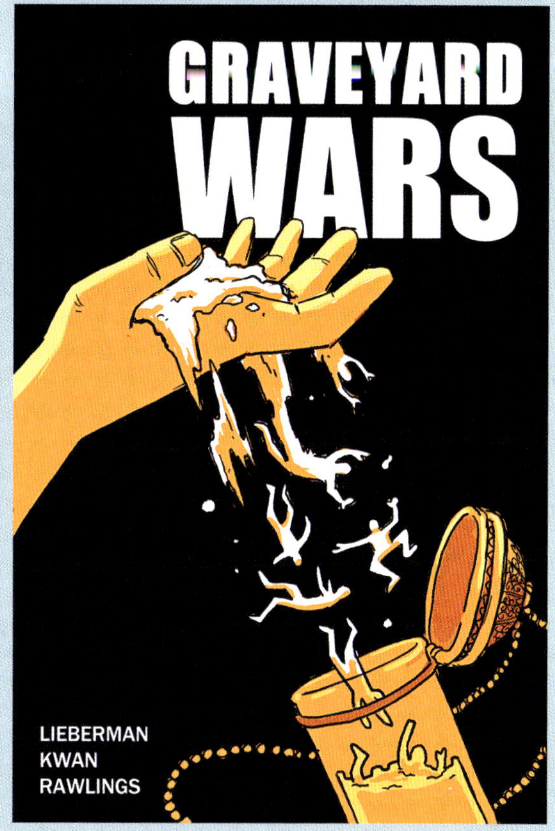
GRAVEYARD
WARS
LIEBERMAN
KWAN
RAWLINGS

The Covers - Probably the most important page in any book is the cover. Here are just a few of the sketches we contemplated as we searched for a the perfect image to sum up the entire book. There are probably ten more we could've added.

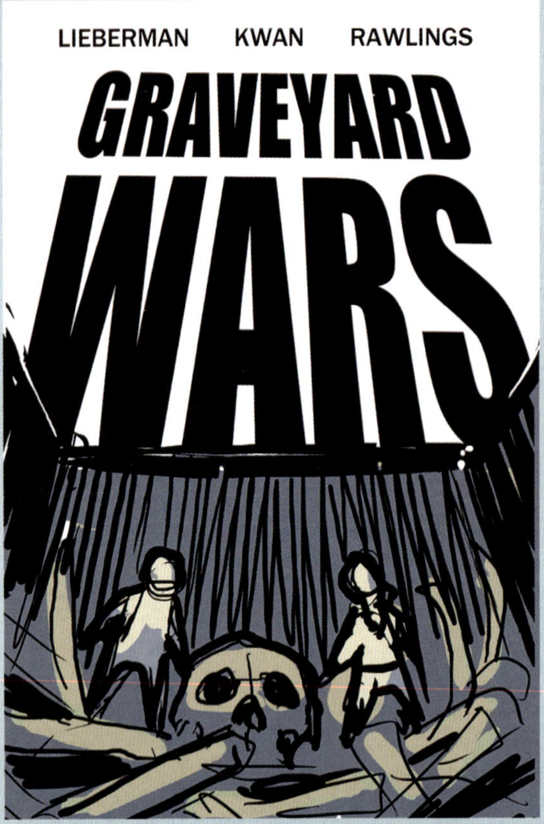
LIEBERMAN KWAN RAWLINGS
GRAVEYARD
WARS
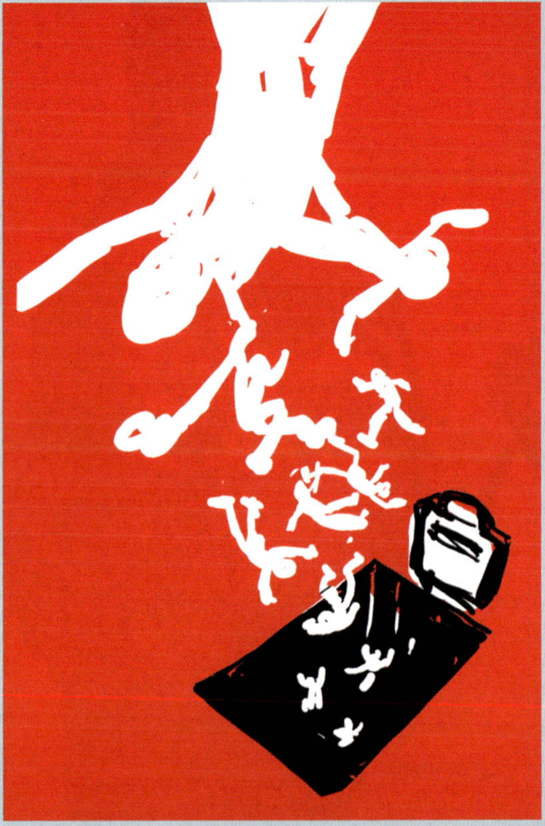
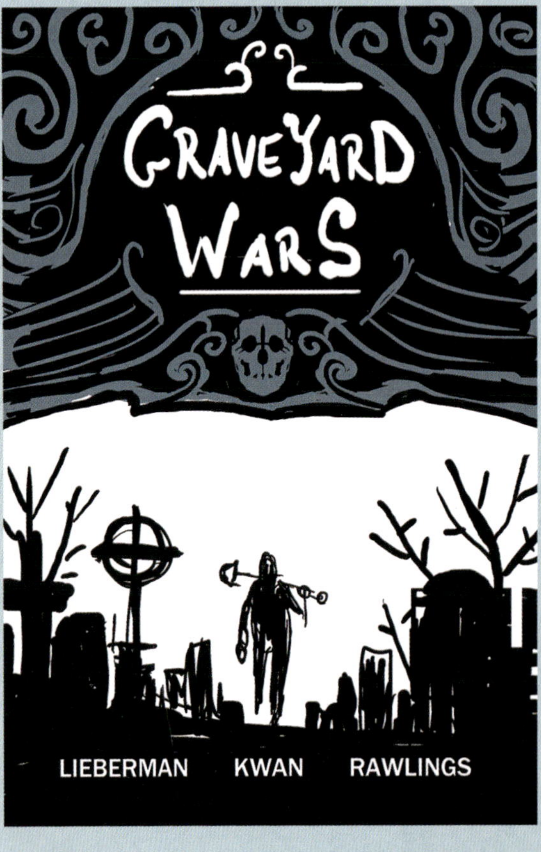
GRAVEYARD
WARS
LIEBERMAN KWAN RAWLINGS
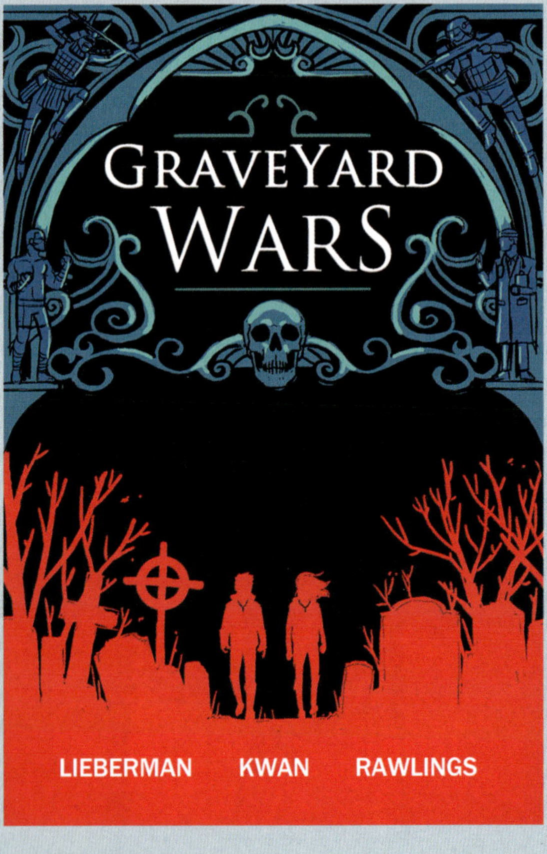
GRAVEYARD
WARS
LIEBERMAN KWAN RAWLINGS

To his credit, Andrew was a design machine.
I finally had the idea of using a head stone as part of the design
and Andrew was quickly able to hone in a really cool design.

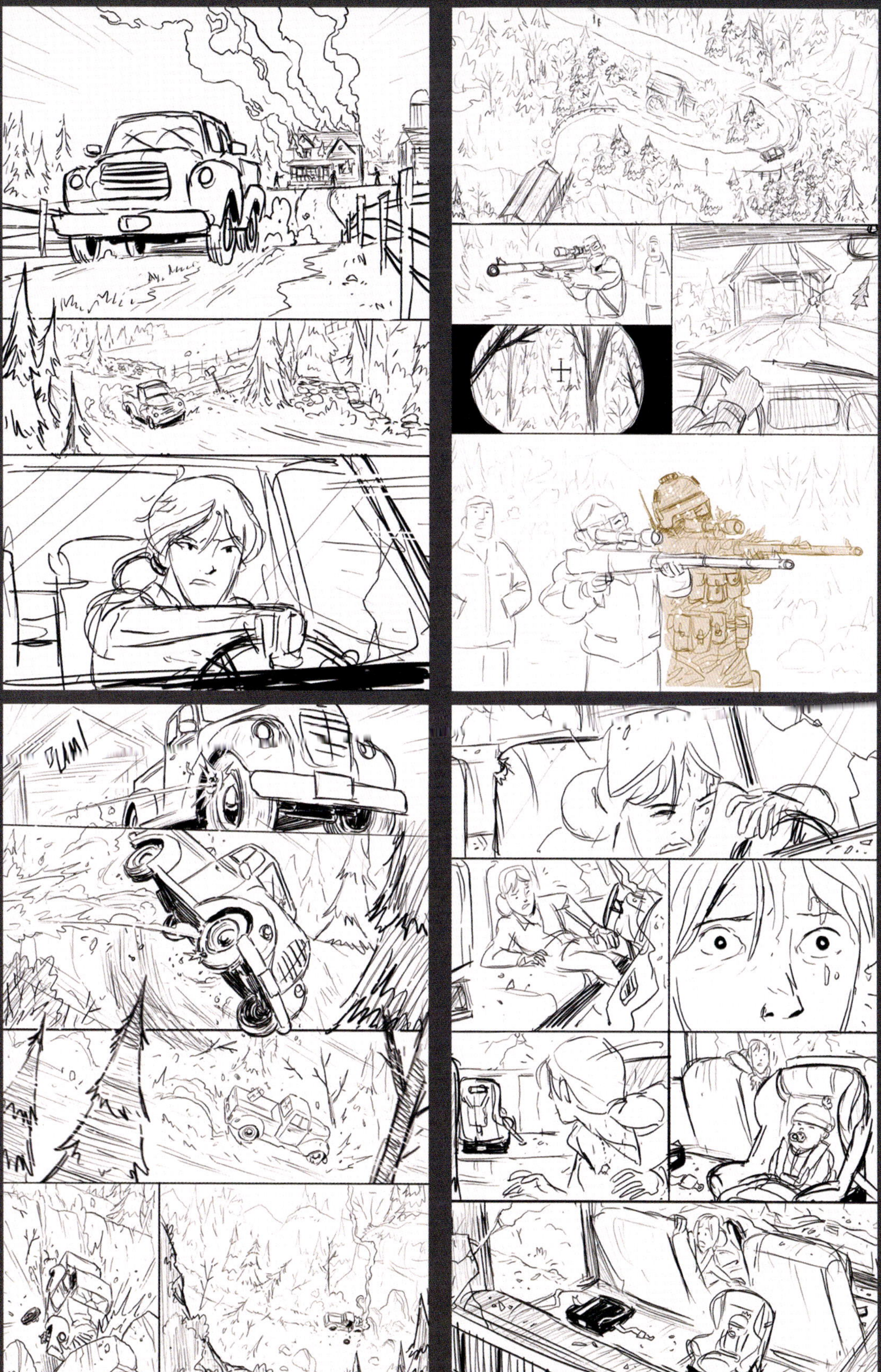

Layout & Design - Obviously, no matter how cool the art is, it won't look good without a great layout design. During the writing process, I worked closely with Rawls as he sketched out rough thumbnails for the book. Here are just a few of his pages.

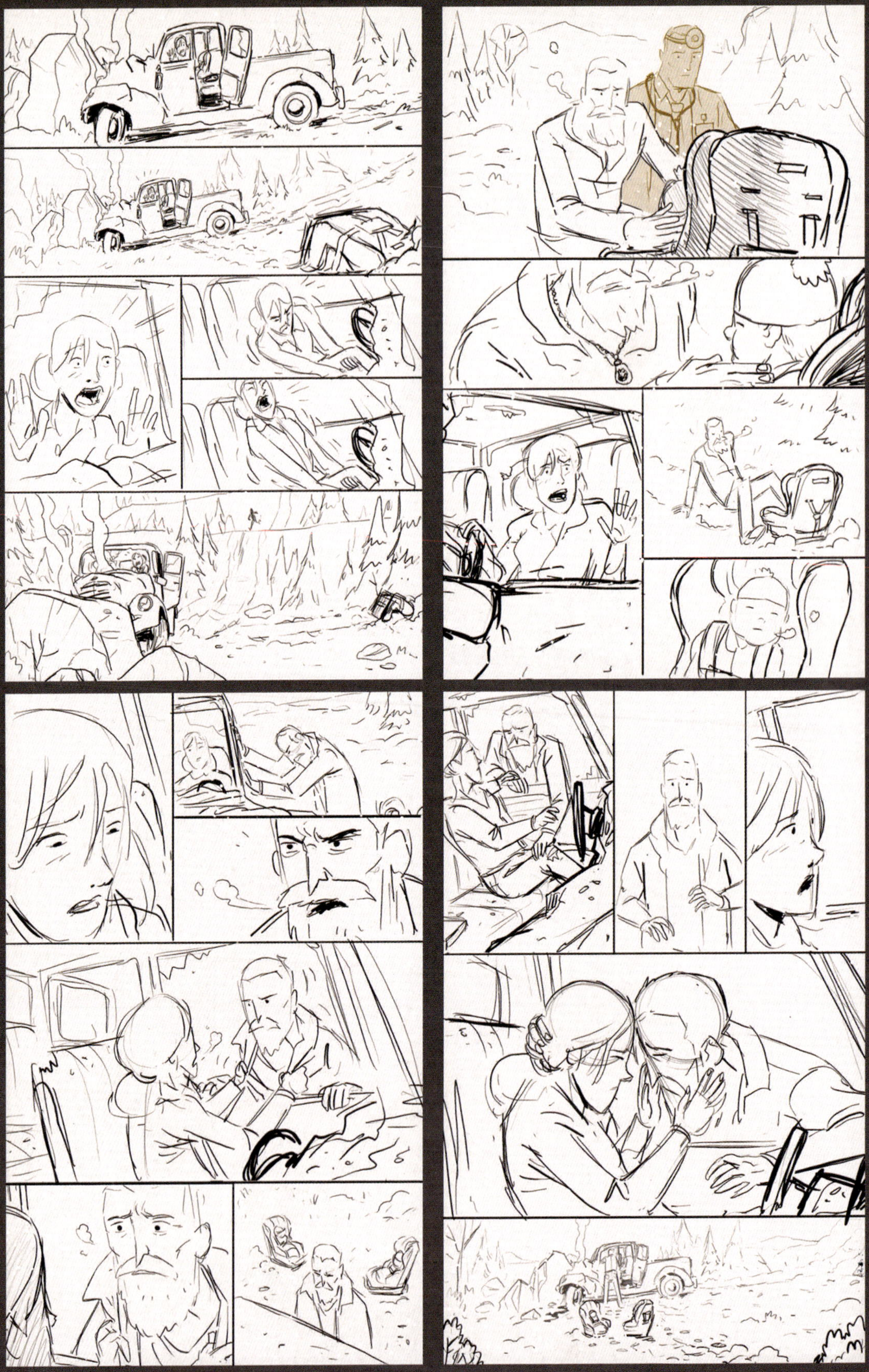

The great thing with Rawls' designs, thanks in part to his animation background, is that he always knows the best way to take the script pages and hone in on and highlight the most important emotional parts of the page.